THURSR

A.F. JANSSON

Paperback ISBN: 978-0-6457228-4-0
Hardcover ISBN: 978-0-6457228-3-3
Cover design by Johnny Greenteeth
Interior illustration by Scott Colliver

*For my young son Alfred without
whom this book would have been
completed a year earlier.*

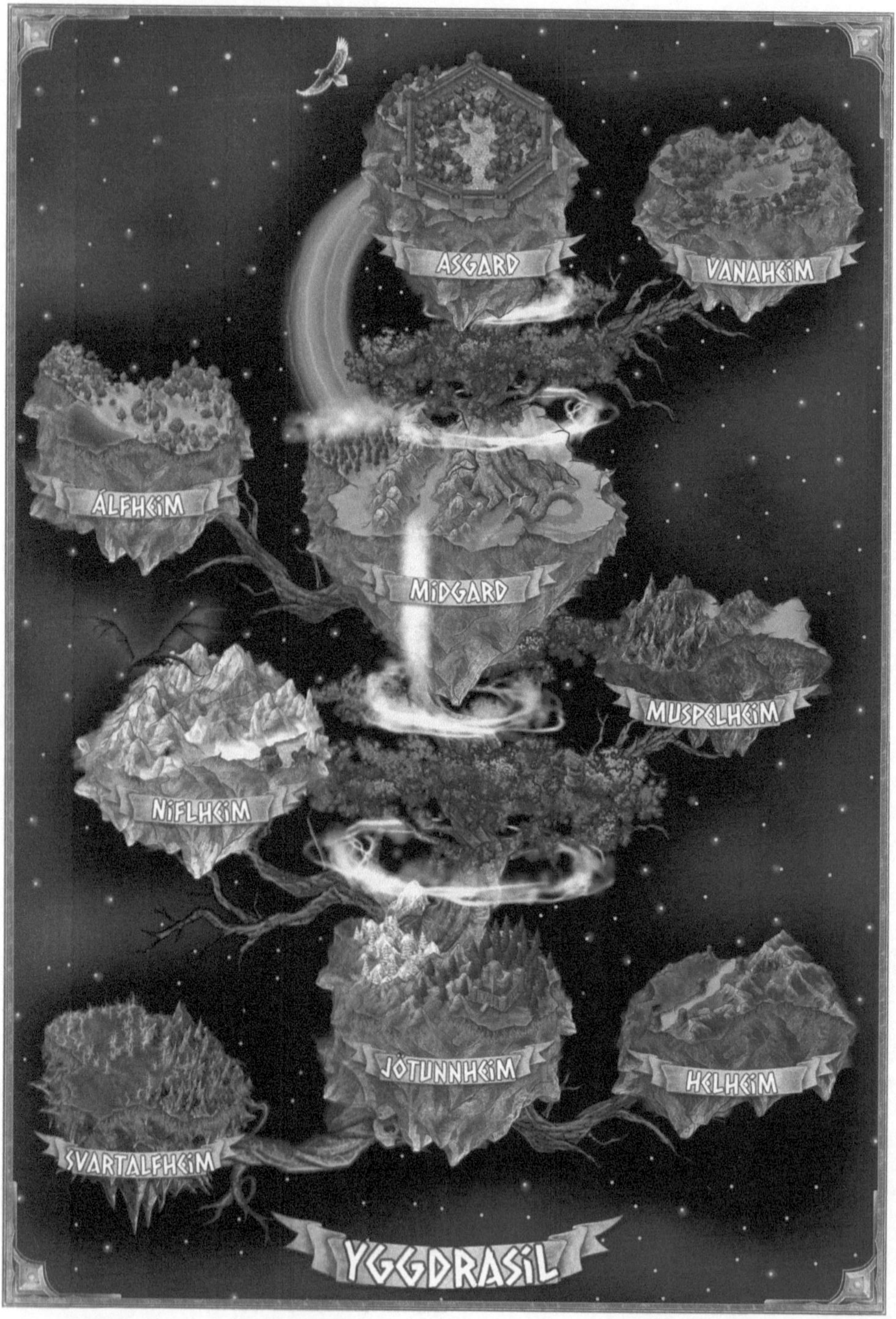

ASGARD
VANAHEIM
ÁLFHEIM
MIDGARD
MUSPELHEIM
NIFLHEIM
JÖTUNNHEIM
HELHEIM
SVARTALFHEIM
YGGDRASIL

JORDR'S MOUNTAIN
GUNDAGANR
BURRUGANDR
NEKK
KELP
UTGARD
BESTLA'S SWAMP
THRYM
JOTUNHEIM

I hung on that tree,
for nine days and nights,
as its roots reached for the heavens.

I gave my eye and was stabbed with a spear,
to my own self given.
I sacrificed myself to myself,
and all was revealed to me.

– Odin, Havamal.

CHAPTER 1

"ASH REACHED INTO THE FORGE WITH A SET OF LONG pliers and grasped the glowing piece of metal inside. Beads of sweat that had formed on his forehead evaporated as he leaned in towards the intense heat blasting out of the magical forge. He pressed his lips tightly together in concentration as he carefully lifted the metal from the glowing bed. On his last attempt, a noise had distracted him and he had dropped the enchanted metal. The subsequent ball of fire had singed half his beard off, giving Eikinri endless amusement for a few weeks until it grew back. It had taken a month of hard work and meticulous engraving, but he was now once again at the point where he had ruined his project the last time.

He carefully turned away from the forge to place the glowing metal on a large anvil behind him. His creation was a round helmet with a protective guard running from the top of the crest, down to the bottom of the bearer's nose. He had based the design on the common Norse helmet, worn by most warriors, but this was no ordinary helmet. Complex bands of dwarven runes had been weaved across every surface and culminated in an engraved troll's head just above the nose guard. With his Stonesight, he could see all the spells and enchantments melding together from the heat of Eikinri's forge.

Ash held the pliers in his left hand and grasped his stone hammer with the right. A tingle of excitement ran up his arm, as it always did whenever he was about to use the magical tool. He was certain the thing had a life of its own. He waited and watched as the glowing helmet cooled and darkened to a deep red. When it had reached just the right temperature, he tightened his grip on the hammer and, with a great overhead swing, struck the helmet with full force.

A great flash of blinding white light erupted from the helmet and he had to use his Stonesight again, because his normal sight revealed nothing but dancing white spots. The enchantments were nearly fused to the metal. Two more strikes and flashes of light later, and he submerged his work into a pool of cold water inside a stone basin next to the forge. The water churned and great plumes of steam rose to the ceiling of the foundry. When it had cooled enough and the water was once again still, he fished out the helmet and turned it over in his hands.

He called it the *Trollhelm*. Although it was made of blackened steel it was as light as a feather. The bands of runes shimmered with golden inlays, and red stones marked the eyes of the troll engraved on the guard. A helmet worth a king's ransom. Or in this case, he thought with glee, a stableboy's.

"You have come a long way, lad."

He turned to look at Eikinri, his Stonesmith master. The surly dwarf stood with his muscular arms crossed over his belly, and his eyes held a rare glint of approval.

"You are already ugly, so I don't understand why you need to make things worse," Eikinri grunted, shaking his head. "Let's see it then."

Ash smiled and slipped the helmet over his head. He felt a tingle run through his body and his stomach heaved like he was falling for a moment.. His master's eyes widened for a second before the dwarf burst out laughing. Ash glanced down at his hands and body, only to find that he still looked the same. He groaned, as he realised all these months of hard work had been a waste.

"It didn't work," he told the dwarf, his voice thick with disappointment. His master didn't answer because now he was roaring with laughter, holding his sides to prevent them from splitting open.

"What?" Ash demanded.

Gasping for air, Eikinri pointed to a large polished shield hanging on the wall nearby. With a suspicious look at the dwarf, Ash walked up to it and gasped. It was no longer him reflected in the shiny metal. Wearing a grimy loincloth, his skin was now pale green, with drab, olive patches. He had short, stubby legs, and a potbelly under a long, skinny torso with spindly, long arms. On the narrow shoulders rested a disproportionally large, round head with a wide mouth, big fleshy ears and a tuft of bright red hair. Even by troll standards, he would be ugly. Seeing the look on his face, Eikinri's body became wracked with convulsions yet again and the man stopped breathing entirely, his face red, with tears running down his cheeks.

"It's not that funny," Ash said, but then he started laughing too.

Ash had returned to Eikinri's foundry after defeating Gurmr and Grundr, to complete his apprenticeship. His master had guided him as he unravelled the secrets of Stonesmithing, deep underground, in Eikinri's smithy. Ash mastered shaping and moulding stone to his will, and he could now travel for longer distances through rock. Eikinri had also taught him breathing techniques and shown him how to relax his body so that it needed far less oxygen while immersed in the rock.

But the most valuable skill Ash had learned was enchanting. Eikinri had shown him how to infuse his Stonesmithing power into a piece of stone or metal and lock it in permanently by engraving it in dwarven or human runes. Although Eikinri had also taught him to read troll runes, he had not learned how to enchant with them, as his master considered it "garbage magic".

It was very taxing, and early on, even the simplest of enchantments, like making a lightning stone, or an iron rod that would heat to boil water, had drained him. He often had to rest for hours, even after just one attempt. But Ash had attacked enchanting with a determination that had even impressed Eikinri, and his skills advanced at a fast pace.

After returning from Midgard, he had spent several years training with the dwarf. His master had recently announced that it was time to complete a Journeyman-piece, to end his apprenticeship. Ash wasn't a master Stonesmith yet, but as a Journeyman, he would need to travel out into the world on his own to gain knowledge and skills. Once he felt ready, he would then return to the dwarf, to present him with a Masterpiece. Only then would he become a fully fledged Stonesmith. Ash longed for the day, although Eikinri had informed him it would likely take decades.

Ash was well aware that he had another, more pressing issue at hand, though. Odin had tasked him with the mission of travelling to Jotunheim to destroy the source of the draugr infestation in his home world, Midgard.

Eikinri's foundry lay inside a branch of Yggdrasil, the world tree, and therefore outside of conventional time. Even though, in Midgard, it had only been a little short of a week since he and his friends had defeated the jotunn Shaman, Ash had spent six long years training with Eikinri. He had now grown into a man. He was tall and muscular, his hands were strong and calloused from endless hours of working with stone and metal. His hair was long, and he kept it in a braid down his back to keep it from singeing while he worked near the forge. He had grown a beard that even his Berserker friend Torsten would be proud of, even if he burned it off in the forge from time to time. The daily weapons practice with the dwarf had kept him agile, and after years of training, he could even best Eikinri from time to time.

They were sitting together at the table in the little kitchen where they always had their evening meals, with the exception that this would be one of their last meals together for a long while.

They had spent years discussing how Ash would go about finding Burrugandr's mountain. After all, Jotunheim was a vast land. Ash would need to go to Utgard, the largest town in the land of the trolls, and from there seek to find out where the jotunn lived. These discussions had prompted the creation of the trollhelm, which would allow Ash to walk undetected amongst the trolls and giants.

"You should leave this for the gods to sort out, lad," the dwarf said for the thousandth time.

Ash smiled at his friend and teacher. "They are, through me. If they got involved directly, it could trigger Ragnarok, the end of the world, far too soon. It is my duty as an Ulfhed to do as Odin bids me. He asked me to go to Jotunheim and destroy the source of the draugr infestation, so go to Jotunheim I shall."

The dwarf harrumphed and ladled some more mushroom soup into Ash's bowl.

"Well, I don't like it," the dwarf grumbled. "By the way, how were you planning on getting there? Jotunheim isn't exactly around the corner."

"Well, I..." Ash stopped. He hadn't even considered that. He had just assumed Odin would take care of that for him, but it had been many years since he had seen or heard from the Allfather.

Eikinri shook his head. "Haven't I drilled it into your head, over all these years, to always plan and consider everything? This is why I am worried about you, lad. You're a bit thick sometimes."

He reached into his tunic and pulled out a pouch, which he slid across the table towards Ash. Ash picked it up, opened it and shook out two round, flat stones into his hand. They had intricate dwarven runes carved on both sides. One glowed softly with a green light and the other with a red. They vibrated gently in his hand.

"Portal stones," his master explained. "The red one will get you to the outskirts of Jotunheim, and the green one, more importantly, will get you back to Midgard, right outside the gates of Gjallarholm."

Ash looked up at his friend. "Eikinri, thank you, I..."

The dwarf silenced him by holding up one of his large, stubby hands. "Say no more about it. If you want to repay me for anything, just make sure you come back in one piece."

Ash smiled and nodded.

"Now, better make sure you get a good night's sleep before you set off." And with that, the dwarf stood and walked into his bedroom, leaving the dishes for Ash to clear. Ash took his time finishing his meal before gathering all the plates and bowls and washing them.

Having finished tidying up, Ash went to his bedroll and lay down to sleep. But sleep didn't take him for a long time, as he stared at the ceiling, worrying about what the morning would bring. He missed his friends, Yrsa and Torsten, and wondered where they were. He would have felt a lot better if they accompanied him to Jotunheim, but he didn't want to put them in harm's way either. Last time he had seen them, they were both seriously injured after crossing paths with Ash. For him that was years ago, but for them not a week had yet passed, and they were most likely still nursing their injuries.

It seemed like madness that he would venture to another world alone, to face untold dangers, on Odin's whim. Eikinri had often warned him of the gods' scheming, and to be wary of them. But he knew it was not only for the Allfather he would go. He was going for himself. He had tasted strength and power for the first time in his life, and it had swept away the fears and loneliness of his childhood. The Ulfhednar had welcomed him like he was family and he had finally felt like he truly belonged somewhere. With a whisper in the dark, he vowed they would never look upon him as a burden, that he would always be worthy of them. He vowed he would be a master Stonesmith, fists crackling with power, that no one would beat him like a stable boy again. He would stand tall, the Ulfhednar beside him, and woe come to those who dared raise their hand against him.

When he drifted off to sleep, it was a restless one as his dreams took him.

Ash floated in a vast empty darkness, far above the gigantic world tree Yggdrasil. In the middle of its trunk, a thick branch held a beautiful, green and blue world, dotted with clouds and basking in sunlight. He knew it to be Midgard, his home world. Above it, in the tree's crown, sat three other beautiful worlds. He knew these would be Asgard, Vanaheim and Alfheim, where the gods and the light elves lived. He drifted downwards, passing the light and fair worlds. Ash drew level with the base of the world tree. Here he found two very different worlds attached to the trunk. One was a world of fire and lava, and the other of ice and frost. He knew these to be Muspelheim and Niflheim, the first worlds to be created at the dawn of time.

Beyond these, the roots of Yggdrasil sprawled out, twisting and curling in space. Three worlds were nestled in the gnarled roots. The first was nothing but shadows, the entire land covered in darkness. This would be Helheim, the land of the dead.

Next to it sat a world hidden in mists, and he knew it was Svartalfheim, where the dark elves and the dwarves dwelled. The last world was larger, made of tall mountains and stone, with deep, purple forests and dark seas nestled in between the peaks. This would be Jotunheim, and this is where he was drifting, getting closer with every heartbeat.

As he passed the two oldest worlds on the trunk, a flash of fire appeared in the corner of his eye. He lifted his head and saw an enormous hand rising from the seas of lava in Muspelheim, the world of fire. The hand grew larger by the second, the fingers opening as it reached for him across the void. When the enormous hand closed around him, the heat became intense, the fire blinding and Ash screamed in pain as his skin seared.

"Wake up, lad, you've slept long enough." Eikinri's gruff voice cut through the dream.

Ash sat up in his bedroll and rubbed his eyes. He was covered in sweat and could smell burnt hair. He looked down to see that the edges of his beard were singed. Ash shook his head to clear the remnants of the dream before he got up and went to his washbowl to splash cold water on his face. He often had dreams these days, and they always ended with fire. Ash revelled in the sensation of the cool water soothing his hot skin. After getting dressed, he packed a few spare tunics, shirts, leggings, as well as a bone comb, knife and an ordinary metal cup he had made as his first metal smithing exercise, in a leather knapsack.

He went to the rock pool in the foundry to fill a waterskin which he hung on the side of his pack. Tying his sleeping roll together with a couple of lengths of leather thongs, he strapped it on top of his knapsack. The last thing he grabbed was a small pouch which contained some gold he had found while working with the stone in the workshop. A speck here and a speck there, carefully extracted over the years, had turned into enough gold for him to make six heavy coins. He tucked the jingling pouch inside his shirt.

It was with great sadness that he picked up the enchanted shield Eikinri had gifted him a long time ago. Both he and his master had agreed that the dwarven runes carved into it would draw far too much attention in Jotunheim, and that he would leave it behind. He vowed to return and collect it someday.

Ash positioned the enchanted shield against the wall and instead picked up a sword in a scabbard that had been sitting next to the shield. He drew the sword and ran his eyes over the blade. It was made from rusty iron and had a few nicks along the blade. The once bronze cross-guard was green and tarnished with age, and the leather wrapping on the handle looked rotten. The pommel was missing entirely.

It was the worst looking sword he had ever seen, but when he ran his finger along the edge, it drew a drop of blood. It was as sharp as any sword could be. Eikinri called it a 'sleeper' and had forged it himself as a gift for Ash. Because of some cleverly concealed enchantments, the steel sword appeared to be a piece of junk that a feeble, low-ranking troll might have picked up. Resting the sword against his backpack, Ash went to find Eikinri.

He found the dwarf in the little kitchen where he was stirring a pot of porridge on the stone stove. Ash looked to their little table and saw several packages wrapped in beeswax paper. He raised his eyebrows at Eikinri and nodded towards the packages.

"Just some things to see you through the first few days, lad. Dried meats and such," the dwarf said, turning around to ladle out the porridge into two wooden bowls.

They sat down and ate in silence, and Ash noticed Eikinri occasionally glancing at him, but turning away when Ash met his gaze. Ash's stomach fluttered with a mixture of anxiety and excitement, but he forced himself to finish the food, since he did not know when his next hot meal would come. When they finished and Ash had washed the bowls, Eikinri spoke.

"Let's get it done and over with."

Ash nodded and left the room to collect his belongings. He slung the pack on his back and strapped the sword to his waist while he carried the trollhelm under his arm. When he arrived back in Eikinri's kitchen, the dwarf was waiting for him.

"Why don't you do the honours, lad?" His master said, nodding towards the wall.

Ash smiled and came to stand next to Eikinri. He concentrated and began singing the oldest song in the world. A wordless song of creation and shaping that Odin and his brothers had sung as they made the world Midgard from the dead body of the giant Ymir.

He felt his Stonesight expand into the stone in front of him as he laid his hand on it. His voice echoed around the chamber and through the very stone under his palm.

The walls here were part of the world tree itself and therefore much harder than normal stone. Sweat broke out on his forehead as he chanted, and he pushed his hand into the wall to his elbow. When his consciousness had permeated the stone in a long cylindrical shape, he released the spell and watched the stone dissipate away from his arm and a long tunnel open in front of him.

Ash smiled and took a deep breath. Eikinri slapped him on the shoulder and they set off at a brisk pace. The spell wouldn't hold against Yggdrasil for long, so they had to be quick.

They arrived on the other side into an underground cave. Ash pulled out a stone from his pocket and whispered "Lyse". The stone emitted a white light that filled the underground cavern. It was the same type of stone that Yrsa had used in the basement of Hornsborg. They were in a small space, dark stone surrounding them. Ash could see well enough when surrounded by stone, using his Stonesight. However, that only allowed him to see the shape of the surrounding cavern, and he wanted to look upon Eikinri with his own eyes as they said goodbye. He turned to his master.

"Eikinri," he started and looked down on his master.

"Don't say another word," Eikinri cut him off, holding his hand up in front of Ash,

"First, show me the portal stone."

Ash was a bit confused but obeyed and took out the pouch the dwarf had given him. He fished out the red portal stone and held it up to Eikinri. It was vibrating softly in his hand.

His master took it from him and holding it up to his eye, scrutinising it, said, "Good. Now put the other one away safely."

Ash tightened the strings on the pouch and tucked it away inside his tunic. When he looked up, he saw the dwarf looking at him through tear-rimmed eyes.

A second later, Eikinri threw the stone at Ash's feet and jumped backwards as a gaping hole materialised with a red flash. Apparently, the dwarf wasn't very good at goodbyes, Ash thought as he fell into the portal, the world going dark around him.

CHAPTER 2

ROGHALD CLUTCHED HIS HEAD IN HIS HANDS AS HE SAT on a log. The voice of the long dead troll he had merged with to transform to a thursr, a battle troll, had grown in intensity since he'd arrived in Jotunheim. Roghald had learned that the troll's name had been Gamir, not that that offered any comfort to him. He could hear the nonsensical blabbering most of the time now, and it was driving him insane. Even when he changed back to his human form, there was no reprieve from the voice in his head.

The last couple of weeks since arriving in Jotunheim had been hard and confusing, even without the mental anguish he was going through. Troll society was brutal. Burrugandr, the jotunn chieftain, had expressed great displeasure at Roghald's failure to capture or kill Ash, and on top of that he also had to endure aggression and challenges from the other thursrs in Burrugandr's ranks. Trolls had a very strict hierarchy based on a pecking order, and any weakness was pounced on and attacked. But being a battle troll, Roghald could heal quickly, and what would be a mortal wound for others, healed in a matter of hours.

Roghald had bested most of the trolls that had challenged him, only yielding to the very oldest, most hardened trolls. He had pondered this, because he hadn't been a troll for very long, but gathered that it had something to do with the strength of the mad troll whose soul possessed him, rather than his own innate abilities. He now questioned if all this power was worth it, considering he was trapped listening to Gamir endlessly.

Roghald had taken to wandering the mountains and deep forests in Burrugandr's land, seeking some respite and peace of mind, and finding very little. Was it possible to escape yourself, he wondered? He looked up at the trees surrounding him. They were much larger than any trees he had ever seen on Midgard, and he doubted twenty men side by side could reach around their trunks. The foliage, many stories up in the sky, was a deep purple hue, as with most other plants in this world. He assumed it was because only very little pale-grey light reached down to Jotunheim, because of its location at the very roots of Yggdrasil. There were few plants to be seen here, and so far he had only found them in these deep pockets between the immense mountaintops. The remainder of the landscape was a windswept and stony wasteland.

Roghald was making his way back to the mountain. A calling had come to him on the wind from Burrugandr's Shaman to return to the chieftain's mountain. It was a shame, because in the last few days, he had discovered a new game he could play whilst wandering the wilderness. Roghald would assume his human form, the shape of a short, portly and pink-skinned servant, who once worked for Jarl Astrid of Gjallarholm. He would walk the wilderness, seemingly weak and vulnerable, until a wild beast would attack, intending to make an easy meal of him. In the last second before the beast was upon him, Roghald would transform to his thursr form and kill it with his bare hands.

Most often the attacker would be a large type of boar, one that stood as tall as a man, with several rows of teeth and tusks in a massive, foaming mouth. Sometimes it was a large cat-like creature with a mottled, purple-tinged coat. One time a group of what could only be goblins - short, green creatures dressed in rotting furs and skins, armed with stone-tipped spears and clubs had even attacked him. He had enjoyed that one the most. Seeing the fear in the goblins' eyes as he throttled them had made him laugh out loud.

But now the fun was over, and he was being summoned back. He pushed off the log and picked up his pace. Burrugandr was impatient and had a foul temper, so keeping the chieftain waiting was the last thing Roghald wanted to do. He jogged along a small river in the bottom of the forested valley until it disappeared into a low cavern and the vegetation disappeared along with it.

Scrambling up the steep walls and out of the narrow gully, a waft of sulphur greeted Roghald like a slap in the face. The next valley was much deeper and broader than the one he had just emerged from and lay in a haze of thin smoke. No vegetation grew there, and he could see no sign of life, only grey and blackened rock. If he were to make his way around the valley, he would lose an hour, at least, so he sighed and clambered down the steep bank. He half slid, half jumped down in a cascade of rocks and pebbles.

Reaching the bottom, he stood still for a moment, staring into the haze. It was eerily quiet and the stench of sulphur, like rotten eggs, made him wrinkle his broad nose. His eyes watered from the vapour and the hot air was stifling. He set out straight across the broad valley, in the shortest way to the other side. The rock underneath his feet was black and lumpy, like someone had poured it out across the valley before it hardened into a thick crust.

If he had not felt the wall of heat just in time, like an invisible wall of fire, he might have stepped into the crevice before he saw it. Roghald pulled up sharply only half a step away from a fissure and what was sure to be a short drop into a fiery death. Looking down, he saw, only a few feet below the opening, a creeping underground river of molten lava, with flames dancing across the sluggish surface.

He could feel his skin stinging from just standing near the opening and had to shield his eyes from the radiating heat. A waft of sulphurous smoke drifted into his face, sending him into a coughing fit, and he decided that the sooner he got out of this place, the better. Skirting the crevice and with his eyes fixed on the ground in front of him, he looked out for more death traps. He hurried as fast as he dared across the volcanic ground.

When he finally reached the bank on the other side, Roghald clambered up as fast as he could. He slipped and slid a few times, but his powerful hands found secure purchases and soon he stood at the top. Roghald filled his lungs with fresh air as a cooling breeze settled like a balm over his overheated skin.

He walked a short while across the ridge before the next valley opened up in front of him. Surrounded by dense forest, stood the broad mountain that was the seat of Burrugandr's power. Burrugandr was a jotunn chieftain who ruled large swaths of land in Jotunheim, but he could usually only be found deep inside his mountain. Although trolls did not like to speak of it, Roghald knew from the sagas back on Midgard, that this was because trolls and giants feared Thor, the Thundergod.

The strongest of the Aesir, and Odin's son, Thor, often made excursions to Jotunheim. He would ride across the sky in his chariot drawn by two massive goats and with lightning and thunder emanating from his magical hammer, Mjolnir, he hunted trolls and giants. So, unsurprisingly, trolls preferred a mountain between themselves and the sky, especially on stormy nights.

Roghald knew Burrugandr was just one of many chieftains in Jotunheim who were engaged in never-ending wars, and scheming for power and land. His master was one of the more powerful ones, though, and his lands among the largest.

Roghald looked up towards Burrugandr's mountain, cradled in a thick forest, and set out for it with a brisk jog. He soon entered the woods and weaved his way through. Sensing movement above him, he looked up to see a small troll sitting on a tree branch high off the ground, glaring at him. Burrugandr's watchers. The entire forest was dotted with them, monitoring anyone who would dare approach, sounding the alarm if needed. He knew there were thursrs stationed closer to the mountain, ready to answer any call to arms by the watchers. He himself had been stuck doing that very task for long, boring days at a time, never hearing a single call from the watchers, because who would dare attack Burrugandr?

As he reached the well-stomped path to the mountain's entrance, he spared a glance toward the heads impaled on spikes along the path. Mostly trolls that had opposed or disappointed the jotunn, they had long since turned to stone, standing forever as a warning to others. There were also a few goblin, dark elf and dwarf heads impaled there, all in various states of decay. Roghald even noticed an old human skull, and was amused to see that even here, some people would dare to venture. He longed for the day when Ash's head would decorate a post along this very road.

Roghald arrived at the wide cave opening and ignored the guards posted there as he pushed past the lower caste trolls waiting to be allowed in. He was a thursr, and therefore part of the upper echelons in troll society, so he did not need to answer to anyone below his rank, let alone some lowly guards.

With long strides, Roghald made his way through the network of broad tunnels, leading deeper and deeper into the mountain. He walked in the middle of the tunnels, with groups of lower ranking trolls parting before him like a ship ploughing through the ocean. They were all shapes and sizes, but none as large as him. Occasionally, one would be slow to get out of his way, and Roghald would encourage it with a kick or a slap, sending it sprawling against the rough tunnel walls.

Although he could see perfectly well in the dark, this was not the case with all trolls, so clusters of carefully cultivated luminescent mushrooms crammed the ceiling, casting a blue and green glow over the tunnel and the trolls milling about within.

Roghald trod the familiar path, following tunnels that led ever deeper into the mountain. The further down he got, the thinner the crowds of trolls became. When at last he arrived at a pair of massive, red painted doors at the tunnel's end, the only trolls he saw were the two imposing thursrs guarding them.

An old, dried-out elf head was fixed in the middle of the red doors, its face a grimace of horror. Roghald, now familiar with the magical seals and wards around his master's hall, reached out his clawed hand and placed a finger on the elf's forehead.

"Burrugandr," he said in his deep voice, and the elf's eyes glowed with a red light as the doors swung inward with a great creaking from the protesting hinges.

Cold, humid air pushed out of the opening, making the hair on his back and shoulders stand up as Roghald entered the hall of the chieftain of the Wasteland Mountains. Pale blue light emanated from flickering torches along the intricately carved stone walls illuminating the massive hall. Roghald had never had time to study the carvings, but from quick glances, he surmised they portrayed battles from the Troll War in which Burrugandr had been victorious and seized power centuries ago. Tattered banners and rusty weapons, all battle trophies, hung on display among other inexplicable items. But nothing in the room drew the eye quite like Burrugandr himself.

A jotunn, the ruling elite of Jotunheim, and a giant, Burrugandr was three times the height of Roghald, even when sitting on his throne. His skin was a dark grey hue with flecks of red over his arms and shoulders, while his massive belly and chest were pale as snow. His enormous body was scarred by intricate runes and symbols, long ago carved into his flesh. Dozens of thick golden bands adorned his arms, enough to buy a kingdom back in Midgard, and bejewelled rings crowded his fingers. Long white ringlets framed a stern face before spilling onto the floor. A massive, broad nose over an enormous mouth dominated the jotunn's countenance, and his face hosted the cruellest set of eyes Roghald had ever seen. They were black and soulless, and Roghald always felt like someone was walking over his grave when they locked on him.

From behind the jotunn's seat, Roghald could see the dark and twisted branches of the source tree reaching up to the ceiling. The glistening boughs seemed to sway gently in a breeze that was not present in the room. A shiver ran up Roghald's spine when he looked at the tree, remembering the horror of being pinned to its counterpart in Midgard. Having the soul of a battle troll forced into him was the best and worst thing that had ever happened to him, and it had all started with this tree.

"Thursr Roghald," Burrugandr's voice was a deep rumble, reminiscent of glaciers grinding rocks.

Roghald laid down, pressing his face into the floor, arms straight out, prostrating himself to show deference to his chieftain. It had cost him a whipping not doing so fast enough last time he had been called to Burrugandr's hall.

"It has finally learned its place," a loathsome snicker rang out from his side.

Roghald got a foul taste in his mouth as he realised that Grinbodr, Burrugandr's Shaman was present. If there ever existed someone meaner and more bloodthirsty than the chieftain himself, it was her. He sensed movement on his left and a shadow fell on his face. Knowing that if he moved now, before Burrugandr had given him permission to rise, he would have earned himself another whipping, Roghald remained fixed to the ground. He would rather die than give Grinbodr the pleasure. A bony finger poked his cheek a few times before a raspy cackle filled his ear.

"Has learned its place, indeed!"

Roghald bit his lip to keep himself calm. A grunt from the chieftain indicated he could rise, and as he did, he shot a murderous look at the Shaman. She was Roghald's height, but where he was muscular, she was gangly, almost spindly. A swell of tangled, dirty white hair covered most of her face and shoulders, with only her long, sharp nose protruding. Her skin was a pale olive, and she wore frayed and dirty red robes that didn't hide the fact that she seemed to be just skin stretched over ancient bones. Although she looked old and frail, hunched at the back and leaning on a gnarled wooden staff, she moved with a youthful vigour and Roghald knew that her mind was as sharp as a knife.

Burrugandr looked to his Shaman and nodded.

"Thursr Roghald," she began, smirking as she pronounced his title. She had made it very clear what she thought about a human gaining rank in troll society.

"A portal from Midgard opened this morning. We believe this is the half-breed, come to seek the source tree."

Roghald tensed at the mention of Ash. He hated the boy with his whole being. Everything that had gone wrong in his life and brought him to this point was Ash's fault.

"The scrying is not clear, and we cannot sense him as we should, but the portal opened in the west, beyond Utgard. If it is indeed the Ulfhed, you will hunt him down and bring him here," Her eyes narrowed and her face turned firm. "Alive," she emphasised.

Roghald gritted his teeth but nodded. He had no intention of letting Ash live a second longer than he had to.

"Do this to satisfaction," the Shaman continued, "And we will remove the soul that shares and plagues your mind."

Roghald inhaled sharply. To be rid of Gamir's presence in his mind would be worth any sacrifice. A gnawing thought struck him that this may be a ruse. Would he lose his troll form, and would he have to spend the rest of his life looking like the hopeless servant whose body he had inadvertently possessed? Wouldn't Burrugandr simply kill him if he was no longer a thursr in his service?

As if reading his thoughts, the Shaman replied, "You have held the thursr shape for long enough. Your soul will always be part troll now and you would remain in this, more superior form, even if the other soul is banished." A cruel smile split her ancient face in half. "To remove it will be... painful, to say the least. Much more so than when you received the blessing."

Roghald remembered the drawn out, torturous experience when Gurmr and Grundr nailed him to the black tree and forced

Gamir's soul into him. He shivered involuntarily. How could anything be worse than that? The voice in his mind was laughing madly when Roghald remembered the painful ritual. He would rid himself of it, no matter the price.

"I will bring the half-breed," he said in a firm voice, and with clenched jaws, he added, "Alive."

"You will take a hunting party with you," The Shaman added. "Thursr Shumbolg and Agash Nightstalker will accompany you on your hunt. They have been informed."

Roghald had to use all his mental strength to not slap his forehead. Thursrs were rare and there were only a few dozen in Burrugandr's service, but Shumbolg was by far the dumbest one. Built like a fortress, the troll was the very definition of brute force, but he had the brains of a chicken. Roghald was unfamiliar with the other name, however.

"Agash?" He asked the Shaman, "That doesn't sound like a troll name?"

"Because she is not a troll, you stupid oaf," Grinbodr cackled. "She is a dark elf tracker, and a highly skilled one at that." Her eyes narrowed. "There will be no escape for Ash of the Ulfhednar this time."

CHAPTER 3

A SH WAS PULLED THROUGH DARKNESS AT GREAT SPEED. He experienced several forceful jerks sideways until he lost all sense of direction. Without warning, a flash of red illuminated the world, followed by a dim, grey light flooding the surroundings. For a moment, he felt weightless before falling hard to the ground.

He blinked a few times and looked up at a grey and sullen sky. Scrambling to his feet, Ash looked around. He stood in a cold, grey landscape, comprising endless mountain peaks as far as the eye could see. There were little dots of purple-tinged vegetation between the mountains, but mostly it was a panorama of stone. Loose boulders were scattered around him, with moss growing in the cracks and crevices. The air smelled metallic.

A chilly wind blew, and he pulled his tunic closer around him. Looking behind him, Ash saw, to his horror, that just a few feet away the ground came to an abrupt end, and he could see nothing beyond but space and stars. He was at the very edge of Jotunheim. A sudden gust of wind pushed him a step toward the verge and he panicked, throwing himself backward, and landed with a clang. He crawled quickly away from the edge.

From the sagas, Ash knew that his home world of Midgard was

surrounded by a tall fence. Odin and his brothers had made it from the slain giant Ymir's eyelashes when they created the world, to keep it safe from the trolls and giants of the other realms. Jotunheim did not have any such constraints. What would happen if he fell over the edge? Would he continue to fall forever until he died of starvation? He shivered at the thought, stood up and started walking in the only direction available to him, away from the edge.

Clouds hung thick in the sky and only a little pale light filtered through. Away in the distance, lightning struck against distant mountains as a storm ravaged the landscape. He hoped it wouldn't find him out here in the open. He adjusted the trollhelm, making sure it was firmly on his head and stopping by a shallow rock pool, he checked his reflection to make sure the disguise was still in place. When an ugly troll face with a mop of red hair looked back at him in the still water, he breathed a sigh of relief. His backpack and clothes were disguised, since the reflection only wore its grubby loincloth, but the sad-looking sword on his hip was still visible.

He needed to find Utgard, the troll capital, and he did not know where to begin. Jotunheim was a vast world, so he had a lengthy journey ahead of him. He scanned the horizon to look for a suitable direction and saw nothing besides a flock of birds circling, slowly coming closer. He wondered what the birds were like here and if they were different from those on Midgard. Then he shrugged and set out in a straight line away from the edge behind him.

As he walked along the rocky ground, following a ridge, Ash glanced up at the birds now and then. When they drew closer, he soon realised that they were larger than any bird he had seen before. Much larger. It also dawned on him that his tuft of red hair and green skin would stand out like a sore thumb against the drab, rocky landscape. If those birds were predatory and looking for a meal, he was likely a prime target.

Glancing around, he saw an outcrop of rock with a few boulders he might squeeze under. He made a dash for it and ducked as he pushed in between the rocks. There wasn't enough room and there was no way he could hide from those things if they came any closer.

Then he stopped and wanted to slap himself. He was a Stone-smith. Ash chuckled for a second before concentrating and sinking his body into the stone. He left his face out of the rock, so he could get a closer look at the birds, but it was well hidden in the shadows of the outcrop. He didn't have to wait long until his wish came true.

A terrible shriek tore through the air and with a loud rustle of wings, an enormous bird landed on the ground where he had stood just moments before. It was facing away from Ash, but he could see it was easily the size of him, maybe even a little bigger. The bird took a few steps on large, clawed feet and swivelled its head, searching the area. Ash got a good look at it when it turned in his direction. Thick, black feathers could not hide the powerful frame as it flapped its wings in frustration. What made Ash's eyebrows shoot up, though, was the fact that under its sharp, predatory beak was soft, white skin and what was an all too human-like mouth with black lips. The smooth skin stretched down to its chest, and it was only at the bird's belly that feathers covered its skin again. Also, it was clearly female.

He wondered if he was looking at a vildvittra, a vicious, but cowardly, predator bird from the sagas. When faced with opposition, they would flee instead of fighting, but a flock of them against a lone traveller would tear him apart in seconds.

"I saw it! I saw it!" the shrieking voice cried to the sky.

Ash felt certain the bird couldn't see his face, hidden as it was in the shadows of the outcrop, and stared at the creature in fascination, even as its gaze glanced over his hiding place.

"Where did it go? Where did it go?" The vildvittra let out a frustrated shriek before jumping up into the air, and with a couple of strong beats of its powerful wings, disappeared from Ash's view. He could hear several other shrieks from the sky above, but soon they grew distant.

Ash remained in his hiding spot a little longer, but he grew tired from the concentration required to stay immersed in stone, so after what he thought was enough time for the birds to disappear, he slid out. He rested for a little while under the partial shelter of the outcrop before he stuck his head out with caution, suspiciously eyeing the skies.

Nothing moved under the heavy clouds. He clambered up and reassessed his plan. At first, he had intended to follow the clear, elevated land, allowing him to see any threats before they got to him. Having encountered the vildvittras, he now considered the added risk of being attacked from above, and decided to travel along the valleys amongst the vegetation. He didn't know what other wild beasts hunted from the skies in this world.

Ash looked at the nearest lowland and its leafy, purple canopy and wondered what dangers lurked in there. Well, he thought, he was about to find out. Ash squared his shoulders and, adjusting his knapsack, set off down the hill.

The ground steepened and soon he found himself not so much walking as much as descending into the valley with a controlled slide, a shower of pebbles and rocks running ahead of him. As he drew level with the canopy of the trees, he realised how enormous they were, stretching several times taller than any tree he had ever seen on Midgard. Their stems were thick and gnarled, with thick boughs spreading out in competition with each other for what little light was available. Ash slid all the way to the bottom and scanned his surroundings. Although the leaf cover wasn't thick, it did cast a gloom on the forest floor, and beside the occasional patch of light breaking through the canopy, it was difficult to see anything down here.

Once his eyes had adjusted to the dim light, a strange world appeared before him. Soft moss covered the ground, growing over the many fallen branches, trunks, and boulders that must have rolled into the gully over time. Patches of a variety of mushrooms and other fungi thrived in the still gloom, and Ash saw that many of them were lightly fluorescent, adding soft blue and green hues to the landscape. The air was still and smelled earthy and fresh, and Ash found it had its own beauty. It was warmer here than up in the highlands, and Ash loosened his tunic again.

From above, he had seen that the valley stretched inland in a reasonably straight line, so he would simply follow it to its end, then decide where to go. He was hoping he would find some kind of settlement where he could ask for directions to Utgard. He set off, and although the walking was harder down here, on account of having to navigate around the many trees, boulders and debris, he made reasonable speed.

It wasn't long before the gloom got even darker and he gathered that the sun was setting. Ash needed to make camp for the night. He had just arrived at a stream that ran along the very bottom of the gully. He was cautious as he approached it, but seeing no movement anywhere, he kneeled on the bank and washed his hands and his face. The water was cold and fresh and tasted crisp, and he stilled his thirst with big mouthfuls of it.

Although he was tired, he felt much better after refreshing himself and walking a little away from the water, he took his backpack off and leaned it against a tree. He unstrapped his sleeping roll and spread it out on the ground before sitting down with a sigh of satisfaction. Ash did not light a fire, in case it attracted whatever creatures roamed the forest at night. Instead, he held his runestone of light in one hand, ready to light it up at the slightest sound, and his sword lay right next to him.

As he sat there, chewing on a dry strip of meat, small lights appeared in the air over the stream. First there were only a few, but soon there were dozens. They were dancing and swirling around each other in a beautiful display that astounded Ash. Fireflies. Ash had only seen a few in his life, and he could barely believe the size of the swarm putting on a light show before him. He leaned back against the tree enjoying the show and thinking that this place wasn't so bad after all.

One firefly drifted away from the rest and drew closer to him. Delighted, Ash held his hand out to it. It was larger than he had thought at first, and a flurry of little wings flapped to keep it suspended in the air. When it was almost at his hand, he saw that its glowing body was about the same size as his finger and it had a humanoid shape, with two thin little legs and arms. The warm glow came from a rounded segment on its torso.

The moment it landed on his hand, he realised it was monstrous. Translucent skin stretched over a tiny skull, which had large, black eyes and a mouth full of tiny razor-sharp teeth. It latched on to his finger and bit down hard, tearing out a small piece of flesh. Ash jumped up, yelping in surprise and pain, and shook his hand until he flung the thing off. His shout and the excited chittering of the creature had attracted the rest of the swarm, which now drifted towards him.

Ash felt warm blood trickle down his hand and the bite burned like fire. He bent down and fumbled for his sword in the dark for a second before closing his hand around the hilt. The blood made it slippery, but years of swinging a smithing hammer and practicing with Eikinri had made Ash's grip like a vice. He stood up, holding it firmly.

As the fireflies drifted towards him, Ash stood still, his sword in a two-hand grip pointed in front of him. The creatures chittered in excitement and the forest behind them came aglow as a swarm of the creatures rose from the undergrowth. There were now hundreds of the little monsters descending on him from all sides, their high-pitched noises an unsettling cacophony. When the first creature came within an arm's length, Ash took a deep breath and Shifted.

Time slowed down, and the familiar calm filled him as the power spread through his body. The world came into perfect focus and he could see with incredible clarity the individual faces of the creatures. They had come to almost a standstill, hanging in the air, little clawed hands reaching out towards him with sharp teeth bared.

Since he had discovered how to unify his two powers of Shifting and Stonesmithing during the battle with Gurmr and Grundr, the jotunn Shaman, he had continued to practice daily in the years he spent with Eikinri. His Shifting had improved, and he suspected he could do it better and for longer than any other Ulfhed. He was a Wolf of Odin after all, and the god's gift was strongest in him.

With sleek movements, he threw himself into a dance of death, cleaving the little creatures one or two at a time with swing after swing of his sword. One by one their little lights flashed, then flickered out until none remained. Darkness and silence fell around him again, and as he let his powers wane, Ash bent down to his backpack for a rag to clean his sword.

He was just hoping that there would be no more surprises today, so he could get some much-needed rest ahead of his long journey, when he heard a voice behind him.

"Well, aren't you a fast one?"

CHAPTER 4

ROGHALD SHOOK HIS HEAD FOR THE THOUSANDTH TIME, trying to rid himself of the troll's voice in his head. It was more a habit now, because it didn't work, but he would not stop resisting Gamir's foothold in his mind. The day he accepted it as part of him would be the day he lost that battle.

Ever since his actual body had perished, and he had taken over Birk, the servant's body, the troll's presence had been even stronger. There were even times, while hunting the forest around Burrugandr's mountain, in the heat of battling a beast, when he lost control of his limbs. His body would keep fighting without his input, the joy and exhilaration clear in the Gamir's laughter, as it took over his bodily functions. Roghald feared the day would come when he would completely lose himself to the mad troll. If so, would he be pushed into a corner of his own mind, forced to live out his life as a helpless passenger in his own body? And trolls lived for a very long time.

As if sensing his anguish, Gamir laughed and babbled incoherently. Roghald pulled himself out of his ruminations and looked up at his companions. Sitting around a large campfire, the only sound was the crunching of bone as Shumbolg the thursr ate his dinner.

Earlier in the day, as they ran along the stony landscape, they had startled a flock of small horse-like creatures that set off with a rumble down the mountainside. In a split second, the massive thursr had dashed into a sprint and run the flock down, slamming his giant fists into the backs of two animals, killing them at once. He had swept them up onto his shoulders and without a word caught up and fell in line with his companions. The additional weight had not slowed him in the slightest throughout the day.

Once they set up camp, the troll lit a large campfire to roast the horse-like creatures. Smelling the burning horsehair had made Roghald's eyes water, forcing him to move a small distance away. The meat was half burned and half raw, but Shumbolg was happily munching away, bones and sinews offering no resistance to his enormous jaw and teeth.

Shumbolg was huge; half again as tall as Roghald, with arms and legs which had more in common with tree trunks than humans. His skin was a dull grey, with small patches of green lichen and moss on his shoulders and on the top of his head. Roghald imagined that if he sat still, he would be perfectly disguised as a rock. The troll wore no clothes of any sort, and his only concession to vanity was a thick gold bracelet around his right wrist. At least it would have been golden at one point, Roghald thought. Now it was dark and coated in grime. Shumbolg looked out on the world through a pair of wide set, beady little eyes, almost completely devoid of any intelligence. He glanced over at Roghald and after a few moments of looking at each other, he held out the half-burned carcass to Roghald, who shook his head. Shumbolg returned to mindlessly staring into the distance, crunching away.

Roghald turned his gaze to the other side of the fire, looking at the complete opposite of the battle troll. Agash's skin was pitch black with long hair, as white as freshly fallen snow. She was slender and agile, and compared to Shumbolg she seemed frail and delicate, but Roghald knew better than to be deceived by her slender frame. The dark elf had kept up with the larger trolls' running pace all day, without breaking a sweat. She had leapt from boulders to fallen tree trunks, scaling any obstacle without effort. She had often pulled away from the trolls to scout ahead, and on one such occasion, Roghald and Shumbolg had come across a small goblin war-band, who had all been cut to pieces. The goblins hadn't even slowed her down enough for the trolls to catch up.

Roghald noticed that her icy-blue eyes never stopped moving, and even now, as she sat rubbing tallow into her bowstring, her eyes were forever darting around, taking everything in. He had never known a dark elf before and found her to be fascinating and quite attractive, with her dark skin, glossy hair, and pointed ears framing her sharp features. She wore tight fitting leathers that showed off her slender figure and when she moved, it was like a predator stalking its prey.

Attentive as she was, she noticed Roghald's appreciative gaze, and in no time pulled out two long, black daggers from her belt and, shooting him a menacing look, twirled them a few times. Agash pulled back her lips and revealed two rows of teeth filed to sharp points. Roghald looked away, and she returned to her bow. He noticed as he lay down to sleep that she hadn't put her daggers away.

They spent the next few days in the same fashion, always running towards the west, through a never-changing landscape. Roghald was becoming bored with the whole affair, when Agash rushed back, not long after pulling away from them. She raised her hand as she approached, and they all stopped in their tracks.

"A band of trolls up ahead," she said, keeping her voice low. "After the next rise. They have been watching us for a while and are waiting for us."

As Roghald scanned the hillcrests ahead of them, seeing nothing of interest, she added. "They have thursrs amongst them."

Roghald raised his eyebrows at this. He hadn't been concerned until she added that bit.

"I wish you would have led with that," he snapped at her, but Agash shrugged.

"Not going to make a difference," she said, dismissing his irritation.

"Shumbolg, look sharp," he told the giant battle troll, who only looked confused. "Be ready for anything, I mean," Roghald sighed.

Shumbolg shaded his eyes with his hand and looked up to the sky, suspiciously scanning the clouds above.

Roghald closed his eyes and took a deep breath. "Be ready to fight the trolls up ahead, Shumbolg,"

Now on much more secure ground, the massive battle troll smiled and slammed his fists together with a dull crack. After Roghald gave Agash a few instructions, they set off again. They crested the rise and in the flat landscape beyond found themselves faced with a dozen trolls in a line, waiting for them.

The trolls were all of different sizes, and most of them were vaettr, the lower class of troll, but in the middle of the formation stood three thursrs. None of the battle trolls were as big as Shumbolg, but were quite sizeable nonetheless, towering over the lesser trolls in their ranks. All of them were armed with clubs, axes or broad iron swords, some even carrying crude shields. They all had a bright red line painted from the hairline down to the tip of the nose.

"Mogthrasir Clan," Shumbolg rumbled in his interpretation of a whisper. "Burrugandr fight a war against them, long time ago."

Roghald nodded, and they slowed their pace as they drew nearer.

The thursr in the middle stood tall with his arms crossed in front of him, a smug expression on his face. He was dark green and his arms and face were covered in scars. Two yellow tusks protruded from the corners of his mouth, but one was broken, and the other decorated with a small silver band. He wore rusted iron-plated armour and a massive sledgehammer was leaning against his leg.

As the thursr opened his mouth to speak, Roghald raised his hand in a lazy wave, which was followed by a quick blur to his left. A second later, a sharp 'thud' to the right of the Mogthrasir trolls made them all turn their heads. Their leftmost warrior had fallen to his knees, gurgling with one of Agash's long, black arrows through his neck. The troll coughed once, spraying dark blood on the ground in front of him, before falling forwards onto his face where he remained, unmoving, turning to grey stone.

The leader turned his head back to Roghald, an incredulous look on his face, the smug smile had vanished.

"Now you know how I feel about surprises," Roghald called to the trolls. "Who are you, and what do you want?"

The thursr's face twisted in anger, and he growled, baring his tusks and yellow teeth. The other Mogthrasir trolls followed his lead, and raising their weapons, they growled and stomped their feet.

Shumbolg, who already towered over everyone, stood up to his full height, raised his fists high in the air and brought them down hard on the ground in front of him. The resonant boom, the broken shards of rock that erupted as well as the tremor it caused took the wind out of the new trolls' sails, and all of them, except the thursrs, took a step backwards. Shumbolg was a living force of nature.

"Again," Roghald said in a bored tone of voice, "Who are you and what do you want?"

The frustration was obvious in the narrowed eyes and clenched jaw of the lead thursr, but he remained uncowed.

"I am Hrungnir," he barked at Roghald. "The great Mogthrasir seeks to know why Burrugandr trolls think they can traverse his lands as they please?"

Roghald raised his head high before answering. "Burrugandr cares not for your dry strip of land. We have an errand to the west and are simply passing through. We will do so with great haste too, because of the smell of this place."

Hrungnir ground his teeth but kept his voice neutral. "What is there for Burrugandr in the west? There is nothing there, but a few small settlements," Hrungnir looked genuinely perplexed.

Roghald stood in silence for a moment, and had just opened his mouth to speak when Shumbolg rumbled, "The Ulfhednar half-breed has-"

Roghald slammed his fist into Shumbolg's arm before the big troll could finish the sentence. If looks could kill, Shumbolg would have been mincemeat.

"Our business is our own," Roghald spat at both Hrungnir and Shumbolg.

Hrungnir didn't hide his mirth at what had just occurred, smiling from ear to ear. "The pup from that wolf bitch and the Stonesmith all those years ago? He is still alive?" Hrungnir was practically radiant with joy. "Burrugandr can't even catch a puppy?"

The Mogthrasir trolls roared with laughter. Roghald lowered his head and clenched his fists. Above all, he wanted to rip Hrungnir's throat out, but even with Shumbolg on his side, against three other thursrs, the outcome was too uncertain. Besides, he had more pressing business at hand.

"Get out of our way, we need to travel through," he growled at the other troll.

Wiping tears from his eyes, Hrungnir stepped to the side with a mock bow, sweeping his arm towards the west. "Best be on your little errand. The puppy might join forces with a rabbit, and then where will you be?"

Their laughter followed them for a long while and Roghald seethed, shooting angry glances at Shumbolg. "Just when I thought you couldn't get any dumber," he snapped at the big troll, who only shrugged and lumbered on. "You'd better hope they didn't read more into it than they seemed to."

As the Burrugandr trolls disappeared over the next ridge, Hrungnir straightened up, all traces of laughter gone from his face.

"Come," he said to the other trolls. "We need to hurry back to Mogthrasir. This is serious."

CHAPTER 5

ASH TURNED TOWARDS THE VOICE AS HE LIT HIS LIGHT-stone and saw a young man climbing out of the water onto a rock in the middle of the stream. The man was handsome with long dark hair, contrasting his smooth pale skin and delicate, almost feminine features. He was also stark naked. The man gave Ash a radiant smile as he made himself comfortable on the rock.

"I owe you my thanks and deep gratitude," he said in the most melodic voice Ash had ever heard. "The glow-fae lingered here for weeks, preventing me from playing my music outside the water.

"Er... You're welcome," Ash mumbled.

The man smiled, bending down to retrieve a glistening fiddle from below the surface. He busied himself picking the strings and adjusting the turning pegs of his instrument. Without looking up from his work, he said. "You are a funny-looking troll."

Ash responded, "I was thinking the same thing."

The man's laughter rang out like a bell over the forest.

"I suppose I am," he chuckled. "I am a nekk, and we rarely show ourselves to others, but I could not bear to stay in the water a moment longer."

Ash's eyes widened for a second. He had heard of nekks from the folklore of his home. They were creatures resembling beautiful, naked men, who would play their fiddles, luring young victims into the waters where they lived, only to drown and devour them. Few could resist the powerful allure of their music's magic. The nekk, sensing his concern, looked up through his ringlets of wet hair and smiled.

"Oh, don't worry. I owe you a debt of gratitude, so you have nothing to fear from me. Besides, you look... sinewy." Then his eyes grew distant as he continued in a sombre tone, "I once lived in Midgard, where most of my kind dwell. A land full of young, plump, delicious humans, unable to withstand my music."

"What happened?" Ash asked, hoping against hope that the enchantments on the trollhelm were working to their full capacity.

"I was banished." The bitterness was clear in his voice. "My presence came to the attention of a Seidwoman in my forest. Unable to kill me, she cursed me to Jotunheim by opening a portal in the middle of my pond. My beautiful little pond." He sighed and hung his head.

"I have to survive on forest animals and the occasional troll. A sad existence indeed."

"Oh. I am very saddened to hear that," Ash lied.

"But, alas," the radiant smile returned. "I can still play my music."

He placed the fiddle against his chin and the bow on the strings. When the nekk played, it was as if magic was spilling from his instrument straight into Ash's soul. It was both exhilarating and reminiscent of the sun's reflection over flowing rivers and waterfalls. It was a song about the waters of Midgard, and a pang of homesickness struck Ash. Eyes closed, the musician played on, lost in the mournful song, swaying to the fiddle's flow. Ash felt compelled to sit down and lose himself in the music forever, to let it sweep him away. He bent his legs, preparing to sit on the mossy ground, but realised with a start that this was the magic of the nekk. He shook his head to clear it and decided to get away before the creature changed his mind about not eating him. Ash quickly gathered his things, took a few steps, but abruptly turned back.

"Excuse me," he called to the nekk, who stopped playing and blinked a few times as if rousing himself from a dream.

"Yes?"

"I would consider your debt of gratitude to me paid if you set me safely on the course to Utgard."

The creature smiled, "But, of course, my ugly friend! Follow this creek until it washes out into The Great Lake. There you can seek a passage across, as Utgard sprawls on its other shore."

"Can't I walk around the lake?" he asked.

"With your short legs, it would take weeks."

"Thank you, I shall be on my way," Ash said.

"Fare thee well, little troll," the nekk smiled. "And take heed even I would not swim in The Great Lake. Beneath its placid surface awaits nothing but a grim death."

And with that, Ash turned around and hurried away. The beautiful music followed him for a long while as he weaved his way around the trees in the dark. When the music couldn't reach him anymore, he sat down, his back against a boulder. Too tired to even spread his sleeping roll out, he closed his eyes and fell asleep.

Ash woke at first light as birds began singing in the canopy above. Sleeping on cold ground left him sore and stiff, but a few stretches and breakfast revived his aching limbs. Soon he was on his way along the little river again. He walked all day, not encountering anyone or anything.

When the light faded in the evening, he had come up with a plan to ensure he could sleep unaccosted. The creek ran in the forested gulley between two mountains, so he didn't have to walk far away from the water to find a rock face. When he reached it, he laid his hands on the uneven stone that the river had carved over eons. He allowed his Stonesight to flow through it. Nothing.

He walked further along and tried again, with the same result.

After an hour's search, he at last found what he had been looking for. Near to the rock's surface, and a little way up, his Stonesight detected a pocket of air. He concentrated and let his hands sink into the stone, and his body soon followed. As he drifted inward and upward, the stone gave way to him, and he soon sensed open air around his hands again.

As he stepped out of the stone and onto an uneven surface, he put his hand in his pocket and lifted out the smooth lightstone. He lit it with a word and waited for the glow of the stone to fill the surrounding space.

Ash stood in a natural cavern inside the stone. It was completely sealed in the mountain, with no openings. It was similar in size to his old loft in the Hornsborg stables. The air felt stale, metallic, and made him lightheaded after a few breaths. Ash had learned well from his dwarven master and could discern the overwhelming presence of natural gas in the cavern. He had to act fast.

Turning to the wall he had entered from, he pressed his hands against it and chanted, channeling his will into the stone. As he worked, the stone melted away from his hands and a tunnel, twice the size of Ash, expanded through the mountain. When it reached the open air of the outside, a gust of cool, fresh air pushed against him and Ash took a deep breath, clearing his lungs. Once the spell faded and the tunnel closed, the metallic odour had vanished, leaving only fresh air in the cavern.

Ash briefly leaned on the cavern wall, exhausted from the tunnelling work. Eating and resting briefly would rejuvenate him, he knew. Ash looked around the cavern. He would have plenty of air to last the night. He spread out his sleeping roll on the flattest surface he could find and dropped his pack next to it. As he sat down, Ash removed the trollhelm and, with a sigh, rubbed his head. It wasn't the most comfortable thing to wear, and he wished he had taken comfort into account when he made it.

He left the lightingstone on as he ate some dried meat and

washed it down with the last of his water from Eikinri's well. When he turned the light off, he laid back on his bedroll in complete darkness. He stayed awake for a while, thinking about his friends, Yrsa and Torsten. It felt like he had not seen them for a lifetime and he missed their companionship. He remembered also all the friends he had lost along the way; Jarl Erik and Jarl Olaf and all the Jomsvikings that had welcomed him as a brother among their ranks. A tear ran down his cheek when he remembered Rani, the Seidwoman. If it had not been for all these people fighting to protect him, he would have been long dead too. The guilt gnawed away at him, and when he found sleep, it was a restless one.

The air was still, but so cold that it threatened to sap the warmth from his very bones. Ash looked around the massive hall. Enormous, frost covered stone pillars held up a ceiling lost in a sea of icicles above and he had to hug himself, sticking his already numb fingers into his armpits. The walls and pillars of the hall were all intricately carved stone, the designs barely visible under the frost. His breath left his mouth as clouds and he felt it freezing and crystallising in his beard.

What was this place?

In front of him stood a pair of immense stone doors, their iron hinges and bands covered by a layer of ice. Sinister runes encircled the doorway and Ash sent a thought of gratitude to Eikinri for teaching him how to read troll.

"*Only Winter Is Eternal*," he translated under his breath.

A sensation of movement next to him made him jerk his head around and his hand searched for a sword that was not on his belt. A tall old man stood next to him, facing the door. Two large ravens, who sat on his shoulders, staring at Ash, fluttered their wings for balance when the old man turned to face him.

"We have not spoken for some time," the man said with a smile that didn't quite reach his one eye. Where the second eye should have been was nothing but dark space, filled with the pinprick light of a thousand stars.

"Odin," Ash said through chattering teeth.

The father of the gods wore a long, tattered grey coat that stood in contrast to his snow-white beard and hair that flowed down his chest and shoulders. He seemed unaffected by the cold, and his breath did not fog like Ash's did.

Ash shivered and his teeth clattered.

"Hugin," Odin said, and one of his Ravens spun its head around to look at him. "Help him, will you?"

The raven cawed once and leapt off the god's shoulder and onto Ash's. As soon as its little clawed feet settled onto Ash's coat, a pleasant warmth spread from the bird, and Ash's shivering body relaxed. It was like sinking into a warm bath on a frosty night and Ash revelled in the sensation.

"Thank you," he said to the bird, but it ignored him. "Where are we?" Ash asked the god.

Odin nodded to the stone doors and spoke, "Beyond those doors lies the throne of Thrym, the Troll King of Jotunheim."

Ash raised his eyebrows and turned back to the doors.

"He is a Frost Giant who clawed his way to power with equal amounts of cunning and brute force. More impressive still is that he has remained in power for a thousand years, which says a lot about Thrym in a place like Jotunheim."

Ash hoped that he would never have to meet this Thrym.

"Walk up to the doors, Ash," Odin said in a low voice.

"We're not going to open them, right?" Ash turned to the old man, wide-eyed.

Odin smiled. "No, that would be foolish. Even in a dream. Place your hands on them."

Ash's mouth had gone dry and his heart raced, but after an encouraging nod from the Allfather, he walked up to the doors, treading as lightly and silently as he could. As he stood before the frozen stone, he looked over his shoulder, and Odin spoke again.

"Place your hands on them and send your mind through the stone."

Ash nodded and placed his hand on the rough, frosty doors. He was met with a biting cold, that even the god's raven on his shoulder could not chase away. He focused on sending his mind through the stone when a wave of hate struck him. It was so strong, it sent him reeling and he fell to the ground, scrambling backwards. Fear consumed him as he stared, unblinking, at the frozen doors. The raven remained on his shoulder, wings flapping.

"That is the hate Thrym has for everything that grows and lives in the warmth of the sun. He was Ymir's first son. After my brothers and I slayed his father at the dawn of time, he made it his life's mission to seek the downfall of the Aesir gods. He wishes to rule eternal over everything we have created as his revenge against us. And he would not be a gentle master."

Ash stood up and walked back towards the god who locked his gaze onto Ash's.

"You can only destroy the source of what is threatening Midgard by getting beyond those doors."

Ash raised his eyebrows. He could still feel the hate and malice radiating from beyond the icy doors.

"How?" he whispered, glancing at the doors. "How can I stand against that kind of hate and power?"

He realised that the reassuring pressure of the raven on his shoulder had disappeared and the cold was once again creeping into his bones. He turned back to Odin, but the god was gone and Ash was alone.

"How?" he asked again into the empty space.

CHAPTER 6

ASH OPENED HIS EYES TO TOTAL DARKNESS. AFTER A moment of confusion, he fumbled around his bedroll until his fingers closed around the lightstone. Its glow chased away the darkness and revealed again the cavern where he'd slept. The air was still and stagnant. He was tired and dazed from a restless night, but knew he could not go back to sleep. Odin's words from his dream weighed on him heavily, and their conversation played over and over in his mind.

The stakes were now even higher, and what had already seemed a hard task now appeared impossible. He sighed as he reached for a piece of bread which had dried up and become as hard as the stone around him. Having drank the last of his water the previous night, he had to do a lot of chewing to swallow it down.

The day wasn't off to a good start, he thought as he packed up his bedroll and pulled the trollhelm over his head. After quickly looking around to ensure he had left nothing behind, he placed his hands on the wall and sank into the stone. He stepped out into a drizzling rain. The forest in the gully in front of him lay shrouded in a damp haze.

"Of course," he muttered, looking up at the thick, low clouds obscuring the distant tree canopy from his view. Before walking off, he turned back to the stone wall and stuck his finger up to the first joint into the stone. He mumbled a spell under his breath and a slight glow appeared where his skin met the rock. He carved the rune Ansuz, the letter 'A', into the wall. When he pulled his finger away, the rune remained, marking the spot of his little cavern. You never know when it might come in handy again, he thought as he turned and walked towards the river at the bottom of the gully.

It wasn't long before an icy trickle of water found its way inside his collar and Ash clenched his teeth, determined to ignore it. When he reached the river, he stood by its bank and eyed it with suspicion for a moment. When no murderous glow flies or nekks appeared, he bent down and quenched his thirst with big mouthfuls of the fresh water. Feeling better, he filled his now empty waterskin and set off downstream.

The next few days were uneventful as he walked through a rain that seemed to have set in for good. Ash spent his nights inside caverns, now adept at finding similar hideouts inside rocks, like the one he'd slept in on the first night. His clothes would just dry out enough overnight for him to be comfortable, only to become soaked again by the same relentless drizzling rain every morning.

Ash would often spot wildlife, strange deer-like creatures with massive antlers, rodents the size of cats and small creatures similar to rabbits, but with much larger, round ears. They all scurried away at the sight of him, except for one massive boar, as tall as a man, that charged him on sight. Ash had scrambled up a tree when the beast had turned to face him and pawed deep furrows into the ground with massive hooves. He had to spend the better part of the afternoon perched on a tree branch as the very persistent animal patrolled the tree in circles. At times, it would turn its beady eyes up at him and bellow. Eventually, the thing gave up and trotted off along the riverbed, huffing in frustration.

Ash had sensed a certain amount of intelligence in its eyes and remained on his branch long after the boar had left. Sure enough, a little while later, he saw its massive head peeking out behind a tree trunk. So, he waited another hour, until he was sure the boar was gone, before sneaking down the tree and hurrying off along the riverbed. Good fortune had it that the beast had disappeared in the opposite direction to where he was heading.

It wasn't long before the creek he followed joined another as two valleys met, and having now doubled in size, the water flowed much faster. Then the forest disappeared as abruptly as it had begun, and Ash found himself standing on a pebbled beach, looking out over the open water of what could only be the Great Lake. With great difficulty, he could make out a thin strip of land on the other side. It was more like an ocean than a lake, he thought.

Looking around to his left, beyond some rocks jutting out into the water, he saw a few ringlets of smoke rising to the sky. Ash made his way over to the rocks and scrambled up the cliff before raising his head over the edge. He looked over a little bay where several ramshackle buildings crowded around a rickety jetty. A couple of barely seaworthy small boats were bobbing next to the jetty, and Ash could see nets hanging from driftwood frames along the shore.

A movement between the shacks had him duck down and he saw a short troll, bent over carrying a large sack, walk down towards the water. He looked an awful lot like Beli, the troll who had plotted his capture and death in Midgard. Jarl Olaf had called him a vaettr. It was ugly and stocky, with an enormous nose and a big mop of black hair, and it waddled along, carrying its burden out onto the jetty. This troll, unlike Beli, had dressed itself in leathery leggings and a jerkin, which Ash could see, even from this distance, was grimy and stained.

The troll got to the last boat on the jetty and dropped the sack into it before straightening up and bending backwards, its hands on its lower back. The thing seemed almost comical, and Ash didn't think it would pose a great threat to him, so he stood up and climbed down the rocks toward the shacks. He jumped the last bit and landed with a crunch on the pebbled beach, startling the troll who swivelled its head in his direction.

Ash put on the friendliest smile he could muster and, waving, he walked towards the jetty. The troll dropped to its knees and reached down into the boat, pulling out a long staff with a rusty hook on the end.

He stood up, gripping the staff in both hands, and as Ash's foot touched the creaky timber of the jetty he called in a shrill voice, "What does he want?"

Ash paused, raising both his hands to show that they were empty, "I mean you no harm. I only need to get across the lake."

He saw the troll's eyes narrow in suspicion. "He can walk for all Felp cares. Go away and leave Felp alone."

"I can pay you," Ash offered. "I have a little gold."

The troll's eyebrows shot up. "How did he come by gold? Gold is won in battle, and he doesn't look the type."

"I, eh... I found it," Ash said. It was the truth, after all.

"Let's see it then," the troll demanded.

Ash shook his head, "Once we get to the other side."

The troll frowned but seemed to come to a decision. "Felp will take him across, but only if he shows Felp once they are on the way."

Ash agreed. After all, the troll had no reason to trust him.

The troll, whose name was Felp explained that he scraped out a meagre living fishing in the lake. He told Ash that he needed to prepare a few things for the journey and disappeared into the closest shack. Ash made himself as comfortable as he could in the back of the little boat. It was a rickety thing of bleached wood. The bottom had a finger-deep puddle of water that stank of fish guts and algae, and it brought the boat's safety into serious questioning. Ash remembered the nekk's warning about swimming in the Great Lake and hoped it would hold together for their passage across.

Felp returned with a sack which he dumped in the prow before jumping in, but he was also carrying two steaming mugs. He passed one to Ash before sitting down on a plank and drank his own in two big gulps.

"Feycockle mushroom soup," he said. "It is cold out on the lake and it will keep him warm and awake."

Ash sniffed the soup and found it smelled earthy and sweet. His stomach gave a rumble, and it reminded him he had eaten very little since yesterday, so he took a small sip. It was smooth and quite tasty and before long, Ash had drunk the whole thing. He passed the empty cup to Felp with a smile and a nod. The troll nodded back and threw the cup back into his sack. He untied the half-rotted ropes that secured them to the jetty and pushed off.

The little boat was bobbing around in the middle of the bay while Felp busied himself with a set of oars lying at the bottom of the boat. A fresh waft of stink rose into the air when he pulled them out of the rancid puddle, but the wind carried the stench away in a moment. When Felp had set up the oars, he rested his arms on them and looked at Ash.

"Now it is his turn to hold up his end of the bargain," he grumbled.

Ash reached into his pack and pulled out his pouch. The jingle when he pulled it out made Felp's ears point up, and his eyes widened when Ash shook out a fat coin into his hand. Felp reached out towards the coin, but Ash tipped it back into the pouch and tightened the drawstrings.

"When we get to the other side," he said in a firm voice.

Anger flashed across the troll's face for a second, but then he smiled, revealing broad, stumpy teeth, and nodded. He grabbed the oars and with a few powerful strokes, they pulled out of the bay. The lake was still, only the smallest swell lifting and sinking the boat gently as they pushed through the dark and somewhat murky waters. The troll was much stronger than he looked, and they moved at a steady, swift pace.

He probably does a lot of rowing, Ash mused, then giggled,

somehow finding it comical. The troll looked up at Ash's titter and grinned. Ash smiled back. Felp was such a nice troll. What a delightful friend he had made. Ash was feeling quite euphoric and as the gentle rocking of the boat tickled his stomach, he couldn't help but laugh again. Felp laughed too, but Ash failed to see the cruel glint in his eyes. Ash's eyelids grew heavy, and he leaned back against his backpack.

"I feel strange," he muttered. His tongue felt thick and furry, and he couldn't help but slur his words a little.

"It's probably the soup," Felp said, still smiling. "Felp added some fallowberries to his."

"Oh, alright," Ash said happily. "Thank you."

"He is welcome," Felp laughed, and Ash laughed with him.

Just before he fell asleep, Ash noticed they were rowing along the coastline instead of away from it.

CHAPTER 7

ROGHALD STRODE THROUGH THE GATES OF UTGARD, his eyes wide, taking it all in. The largest settlement in Jotunheim, Utgard housed every kind of troll imaginable, from foot-high little runts to massive thursrs. Roghald even spotted a few dark elves, goblins, and a dwarf in the throng of trolls milling around the streets.

Inside Utgard's enormous walls stood tall and warped buildings, each one stranger than the other. The town was known as Jotunheim's trade hub and at its very centre, lay the largest open-air marketplace of their world.

Utgarda-Loki, the jotunn ruler of Utgard, showed no fear of the Thundergod and built the settlement in the middle of an open plain next to the Great Lake, ruling it with an iron fist. The giant had declared his peace on the settlement and enforced it with brutal violence from his ranks of battle trolls. If any creature, troll or otherwise, were to raise a fist or a weapon against another within his walls, Utgarda-Loki would mete out swift and cruel punishment. His firm rule allowed for uninterrupted trade to occur in the marketplace and made Utgarda-Loki one of the wealthiest trolls in Jotunheim.

A drizzly rain had been falling since the morning, and the heavy foot traffic had churned the unpaved streets into a mud field, so when a short vaettr ran past, he splattered Roghald with the foul muck without so much as a glance back. Roghald clenched his fist in anger, the impulse to crush the little troll for his insolence only curbed by Agash's firm grip on his arm. The dark elf had explained to him Utgarda-Loki's peace before they entered the town. With a stern shake of her head, she compelled him to swallow his anger.

"Let's go," he snapped. "The sooner we are away from this place, the better."

"This way," Agash replied and took the lead through the winding streets. They avoided the marketplace altogether by skirting close to the walls and soon found themselves at the edge of the lake. Dozens of boats were moored in the shallows and along several sturdy jetties. Even through the rain, the air was thick with the smell of rotting fish, kelp and general refuse that always seems to accumulate where people gather boats.

Amidst a hive of activity, they walked out onto the largest jetty, where workers were tying up and loading several broad ferries. Roghald walked up to the closest one, a wide barge half loaded with goods. Along the railings of the barge, he saw trolls seated in pairs, chained to each other and the bench they sat on. They looked altogether miserable, and several of them were sporting dark bruises on their backs and shoulders.

A grey, fat troll was reclining on a sack, eating a large turnip-like vegetable, and he looked up when he saw Roghald's group approaching. He had a thick wooden rod across his lap.

Roghald addressed him, "We need to get to the western shore as soon as possible."

Turning his attention back to his food, the troll replied, "A finger of gold for you and the mud-fairy and a finger of gold for the walking mountain."

Roghald felt Agash tensing up next to him at the slur for dark elves. He took a secret delight in her affront. Her arrogance had been getting on his nerves of late.

"We need to leave right away," Roghald said.

The ferry troll snorted, spraying little bits of turnip on the deck in front of him.

"We'll leave when I'm good and ready. I'll still have room for cargo, even with your big pet on board."

"You'd be wise to show some respect for your betters."

The troll looked up at him calmly. "I don't see why I have to," he sniggered. "Utgarda-Loki's peace holds here on the jetty too, and even a brute like you would have enough sense not to shed any blood while on the Great Lake. Since I never leave this barge, I need not fear anything from the likes of you."

Agash had explained to Roghald that a breed of enormous eels infested the Great Lake, and though they were blind, they possessed an exceptional sense of smell. They could detect just a few drops of blood in the water, and this was enough to send them into a frenzied attack. Because of their enormous size and ferocity, they could destroy even the largest of barges in a matter of minutes. That explained the bruises on the rowing-slaves' backs and shoulders. The barge troll would use a thick rod instead of a whip, lest he doom them all to a terrible ending in the stomach of an eel.

The fat troll heaved his bulk up from the sack with some difficulty and threw what remained of his turnip to the nearest pair of slaves who wrestled for the scrap.

"You are free to go elsewhere, but few of the barges are large enough to take your thursr." He walked up to the railing, placed his knuckles on it and leaning forwards looked Roghald straight in the eyes, "Now, pay up or get out of my sight."

The anger that burned inside Roghald had the troll in his head screaming with laughter. He closed his eyes and took a deep breath. Once he was calm enough that his hands stopped shaking, he reached into his pouch and pulled out a coiled length of gold that Grinbodr had given him for the journey and pinched off two finger lengths of gold with his nails. He gave the smiling ferry troll a dark look when he handed him the gold and vowed that should the opportunity present itself, he would tear the bastard to pieces.

"Wait on the jetty until we are ready to set off, so you don't get in the way."

Roghald turned just in time to see Agash's smile disappear from her face as she assumed a neutral expression. His predicament amused her. When this business was over, he would teach her a lesson or two. He shoved his way past the dark elf, who had to take a few steps back to regain her balance, and walked up to a stack of crates in the middle of the jetty where he sat down. Shumbolg followed him obediently, and eventually Agash sauntered over too.

After a long silence, Agash spoke in her low voice, "I need to stress the importance of not spilling blood on the Great Lake." With a meaningful look at Roghald, she continued, "And if you are considering throttling someone instead, be aware that the barge troll has a knife on his belt and he seems the type who would take everybody down with him."

Roghald scowled but said nothing. They spent the rest of the morning in the rain, waiting for the signal to board. By the time the bargemaster waved them over, they were thoroughly soaked and Roghald's mood had worsened.

"The walking mountain needs to stay in the middle of the barge at all times, lest we capsize," the troll said. "You two can sit down wherever you find room."

Crates and sacks covered everywhere else on the boat, except for the clear area in the middle reserved for Shumbolg. When the massive thursr set his foot on the deck, the whole barge dipped to the side, and the waterline came close to the top of the railing. A few of the slaves yelped and gripped their benches, but as soon as Shumbolg took the next step and placed himself in the middle of the flat vessel, it righted itself again. Roghald and Agash jumped on and went to opposite ends of the boat, making themselves as comfortable as possible.

When the fat troll approached him, Roghald asked, "How long?"

The bargemaster looked up at the sky, then out over the lake.

"Not much wind and the lake is calm, so probably around noon tomorrow."

A whole day and night, Roghald thought. And the entire time Ash would get further and further away in who knows which direction. He didn't think that the stupid lout would have a snowflake's chance in a smelter of actually reaching Burrugandr's mountain, let alone destroying the source tree, but he couldn't live with the embarrassment of Ash eluding him again. Besides, he was getting desperate to get rid of the voice in his head. Since he more or less spent all his time in his troll shape nowadays, there was no reprieve from it. Its meaningless wailing and blabbering was slowly driving him mad.

He sat down on the deck and propped his muscular bulk against a coil of thick rope. Holding out his clawed hands, he flexed his fingers. Roghald liked his troll shape. It was strong and powerful, and he felt almost indestructible in this form. He would be happy to spend the rest of his life like this, if not for the curse of Gamir's voice that came with it. He would find Ash and bring him back to Burrugandr alive. Then, once Grinbodr had removed the troll from his head, Roghald would kill Ash, if the jotunns hadn't already. After that, he'd find a way back to Midgard and let his wrath loose on the world of humankind. If they thought Gurmr and Grundr were bad, then they were in for a shock.

With a smack of his stick, the barge troll sent one of his slaves to untie the mooring ropes, and several others pushed off the jetty with their oars. The vessel drifted away from the jetty and on the bargemaster's barking command, a goblin, who seemed to be on the brink of starvation, started beating a steady pace on a wide drum. The rowers dipped their oars in the water with long strokes, paced by the rhythm of the drum. It took a moment for the barge to build up speed, but they made their way out of the cove at last, leaving Utgard behind.

Roghald stood to watch the strange town disappearing at a snail's pace. The drumming aggravated his already irritable mood, and the drizzling rain didn't help matters. He sat back down with a sigh. This was going to be a long trip.

They bobbed along the grey waters all day long and just as Roghald could make out the coastline of their destination through the rainy haze, the world darkened and night set in. The fat bargemaster walked around the railings lighting big metal lanterns that hung on sturdy posts evenly spaced along the ship. A yellow light now glowed over the vessel. It seemed as if they were alone in the world, just a small sphere of light, drifting in an endless universe of mist and darkness.

Later that night, a breeze came through and swept the rain away. The otherwise black sky revealed a few shining stars. It would have been a tranquil moment, if it hadn't been for the incessant drumming, Roghald thought. He stood up and sat on the railing to dry out in the light wind when the bargemaster approached.

"I wouldn't get much closer than that," the troll said with a sneer. "The eels leap out of the water and snatch people if they get too close."

"They are supposed to be blind, are they not? They hunt by the smell in the water." Roghald replied in a dry voice. He had no time for the troll.

"This is true, but if I can smell you across the barge, I'm sure they can too," the troll snickered.

"Go away."

"I have come to tell you that the plans have changed. I have decided to deliver my goods to the northern shore first, so the rowers won't have to work against the wind on the last leg," he grinned at Roghald. "Unfortunately for you, that means that you will have to enjoy our company for a few more days, as the western shore will be our last destination."

Roghald said, with an edge to his voice, "That is not what we agreed upon."

"My barge, my decision." The troll added with a laugh, "You can always swim if you don't like it."

Roghald clenched his fists in frustration.

"Or," the troll began, his voice now like silk. "You can always encourage me to stick to the original course." His eyes drifted to the pouch on Roghald's hip where he kept the length of gold.

So that was his game, Roghald thought. He would press his passengers for more pay, once trapped in the middle of the lake. The arrogant smile on the troll's face sent a wave of fury through Roghald's chest.

"Oh, please," Roghald said through gritted teeth. "Allow me to encourage you." With that, his arm shot out, quick as lightning, and seized the troll by the neck. He squeezed hard and the troll's face turned first red, then purple, as his eyes bulged from his head. His hands gripped Roghald's wrist to pull the hand off him, but Roghald was a battle troll, and the bargemaster would have no hope of breaking his grip.

"No blood in the water," Agash's smooth voice was at his side. She seemed to appear out of nowhere.

Roghald turned to the dark elf. "I know what I'm doing. Stay out of it."

While Roghald's attention was on Agash, the barge troll seized his opportunity and pulled the knife from his belt. Roghald felt a flash of pain in his arm and when he turned back to the troll, he could see the long knife buried to the hilt in his wrist. The smaller troll tore the knife out and raised it to strike again, so Roghald shook him like a rag doll.

He stopped when he heard the 'plop' from the blood-covered knife landing in the water a few yards out from the barge. The world seemed to stop as everyone on the barge stood or sat perfectly still and held their breaths, listening hard. Then the water churned once. Then twice. Roghald glimpsed a long, glistening body in the torchlight and the barge rocked slightly. A soft wail was heard from the rowers.

"You idiot!" Agash snapped. "You have doomed us all."

Roghald returned his attention to the bargemaster, who had gone pale with fear. A terrible idea struck him, but right now anything was worth a try. He winked and smiled at the troll before lifting him up by the neck. He took a few running steps towards the railing and threw the troll as far out as he could. The bargemaster landed at least twenty paces out into the water with a splash and the surrounding sea erupted in a wild churning as long, slippery bodies began tearing him apart.

"Lift your oars up!" Roghald called to the rowers who, used to obeying commands, did so even amid their distress. "Everybody quiet!"

The screams of the fat troll lasted only a moment, but the churning in the area where he'd landed carried on for several minutes. They stood in silence on the barge, slowly drifting away from the scene. Once the feeding frenzy had quieted down, they felt a few bumps against the hull of the barge. A few of the rowers yelped at this, but when Roghald gave them a murderous look and pointed first to them, then the water, they clamped their hands over their mouths.

It wasn't until long after the water had settled that Roghald decided they were in the clear and told the rowers to dip the oars in the water once more. They set course for the western shore, but they'd have to do without the drum. As soon as the goblin began striking out the rhythm, Roghald snatched it from him, and threw it overboard.

Chapter 8

Ash woke up with a throbbing headache. A wave of nausea swept over him, and he kept his eyes pressed shut as he took slow, deep breaths. He realized that someone had tied his hands behind his back and also tied his feet together. That weasel Felp must have drugged him. Ash wanted to slap himself for being so naïve and accepting a drink from the unknown troll.

Once the wave of nausea had passed, and he could open his eyes, he found himself lying on the dirt floor of a small, rickety hut. It was dark, but a sliver of light coming around the ill-fitted wooden door was enough to illuminate his surroundings. There were a few shelves along the walls, and he eyed them off in search of something to cut his bonds with, but saw only old buckets and lengths of rope.

He heard footsteps approaching and looked down to see the shadows of two feet approaching underneath the door. As the door opened with a creak, Ash shut his eyes and pretended he was still asleep. That turned out to be a mistake, since it might have spared him having a bucket of icy lake water dumped on him. He gasped and spluttered a few times as the water found its way into his nose.

"Up you get," a harsh voice chuckled.

Ash looked up at a squat, short troll. It was green skinned with

drab, olive hair on its head and muscular shoulders. A nasty looking, iron-studded cudgel hung from a thick leather belt around its
waist. It looked quite worn.

"Where are my things?" Ash asked the troll.

"Belongings are no concern of yours anymore," the troll laughed,
spreading his arms in a gesture of generosity. "All you will ever
need from here on will be provided for you, you lucky bastard!"

Ash knew there was nothing lucky about the situation he found
himself in and sighed.

"What do you mean?"

The troll bent down and put his bulbous nose closer to Ash's
face than was comfortable and gave him a broad grin.

"You are to be a barge rower. You can look forward to years of
exercise in the fresh air with all your needs taken care of and very
generous pay on top. I envy you, I really do!"

Ash didn't miss the wicked glint in the troll's eyes as he stood
up.

"Pay?" Ash questioned. Being tied up didn't seem to go hand in
hand with getting paid.

The troll kicked him in the stomach.

Ash groaned as it winded him and the nausea returned a hun-
dredfold.

"There is your first payment," the troll laughed before bending
down and lifting Ash by the neck.

"You're heavier than you look. Maybe you won't be as scrawny
a rower as I thought." With that, he carried Ash out into the daylight.

They were on the shore of the Great Lake in a small cove that
seemed well hidden and protected by cliffs on all sides. Only a narrow gap between the cliffs revealed a pathway leading into a deep
green forest. Several sturdy stone buildings leaned up against the
cliffs, and a well-built timber jetty stretched a short way into the
lake. Several other trolls were busying themselves carrying goods
out of the buildings and stacking them on the jetty. All of them

closely resembled Ash's tormentor, leading him to assume they were related.

The troll set him down on his feet when they got outside the little building.

"I am going to untie your legs, but if you try to run, you will bitterly regret it. Understood?"

Ash nodded.

The troll bent down and worked on the knot around Ash's ankles. As soon as Ash could feel the bonds fall off him, he drove his knee as hard as he could into the troll's nose. The troll staggered backwards, a look of disbelief on his face and now sporting a broken nose gushing with blood.

Ash smiled at him, "There's your change for the payment."

Then he ran. He ran straight for the pathway leading into the forest. Ash figured his best chance was to hide among the trees. He had only taken a few steps when the troll had recovered enough to let out an angry roar. Ash sped up. It was difficult to run with his hands still tied behind his back, and he still felt a little off from being drugged, but he reached the forest and set off down the track.

In stark contrast to the bright cover, the forest was silent and gloomy. His rapid footsteps on the well-trodden path rang out around him. He heard shouts behind him, and he chanced a look behind. Three trolls were just entering the forest, but it wasn't them he was worried about. In front of them, on a chain held by one troll, was a squat, toad-looking creature. It had big reptilian eyes on top of its head and a broad mouth which spanned the entire width of its head. The glistening brown skin was covered with black spots, but unlike a toad, it had long, muscular limbs that were now churning at the ground in a frenzy to get to Ash. Its broad paddle-like toes dug into the soil as it strained against the chain.

Ash Shifted, and the world slowed down. As the trolls and their creature came into perfect focus, Ash could see the grin on the troll's face and the excitement in his eyes as he let go of the chain and the toad shot forward. Ash jumped and brought his tied-up hands under his feet and around to the front. As soon as he landed, he set off running like mad along the path.

For a moment, he heard galloping behind him, but then it fell silent. Ash risked another glance behind him and saw that the pathway behind him was empty. He caught a movement above him and looked up to see the thing leaping from tree to tree, its broad head fixed on him. It was moving as fast as Ash. He cursed and ran faster. He was pulling away from the creature but knew it would not be long until he ran out of energy while Shifted. And he needed energy to fight. With his hands tied and no weapon, it was going to take a miracle, but he had no option. He sprinted faster to get a little further ahead of the toad. He knew his only chance was to take the fight to the creature.

A plan was forming in his head, when something hit his right leg and yanked it back, sending Ash sprawling towards the ground. He landed face first on the path and turned around to see the creature up in a tree, its mouth open wide and a long tongue stretching down to the back of Ash's leg. The tongue ended in a sticky ball that had half wrapped around his thigh and it was slowly retracting, pulling him closer.

Ash shook his leg, but the sticky tongue held firm, dragging him through the dirt. He looked around in desperation for something to use as a weapon, but there was nothing except pebbles within his reach. Then he almost laughed, cursing his own stupidity, and scooped up some pebbles between his hands. Granite, mica, and shale. He channelled his will into the stones, forcing the minerals to merge into a solid orb. Next, he forced the lump to heat, using the same technique as when he had carved into the rock face to mark his cave.

The solid orb now glowed a deep red as the stone came close to its melting point. Ash could feel the heat radiating from it. Then he slammed it into the tongue. The toad let out a drawn-out squeal, distorted by the slowing of time, and the tongue let go and retracted, leaving only strings of slime along Ash's leg.

He got to his feet just as the toad landed on the ground in front of him. It opened its mouth wide and crouching down on its powerful legs, it hissed at him and dug its feet into the ground. It launched itself straight at Ash, but he was still Shifted and leapt to the side as the creature shot past him. Ash still held the glowing lump of stone, and now running his fingers over it, shaped it into a foot-long spike.

The toad spun around and once again shot forwards towards Ash. He almost felt sorry for the creature as he stepped to the side, and as it came level with him, slammed the spike into the base of its neck. The momentum of its leap carried the toad through a few rolls on the ground, but by the time it came to a stop, it was dead. The still heated spike sizzled as a few tendrils of smoke escaped the wound.

Ash stopped Shifting and drew a relieved breath just as something slammed into him. Some kind of rope with hard leather balls on the end spun several laps around him, pinning his arms to his sides, and knocking him over. He had forgotten about the trolls. Soon, all three were upon him. He saw that one of them had Ash's own sword stuck in his belt. He doubted the troll knew what a formidable weapon it was. The troll with the broken nose walked up to the toad and bent forward, placing his forehead on the dead creature's head. He let out a long wail.

One of the other trolls walked up to Ash and kicked him in the head. There was a metallic clang as the kick hit the trollhelm, leaving Ash unscathed. The troll grunted in surprise. Ash's disguise had a tuft of red hair but didn't wear a helmet to make such a noise. The troll bent down and felt around Ash's hair and seeming to find a purchase, yanked and pulled the helmet off. Ash felt a tingle as the spell left him. The troll stumbled back a few steps, its mouth open in utter surprise, staring between Ash and the trollhelm that had materialised in its hands.

"It's… it's a human…" he whispered, before turning to his companions. "It's a human!"

Broken-nose now stood up, tears streaking his face. He looked at Ash for a moment before his eyes darkened. "It's a dead human, is what it is," he said, walking with determined steps towards Ash, yanking his cudgel from his belt.

"No, wait," said the third troll, moving to block his way. "It could be worth a lot."

"I don't care! It killed Glop!" broken-nose roared, pushing the other troll out of the way. Walking up to Ash, he raised the cudgel above his head. Ash struggled against his bonds, but he was wrapped up tight and couldn't move. The murderous expression on the troll's face remained even as a spear slammed into the side of his neck and penetrated through to the other side. He fell to the ground, already turning to stone.

The other two trolls spun towards the forest where the spear had come from, and their faces paled as Torsten the Berserker, in all his might, stepped out of the trees. The enormous man, wearing a bearskin over his shoulders, had a crazed look on his bearded face as he towered over the trolls, who had become frozen on the spot. Torsten roared and leapt into action. Swinging his massive axe, he threw himself forward at the first troll who shrieked and turned to run. The troll didn't even get to take a single step before Torsten's axe cleaved it in two at the waist.

The other troll was already running down the path before his friend's halves had hit the ground. He did not, however, make it many steps until something shot out of the forest, quick as lightning, and slashed him across the calves. The troll fell face first onto the path and began crawling away using only his arms, horror-struck.

Yrsa stopped Shifting as she strolled up to the troll casually and bent down to cut his throat. She wiped her seax on the back of the troll just before he turned to stone. She stuck the weapon back in her belt and turned to Ash, a big smile on her face.

"Well, well, well... I guess the big Stonesmith still needs rescuing, ha?"

CHAPTER 9

THE BARGE BUMPED INTO THE WOODEN JETTY. Roghald let his eyes run over the small, protected cove, looking for any signs of movement, but there were none. The sheltering cliffs surrounding the cove had several sturdy stone houses built up against them, with one of them having its door unlatched and swinging gently in the breeze. The trading station seemed abandoned. His suspicion grew as he observed stacks of cargo neatly piled up on the jetty.

"Keep your wits about you," he told Agash and Shumbolg, his eyes never leaving the shore. "It could be a trap."

Agash had her bow drawn and an arrow resting on the string as she leaped onto the jetty before the trolls had even secured the lines. Once the barge was tied off, Roghald also jumped onto the jetty, followed by Shumbolg, who once again threatened to capsize the barge. They began moving along the jetty with caution when there was a cough behind them.

"Ehrm, what do we do?" one of the rowing slaves asked sheepishly.

"Do as you please," Roghald told the slave. "You are all free, as far as I'm concerned."

All the slaves straightened up in their seats at his words, wide eyed. The slave who had spoken lifted his hands up in front of his face, showing Roghald the thin loops of chain that bound his wrists to the rower next to him.

Roghald rolled his eyes. "I suppose the keys were with the bargemaster?"

All the slaves nodded.

He sighed and looked around him, his eyes falling on a flat bar lying next to the cargo on the jetty. It was likely used to open crates. He tossed the bar to the slave who almost missed it, managing to just grab it before it fell overboard and Roghald turned his attention back to the shore.

Shumbolg had moved off the jetty and stood resting on his knuckles, scanning the surrounding buildings. Agash was on one knee near a small timber shack, poking at the ground with an arrow. Roghald walked up to her, and she raised her head, looking toward a small opening in the cliff where a path wound its way into a forested area.

"There was blood spilled here, no later than this morning." She pointed to a dark patch on the ground, next to a short length of rope. "Then someone was chased into there, and they did not come back." She nodded toward the forested path.

Roghald turned to Shumbolg, who was poking his head into one building.

"Let's go. This doesn't concern us, but we might get caught up in it, so be alert."

Agash scouted ahead as they set out along the path into the forest. The creaking sounds of chain brackets being pried from the barge hull, accompanied by excited voices, followed them as they left the cove.

The forest was silent and Roghald followed the path, with Shumbolg lumbering along behind him. In his mind, the troll was blabbering with excitement again, and Roghald knew that meant something was nearby. As they crested a small rise along the path, they saw the three mounds in the shape of trolls spread out before them, with one mound clearly cut in half at the waist. Agash was kneeling next to a dead froglike creature. Roghald scanned the surrounding forest, but could see nothing.

The dark elf stood up and walked towards him. Her hands, covered in blood, held something elongated as she walked towards him. She approached Roghald and handed him a blood covered item. He reluctantly took it and seeing it was a smooth and sharp piece of rock, he looked at her, raising an eyebrow.

"Stonesmith," she said.

Roghald's eyes widened for a second, before a grin split his face in two. "Ash," was all he said, and the troll in his mind laughed and laughed.

CHAPTER 10

ASH COULD NOT STOP SMILING AS HE WALKED ALONG the path with his friends. They headed towards Yrsa and Torsten's last campsite, which was nearby.

"A Seidwoman came to Gjallarholm from the south," Yrsa explained. "She said she had a message for me and Torsten from the gods."

"We were both injured after our battle with the jotunn," Torsten cut in. "But she sang over us and tattooed some runes around our injuries and they healed overnight!" He lifted his bearskin to show several pink scars that were all that remained of the draugr bites and slashes he had endured during the fight with Gurmr and Grundr. One could see several fresh black runes around the existing swirling tattoos on his torso.

"Looks pretty good, I think," he said with a smile.

"Anyway, like I was saying," Yrsa said with a stern look at Torsten. "The message was that you had left for Jotunheim and Odin wanted us to go with you, and a good thing he did, from what I just saw back there."

Ash ignored the taunt and just smiled. "Well, it is very nice to see you both," he said.

"The Seidwoman gave us these portal stones and before we

knew it, we found ourselves in this strange land. We gathered they would have sent us close to you, so we looked around near where we arrived first. When we found the rune for 'A' carved at the foot of a mountain, we figured that few people around here could carve in stone, so it had to be you. After we found the next rune, we were sure that we were on the right track."

Ash was very glad he had carved those runes, or his friends might never have found him. Certainly not in time to save his life.

"Then we came along this man in the nuddy, sitting on a rock in the river." Torsten rumbled. "He played a fiddle and Yrsa became all smitten and waded out to him, dropping her weapons and un-buttoning her armour."

Yrsa's face flushed as she scowled at the Berserker. "It was a spell, Torsten. I have no memory of it!"

Torsten chuckled. "Anyway, when he smiled at Yrsa, I saw he had a mouth full of fangs, so I knew something wasn't right, and I threw my axe and buried it in his head."

"That was a nekk!" Ash blurted out. "It's spell didn't work on you?"

"I guess I've never had much of an ear for music," Torsten rumbled.

Yrsa, having recovered from her embarrassment continued. "Eventually, we found a vaettr by the lake, just as he docked and unloaded a deerskin knapsack that looked an awful lot like the ones we use in Midgard. It didn't take too much convincing to get him to confess the entire story of drugging and selling you to the other trolls. He kept insisting that it was another troll, not a human he had abducted, which now makes sense."

Ash tightened the straps on the pack that his friends had hand-ed him back when they found him.

"We were on our way to where the troll said he had left you when we heard the fight. Peeking out from behind a shrub, we saw three trolls had overpowered a smaller one. That was none of our business and we were just about to leave when one of them yanked your helmet off and suddenly, there you were! It turned out to be a fun little fight. Haven't killed many trolls before," Torsten mused. "Gives me the shivers how they turn to stone when they die, though."

They walked in silence for a while.

"You've aged a fair bit," Yrsa remarked, eying him up and down. "How long were you there this time?"

"Six years," Ash replied.

Torsten whistled. "Long time to be stuck underground, lad. At least it gave your beard a chance to grow in." The Berserker laughed and reached over to tug at Ash's whiskers. "And you're now older than Yrsa, so I guess she can't boss you around anymore!"

Yrsa punched both of them in the arm with two quick thuds, which ended Torsten's laughter. "You'll both do well to listen to me. If you two fools were left to decide for yourselves, we'd all be dead.

Ash avoided Torsten's eyes as he opened and closed his fist, trying to regain some sensation in his throbbing arm.

"So, where to?" Yrsa said, changing the subject. "Where in these gods-forsaken lands might we find this source tree we seek?"

"I don't exactly know," Ash started. "It is under a jotunn chieftain named Burrugandr's mountain. But first we need to face Thrym, the Troll King of Jotunheim. He lives inside a frozen fortress, but I have only seen it in my dreams, so I don't know where to look."

"Erh," said Torsten. "How sure can we be sure that it wasn't just a... eh, dream?"

"Well," Ash said. "Odin was there."

"Right, right," Torsten said whilst giving Yrsa a look that suggested that maybe Ash hadn't had a lot of fresh air during his years in Eikinri's smithy, but she only glared back at him.

"Of course, the boy is right," she said in a firm voice. "He is a Wolf of Odin, and the Allfather guides him. And we were sent here, were we not?"

"Right, right," the Berserker repeated, raising his hands in resignation. "So, where do we go?"

"I was going to Utgard and in my disguise, I was going to seek directions to the troll king's fortress. Apparently, he is a frost giant."

Both Yrsa and Torsten stopped in their tracks. Ash, who was a few steps ahead, stopped too and turned to face his friends.

"A frost giant?" Yrsa said in a low voice.

"Yes." Ash replied.

"And we need to face him?"

"Supposedly, yes."

"Getting past one of the oldest and fiercest enemies of the gods and humankind is the way to find the source tree?"

"So I am told, yes."

Yrsa and Torsten exchanged sceptical looks.

Then Yrsa shrugged and said, "I suppose you always need to have a bit of faith when dealing with the gods."

She must have seen the expression on Ash's face as he looked over her shoulder, because she ducked just in time for an arrow to pass over her head and slam into a nearby tree. They spun around to see a woman holding a bow standing in the middle of the path. She was slender and tall, wearing tight fitting leathers that would have made Ash blush under other circumstances. She had a brown cape over her shoulders, its hood shrouding her face in darkness. The friends all looked at her in a moment of confusion, until she reached her hand over her head and pulled a long black arrow from a quiver on her back, and they all sprang to action.

Torsten pulled his large round shield from his back in a well-practiced, smooth movement, whilst Ash and Yrsa both Shifted. At a hand signal from Yrsa, they split up and ducked into the forest in separate directions to flank the archer. Torsten roared and raising his axe in one hand, held his shield in front of him and ran straight for the woman. The thud of an arrow slamming into flesh could be heard, but even with the shaft sticking out just above his knee, Torsten did not slow or falter. He had entered the raged state of the Berserkers and neither pain nor wounds would stop him now. He appeared taller and his long strides carried him towards the woman.

Drawing close to her, he swung his axe in a blow that would have cleaved her at the waist had she not leapt straight up into the air. With a rustle of leaves, she disappeared in the purple canopy above. Torsten stood staring straight up, searching for their attacker, when a rumble caught his attention. He lowered his gaze to see an enormous creature lumbering towards him. The thing seemed to be made up of weathered stone, and was large enough to shoulder young trees out of the way, snapping them off without slowing its pace.

The Berserker roared a challenge that was answered with a bellow from the attacking thursr in a display of yellowed teeth and tusks. Torsten raised his shield and axe again as the massive troll came at him like an avalanche. As it drew near, the troll lifted an arm the size of a tree trunk in front of its chest and swung a heavy backhand to crush Torsten. It would have succeeded if Yrsa hadn't slammed into Torsten at full speed, throwing them both to the side and clear of the blow. Ash, who had just arrived from the other side, saw his friends land on the ground in front of him.

"You idiot!" Yrsa snarled as she leapt off the berserker's back and spun around to face the thursr. The enormous troll needed several steps to slow down from the momentum of its run and was clumsily turning around further down the path.

"Don't let it catch you in the open, it is too powerful," Yrsa said before turning a stern look on Torsten. "That especially goes for you."

Torsten gave her a sheepish smile and shrugged. "It's a good death, to die fighting a troll that size. My seat in Valhalla would be assured."

Yrsa rolled her eyes, and then the troll was near again. They raised their weapons and spread out to flank the massive creature when another roar rang out, and a second troll stepped out of the forest. This one was nowhere near as large as the first, but still towered over the humans. It was muscular, with long arms that ended in clawed fingers. Two horns curled backwards over his head, while short, bone-coloured spikes sprouted on his shoulders and upper arms. In just a second, Ash identified Roghald, who had his eyes fixed on him.

Ash stopped Shifting for a moment and called to his nemesis, "I thought you were dead."

Roghald let out a guttural laugh. "I'm harder to kill than you would think, whelp."

"Don't worry," Ash called, a smile on his face. "This time, I'll make sure you stay that way."

Roghald went into a state of blind rage and threw himself towards Ash, running as fast as he could. He was so focused on getting to Ash that he didn't see Yrsa coming from the side, stabbing her spear into his thigh, and sending him sprawling onto the forest floor. That's how the Ulfhednar fought. Just like wolves, one would distract the prey, and the others would attack from the side or behind.

Yrsa's face was murderous, as she too now recognised the troll that killed her father, Jarl Olaf. Torsten had his hands full, ducking and weaving around trees, only just staying out of the big thursr's grasp, whilst landing the occasional quick swing of his axe on the troll's legs or torso. He did well avoiding the troll, until a long, black arrow slammed into his back and he stumbled. His foot got caught on a tree root and he fell with a yelp.

Yrsa, in her Shifted state had kept an eye on both thursrs and pulled her spear from the fallen Roghald's leg. With a look of frustration, she turned her head between Torsten and Roghald a few times before deciding to sprint to her friend's aid, and abandon fighting her father's killer.

Ash had followed the direction the arrow had come from and glimpsed a brown hood behind a nearby cluster of rocks. He Shifted again and ran as fast as he could towards it before the archer would have time to draw and release another arrow at Torsten. He didn't slow down when he reached the boulders the archer was hiding behind, he simply dove headfirst into them. Shifted and using his Stonesmithing powers, the rock parted like water before him and he crashed into the archer on the other side, locking his arms around her waist and knocking her over.

They tumbled backwards in a tangle of weapons and capes, but Ash being much faster pushed off the ground and landed with a knee on her belly and in one smooth movement pulled his seax from his belt. No sooner had he raised it towards the archer's throat than her hood fell back.

Ash froze for a second as long white hair cascaded out around a smooth, pitch-black face. She had almond-shaped, ice-blue eyes above high cheekbones and her ears were pointed at the top. She was the most beautiful thing he had ever seen, and his heart stumbled, skipping several beats. He was suddenly acutely aware of her slender body beneath him.

She had a look of confusion for a moment before her eyes filled with understanding. Then they narrowed, and she parted her lips, revealing two rows of teeth that had been filed to sharp points, and growled at him. Ash was so taken aback that he flinched and lost his concentration and therefore his Shifting, only a split second before she slammed her fist into his face.

It felt like being hit by a hammer, and Ash tumbled to the side, landing face first on the mossy ground. He raised his head and shook it to rid himself of the ringing in his ears before remembering what was going on. In a flash, he rolled onto his feet, his seax held out in front of him, but the archer was gone. He spun around a few times and looked up into the tree canopy, but there was no sight of her.

"Ash!"

Yrsa's voice made him turn and scramble back over the cluster of rocks. He looked down, and his heart dropped. An unconscious

Torsten was held around the waist by the massive troll who used him as a club, swinging him wildly to get at Yrsa. She was Shifted and moved around the blows easily, thrusting her spear over and over into the body, arms and legs of the monstrosity. Her blows did not, however, appear to affect the troll in the slightest. He kept swinging Torsten like a rag-doll. Several trees lay toppled around the giant, having not been able to withstand the force of nature that was Shumbolg.

Ash saw Roghald, his leg wound now healed, running towards Yrsa from behind. With no time to think, Ash Shifted and Roghald's pace slowed down to that of a snail. As the scenario in front of him came into sharp focus and Ash took it all in, he sprinted towards his friends. He noticed that even Yrsa, despite being Shifted and much faster than the trolls, had also slowed down. After years of training, Ash had reached his full potential and was now faster than her. Much faster.

He sprinted up behind Roghald and, with one swift movement, pulled his sword and sliced through the thursr's Achilles tendon, almost cutting off his whole foot. His blade had cut so fast that Ash couldn't even see any blood leaving the wound yet. He was now right behind Roghald, so Ash jumped high and slammed the pommel at the bottom of his sword hilt as hard as he could into the back of Roghald's head.

The troll was toppling forwards, and Ash let his momentum carry him over the thursr, towards the enormous battle troll. The beast still had Torsten in its grasp, and the fear Ash felt for his friend propelled him forward. He darted past Yrsa, who had just ducked beneath a wide swing with the Torsten club. Ash leapt forward and up at the troll. With the sword raised above his head in two hands, Ash brought it down in a deep cut from the troll's jaw, all the way to its belly.

The wound closed almost as fast as Ash had made it. He was so stunned that he almost forgot to duck when the troll's empty hand swung around to grab him. Ash rolled backwards and away from its reach.

How could you kill something like that? It would just be a matter of time until the troll wore them down and they made a fatal mistake and it would all be over. And Torsten's chances of surviving were diminishing by the second. Ash launched forwards again in a barrage of stabs, cuts and thrusts, to every part of the troll's body, only to see the wounds healing before his eyes. The troll did not falter for even a moment.

He felt the first twangs of exhaustion as the Shifting took its toll, and he noticed Yrsa had stopped using her Ulfhednar power altogether. He had to do something. In a desperate attempt he feinted to the left and once the troll's enormous bulk moved in that direction, he darted right and springing off a fallen tree, he leapt up and with a pull of the thursr's loincloth strap, he swung himself up onto its back. As the troll was hunched over, Ash found enough perch on its rough skin to not fall off and started hacking at its neck. Let's see if you can live without a head, he thought.

But every blow he landed, no matter how deep he cut into the monstrosity's neck, had already healed by the time his next blow struck. He screamed in frustration when he realised he could never cut through fast enough. This troll healed far faster than any he had ever seen. Only an outright mortal blow would kill it.

"You cursed, useless lump of rock, why won't you die?!" he roared, his voice cracking with fear and frustration, but then a thought dawned on him. Trolls were formed from rock and when they died, they returned to just that. It was part of what they were. And if Ash knew anything, it was rocks. He placed his left hand on the troll's shoulder and concentrated. He could feel its muscles tensing as it reached behind its head to pluck him off. There wasn't much time.

Ash sent his Stonesight into the large body and although most of it was organic stuff, blurry to him, he picked up a fine network of shale and mica, throughout the thursr's body. It was in its blood, in fine particles, pumping and pulsating through its veins. All the veins congregated towards a small central point deep inside its chest before being sent out to all the limbs. Ash knew he had found the thing's heart.

He set the tip of his sword next to the troll's spine and pushed. Eikinri's sword slid in through the tough flesh when Ash put his weight on it and the tip moved towards the heart. The hilt hit the troll's back with only a few inches to go, stopping just short of the heart. But Ash was not done. Stone is stone, he thought, and concentrated. He started singing a song, so old that very few people had ever heard it, let alone known the meaning of the words or the power in it. Very few people besides the Stonesmiths, that is. It was the song Odin and his brothers sang when they created the world of Midgard from the giant Ymir's bones. It was the song of shaping stones and mountains. The minerals in Shumbolg's body listened and remembered and conformed to Ash's will.

The troll froze as the hilt of Ash's sword sunk into its body in a spray of blood. Shumbolg let out a drawn-out wail that was cut short as soon as the tip of Ash's sword pierced his heart. The troll slowly toppled sideways and when his enormous, now turned-to-stone body hit the forest floor, its weight was so great that it broke into a thousand pieces.

Ash stopped Shifting and ran into the pile of gravel and stones. Fortunately, Torsten was lying to the side and was not caught underneath the behemoth when it fell.

Ash suddenly remembered Roghald and spun toward where he had fallen, his sword raised and ready to strike, but his nemesis was nowhere to be seen. He scanned the forest around him as he returned to his friends, but there was no sign of Roghald. Yrsa was kneeling next to Torsten, a worried look on her face.

"He is still breathing, but it's very shallow. I think that thing crushed his ribs."

Ash looked down at his big friend who looked paler than usual and could see that pink spittle was bubbling at the corners of his mouth with every breath.

Yrsa turned to Ash, and he noticed her eyes had a glazed look and her voice sounded thick as she spoke. "I can't lose him too, Ash. Not after Olaf..." She bit down hard and looked back at Torsten. Then she took a deep breath and sat in silence for a moment before she squared her shoulders and stood up.

"Come. We'll make a stretcher and pull him with us. We have to get away from here before the others come back." Her voice was as steady as always, and the tears were gone from her eyes.

Ash nodded, and they set to work.

CHAPTER 11

ROGHALD JOGGED ALONG THE TRACK, AWAY FROM THE battle that marked the end of Shumbolg. How could Ash move so fast? Even compared to that Ulfhednar shieldmaiden, he was fast. And he had aged a lot in the short time since Havbodr, the sea hag, had killed Roghald. His jaw had dropped when he saw Ash move in what could only be described as a blur and saw him single-handedly kill the largest thursr in Burrugandr's horde.

When Roghald realised that the tide had turned against him, he had fled, running back towards the barge. Agash materialised next to him and kept his pace in silence.

"Where were you?" he snapped at the dark elf. "You could have shot him while he was busy with Shumbolg."

Agash shook her head, "He's too fast. It would have only given my position away had I shot another arrow, and I only narrowly escaped him the first time. I have seen the Ulfhednar fight before, but this one, he's different. Much faster."

"Burrugandr will hear of your cowardice," Roghald replied through gritted teeth.

"As he will hear of yours," she said, her face neutral.

Roghald scowled but said nothing as they broke clear of the

woods and into the cove. The barge lay where they had left it, bobbing alongside the jetty. About half of the rowing crew had freed themselves and were working hard on breaking their remaining comrades' fetters. Roghald landed on the barge with a thud that sent it rocking.

"Back to your benches," he yelled. "Take us out."

The slaves all looked at him with a mix of fear and surprise.

"But... You freed us," said the skinny goblin.

"Consider yourselves un-freed."

The trolls looked at each other, and most ambled back onto their benches with slumped shoulders. Two of them, who had been standing on the jetty next to the barge shared a quick glance before sprinting down the jetty toward the beach and the forest beyond.

The first one was still on the jetty when Agash's arrow slammed into him between his shoulder blades and sent him sprawling forwards. The second troll did much better than his companion, actually managing several steps onto the beach before an arrow shot clean through his throat in a spray of blood. Roghald, having watched the spectacle, turned back to the rowing crew.

"Anyone else feel like taking their bid for freedom? No? Then get to work."

He released the ropes mooring the barge to the jetty and pushed away from it with a kick. The rowers dipped their oars, and the barge made its way out of the cove with much greater speed than before, since Shumbolg's weight was no longer slowing them down.

"Back to Utgard," Roghald told the crew. The rowers fell back into rhythm with long strokes and the barge cut through the dark waters, leaving the little sheltered cove behind.

Standing at the railing, Roghald looked back at the forest they had left behind, his mind was churning. How could he defeat Ash when he wielded such formidable powers? He could not defeat him in a direct confrontation, that much was clear. The whole situation seemed utterly hopeless. Roghald, however, had an uncanny ability to find people's weaknesses and had more than once exploited them for his own gain. It didn't take long until Ash's weakness was obvious to him, and he smiled to himself. Ash was too trusting. That was the key. The way to capturing Ash was not through brute force, but with deception and cunning. Roghald hummed a joyful little tune as a plan took shape in his mind.

"We need to find a Shaman when we get to Utgard," he told Agash. "Someone discreet who will work for gold."

The dark elf looked at him with a critical eye. "I may know of someone," she said, and her eyes grew distant. "But she is... difficult. She lost all her children in the Troll Wars, and sorrow and madness have overcome her. There was a sad resonance in Agash's voice that did not go unnoticed. "She has no loyalties to any chieftain, as a matter of fact, she despises them all. There are no guarantees she will help us, even for gold, but for what you are asking, there is no one better."

"Perfect," Roghald smiled and sauntered over to a stack of empty sacks where he made himself comfortable with his hands behind his head. And the troll in his head laughed.

The next morning the barge bumped against the dock, and Roghald was once again looking out over Utgard. He didn't like the town the second time around either, but at least it had stopped raining. The rowers that had broken their chains on the other side of the lake simply stood up and smiling, walked off the barge and onto the docks. They were well aware of Utgarda-Loki's Peace that applied here and that Roghald could do nothing to stop them leaving. The freed rowers, not willing to risk their freedom any further, ignored the cries of their still-chained comrades as they vanished into the streets of Utgard.

Roghald and Agash jumped ashore and set off into town. Roghald eyed all the mismatched buildings and creatures as they made their way through the winding streets. No two buildings were alike. Crowded together, the buildings displayed a variety of architectural styles. Some were made of intricately carved stone, adorned with beautiful reliefs of dragons and snakes over the doorways. Others were little more than hovels, hastily constructed from driftwood salvaged from the lake. Some had sturdy, iron riveted doors, while some only had tattered curtains to keep the eyes of the world from peering inside.

The streets were again milling with a multitude of trolls and other races, but what caught Roghald's eye was a human walking through the street. He wore Midgardian garb, leggings and a tunic, and although some of the surrounding trolls glanced curiously at him, he walked through the street without being approached and soon disappeared around a corner. Agash gave Roghald a bemused look. "The Peace applies to all within the walls of Utgard, even humans and some do find their way here."

Not in the mood for small talk, Roghald changed the subject. "Where did you say this Shaman lived?"

"A few days north of here. She doesn't like company."

"Well, she's about to have some, whether she likes it or not."

They made their way through the town, toward the main gate. Here, they found their passage was blocked by several large thursrs. Although not as big and hulking as Shumbolg had been, they were not far from it. One of the battle trolls reached out and with its massive arm gave two sturdy knocks on the solid door of a stone gatehouse.

"Get out of our way," Roghald said through gritted teeth. He had had just about enough of Utgard, having been bumped in the street by insolent lesser trolls the entire way from the docks. Agash placed a warning hand on his arm. "Utgarda-Loki's guard," she whispered, so only he could hear it.

The guardhouse door opened and a tall, but very skinny troll stepped out and blinked a few times in the daylight. She had elongated, thin limbs and reminded Roghald of the stick puppets the children of Hornsborg used to play with. She had long, deeply red hair that fell straight down and beyond her waist, and she wore a green woollen tunic that reached just below her knees. Her skin was so pale that it was almost translucent and she seemed young, but then again, you never knew with trolls. Several thick gold bands encircled her upper arms and one adorned her neck. When she scrutinised Roghald and Agash, she did so with dangerously intelligent eyes, and the second warning touch he received from Agash was completely unnecessary.

"I am jotunn Blodheid," her voice was deep and resounded between the wall and the closest buildings. "Are you not a thursr of Burrugandr's horde?"

"I am thursr Roghald of Burrugandr's mountain, yes." Roghald had squared his shoulders and refusing to be intimidated by her superior class or guards, met her gaze with confidence.

She seemed amused when she replied, "Utgarda-Loki requests a word before you depart his town, thursr Roghald." Her words were civil, but her tone conveyed as much 'if you please' as one usually finds in 'stand and deliver'.

Roghald clenched his fists and glanced at Agash who gave such a minute shake of her head that he wasn't entirely sure he had seen it at all. Relaxing his hands with a sigh, he grumbled to Blodheid. "Gladly."

The jotunn threw her head back and laughed before walking away, waving to Roghald and Agash to follow. Three of the giant thursrs fell in behind Roghald, barring any escape. After walking along the wall for a short while, the surrounding houses ended, and the street opened up to a paved courtyard. In the middle of it, there sat a stronghold constructed from square, grey stones the size of wagons back in Midgard. The squat but sprawling building took up a vast part of the town, only slightly lower than the city walls themselves. It was a forbidding building, with only a few small windows and the grey stone contrasting with the black shale roof. The stronghold, although not as tall, dwarfed Gjallarholm, which up to this point had been the most impressive fortress Roghald had ever seen.

"Behold, the fortress Utgardar," Blodheid said when she noticed Roghald staring at the building. "A fortress so mighty, even the Thundergod dare not attack it."

Roghald doubted very much that it was fear that had kept Thor the Trollslayer from levelling the fortress, but he kept his mouth shut. She led them through a gate that closed with what was, to Roghald, an ominous boom, behind them. The thursrs had stayed behind when they entered Utgardar and Blodheid took them through another courtyard in silence, before entering the building proper.

To Roghald's surprise, the building was one entire great hall, spanning far in each direction. The stone roof of the building extended an impossible length with no pillars for support. Roghald knew magic was in play to hold it up. A closer inspection revealed glowing runes both on the ceiling and the doorway through which they had entered, confirming his suspicion. The hall was lit by dozens of immense fireplaces dotted along the wall, and almost all of them were cooking some sort of animal. Hundreds of caged lanterns hung on chains from the ceiling, casting a dim light over the hall. Roghald craned his neck to look inside one cage and saw a small, winged creature with a glowing body pulling at the thin bars, trying to break out. The thing looked vaguely human, with black eyes over a mouth full of sharp teeth.

Large skins and furs covered the floor, while small groups of trolls were scattered all over the place, eating and drinking. Some played strange stringed or percussion instruments. The din in the hall was chaotic and almost deafening, as waves of sporadic guttural laughter echoed under the vast ceiling.

Blodheid set out across the floor, weaving her way between the many groups, and Roghald had to quicken his step in order to keep up with her long strides. At the end of the hall, on a mound of thick furs, sat the fattest troll Roghald had ever seen. He was a giant in his own right, but his girth was such that he was as wide as he was tall. His skin was as pale as Blodheid's, but the two couldn't be any more different. He had rolls of fat that started under his broad mouth and continued to what was the most impressive belly Roghald had ever seen. He doubted the troll had even moved from the spot in centuries, if ever. Gold armbands, as thick as a man's thigh, adorned his massive arms, and his fingers were crowded with rings. The jotunn had more wealth on him than all the kingdoms of Midgard combined. He had a broad nose that spanned almost from one massive ear to the other and beady eyes under a broad forehead. All the gold and the sheer shape and size of the troll diminished what would have been an impressive swell of red hair.

Around him sat several other jotunns, all laden with gold, but to a much lesser extent.

In one hand, Utgarda-Loki held an entire roasted ox-like creature and would intermittently gnaw at it, grease and juices trickling down his many chins while he talked and laughed with the other jotunns.

Blodheid stopped and stood still a short distance from the group, with Roghald and Agash only a step behind. Some jotunns gave them curious looks, but Utgarda-Loki did not so much as glance at the trio. He kept on eating and talking with the jotunn next to him. Roghald, already irritated at this delay, started fuming and was just about to call out, when the chieftain waved a meaty hand and Blodheid took several steps forward. She bowed low, which with her gangly frame seemed almost comical.

"What has my daughter brought me this time?" Utgarda-Loki rumbled.

All the jotunns were now staring at Roghald and Agash expectantly, except the one on Utgarda-Loki's right, who sat with a smug expression, her arms crossed in front of her. She was tall and lean, but where Blodheid was skin and bones, this jotunn was muscular. Her grey-mottled skin was riddled with scars, where runes had been carved into her flesh. Since trolls healed almost any injury, Roghald knew these would be magical runes, or at least put there by magical means. She wore nothing more than a loincloth and a vest of grey fur, with her pitch-black hair tightly braided and cascading over one of her shoulders. Her features were harsh, with sharp cheekbones and a broad jaw, and two tusks pulled her lips into a constant scowl. But what caught Roghald's eye was the bright red line painted from her hairline down to the tip of her nose.

"Mogthrasir." Agash's whisper was little more than a breath, but she needn't have bothered. Roghald remembered the confrontation with the Mogthrasir clan on the way to Utgard.

"This is thursr Roghald of Burrugandr clan, as you requested, father."

Utgarda-Loki chuckled, and his eyes fell on Roghald.

"Doesn't look like much does he?" he said to the room and was rewarded with a murmured consent from the attending jotunns.

"I am told there was another thursr with them."

"So I was informed, yet only this one and the dark elf came back from the lake."

"Interesting," rumbled Utgarda-Loki, rubbing one of his many chins.

"Did trouble find you in the west, thursr Roghald?" There was amusement in his voice as he spoke.

"He is occupied elsewhere," Roghald replied in a curt tone. This lump of lard was getting on his nerves.

"No doubt," smiled the chieftain. "Did you find your wolf pup?"

Roghald froze for a second and that was all the confirmation Utgarda-Loki needed, because he chuckled, "I guess not." The jotunn sat in silence for a while, scrutinising Roghald, a thoughtful expression on his face. "There is no love lost between your master and I," Utgarda-Loki went on. "And his errands often work against mine. As you can see, I am the most powerful chieftain in all of

Jotunheim, second only to the Troll King. Even Thor of the Aesir does not dare to strike my settlement."

At the mention of the Thundergod, all the jotunns flinched and ducked down low, making a protective sign with their right hand. Utgarda-Loki only laughed.

"My settlement has sat here, untouched, for centuries, and my power has grown and the trade has made me very wealthy. Few chieftains dare oppose me anymore, but your master is one of them." His face turned serious. "I know your master does not have the support of the Troll King, who is biding his time inside his frozen wasteland, yet Burrugandr's magic is powerful. Strong enough to send a root of corruption all the way to Midgard, which is beyond even me and my Shamans. So, where does he get his power, I ask you?"

Roghald shrugged. "I am but a lowly thursr," he said in a casual tone. "The business of the jotunns does not concern me."

"It is always wise to know one's place, that is true," Utgarda-Loki said in a low, dangerous voice. "But my magic is great, and I see things and I hear things that are hidden from others. I know that his power comes from outside Jotunheim, but from where, I cannot tell."

Roghald stood stone faced and said nothing.

"It would be serious if the dwarves or the dark elves aided him, and since one stands next to you, that is possible. But then again, we all hire dark elves to do our bidding from time to time, so it means nothing that she is here. It would not be the Aesir, since they treasure Midgard above all, nor do I think the Vanir would betray their treaty with Asgard. The frost giants of Niflheim? Perhaps, but our Troll King is a frost giant, so, again, unlikely. The light elves, then? No, never would they aid a troll in anything. So that leaves only two possible answers: He is aided either by Hel, the kingdom of the dead or by Muspelheim, the land of the fire giants. In the latter case, it would be a great betrayal of the Troll

King and could only be interpreted as Burrugandr's ambition to rule Jotunheim."

All eyes turned back to Roghald when the jotunn had finished speaking. He kept his face expressionless when he answered. "I know little of these things, but my chieftain remains the loyal servant of Thrym the Troll King. We hunt for the whelp of the Ulfhednar bitch who defied Burrugandr, as these things cannot go unpunished, or they bring shame to the great Burrugandr."

Utgarda-Loki grinned. "Why, of course he is still a loyal servant of the king! Burrugandr has always acted honourably and would never use deceit or cunning for his own personal gain."

At this, all the jotunns broke out in roaring laughter, every troll in the hall turning to see what the commotion was about. Roghald stood fuming at the joke, watching the jotunns guffaw at his and his chieftain's expense. Some of them even had tears rolling down their ugly faces. As the laughter died down, Utgarda-Loki gave him a dismissive wave of his hand.

"Off you go, little thursr, on your master's errand, but remember that we are watching."

Red in the face, Roghald turned around without a word and stomped away through the hall, eager to leave Utgard behind forever. He had only taken a few steps when one jotunn mumbled something and another round of howling laughter broke out. Roghald hurried along, Agash close behind him as they stepped out into the daylight.

As the laughter died down, Utgarda-Loki watched Burrugandr's thursr leave the hall.

Mogthrasir leaned into him and said, "Do you believe him?"

He shook his head, sending his many chins jiggling. "Not a word. Burrugandr is making some dangerous moves, and whatever his plans, I intend to stop him. He was always ambitious, and he has lusted after the Troll King's throne for centuries, but I will be damned if I am to be ruled by the likes of him."

"What do you suggest?" Mogthrasir had a wicked grin on her face.

"Send your people west and find the pup before they do. Blodheid will accompany them. Whatever the human did to elude Burrugandr's thursr, she will overcome as her magic is strong."

CHAPTER 12

ASH KNEELED NEXT TO TORSTEN AND PLACED HIS HAND on his friend's chest. His breathing was shallow and ragged and the Berserker was ghostly pale. Yrsa had fashioned a stretcher from two long branches and Torsten's cape, and they were dragging him northwest along the forest path, away from the lake. Both Ash and Yrsa would glance with concern at the two furrows that the makeshift stretcher was leaving behind in the dirt as they pulled the heavy man along. A child could follow their trail. They would often turn their heads and scan the path and forest behind them.

"We need to find shelter," Yrsa said as they stopped to catch their breaths. "It will be dark soon and bumping along like this isn't helping him."

Ash nodded. They needed to get away from the open path before night fell. He knew only too well of the dangers in Jotunheim, and he would wager there were plenty more that he hadn't experienced. Yet, he thought.

They were in a flat, forested area, the ground thickly carpeted in deep moss and clusters of ferns. Ash looked at the surrounding mountain peaks. The bases of the mountains were all further away than they could drag Torsten before darkness fell, so finding shelter in a cave or cavern was out of the question.

"Let's go a little away from the path and set up camp. It's the best we can do. At least we will have time to gather firewood before it gets dark." Yrsa said, and they turned the stretcher off the path and into the forest. Their progress was slow. Ash cringed at every rock and root they had to drag Torsten over, causing small moans to escape the large warrior at every bump. When they entered a small clearing, shielded by several wide tree trunks, Yrsa stopped.

"This is as good as it's going to get," she said, and they carefully lowered Torsten to the ground. "Set the camp and gather some firewood and I will see what I can do about the tracks we left behind."

Ash stretched his back as Yrsa disappeared back towards the path. He was much taller than the shieldmaiden these days and had had to stoop to keep Torsten level as they dragged him along. Ash's back was aching from the effort. He set about his tasks, laying out their bedrolls and collecting firewood. He had a decent stack of dry twigs and fallen branches by the time Yrsa returned.

"It will not fool a tracker, but for anyone else the tracks continue on for a good while past us, before disappearing."

Ash remembered the archer he had tackled. She seemed very much like the tracking kind, so Yrsa's efforts didn't add to his sense of security. Then he remembered the strange moment they had shared in the middle of the fight. He couldn't help but blush when he was reminded of her slender figure or the savage beauty as she bared her filed teeth at him.

"Pay attention!" Yrsa hissed. "We are well behind enemy lines, and that is no place to daydream."

Ash shook his head and busied himself lighting the fire. Although it increased their risk of being discovered, they needed one to keep Torsten warm through the night. He lit it near the Berserker, ensuring that the slight breeze drove the smoke away from him, and Yrsa inspected the man's injuries.

"He only has a few superficial cuts," she said when she was done as she pulled a blanket over Torsten. "All the damage is inside of him, from being crushed and thrown around by the thursr."

Ash looked at his friend who was still breathing, but even more shallow than a few hours ago.

"It is not looking good, Ash."

Ash tried to swallow the lump that had formed in his throat, but it wouldn't budge.

"Surely, we can do something?"

"He is as tough as old leather, so who knows, he might pull through, but there isn't much we can do. Maybe if we had a Seid-woman to help us, but the closest one is a world away. We are on our own here," she said, her voice faltering to a whisper, and tears brimming in her eyes.

Ash's stomach twisted as what she said sunk in and he faced the reality of their situation. Torsten would die if something wasn't done.

Yrsa wiped her eyes and squared her shoulders. She turned to him and saw the defeated look on Ash's face and said, "Let's see what tomorrow brings. The world is a strange place, and this place is even stranger. We will sleep on it and in the morning, we will make a plan."

Ash gave her a half-hearted smile. "Sure. I'll take first watch," he offered. "I don't think I could sleep, anyway."

Yrsa nodded and with a final smoothing of Torsten's blankets, she laid down on her bedroll and closed her eyes, just as the last of the sunlight faded away and darkness fell. Their world shrunk to the small circle of light around the fire. Ash sat listening as the sounds of the night crept in. They were not unpleasant, but very different from the sounds in the forests back home. He heard chitters and croaks and somewhere in the distance, something bawled and Ash hoped he didn't have to find out what creature made such a noise. He couldn't stop ruminating on Yrsa's words of how alone and far from home they were. Everything and everyone they had ever known was literally in another world, and one of his best friends would probably die because of it.

"Beware the gods, lad. Their dealings are their own and nothing good comes from being involved with them." Eikinri's words echoed in his mind, and Ash now understood the wisdom in them. Eikinri! The thought of his master reminded him, and he fumbled inside his tunic and pulled out the small leather pouch the dwarf had given him. His hands shook as he opened the drawstrings to retrieve the portal stone.

This was it. He could send Torsten back to Midgard. He would get help in Gjallarholm and would live. Sure, Ash and Yrsa would be trapped here, but they would find another way to get home. Either way, it didn't matter, because Torsten would have a much greater chance of surviving. Ash held the stone close to the ground and felt it vibrating in his hand. Excellent. They were in a low enough point of Jotunheim that it would work. He looked at his unconscious friend and steeled his resolve. Ash didn't care if he had to live in Jotunheim for the rest of his life, so long as he knew the Berserker had a fighting chance to live. He raised the stone over his head to throw it on the ground next to Torsten.

"It is very noble of you to sacrifice your means of return for your friend."

Ash nearly fell over from the shock of hearing the voice and spun around to meet it. Only a few steps away from him, on his knapsack, where a second ago there had been no one, now sat a woman. She was fair and beautiful, with golden ringlets spilling down her back and shoulders all the way to the ground. She wore a pristine green dress with intricate red and gold patterns embroidered on the sleeves and around her neck. The woman sat with crossed legs and cradled a tabby kitten in her lap, affectionately stroking and playing with it, while smiling down at it. Ash pulled his seax from his belt and glanced at Yrsa who hadn't stirred.

"Who are you?" he stuttered, finding himself lost for words, pointing the weapon at her. She looked up at him, and the smile she had reserved for the kitten was now aimed at Ash. He felt his knees go weak as the full beauty of her hit him like a blast of fire. It had to be a spell, he thought.

"I am Freya," she said in a voice as melodious as the ringing of bells. Ash, still stunned, could only stare at her, his mouth open. Her attention returned to the cat, and he felt his mind functioning again.

"The goddess?" he whispered in an incredulous voice. She laughed, and it was the most beautiful sound Ash had ever heard.

"Some call me that, yes."

Ash sat back down on his bedroll and laid his weapon on the ground. Freya continued to play with the kitten, but her face grew serious.

"You cannot send the Berserker away," she started. "If he leaves you, you will fail. Odin has foreseen it."

"But he will die," Ash whispered.

Freya looked over at Torsten, who was now taking such shallow breaths that they were almost imperceptible. "Perhaps," she said thoughtfully, "But perhaps not. I can give him some life, sustain him for a few more days, until you can take him to a place where he can be healed.

Ash felt confused. "I thought the gods couldn't get involved?" he said. "Is this not breaking the rules?"

She looked back at Ash, her face dead serious. "It is, and it will cost us dearly. It will mean that the opposing powers may aid their champion, so it is no small price to pay. This is why we can only give you a little help. The aid they will give their champion will be proportionate to the aid we give you. Do you understand?"

"Yes. Please help him. No cost is too high if it saves his life."

"You speak like you have sense, young Ulfhed," Freya looked at him with disapproval. "Be cautious that you do not doom the world with your careless words."

She raised a slender, perfect finger and tapped the kitten on the head. In a second, it grew to a fully grown cat, and Freya bent down and whispered in its ear. The cat sat up and leapt off her lap and landed on soft paws next to Torsten. Then it simply walked into the sleeping Berserker and disappeared. As soon as it entered his body, Torsten took a deep breath and Ash thought he could see a bit of colour return to the man's cheeks.

"Thank you," Ash whispered, the lump had returned to his throat. "Now, where do we take him to be healed?" he asked the Goddess.

Freya told him, and Ash got his second shock of the night.

CHAPTER 13

R OGHALD LOOKED OUT OVER THE MARSHLAND.
"She lives in a swamp?"

The air was thick with the stench of stagnant water and rot. A narrow strip of land snaked between two sheer cliff walls, bending out of sight almost immediately. Naked trees, long dead, dotted the waterlogged little valley. The only sound Roghald could hear was that of buzzing insects.

"I told you, she doesn't like visitors." Agash said, lacing her boots after tucking her leather pants inside them. When Roghald raised an eyebrow at her, she simply said, "Leeches."

He looked down at his bare legs beneath his loincloth and sighed. Of course.

"You go first," Agash said, hanging her bow around her neck. "You are much taller and won't fare badly if there is a sinkhole."

Roghald grumbled but started walking. At first, the ground was just damp and squishy under his bare feet, but before long, he sunk down to the ankles with each step. The first painful sting caught him by surprise, and he yelped as he swatted the back of his neck. He looked down inside his hand and saw the crushed body of a flying insect the size of a sparrow, with a stinger the length of a human finger. The second sting came only a moment after, in his thigh, and he slapped his leg with a loud smack.

Agash's echoing laughter resounded behind him. He spun around enraged, only to see the dark elf grinning, baring her sharpened teeth.

"Troll-flies." She said in a jovial voice. "Stings like a bastard, I'm told."

He glared at her, watching one of the overgrown insects swoop right past her head as it honed in on him. He slapped it out of the air as it drew near.

"How come it ignored you?" he asked her with some indignation.

"Dark elf," she said, tapping her own chest. "They feed on the minerals in your blood, and since I am so much more than a walking lump of rock, I do not interest them."

Roghald stared at her with murder in his eyes. How he loathed the snarky tracker. He vowed to himself that the moment she was no longer of any use to him, he would snap her neck like a twig.

"So, what do you suggest?"

"Cover yourself in the mud. You'll still get a few stings, but it will deter most of them."

Roghald swore to himself and shook his head, but a fresh sting between his shoulder blades had him arching his back a second later. After eventually dislodging the sucking insect from the hard-to-reach spot, he plunged his hands into the mud and pulled up big handfuls of it. He slapped the stinking mud over every bare bit of skin on his body.

"Don't forget your face and hair," Agash grinned at him. Roghald cursed her a few times but followed her advice.

They set off again, heading deeper into the putrid swamp. Roghald would still get a few stings and although she didn't make a sound, he could feel the glee radiating from the dark elf behind him every time he flinched and slapped himself. The water got deeper as they pushed on and soon it reached halfway up Roghald's thigh. He could hear a muttered curse behind him and turned to see Agash with water and mud to above her waist. Now it was his turn to laugh.

"Keep up, shorty," he said with mirth.

She glared at him, moving forwards through the putrid water.

"I can carry you, if you want?" He said with a wink.

"I would rather drown in this muck whilst being eaten alive by the leeches than be that close to you," she growled at him. Roghald laughed and pushed on.

The light faded in the already gloomy swamp-valley. Just as he was about to berate the dark elf for failing to foresee that they would be caught out by night-time, he caught sight of a soft light up ahead. He picked up his pace, eager to get out of the muck. It wasn't long before it got shallower as the bottom started rising. Roghald took the first step onto dry land at last.

Looking down at his legs, he saw they had swollen and were full of bulbous pustules. Horrified, he tentatively reached down and touched them, but they moved beneath his fingers. That's when he realised they were leeches. Disgusted, he began picking them off and crushing the vile creatures beneath his feet. By the time he had finished, the last of the daylight had faded and night had crept in.

He lifted his head and looked at the light ahead of him. It came from a fire in front of a small shack, nestled between a few living trees and shrubberies. A small cauldron hung above the fire, suspended by a chain from three crossed branches, tied together with a strip of bark. A round stone had been placed next to the fire, seemingly for someone who liked to sit close to it. Despite the stagnant air, there was also a fresh aroma, a sweet floral scent, and he saw that the purple shrubs growing around the hovel were speckled with tiny white flowers.

Roghald realised with relief that he hadn't felt a sting for a while now and relaxed somewhat. Although he healed any injuries rapidly, the dull ache from the nasty stings seemed to linger quite a while, and his entire body felt like it was throbbing, thanks to the dozens and dozens of bites.

When Roghald walked close enough to the fire that he could feel its warm glow on his skin, a voice startled him.

"Go away."

Roghald searched for the source but could see no one.

"Hello?" He ventured.

"Go away."

It sounded like it came from the ground, and he looked down at the fire.

The stone next to the fire moved and Roghald realised it was not a stone, but a tiny troll, no larger than his foot, wrapped in a worn, grey blanket. A round face that consisted almost entirely of wrinkles peered up at him under long, matted grey hair.

"I don't want visitors. Go away, or I will curse you back to the stone whence you came."

"Mother Bestla," Agash began, "We are sorry to bother you, but we need your help."

"I care not for your plights or your affairs. I am merely awaiting Ragnarok and the end of days, when Surtr will burn this cursed world as it deserves." She squinted at Agash. "I remember you, dark elf. Once, I allowed you to shelter here for a night when the trolls whom I despise were hunting you. I see I have come to live to regret it, because here you are, and you have brought a damned thursr to my fire. Now go away!" The little troll started rocking backwards and forwards, muttering to herself, shaking her head.

Roghald fumed. Roghald fumed as he waded through a stinking swamp all day, getting stung countless times by insects and eaten alive by leeches, all for nothing. It was Agash's fault, of course. His rage was building again, and he opened and closed his fists, imagining them around the dark elf's neck. Gamir, fed by his fury began roaring and laughing in his mind, egging him on to kill the elf.

The little troll by his feet stopped her rocking and cocked her head as if listening. Agash said something, but the old troll lifted her hand, demanding silence. Her head swivelled around and her eyes rested on Roghald. She squinted at him for a long moment before her eyes widened and her eyebrows shot up.

"You carry the fire of Surtr inside you." Her voice was barely a whisper. "You carry the beautifully devastating fire that will one day burn the worlds." Her eyes were shining with reverence and her face wrinkled up even more as a toothless grin twisted it in a grimace of pure madness.

She was clearly insane, but he needed her, so Roghald smiled back at her. "Yes, I carry the fire," he lied. "And I need you to help me burn the worlds."

The little troll cackled and started rocking back and forth at a much faster pace. Roghald thought she might topple over in her excitement.

"Sit. Sit by my fire." She spread her hands out in a gesture of welcome, and Roghald and Agash sat down. The fire was warm, and they were cold and tired from wading through the swamp, so it was a welcome respite.

Roghald studied the little troll as she rocked back and forth like a little child.

"You are a Shaman?" he asked, trying to keep the scepticism from his voice.

The little troll nodded in excitement. "The best," she said, but then her face changed as if a great sorrow came over her. With slumped shoulders, her rocking slowed down and her eyes grew distant. "At least I was," she whispered.

"A long time ago, the usual squabbling of the chieftains came to a head when one accidentally poisoned another's mate instead of the chieftain herself. In a rage, the bereaved chieftain declared war and called on all her allies. Bound by their oaths of stone, they had no other choice but to join her, even though it was a pointless war, declared in anger over a trifling matter. The other side had allies too, and before anyone knew it, another Troll War had erupted and was raging all over Jotunheim. It lasted for decades and soon all the able-bodied trolls had been called upon by their local chieftains. Including my sons. My beautiful sons." The little troll paused as she wept, slowly rocking back and forth. After a moment, she stopped and used the blanket wrapped around her to blow her nose.

"When the war ended and the armies dispersed, the trolls returned home. I waited and waited, but every day my heart grew heavier when none of my sons returned. When a year had passed, I gave up hope and my heart broke. I went to Utgarda-Loki, who had called upon my sons, but when I asked about them, he laughed me out of his hall. He said he was too important to keep track of a bunch of vaettr on the battlefield, and that if they were dead, I should be grateful that I could make a sacrifice for my betters."

Her eyes filled with rage and her entire body shook as if by convulsions. "I live only to see them all burn in Ragnarok; to watch Surtr's fire melt their flesh from their bones!" Spittle flew from the corner of her mouth as she raised her tiny clenched fists in front of her.

For a while, the campfire echoed with the sound of her rapid breathing, before it too subsided and she resumed her slow rocking.

"I never served another troll as a Shaman again, even though a hundred years have passed, nor will I, in another hundred years." Her eyes turned back to Roghald. "When will you burn the world?" she asked him.

"Soon," he said, his face splitting in a grin. "As soon as I can."

The little Shaman turned back to her fire and stared into the flames, still rocking. "Then I will make an exception and help you."

Roghald's smile broadened as he studied the little Shaman, but he didn't notice that behind him, Agash was watching the exchange with a worried look on her face. Mother Bestla looked at him as if seeing him for the first time and raised an eyebrow.

"Why are you covered in mud?"

"To keep the troll-flies away."

"Pfft. The only thing that keeps them away is the scent of these danar blossoms. Who told you such nonsense?"

Roghald heard a snorting laughter behind him. He was definitely going to kill the dark elf.

CHAPTER 14

Yrsa sat on a rock, rubbing her temples with her eyes closed. She was getting a headache.

"Tell me again, slowly," she said, looking up at Ash who stood in front of her, looking everywhere except at her. In many ways, he was still the boy he'd been the day she started training him, for all his muscles, beard and abilities. He also had an astounding talent for finding himself in extraordinary situations.

"Well," Ash started. "So, Freya"

"The goddess of love, fertility and seid-magic," Yrsa inserted.

"Yes, the goddess of love, fertility and seid-magic," Ash confirmed. "Came here last night while you were asleep and told me that instead of me sending Torsten back with the portal stone–"

"Which would have likely saved his life," Yrsa added.

"... which would have likely saved his life, we instead need to take him to Gundaganr–"

"Your paternal troll grandmother,"

"... my paternal troll grandmother–"

"Who not only orchestrated the death of her son, your father, but also tried to kill your mother, and by extension, you."

"Yes. And she must heal Torsten, because without him we are doomed to fail," Ash finished.

Yrsa went back to rubbing her temples. "Yeah, that's what I thought I heard," she mumbled.

She looked over at Torsten, who was breathing a lot easier than yesterday, and his skin wasn't as ghostly pale either.

"Fine," she said, slapping her knees with both hands before standing up. "Let's pack up and be on our way." She knelt down and started rolling up her blankets, but paused. "I don't suppose the divine and almighty Freya gave you directions to your grandmother?"

"About two days' travel north."

"I'm surprised," Yrsa grumbled. "I expected us to have to find out where by reading the entrails of a goat or something."

Ash ignored Yrsa and busied himself packing up their little camp. He had felt increasingly frustrated by the dealings of the gods himself. It was rarely a straightforward affair, and always riddles and mysteries. He sighed to himself. He might as well get used to it, his life was tied to the gods, and he couldn't see how it could be otherwise.

Once they had packed up, they took their positions on either side of Torsten's stretcher and, grabbing one of the long branches each, lifted him up. They nearly flipped the injured man over, as he was now as light as a feather. Ash looked down and saw a small rune burned into the timber next to his hand. He looked over at Yrsa's branch to see the same rune repeated on hers.

"I guess the gods can be a little helpful at times," Yrsa muttered.

They set off, and this time travelled at a much faster speed than the day before. Ash was pleased to see that the dragging stretcher hardly left a track at all, compared to the deep furrows it had carved into the ground the day before. They followed the forest path, which snaked north for the rest of the day. By the time the distant sun was setting, they had had to veer off the path as it turned west. The trees had thinned for the last couple of hours, and barren stone replaced the lush purple tint of the surrounding foliage.

When they set out the following day, having spent another night in the open, they soon found themselves in a drab stone tundra. They set out the following day on a drab, stone tundra with occasional dry patches of grass that swayed in the strong winds of the open plain. They were gradually climbing higher until Ash noticed a magnificent view of the Great Lake on their right, surrounded by lush forest on all sides. The lake's size amazed him, and a part of him felt relieved that he didn't have to cross it. Felp, the troll that had kidnapped him, had told him of the eels that inhabited it.

Yrsa grabbed his arm and pointed to a small hollow in the stone, where dust and dirt had gathered, protected from the wind. In it was a clear footprint, twice as big as a human foot. It also had only four toes, and the end of the footprint gouged the ground, as if by claws. "That's fresh," she said, scanning the surrounding landscape for any movement.

"Let's see where it's headed."

They grabbed Torsten's stretcher and followed in the footprint's direction. Ash sent a worried glance at the Berserker who seemed to get worse as the day wore on. The big man now gurgled and wheezed with every breath.

They spotted several more footprints. The troll had walked straight in one direction, towards the closest mountain peak. It wasn't long before they crested a rise and looked down upon a small gully, as barren as the rest of the landscape. The difference here was that there was an enormous cave mouth that opened up into the side of the mountain, as well as a lot of debris spread around outside it. Most of the debris, Ash could see, were bleached bones. This was possibly his grandmother's cave.

"Wait here with Torsten," he told Yrsa, who opened her mouth to protest. "No point having him down there if there is a fight," Ash cut her off. "If it's too much to handle, I'll just run away. I'm bound to be a lot faster than anything coming out of that cave."

Yrsa did not look happy, but since she didn't have a better alternative, she gave him a curt nod and they set Torsten down. Ash reached into his pack and pulled out the trollhelm and put it on his head. Yrsa didn't spare him a glance as the illusion took hold, since she and Torsten had made him perform that trick several times since they reunited. They had found it quite amusing.

Before setting off down the gully, Ash loosened his sword in its scabbard so he could draw it in a flash if he needed it. Every fibre in his body screamed for him to run as far from this place as he could, but he kept putting one foot in front of the other, knowing that his friend's life was in the balance.

He walked up to the cave's opening and peered into the gloom. He saw nothing but a broad passageway that curved out of sight a short way into the cave. The opening was large, at least three times as tall as Ash, and just as wide. He turned around to look at Yrsa who gave him a reassuring wave. He turned back to the cave and took a deep breath. Cupping his hands around his mouth, he shouted. "Hello!"

He stood back a few steps and waited for what felt like an eternity, but nothing happened. He looked back at Yrsa who shrugged and raised her hands. Turning back to the cave he raised his hands to his face, preparing to call out again, but he let out an involuntary yelp when a massive body materialised out of the darkness. Ash stumbled back a few steps.

The troll was huge, almost filling the entire cave opening. It was a rotund creature, with thick arms and legs, and its lower body was wrapped in a patchwork of skins and furs, tied together at the waist with a broad leather belt. Its skin was grey with a myriad of dark flecks on its arms, shoulders and hands, while its belly and chest were so pale, they were almost white. It had long, matted black hair that hung down in tangles on the sides of its broad face. A strange necklace, made up of five white bird skulls tied together with string, dangled on its chest. The face had two large, yellow eyes and a wide, bulbous nose over a square jaw. The creature looked down at Ash, perplexed.

"Erh," Ash started, tense and ready to Shift at a moment's notice, but the troll just stood there, just staring at him. He took another deep breath and spoke in a firm voice. "I seek Gundaganr."

The massive troll raised an eyebrow. Yrsa must have moved, because its eyes flicked up and as it looked beyond Ash, its eyes narrowed. "She has no interest in the likes of you," the troll rumbled in a deep voice. "Go away." He started turning to go back into the cave.

"Wait," Ash called to the troll. "She is my grandmother."

The troll halted, and a smile crept onto its face.

"You are not the first bastard to come here seeking a handout. Gundaganr has many sons who travelled far and left many offshoots behind. Begone. There is nothing for you here except a beating if you don't heed my words." The troll paused, then bent down and took another good look at Ash. "You are quite the runt, aren't you? Which one of my brothers spawned such a weakling?" There was some curiosity in his voice, but mostly glee.

"My father was Jordr the Stonesmith and my mother was Gunnr Ulfsdaughter the Ulfhed. I am Ash Jordrson, the last of the Wolves of Odin." At his last words, Ash removed the trollhelm, breaking the enchantment of his disguise. Ash didn't think it was possible for a creature to open its mouth as far as the troll did. Its eyes were as big as saucepans and perfectly round as they bulged out of the creature's head. The troll stared at him, flabbergasted. Ash shot the troll a winning smile and continued in a cheerful voice. "I guess that makes you my uncle."

Gundaganr was an impressive troll. She was half again as tall as Ash, and she held herself like a queen as she sat on simple furs by the fire, across from Ash. Once Ash had revealed his identity, the troll had, after its initial shock, disappeared back into the cave. Upon its return, it silently and anxiously guided them into the cave through a twisting and winding tunnel. If the troll had been worried, it was nothing compared to how Ash felt when they entered a great cavern only to see at least a hundred pairs of eyes staring at them in the gloom.

Inside the cavern, Ash heard a cacophony of whispers as they were led down the middle of the large group of trolls. Some were enormous and Ash could see them hefting large clubs and spears as the tension rose thick enough in the cavern that he could have cut it with his seax. The cool and damp place carried the sour musk that Ash had come to associate with trolls. His eyes fell on a fire crackling in the middle of the cavern. The surrounding space was empty but for one figure, although the densest concentration of pressing troll bodies was just outside the furs spread out around it. Ash also noticed that the largest of all the trolls seemed to have gathered there. They were protecting their matriarch.

Gundaganr's eyes were the only ones not on him. She sat with a straight back, her head held high, but her eyes were closed. A thick swell of grey hair spilled down her shoulders and lay in thick ringlets on the surrounding furs. She herself was also wrapped in furs, with a thick apron on, but Ash could see her skin was grey with the same dark flecks on her hands, neck and long pointed nose as the troll who had escorted them in. In fact, all the trolls in the cave had the same skin. Gundaganr's sons, every one of them. He could feel the tension radiating from Yrsa, who was next to him, and he didn't have to look to know that her hands were close to her weapons. They stopped in front of the fire and the troll that had led them in now vanished into the mass of bodies around them. For a moment, all that could be heard was the crackling of fire and Torsten's gurgled breaths.

Then Gundaganr opened her eyes. They were yellow with a golden centre. The intelligence and wisdom in them struck Ash, but he could also see malice. This was not someone to be toyed with.

"Grandmother," Ash said, in the firmest voice he could muster.

Hisses and snarls erupted all around him and the bodies surrounding them pressed closer, and he heard Yrsa draw her spear from the sheath on her back. Gundaganr raised her hand a few inches off her lap and the cave fell silent again.

"He knows not of our ways," her voice, deep but surprisingly soft, filled the silence and echoed throughout the cave. "We will give him leave this one time."

Ash held his tongue. This seemed very much like a 'speak when spoken to' situation.

Gundaganr scrutinised him for a long moment. He read anger and exasperation in her eyes, but also something else. Was it... sorrow? Then she slumped slightly forward, and she looked much older, like the centuries pressed down on her shoulders. She gazed down at her hands in her lap. When she looked back up at Ash, her features had softened, and he could see no trace of the anger.

"You have his eyes," she whispered, then she added, "As they were after he transformed to pursue that... your mother." Her back straightened, and some of the steel returned to her presence. "I had every intention of killing you when I was told you were foolish enough to come to my doorstep. Your existence has been a matter of great shame to me. But seeing Jordr look back at me through your eyes, I know now that I could not."

Ash swallowed. It seemed like he had almost made a fatal mistake coming here. A part of him had rejoiced when Freya gave him directions to find his grandmother. He knew very little of his father, beyond the fact that he was a Stonesmith, and this was a pathway to learning and reconciling his past.

"I know almost nothing of him," he said in a low voice, "but there is a hole in my heart left by him."

She looked deep into his eyes, seeking for any untruth, but when she found only her own grief mirrored, she took a deep breath and spoke.

"I love all my sons, but Jordr was always different, even as a little trolling," her voice was low and full of sorrow. "He was smarter than the others, wilder, with a curiosity that almost saw him killed several times. I could sense that the magic was stronger in him than the others. Much stronger. So, I paid a fortune to have him apprenticed as a Stonesmith. He excelled and the magic within him blossomed, and I believed that his, and our, fortune were assured.

Then her eyes darkened, and a hint of steel entered her voice. "But a Stonesmith can be a powerful weapon, and he was noticed by the Shamans and chieftains, but also by the Aesirs in Asgard." At the mention of the gods, she spat into the fire, sending sparks flying.

"That is why most Stonesmiths choose to work hidden away, deep inside the mountains, but Jordr refused to be contained like that. He enjoyed travelling all over Jotunheim, plying his trade. He made a great name for himself, but that would be his undoing."

Gundaganr sat in silence for a while, her eyes distant. "One day Odin the Destroyer sent his Wolf for him. Not to kill him, but to twist him to become yet another of his many tools. Odin corrupted him, tempted him with the fire of the gods, which he placed in his hammer."

She raised her head and her eyes met Ash's. "Beware the one you call the Allfather, boy," she hissed at him. "He walks only his own path, and you are but a means to reach his own ambition. Therefore, I called upon Burrugandr to save your father from the clutches of the Aesir and their schemes."

Ash could only nod, hanging on the troll's every word.

"When he met your mother, he fell in love. I was very suspicious, and I scried and searched, but there was no spell behind his infatuation, he was truly in love. When he came to visit, he would tell me of her, of her beauty and her iron will. He said she was like one of his precious metals come alive, unbending to the storm. We fought and argued, but he would not see it my way. The last time he came to see me, he had transformed." Her voice was dripping with sorrow for a child lost long before he died.

"His powerful frame and beautiful skin were gone, and before me stood a pink and fragile human." A lamenting murmur rose from the surrounding trolls. "I could see where he had carved the runes into his flesh. Hundreds of runes and spells that had changed him and shaped him, no doubt to make himself more pleasing to your mother, in what would have been a very painful process. But I knew it was only an illusion. You cannot change your essence, so there was still hope. In his heart, Jordr was still a troll. I spent weeks in a trance, scrying and unwinding the spells that protected them, and soon I found where they lived. Jordr had made a home inside a mountain in the east, where they both lived. I also learned that your mother was with child, carrying you, and that they were preparing to move to Midgard. I was to lose my son forever."

Gundaganr was wringing her hands, but Ash could see that she was doing so to hide the slight tremor that had come over them. "In desperation, I sought Burrugandr, the jotunn chieftain in that area, and I told him all that I had learned. I didn't expect his own greed and ambition to be so great. Instead of preserving the pride of Jotunheim, he saw only an opportunity to secure the powerful weapon you could grow up to be. He did not hesitate to cast my beautiful son, and all that he was, to his death in the mountain." She fell silent and Ash could see the tears streaking her face. When she looked up at him, the anger had returned to her eyes. "Although Burrugandr killed my son, this is the work of the Aesir and your mother, so you will understand why I intended your death when you announced yourself as a Wolf of Odin on my doorstep. To me, the part of you which comes from my son has been pushed aside by the Aesir, and I see now that, beside your eyes, nothing remains of him." Tension rose in the cavern as the trolls again shuffled closer, and angry snarls and grunts echoed around the enclosed space.

Ash bent down and pulled aside one of the big furs in front of the fire, revealing the cold stone beneath it. He pressed his hand against the floor and let his hand sink into the stone to his wrist.

The whole cavern fell silent once again. He sang a low wordless song, and a glowing circle appeared a few inches out from his hand. After a few moments, he lifted his hand out of the ground, taking along the stone which had been inside the circle, leaving only a hole behind. Standing up, he held the chunk of stone in his hands and, still singing, his voice echoing around him, began shaping the stone. In seconds, he had created a perfect orb. It had a striped appearance, as the different minerals that made it up had separated into what looked like strata. He took a few steps forward around the fire and placed the orb at Gundaganr's feet. He again saw her eyes fill with tears when he spoke.

"A lot of my father remains in me."

CHAPTER 15

ROGHALD STEPPED OUT OF THE SWAMP AND BENT DOWN to pick the leeches off his legs. He took the pack he had been carrying on his shoulders and strapped it back on his hip, after checking that it was still dry. He lifted the lid to make sure that the talisman was still intact. It seemed so fragile, given that it was made up only of twisted twigs, but Mother Bestla had assured him it was nearly indestructible. She had sung and chanted for two days and nights, weaving the sticks together into a complicated knotwork. When she had finished, the old Shaman had almost collapsed from the effort, but she had accomplished her task. She had made a bracelet that bestowed the most powerful blessing a troll could receive, and she had made it for him to give to Ash.

Before they left her island in the swamp, the little Shaman had clung to his ankles and begged him again to burn the world, to let the fire within him out. It was clear to Roghald that she was mad, and not wanting to upset her, he assured her he would burn the world as soon as he could and untangled himself from her tiny, clawed hands.

They waded through the swamp in silence. Agash had fallen unusually quiet and broody, but Roghald welcomed the change as he had had enough of her.

"We should report back to Burrugandr," It was the first time she had spoken all day. "Several weeks have now passed and we need further support and instruction before we take on the humans. We underestimated them."

Roghald scrutinised the elf. There was something else she was worried about. Something she wasn't telling him. The doubt in her eyes was as clear as day. "We have everything we need right here," Roghald said, patting his pack. "You just worry about the tracking, I will take care of the humans."

"I really think-"

"Enough!" Roghald roared. "You were hired to do a job, so do it!"

He saw the conflict of emotions on Agash's face. Anger, resentment, but also a touch of... fear? After a moment's silence, she cast down her eyes in resignation.

"As you say," she said through clenched teeth.

Roghald snorted in disdain and turned around and resumed walking. He could feel an itch between his shoulder blades and waited for one of her arrows to slam into him. But nothing happened, so he kept walking. Weakling, he thought.

They travelled throughout the day and night, finally reaching Utgard when the sun stood at its highest on the second day. Utgard looked the same as it always did, and to Roghald's surprise, they were able to enter the gates without being stopped. He had expected at least some harassment from Utgarda-Loki's trolls, but beside a few appraising looks, they were allowed through with no fuss. They pushed their way down towards the docks and began the search for another ferry to carry them across the lake.

As all the ferries left in the mornings, to minimise the nights spent on the dangerous lake, they had no option but to wait for the next day. Roghald secured a space for them on a barge that was currently unloading. It was smaller and seemed to be rowed by free trolls. It also had an elaborate sail with multiple beams coming off a central mast. The bargemaster, a thin, grey-skinned troll, advised they could spend the night on the barge, if they so wished, once they had finished unloading. They would set out at first light, and he would prefer if he didn't have to wait for them.

Roghald sent Agash to purchase some food to replenish their dwindling supplies, while he made himself comfortable on the jetty. Although his troll form was more powerful and durable than his human shape had been, he felt exhausted from the long days of travel. He leaned his head back against a tall mooring post. He was just going to rest his eyes for a moment.

When he opened them up, the world had gone grey. It was as if all the colour in the world had been washed away. Roghald looked around and saw the trolls, who had been busy unloading the barge, frozen and unmoving, as if time itself had stopped. He caught a movement and turned to see the bargemaster walking towards him. The troll moved towards Roghald in a strange, jerking fashion, like he wasn't used to moving in a body.

Roghald could hear the mad troll in his mind roaring in ecstasy, its joy spreading throughout his entire body. The bargemaster had a horrible grin plastered on his face and drew closer. Roghald tried to rise to meet this threat, but found he was stuck to the jetty and completely paralysed. He could only watch in horror as the creature drew nearer and stopped in front of him. When the troll bent down and put its face uncomfortably close to Roghald's, he gasped when he saw its eyes glowed like fire and molten rock. It was the only sliver of colour in the otherwise drab world.

"Is this a dream?" he asked, surprised at how firmly his voice held.

The creature grinned even wider.

"Maybe," it said. Its voice sounded like a dozen voices speaking at the same time.

"The enemy has aided its champion. The enemy has breached the agreement and we may instruct you.

Roghald was confused. What champion?

"You need to ascend to the greatness within. Join the two, to make a whole and rise to power in His glory."

Roghald was getting increasingly uncomfortable as the creature's fiery breath washed over his face in a stench of sulphur. He wanted this thing gone at any cost.

"I don't understand. What do I need to do?"

The thing paused, and its wide grin crept back.

"Burn, thursr Roghald. You need to burn."

With those words, his world erupted in flames, and Roghald screamed.

He opened his eyes to the bleak sunlight. The colours of the world had returned and in a moment of confusion, he watched the movement of the trolls unloading the barge, a blank look on his face. It had been a dream. But it had felt frightfully real. The bargemaster stood on the railing of the barge, overseeing the offloading of the goods. Roghald eyed him with suspicion for a moment, but there was nothing unusual about the troll anymore.

A sack landed next to him, startling him, and he looked up at Agash.

"Bit jumpy for a thursr," she remarked.

Her attitude had returned over the last day or so. Roghald bared his teeth at her and opened up the sack. He pulled out a leg of meat and devoured it in a flash. Soon, the barge crew had finished unloading and began loading their new cargo. By the time the sun was setting across the lake the loading was complete, and the bargemaster waved them over. They settled in and made themselves comfortable for the night.

Roghald leaned his back against the railing. He opened his pack and took out the bracelet Mother Bestla had made. He tried to follow the complicated network of twigs, but it made his head spin if he focused on it too hard. It reminded him a bit of a bird's nest. He couldn't sense anything from it, and a small part of him was sceptical that it would work. It had better. Putting it back into his pack, he closed his eyes, determined to get some sleep. He knew he had some long, hard days ahead of him.

Roghald woke to Gamir babbling in excitement, and sighed. The troll would be the death of him one day. But then he was reminded of the time when on a boat, travelling towards Gjallarholm, the troll had woken him up because there was danger nearby. It seemed similarly distressed now, but there was also a hint of outrage.

Roghald lay still for a long moment, listening intently to the world around him. He felt the almost imperceptible bobbing of the barge on the still water of the lake. He heard the soft creaks from the ropes securing it to the jetty, and in the distance the laughter of some revelling trolls, but within his immediate vicinity all was quiet. Peering through one eye, he scanned the barge. All was still in the night. The soft glow of two lanterns at either end illuminated the vessel as bright as day to his night vision. He saw the sleeping forms of the crew at the opposite end of the little ferry and Agash's pack and blankets a little way away from him. The dark elf was missing. When he thought of the archer, the troll in his mind growled like a dog. He sat up and looked around the barge and jetty. As he did so, he managed to just glimpse someone slinking around the corner of one of the harbour warehouses.

What was she up to? He didn't trust the elf, and his mistrust for her had only grown since they first set out. She was up to something, and he decided he was going to find out what. He got up, stepped onto the jetty and set off towards where he had seen the movement with fast but silent strides. He stopped at the corner and listened carefully for a second before poking his head around.

It was a long, narrow alleyway between two long warehouses. There was a lot of debris and rubbish piled up against the walls of the two buildings, but he could see down the middle of it. Two dark shapes stood at the end of the alleyway. One was a large, hulking troll, bent down towards the smaller, unmistakable shape of Agash. His night vision was excellent in his immediate vicinity, but it did not reach very far, so he could not make out any more details around the two who were deep in conversation, their heads close together. They kept their voices low, and he could not hear a word. But he knew that whatever was being said did not bode well for him.

He watched the two part ways, and Agash headed back towards him. He dragged his head back to avoid drawing her attention, and then tip-toed as fast as he could around the corner, pressing himself against the wall. It wasn't easy hiding a bulk as large as his, but he relied on his muted colouring to blend into the shadows. He held his breath as Agash walked past him on her way back to the barge. She moved in dead silence, and not once did he hear the fall of a single footstep.

When she was far enough away, he slipped back around the corner and with a few long, careful strides he was standing in the alleyway from where she had emerged. He hurried along it, trying not to upset anything or leave signs he had been there. Soon, she would realise that he was not on the barge and might backtrack to ensure he hadn't been spying on them. He had very little time.

The first thing he noticed was that there was a chill in the air where the two had spoken. It was a lot cooler than the rest of the alleyway. He felt a sharp chill in his bare feet and, looking down, he saw the last remnant of frost melting on the rough cobblestones beneath him. He could also see the vague outline of a footprint and squatted down to get a closer look at it. The ice crystals melted and turned to moisture on the worn stone surface as he watched, removing any trace of the creature having ever been there.

Aware that he had already lingered too long, Roghald stood up and after checking that no one was watching him, he took off down the other end of the alleyway than the one from which he'd come. He wandered the streets of Utgard while pondering his situation. Who had Agash met with? Was it someone from Burrugandr's mountain? Did they not have faith in him and needed her to check in? Or was foul play afoot? He had more questions than he had answers, and he was none the wiser by the time he had circled back and stood once again in front of the barge.

As he clambered aboard, he saw Agash's eyes flicker open and they watched each other in silence for a moment.

"Late night walk?" she asked him.

"I felt restless," he grunted. "Where were you?"

She rolled her eyes before answering. "Nature called, and I wasn't particularly thrilled about having to relieve myself in front of a barge full of vaettrs."

Roghald shrugged and went back to his spot. He closed his eyes, forced to listen to Gamir's mad ramblings in his mind. For a long time, he could feel Agash's eyes on him. He did not sleep at all, lying alert for the rest of the night.

CHAPTER 16

ASH FELT EXHAUSTED. THE RITUAL HAD BEEN GOING through the night, and he knew the sun had long risen outside the cave. Gundaganr sat cross-legged next to Torsten's prone, naked body by the fire in the middle of the vast cave. The drawn-out monotonous chanting that flowed from the troll matriarch felt like it had spanned eons. Her many sons, close to a hundred he had estimated, sat kneeling in a crowd around her, swaying from side to side in unison with her chanting. At some unseen signal, they all raised their right hand in the air and brought down their palms in a great combined slap on the stone floor from time to time. The thundering sound jolted Ash each time, his frayed nerves on edge.

His eyes were drawn to the dead stag-like creature lying on his grandmother's right side. The majestic beast had been dragged into the cave by two of the trolls, and Gundaganr had slit its throat with an experienced hand. As the lifeblood spilled out of the mournfully baying creature, she caught it in a deep stone bowl. That bowl now sat to her side and as she chanted, she would dip the leaves of a tree branch in the blood and splatter it on Torsten.

At first his friend had tensed and arched his back, an inhuman sound escaping between his clenched teeth. Ash had stood up in panic, but an angry glare from his grandmother and Yrsa's hand on his arm brought him back down to the stone floor. Torsten was now fully bathed in the clotting blood and his body continued to spasm as the troll kept up her relentless chanting. Gundaganr would occasionally draw a complicated rune in the blood covering Torsten, and Ash could swear that the rune would glow softly for a moment, before the film of blood would again close over his skin.

Three rumbling rounds of slaps rung out in the cave, and Ash realised that the chanting had stopped. The blissful silence felt like a breath of fresh air, and Ash stood up to get a better sense of what was happening. All the trolls sat perfectly still, watching Torsten's unmoving body. He realised his friend wasn't moving at all, and his heart sank. Gundaganr signalled to one of her sons who had been standing by and the troll lumbered forwards carrying a barrel. Stopping in front of Torsten, he upended it, and a swell of water splashed onto the man.

The string of swearwords that erupted from the Berserker was like music to Ash's ears and he and Yrsa darted forward to their friend. Bewildered and still half covered in blackened blood, Torsten sat up, blowing his nose and wiping his face, trying to rid himself of the water.

The cave erupted in laughter. A wide-eyed Torsten reached for the axe on his back that was no longer there, as he found himself naked and surrounded by a host of ugly trolls. When he saw his friends and the relief in their eyes, he relaxed somewhat, but he was suspiciously eyeing the surrounding trolls. Ash looked at his grandmother, who sat to the side, as regal as any queen, and when their eyes met, he bowed his head in gratitude. She just stared at him, but Ash didn't miss the warmth in her eyes this time around.

The trolls had butchered the stag and some of them had gone out into the forest and returned with skins full of strange mushrooms, roots, and tubers. A large cauldron appeared from the back of the cave, and Ash watched as they cooked a stew on one of the several fires that had been lit around the cavern. Ash found the stew to be delicious, and his ravenous appetite surprised him.

Still, it faded next to Torsten's, who had devoured three full bowls, seemingly not even chewing.

"Slow down," Yrsa had scolded him. "There are bones in there, and I'd hate to have gone to all this trouble just to see you choke to death, like a dog who hasn't been fed for a week."

Torsten just shrugged, helping himself to a fourth bowl. Having eaten their fill, they sat around the fire, lost in their own thoughts, when Gundaganr spoke.

"In Jotunheim, there is a saying," she started, her eyes on Ash. "Nothing comes from nothing."

Ash remembered where he had heard those words before. Beli had spoken those exact words when he tried to trick Ash into travelling alone to Gurmr and Grundr's cave.

"I have healed your friend, at no small cost to myself," she said.

Ash knew that the ritual had taken its toll. The troll Shaman had dark rings around her eyes and her skin looked paler than before.

"Now I want recompense for doing so."

Ash steeled himself for what she would demand and nodded to his grandmother. After all, no price would be too great for the life of his friend.

"When your father was killed, one of Burrugandr's thursrs cast him down into a deep chasm. I have sent my sons several times to retrieve the stone that is left of him, so he can rest here, close to his family. But the chasm is deep and treacherous, and they could not make it all the way down. You, as a Stonesmith, can," she said, her eyes never leaving Ash's. "The price I demand for healing your friend is that you bring my son home to me."

Ash thought it over for a second. He had little time to spare. Every day the enemy grew stronger as they grew the source tree again towards Midgard. But the thought of being able to put his father to rest among his family was one that sparked a sense of pride and purpose within him. He looked over at his friends and Yrsa gave him a minute shrug, leaving the decision to him. Torsten was busy with his bowl of stew and hadn't even looked up. Ash turned back to his grandmother and bowed his head in agreement.

"Very well," she said, and gave him a quick smile. "Your sense of duty mirrors your father's," she said with approval. "Jordr's mountain lies between here and Burrugandr's, only a few days travel from his black mountain. But you must take care, lest he find out that you are near. No doubt he is still searching for you, even after all these years."

Oh, no doubt, Ash thought.

"And I would avoid Utgard altogether if I were you," she continued. "Although there is no friendship between Burrugandr and Utgarda-Loki, he is sure to have trolls loyal to him in the settlement, and you are quite the conspicuous lot, after all." With this, she eyed Torsten and Yrsa with a frown.

"You might even draw Utgarda-Loki's attention, and that would be bad indeed. He is cunning, arrogant and cruel, and since he managed to trick Thunder-Thor himself, he no longer fears anything."

At the mention of the Aesir, the trolls that were listening ducked down with a careful glance upwards, whilst making a protective sign by pressing their little fingers and thumbs together. Gundaganr snorted and gave them a disdainful look.

"Tricked Thor?" Ash asked.

"Yes. Once, when old Thunder-Thor travelled across Jotunheim, he came across Utgarda-Loki's lodge, where a big feast was being held. The Aesir, who loves a feed and a drink, put his animosity towards trolls and giants aside for a night to join the festivities. However, as Thor entered, Utgarda-Loki declared that none may sit at his table unless they could perform a great feat. He had also recognised Thor by the hammer hanging off his belt, and added that if Thor should fail in his feat, he would have to swear to never harm Utgarda-Loki or any of his descendants. Thor, confident in his capabilities, drew his chest out and dared Utgarda-Loki to name a challenge." Gundaganr paused for a moment to drink from a hot brew in front of her.

"Utgarda-Loki sent for his largest drinking horn. As it was carried in by two thursrs, all could see that it was full to the brim with mead and was so large that it didn't fully fit inside the hall. Utgarda-Loki declared it would be a feat indeed to finish the entire horn in one draught. Thor, never fearing a challenge, reached out and put the horn to his lips. He drank and drank until his face turned purple. At last, he had no choice but to put the horn down, or he would suffocate. When Utgarda-Loki inspected the horn, only a hand's width had been drunk, and Thor had failed the challenge."

Torsten, a Berserker, had a bond with Thor, who had granted some of his powers to the first of Torsten's line. He started to protest, but an angry look from both Gundaganr and Yrsa silenced him.

"Utgarda-Loki found great mirth in Thor's failure and declared that an easier challenge needed to be set. With this, he pointed to a cat that had come wandering into the hall. "Lift my cat, Thunder-Thor, and I shall consider that your feat," he declared. Thor, who felt the rage burning inside him because of the humiliating words, stomped up to the cat and surely meant to pick it up and throw it through the ceiling. But as he put his hands underneath it and lifted, the cat stretched to become impossibly long, and try as he might, he could not lift it off the ground. Struggling under its weight, Thor used all of his strength and pushed high over his head, but only got the cat to take one paw off the floor.

"Setting the cat down, he knew he had failed the second challenge, and the rage that he is so famous for was now blossoming within him. He challenged anyone in the hall to fight him as his last attempt at a feat. However, none stepped forward. Smiling, Utgarda-Loki declared it would be demeaning for anyone there to fight someone who was so weak that he could not even lift a cat. As Thor reached for his hammer to attack the obnoxious chieftain, Utgarda-Loki held up his hand to stay him. If Thor could defeat his old nurse in a wrestling match, he declared, then he could stay and drink in the hall, as he at least would not be the weakest one there. Thor, whose thirst had not been quenched by the long draught of the horn, agreed, as long as he could feast at the end.

"An old and bent troll woman lumbered forwards and Thor went to make quick work of her. But when they gripped shoulders, he found she was incredibly strong. He put his best effort in, but however hard he fought, the old woman fought harder and stronger. Before long, she forced Thor's knee onto the ground, and having lost the third challenge, he left the hall in shame. Utgarda-Loki walked him out, an arm around his shoulder. Here he declared that Thor had lost the wager and was now sworn to never harm Utgarda-Loki or any of his descendants."

"This cannot possibly be true!" Torsten was enraged, bits of meat and vegetable spraying from his mouth. "No one, especially an old troll woman, could best Thor of the Aesir in combat!" His face was red, and he was panting, his eyes daring the Shaman to disagree with him. Tensions rose in the cavern as many of the surrounding trolls growled and stood, opening and closing their clawed hands.

Gundaganr's cackle broke the tension. The old troll woman laughed, a finger pointed at Torsten. "As touchy as the god you follow. I'm sure you would make him proud."

The trolls sat back down, but kept a wary eye on Torsten.

"You are right, of course," she mused. "It was all trickery by Utgarda-Loki's magic. The mead in the horn was the entire ocean, and it baffled all that Thor had drunk a hand's width. The cat was none other than Jormungandr, the serpent that wraps around the entire world. It struck fear in all their hearts when Thor lifted one of its paws off the ground, for he had held almost the entire serpent to the sky. Finally, the woman he wrestled was none but Old Age, which no one can defeat. So, now you see the cleverness behind Utgarda-Loki's challenge. He is now safe from Thor, free to live in the open, unlike the rest of us."

"How do you know this, if Thor himself doesn't?" Yrsa asked the old Troll.

"Oh, a few of my sons you see here were fathered by Utgarda-Loki, and he likes to boast when between the furs."

The humans gave the surrounding trolls a nervous look.

"Don't worry," Gundaganr smiled. "My sons are fiercely loyal only to me."

She gave Ash a long, scrutinising look. "Although Utgarda-Loki is bad, the one to beware of is Burrugandr. He walks his own path and is ruthless to those who oppose him. His ways are not the ways of Jotunheim, and many trolls would not rally behind his cause. Some would, but not all. The Troll King has been asleep in his fortress of ice for generations, and the chieftains are free to run wild on his land. They hold the most power and for some, it has corrupted them. For a long time, they had been busy fighting and squabbling with each other, but factions have formed. We may have another Troll War on our hands before long. Woe to the worlds of Jotunheim and Midgard, should Burrugandr emerge as the victor."

She stood and wiped her hands on her apron.

"You may sleep by my fire tonight, but tomorrow you must leave." With that, she walked away and disappeared among the mass of trolls in the cavern.

Ash and his friends made themselves comfortable and laid down. Besides the stink of a hundred trolls, it was quite pleasant lying by the fire, their bellies full from a hot meal.

"And I thought my family was strange," Yrsa said in a low voice to Ash, gaining a snort from Torsten. Ash said nothing, pressing his lips shut in what he felt was a disapproving grimace.

"You do realise that every single troll in here is your uncle?" Yrsa continued, grinning like a wolf. "So, at least we know where you get your looks from." Torsten's body shook in silent laughter as the big man buried his face in his hands.

Even Ash couldn't pretend to be upset anymore and smiled.

"Maybe I'll introduce you to one of my cousins one day," he told her, wriggling his eyebrows.

Yrsa looked horrified.

"Although it might be cruel to match someone with such a savage beast," he continued. "Even trolls don't deserve that."

Torsten couldn't contain himself anymore and burst into a loud guffaw, soon followed by his friends. Some trolls turned their heads to look at them, but most just ignored the noisy humans.

When the laughter had died down, Ash turned to his friends, his expression more serious.

"Going to retrieve the remains of my father will set us back," he told his friends in a low voice.

Yrsa shrugged. "Small price to pay to keep Torsten with us," she started, before the Berserker nudged her in the ribs and winked. "Although I am already regretting it," she said, scowling at the big man.

"We still don't know where Roghald has gone, but I'm sure we can count on him being back before we know it," Ash said.

His friends nodded with sombre faces. They had been surprised by Ash's tale of his old stable master who had somehow turned into a troll and joined the enemy's ranks. To them, it was unthinkable that a human would betray their gods and their kin.

"We will deal with him when the time comes," Torsten rumbled. "He may be powerful, but even he is not immune to a well-placed axe."

With this, they all stretched out on the soft furs, and soon Torsten's snores echoed throughout the cavern, rivalling even that of the surrounding trolls. But Ash laid awake for a long time after his friends had fallen asleep. A lot had happened in the past week, and he struggled to process it as his mind drifted to the events unbidden.

He would almost certainly have died in the forest, had it not been for his friends. He did not fear death anymore, since he knew that his mother, a Valkyrie, would collect his soul from the battlefield and take him to Valhalla, the hall of the gods. A part of him even longed for the day, so he could once again see her face. A face that held nothing but love for him. Just as Gundaganr had nothing but love for her son Jordr, his father. Or his father transforming himself, leaving his old life and family behind, all for the love of his mother.

It stirred up no small amount of confusion in him to find out that trolls loved like humans did. In the stories he was told as a child, trolls were always cruel and sinister creatures, hiding in the forests, longing to eat the flesh off the bones of any careless wanderer. Maybe that was not entirely true? Yes, since he arrived, he had mostly encountered hostility, but Jotunheim was a hostile world. Maybe some trolls were the way they were because it was a matter of survival in a harsh environment? Eat or be eaten. It was a lot easier to think of the trolls as a united group of enemies, set out to destroy humanity, but he learned that there were factions within their society, too. And he was part of this world as well. At least half of him, anyway. The side that was his father. A good troll. A loving troll.

Ash stayed awake for a long time, but when he eventually fell asleep, it wasn't a restful one.

Ash opened his eyes. He stood on a sun-drenched hill, looking out over the unmistakable landscape that was Midgard. Its warmth and beauty struck his heart, and he longed for his home world, more than anything else, because he knew it was a dream. He heard a flutter of wings next to him and turned to see Odin by his side, his two ravens perched on his shoulders. The old god was wearing his usual grey tattered robes and held a long spear in his hand as he wistfully gazed out over the landscape.

"Beautiful, isn't it?" Odin said. "The finest thing we ever created. Before humanity, my brothers and I would spend weeks at a time walking across these lands, marvelling at their beauty. But after we created the first humans, and they settled this vast land, it truly reached its purpose and perfection."

"Could have done without the long winters," Ash offered, remembering fingers and toes numb with cold while fetching water from a frozen well.

The old god laughed. "There is beauty in all seasons. The joy in spring of all things living would not be possible without winter. The seasonal changes drive life and make it flourish." He turned to Ash. "See it as the land breathing. Each year is a breath in and a breath out." The old man leaned on his spear and his eyes grew distant. "Stagnation is death," he whispered.

A flash of light appeared in the distance. It was so bright Ash had to squint when he looked at it. It glared for a few seconds before settling, revealing what appeared to be a long rift in the very air, just above the ground. Ash could only look in horror as creatures began spilling out of the rift. They were trolls, but unlike any trolls he had ever seen. They had flames licking their skins, and swords and spears of pure fire. Some were giants, entirely made of flames, with only glowing embers for eyes.

They set upon the landscape, and all that they touched burned to the ground. Cities and towns fell before them, and soon the entire land was ablaze. The screams and moans of the innocent carried to Ash on the wind along with a slow rain of ashes and embers.

Ash turned to the god and saw that he was smouldering, the fires slowly consuming him.

"Is this the future?" Ash demanded, fear and sorrow permeating his voice.

"It is a future," Odin replied before he disintegrated, and the wind carried away his ashes.

CHAPTER 17

T HE BARGE BUMPED AGAINST THE WOODEN JETTY. Roghald looked around the familiar little cove. The bodies of the
rowers Agash had shot down last time they were here lay where
they had fallen, nothing more than small mounds of stone bearing
testament to their lives. He jumped onto the jetty, followed by
Agash, who had an arrow resting on her bow. Without a word,
the barge set out again, the bargemaster having been paid for his
service in advance.

"Find their trail," Roghald barked at Agash, who immediately
set out towards the forest.

Once they caught up with Ash, Roghald decided he would kill
the dark elf. Not only was she a coward, running away when the
tide of the battle turned, she was deceitful as well. He only needed her to find Ash, then her life would be forfeited. His fingers
twitched and, in his mind, Gamir laughed as Roghald imagined
throttling the life out of her.

They set off through the forest and it wasn't long until they
arrived at the scene where they had last encountered Ash and
his friends. The large mound of stone that had been Shumbolg
stood as a monument to the once powerful thursr, surrounded by
snapped trees.

Two parallel furrows carved into the ground led back towards the forest path.

"Looks like the Berserker didn't quite die," Agash remarked, pointing out the trail. "They dragged him off."

"Makes little difference," Roghald said. "Doesn't look like he'll be in any shape to fight when we catch them, anyway."

"It is not him I'm worried about," Agash said. "The boy moves like nothing I have ever seen, and he's a Stonesmith. I'd rather fight ten Berserkers than take him on again."

"You're a coward," Roghald spat in a disgusted voice. "Leave the brat to me, you just find him."

Agash's eyes narrowed at Roghald's words. "You left the battle too, Roghald, and you were far better equipped to fight him than I was."

"Tactical retreat," he mumbled, and gave her a dismissive wave of the hand. "Now, find the boy."

Agash gave him a quick, hateful glare before setting off again along the trail.

They found the camp where the humans had spent a night and immediately set after their poorly concealed tracks.

"The trail is around four days old," Agash had said when they set camp for the night. "They move slowly, so we should be able to catch up to them in a day or two."

The next day found them crouching low, looking down on a stone gully. The two parallel drag marks they had been following could be seen as faint white scratch marks on the stone. They led straight into a cave opening and did not come out again.

"They are in there," Agash whispered.

"Then I am going in," Roghald rumbled.

"Could be an ambush," she cautioned.

"Doesn't matter," Roghald said, tapping his hip pack. "I will hobble our little wolf when I see him.

There was movement toward the cave, and the two ducked

down lower. A troll had appeared in the opening and stood blinking in the sunlight.

"If they were inside," Agash whispered, "they are likely dead."

Roghald's eyes narrowed as he watched the troll exit the cave and move up the gully to the side.

"No. That troll might be big, but he's only a vaettr, and could never overpower them."

"Unless there is a large group of them living in there," Agash said, her eyes taking in all the refuse in the gully. "A couple of dozen trolls that size could defeat them if they stumbled into their dwelling.

They watched the troll clamber out of the gully and disappear into the forest.

"Let's go ask him," Roghald said.

They pulled back and circled around to their left. It didn't take long for Agash to find the troll's tracks, and they followed it deeper into the woods. They advanced slowly and soon glimpsed the vaettr between the trees. The troll had squatted down in a patch of low shrubs laden with violet berries. He was picking and dropping them onto a skin that was spread out on the ground next to him. Engulfed in his task, carefully picking the plump berries with his thick fingers, one or two at a time, he did not notice Roghald until his shadow fell on the bushes in front of him.

The troll frowned and, turning his head, glanced up. Seeing the horned battle troll towering over him, his expression changed from one of annoyance to concern as his eyes widened. The sound of footsteps behind him made him swivel his head around further to see Agash stepping out from behind a tree, a black arrow resting on her bow. He stood up slowly, turning to meet Roghald's gaze.

"Hello, friend," Roghald said in a cheerful voice.

The troll kept his mouth shut, staring at Roghald. He stood with his head tall, appearing defiant, but Roghald could see that he was nervously fingering an ugly necklace made from bird skulls.

"Not a chatty one, eh?" He smiled at the troll. "Don't worry, we mean you no harm. I just have a few questions."

The troll visibly relaxed.

"We are looking for three humans, one of which is injured. Seen them around?"

The troll's eyes widened again a split second before he shook his head.

"Not seen any humans at all?" Roghald said, as cheerful as ever.

"N-no," the troll said, a quiver in his voice.

"You know," Roghald grinned, baring his teeth. "I was hoping you would say that."

Roghald watched the troll's body turn to grey stone. He had held out longer than Roghald expected, but eventually he had cracked. Only this morning, the humans departed, heading north-east. Why the trolls had let them live, he did not know. By the time he got to that line of questioning, the troll was in pretty bad shape, mumbling 'family, family' through its broken teeth. Pathetic, Roghald thought. Especially when the troll's last words were calling for its mother as Roghald pummeled its head and body with his meaty fists.

Roghald wished he had the time to clear out the cave of trolls, just for aiding the humans, but he needed to catch up with Ash before the trail turned cold. He had also derived some small pleasure in Agash's discomfort at the torture he had put the vaettr through. He noticed her turning away from him as he was working on the troll. This just confirmed what he already knew; she was weak.

They pushed on and in no time, Agash had picked up the humans' trail, winding its way northeast, just as the troll had said. Roghald, getting excited as they drew nearer, demanded the fastest speed Agash's tracking would allow, and they moved at a mile-eating pace and didn't stop when night fell.

As the sun set the next day, they looked down from a ridge, onto a rocky valley where three small dots were setting up camp for the night, next to a copse of gnarled trees. They drew back from the ridge with caution, to avoid drawing the humans' eyes with their movement.

"We best wait for the night and see if we can take them by surprise," Agash said.

Roghald grunted his agreement, and they pulled back further from the ridge to rest for a few hours.

"I will take the first watch," Agash said, sitting down on a fallen log. They had moved down into the neighbouring gully and the cover that the many trees offered.

Roghald, saying nothing, laid down on his back, resting his head on his hands.

"Two hours, no more," he told the dark elf as he closed his eyes. But Roghald had no interest in sleep. He laid on his back and after a short while he forced his breathing to slow, making it seem like he was asleep. He did not hear a single sound from the dark elf, but when, after half an hour, Gamir began blabbering in excitement, he knew she was moving.

Roghald opened one eye a fraction and saw her as she slipped around a tree. She had made no sound at all. He waited a few more minutes before easing himself up as quietly as he could. Peering around the tree where Agash had disappeared, he saw a soft blue light from behind a thicket up ahead. What was she up to?

Roghald crept towards it, carefully avoiding every twig and fallen branch in his way, which was easier said than done, since he had rather enormous feet. He flinched and cringed when, despite his utmost effort, one snapped beneath him. Roghald stood still for what felt like an age, but there was no movement from the thicket in front of him. Deciding he had gotten away with it, he started forwards again and, in a few minutes, was craning his neck to look over the bushes.

An icy jewel laid on a rock, emitting the soft blue light. Even from where he stood, he could see the frost that had formed on the stone it was resting on. There was no sign of Agash. That was when he felt two feet land on his back and a blade press against his throat.

"You're not the first person whose last lesson in life was to never try to sneak up on a dark elf." Agash's lips were close to his ears, and her voice was almost purring. "Don't think I wasn't aware that you followed me in Utgard as well, you stupid troll. You should have stuck to fighting and left the sneaking to the experts," she hissed. "I always knew I would kill you, Roghald, but I didn't expect it to come so soon. My employer doesn't want the Ulfhed to die just yet.

"What employer? You are paid to aid me by Burrugandr," Roghald growled.

"Maybe someone paid me more," she giggled, then with one smooth movement she pulled her dagger to the side, cutting deep into his throat.

He swung his arm around, trying to swat her, but she had already jumped away. He spun and stood up as a swell of warm blood ran down his chest. Stupid elf. Trying to kill a battle troll with a dagger. All he needed to do was keep away from her for two seconds, and the wound would regenerate and heal. He coughed and sent a spray of blood into the air. The pain in the throat was burning, and he was finding it hard to breathe. The whistling sound from his neck every time he took a breath was disconcerting. With a shock, he realised the wound hadn't even begun to heal, and his eyes widened. He heard another giggle from Agash.

"What's the matter? Not healing up?" She grinned at him and her sharpened teeth making her look even more ferocious. "Aesir steel," she added, holding up the now blood covered black dagger. "From the forges of Eitri and Brokkr, the master dwarves who made Thor's very hammer." She looked at the dagger almost lustfully. "It kills trolls." She turned her eyes back to Roghald. "It is my payment for the service I am about to perform, and I must say that this is the best and most enjoyable bargain I have ever struck."

Roghald held his hand pressed against his throat, but the blood kept trickling out between his fingers and he was feeling light-headed.

"Damn you, you stinking elf!" he rasped in a hoarse voice.

Agash was crouched low, circling him like the predator she was. He kept turning to face her, but the moment he stumbled, she found the opening she was looking for and darted forward. He saw her coming and swung his free arm to grab her, but she had only feinted and ducked low, well under his arm. Rolling past him, she sliced deep into his thigh, sending another spray of blood onto the mossy ground. Roghald roared as the pain exploded in his thigh, causing another gush of blood from his throat. He swung down, but she had already rolled away. He felt like he was moving in mud. The pain in his wounds was agony, and his ears were throbbing with every slow and irregular heartbeat.

Agash was back on her feet and circling him once again, and Roghald found it difficult to focus on her now, her dark skin and leathers blending well with the shadows. He knew he only had one chance. He fumbled with the strap of the pack on his hip while monitoring the circling dark elf. Roghald just managed to get it open and stick his hand inside it when Agash lunged forward. He threw himself backwards away from her and pulled his hand out of the pack.

"Esh!" he called in a raspy voice, and a blinding light exploded from his hand. Agash screamed as the light struck her and threw her hands up, shielding her face. She threw herself to the ground and Roghald could see the blisters already forming and bubbling on her hands. She was whimpering, cowering away, but he kept the cone of light trained on her as he stumbled back onto his feet.

"What's the matter, mud elf? Bit of sunlight hurting you, is it?" he croaked.

Svartalfheim, the world of the dark elves, had no sun at all. The weak sunlight that filtered through to Jotunheim wasn't enough to cause them any harm, but direct sunlight, as it shines on Midgard, would cripple a dark elf. And this object was much more powerful.

"Mother Bestla warned me of your intentions," he told the cowering elf. "She said she sensed treachery in you and gave me this little thing. Years' worth of sunlight stored up and released at once."

Agash moaned and Roghald took delight in seeing the blisters on her hands and the parts of her face she wasn't able to shield, burst and weep a clear liquid as she writhed in pain. He walked towards the elf but felt lightheaded and had to lean against a tree for a moment or he would have fallen. He felt his wounds tingling and was relieved to see they were slowly closing up, but he was still losing blood. His head was spinning, and he had to rest his entire body against the tree, all his concentration focused on keeping the light on Agash. Then it flickered twice before going out. The world was dark once again.

Agash pulled herself up to her feet. Her face was a grimace of pain. There were horrible burns on the edges of her face that she could not shield. The dark elf held her hands out in front of her, her palms a mess of burst blisters and burned flesh. She was breathing in short gulps, and her eyes were wide and distant as she looked at Roghald in shock and horror. She blinked a few times, then looked down at the dagger at her feet.

Roghald could only watch, unconsciousness threatening to take him, as she bent down and reached for the dagger with both hands. She sobbed in pain as she picked it up clumsily, holding it between the two savaged hands. She straightened up and with a last look at Roghald, turned and staggered off into the trees. He sat there for a while, listening to her crash through the forest, all her stealth gone, until he felt she was far enough away that he could allow himself to slide into blissful unconsciousness at last.

CHAPTER 18

Ash and his friends stood in the dark, just beyond the edge of the grove of trees where they had set up camp. For several minutes, they had been watching a strange, bright light from over the ridge to the west. It flickered twice and then it went out, only the dark outline of the ridge now visible as a silhouette.

"What do you suppose that was?" Torsten asked.

"No idea," Ash said. "Maybe lightning?"

"Don't be daft," Yrsa scolded. "That's Torsten's job."

The Berserker muttered a few swearwords under his breath before turning around and walking back to their camp. "I don't care what it is, my feet are sore and I want something to eat," he declared to the world in general.

Yrsa and Ash remained, eyes fixed on the ridge.

"You go feed the bear," she said. "I'll stick around here for a while."

Knowing better than to argue with the shieldmaiden, Ash turned back to the camp and unpacked provisions from his pack. Yrsa kept her eyes trailed on the ridge until long after the light had disappeared, but when all was still an hour later, she shrugged and turned back to the camp.

They rose when the first light of dawn reached them, and after a cold breakfast, they set out, eager to be on their way. Yrsa took the lead, her eyes scanning the trees and ridges around them. Torsten and Ash, a few steps behind, paid less attention to their surroundings.

"So, when we get back to Midgard, we gather what's left of the Jomsvikings and sail east. There are still many rivers that we haven't explored, and a summer of raiding unknown lands is just what we need to relax from all this troll business," Torsten said in a cheerful voice. "We have enough people to fill two longboats, and I think we deserve a break, don't you?"

If anyone had asked him to go raiding ten years ago, Ash would have jumped at the opportunity, but the prospect had lost some of its charm to him. He had seen enough death and violence to last him a lifetime, and he wasn't sure that he felt comfortable attacking sleepy towns, burning them to the ground and taking their valuables. It seemed like something Burrugandr and his people would do.

"Let's just worry about making it back for now," he told his friend, but Torsten wasn't listening.

"Some of those lands are laden with riches, guarded by lazy people who have grown fat from too many big dinners." His eyes were distant, and a dreamy smile spread across his face, "We might even need to bring a third ship, just to load the loot onto."

Yrsa's hissing pulled the giant man from his daydreaming and Ash from his pondering. They all drew their weapons, and Ash saw what had drawn her attention. A creature was staggering towards them. Its head and shoulders were wrapped in a worn blanket, and a hand reached out towards them as it stumbled along. Torsten, axe in hand, turned around and eyed the trees and ridges around them with suspicion while the creature drew nearer. They spread out to flank it better if it attacked one of them.

"Oh, thank the gods! You are from Midgard!" The voice was high pitched and nasal.

Ash's eyebrows flew up as the creature pulled the blanket off the top of its head and a pink, pudgy face looked back at him. It was a human. The man was short and portly, with a round head and a small mouth with buck teeth, and his face seemed to be permanently occupied by an arrogant sneer.

"You're human?" Yrsa asked suspiciously.

Torsten paid the man little attention, continuing to survey their surroundings. "This feels like a trap," he rumbled.

"Yes, yes, I am human," the man said as he sunk down to the ground, his body relaxing in apparent relief.

Yrsa was eyeing the man. "You are no warrior," she said matter-of-factly. "What are you doing here?"

"I am Hagan. I am a servant of King Harald of Hammershall," the man said, straightening up where he sat.

"The King?" Ash asked incredulously. "Why is the King sending someone like you to Jotunheim?"

The man gave Ash a defiant glare. "I was sent as part of a larger retinue," he said, as if talking to a child. "The King's Seidwomen opened a portal and sent us on a diplomatic mission to seek trade with Utgard. However, we were attacked by these, these monsters. I only just escaped, but the rest were all slaughtered."

"Don't worry," Yrsa told him. "You'll soon be joining them. Can't see someone like you making it very far here."

The man's eyes widened, and his jaw dropped.

"Y-you have to help me," he demanded. "I am the King's man. It would be treason not to."

"Really? And where was the King when the north was overrun by the draugr, huh?" Torsten spat, his eyes filled with anger. The only kindness I will extend to the King's man is a quick death to spare him any unnecessary suffering."

Ash placed his hand on his friend's arm to calm him. "We can't just leave him," he told them both. "We can't betray our own kind, or we'd be no better than Roghald."

Ash didn't notice how the man had stiffened at his words and how his eyes had for a moment filled with hate, but in a moment, his gaze had returned to normal.

Torsten looked at Ash. "It feels wrong, Ash. I have heard that the old King has reverted to childhood and sits dribbling on his throne. How could he have come up with the idea to send people to Jotunheim?"

"He has advisors," Hagan said. "Several of the Jarls that were close to him are interpreting his wishes."

"We'll keep a close eye on him," Ash reassured his friend. Torsten gave him a long look before nodding once. "Fine," he said, turning back towards Hagan. "But if this smarmy bastard as much as scratches his bottom in a way I deem suspicious, I'm killing him." He followed his threat up with a fierce grimace, bending down towards the servant, making the man flinch and pull back from him in fear.

"It's alright," Ash said to Hagan, offering his hand to help the man up. "He'll grow on you."

Yrsa had fallen quiet, but Ash noticed she was drumming her fingers on her spear whilst looking between Ash and Hagan. He could see that she had conflicting feelings.

Hagan, it turned out, was a most disagreeable fellow. It didn't take long for his nasal voice and pompousness to get on everyone's nerves. Ash regretted taking the man under his wing after only the second hour of the man's complaints. There was just something unlikable about him. Ash also had a niggling feeling that he had seen the man before, but he couldn't quite place him. The man insisted that he had never left Hammershall.

Torsten, famous for his short temper, had pulled ahead of the group to avoid accidentally beheading the man after one unusually long tirade about the composition of the Jotunheimian landscape.

Yrsa, Ash noted, fell increasingly further behind, until she too was out of hearing range. That left Ash alone to suffer the constant whining. He wondered if the teasing of his friends would be worth it if he went back on his word and killed the man, but he dismissed the thought as quickly as it had come.

"I would like to thank you, Ash, for speaking up on my behalf earlier," Hagan started. "You are a man of honour, doing what few would have done in that situation. I do realise that I may present as somewhat of a... burden to your group, since I am not a warrior."

Ash felt ashamed for having considered killing the man only a moment earlier.

"Oh, it is no trouble, Hagan," he told the man. "Think nothing of it."

"I wish to express my gratitude in some way, but I find myself without means to do so," Hagan said.

"Really, don't worry a-" Ash got out before the rotund man interrupted him.

"There is this," Hagan said, having lowered his voice.

He had pulled a round circle from the depth of his clothes. It seemed to be some kind of bracelet, made entirely from twisted twigs. There was no pattern to them, but the twigs seemed to be a haphazard weave of twists and bends.

"This is a blessed bracelet made by the King's Seidwoman herself. It gives a warrior strength and power in battle, allowing him to defeat all his foes." The man looked at it reverently. "I would like to give it to you, to express my eternal gratitude," Hagan said, holding it out to Ash.

Ash looked at the bracelet. It seemed harmless enough, and he didn't get a bad feeling from it. He was about to reach out his hand to accept the gift, just to shut the man up, when he looked up and saw the look in Hagan's eyes. Hunger. Excitement. Malice. Ash kept his hand down.

"No need," he said. "You keep it."

"Please," Hagan said. "It would mean a lot to me if you accepted this small gift."

"I'm not one for jewellery and ornaments," Ash continued. "Besides, it sounds like it is not yours to give away."

"Oh, but I insist," Hagan pressed him. Ash couldn't help but hear the note of desperation in his voice.

"No," Ash snapped. "Put it away or I will give your fate to Torsten to decide over."

Hagan grumbled and put the bracelet back in the folds of the blanket. Ash pulled ahead to Torsten, leaving the pudgy man to stare daggers at his back as they carried on through the day.

They had walked east in a gradually descending landscape. By the end of the day, grass and mosses had replaced the stone underneath their feet and they found themselves under a purple canopy of giant trees in another forested valley. The air was richer here, and a there was a touch of humidity in the air.

Setting their camp by a shallow creek, Ash sat listening to it burble as it rushed along its bed, bubbling over rocks and branches. Torsten was cheerfully building a fire, his eyes drawn to the two round-eared rabbit-like creatures Yrsa had speared as they came across them earlier that day. Ash shared Torsten's excitement. Their field rations were nothing short of boring and he had been eating as a chore rather than any kind of enjoyment in the last few days.

Hagan sat off to the side. He had been keeping to himself ever since Ash had declined his gift. Everyone had taken the man's sulking as a gift from the gods, since he hadn't uttered a word since. Ash walked down to the creek to wash. He revelled in the sensation of days' worth of grime being washed away by the clear, fresh water. The creek was shallow, but if he laid down on his back, it was just deep enough to submerge his body. He got out of the water, almost slipping several times on the rocks as he clambered out and walked up to the fire to dry out.

By now, Torsten had it burning merrily and Ash's mouth watered at the smell of the now skinned and gutted rodents roasting over it. After cooking the animals, Ash and his friends ate to their satisfaction. Torsten then buried several tubers, which were given to them by Gundaganr's sons, in the coals. They sat around, patiently waiting for the tubers to roast.

"I would like to take a watch tonight, to do my part," Hagan said from his spot to the side.

"No." Torsten said, not even looking at the man as he attempted to dig a tuber from the fire.

"Why not?" Hagan said indignantly.

"Because." Torsten grumbled, more focused on the food than the man talking.

Hagan gave Ash a pleading look, but Ash just shook his head. He had seen something disturbing in the man and had no trust in him. Hagan went back to his sulking as Torsten triumphantly held up a cooked tuber for all to see. A second later, he yelped and began tossing the hot root between his hands.

Yrsa laughed and Ash smiled, the bitter servant all but forgotten. They lingered by the fire for a while before spreading out their blankets and laying down to sleep. Ash, who had the first watch, sat staring into the fire for a while. When Torsten's quiet respirations turned to a cacophony of snores, Ash got up and moved away from the fire. If anything approached their camp now, he would not be able to hear it over the Berserker, so he had a habit of walking the perimeter when on watch. He looked out over the landscape, vaguely lit by the distant moon. He let his eyes wander, familiarising himself with every shadow. What he didn't notice was that behind him, Hagan's eyes had followed him this whole time, and now the man was slowly rising from his blanket.

CHAPTER 19

ROGHALD WATCHED ASH WALKING AWAY FROM THE fire. It had been difficult for him to control himself when close to the man. Temptation had almost gotten the better of him several times, and it was with great effort that Roghald stayed his hand before he struck. He knew that once he revealed himself, it would all be over. Ash's abilities would allow him to overpower Roghald in a moment, just like he had with Shumbolg. Not to mention the Berserker and Ulfhed-bitch that rarely left Ash's side.

It had taken Roghald the entire night to heal his injuries from Agash, and some cuts still ached and throbbed even after the skin had closed over. He regretted not having been able to finish her, and his eyes darted between the shadows surrounding the camp. Roghald would now have to look over his shoulder for a long time, worrying about the dark elf. He would not let her get away again the next time they met.

Once more, he thanked the Norns for spinning his web so that he had possessed Birk the servant's body. He was worried that the humans might have recognised him from Gjallarholm, but they didn't seem to. After all, servants blended into the background, invisible to the high and mighty Jomsvikings. His plan of embracing the persona of the annoying servant, as he remembered him, had worked, and he had driven the two warriors away, often leaving him alone with Ash. Unfortunately, he could not persuade the man to accept the bracelet, and now Ash was suspicious of him. His only chance was to take a more direct approach.

Roghald watched Ash lean against a tree trunk, just beyond the light of the fire, and scout the landscape. He would not get a better opportunity than this. Pushing off the blanket, he stood up, careful not to make a noise that would wake the other two. They did not stir and the Berserker's snoring covered what slight noise he made as he walked over the mossy ground towards Ash's back.

When he was only a step or two from him, he whispered, "Ash."

His nemesis spun around, his hand on his sword, but did not yell out.

Roghald held up a hand and smiled at the boy. "My apologies," he whispered. "I did not mean to startle you."

Ash eyed him with distrust, but soon relaxed and let his hand fall from the sword.

"I wish to apologise for my behaviour today," Roghald said, conjuring up the most earnest expression he could. "All this is very hard for me and I feel lost in this gods-forsaken world. I know I have acted strange and I should not have pushed you to accept the bracelet. Can you forgive me, so that we may get along until this ordeal is over?" It was with great satisfaction he saw Ash's eyes soften. He smiled at the boy and extended his right hand towards him in a conciliatory gesture.

Ash looked at the hand for a moment, but soon returned the smile and reached his own hand out towards Roghald. That's when Roghald revealed his other hand, which he had concealed in the blanket over his shoulders, and deftly slid the bracelet over Ash's outstretched hand. The boy recoiled as if a snake had bitten him and shook his hand. He tried to pull it off with his other hand, but it would not budge. He looked like he was about to call out, but then Ash stopped and blinked a few times, a look of surprise on his face.

"I-I feel great," he said, his eyes finding Roghald's.

"I told you, it is a blessing. My apologies for forcing it on you, but the depth of my gratitude knows no bounds," Roghald said, bowing his head.

Ash's mouth fell open, and he spun to look around him.

"I can see in the dark!" Filled with awe, he exclaimed, "I can see in the dark!" and rubbed his eyes before looking around again.

"What's the ruckus about?" Yrsa's voice cut through the night like a knife. "Carrying on like this is an excellent way of drawing down every monster in Jotunheim on us." Crossing her arms, Yrsa scowled at Ash and gave a suspicious glare to Roghald.

"Nothing, sorry," Ash lowered his eyes from the glaring shield-maiden.

"You. Go to bed. You. Keep a proper watch and shut up." She pointed at them in turn and was just about to turn around when Roghald spoke.

"The only one making noise now is you." He could not suppress his irritability any longer.

Yrsa's eyes changed from stern to furious in a split second. She took a quick step toward Roghald, and unfortunately for him, it saved her life. A massive spear shot past where she had been standing and slammed into a nearby tree, splitting it with a loud crack. They all stared at the quivering spear for a moment before Yrsa yelled, "Defensive positions!"

Roars went up in the trees all round them, and as they were all backing towards the campfire, Roghald could see large shapes moving through the trees, sending the canopies waving. When the first creature pushed into the clearing and became visible by the light of the fire, it only took him a second to recognise the thursr as being from Mogthrasir clan by the bright red stripe painted from his forehead to the tip of his long nose. He was ashen in colour with a swell of black braids, and in his muscular arms he held a spear like the one that had been thrown at Yrsa.

The massive troll roared a challenge and drew his spear back to launch at the group of defenders. However, he never had time to throw it, since Torsten's axe came spinning head over shaft through the air and slammed into his face. The Berserker, with a roar of his own leapt forwards and caught the axe as it fell when the troll's body crumbled into a pile of rubble.

More trolls ran into the clearing and Roghald saw to his dismay, that they were all Mogthrasir and they were all battle trolls. His carefully laid plans fell apart. He had intended to pick off the Berserker and the shieldmaiden one at a time until there was only Ash left. The boy would not have been able to resist him, now that the bracelet was on and Roghald would have had his victory and revenge. Now he would be lucky to make it out alive. His only hope was to breach the Mogthrasir lines and escape into the night.

As the thursrs and humans clashed in a frenzy of clanging weapons and shouts, he prepared to change into his troll form. Then he heard a familiar voice ring out over the din of battle.

"We need them alive, you idiots!"

Blodheid, he thought. The jotunn from Utgard; Utgarda-Loki's daughter. The Shaman materialised from the trees but kept away from the battle. Her skinny frame and long limbs made her look like a big white spider by the glow of the fire. The trolls ignored Roghald as he ran off to the side, not posing a threat to them. He ducked in between the large roots of a nearby tree where he had a clear view of the fight.

"Shift, Ash! Shift!" Yrsa's call rang out. She was fighting a thursr wielding a large, iron studded club. She was avoiding his blows with ease, jabbing her spear into its green body, but the beast showed no sign of slowing down.

"I can't!" The desperation was obvious in Ash's voice. "I can't make the Shift!"

Roghald knew why. The blessing. It was the blessing of True

Troll, a spell that made a troll connect fully to the magic within. It strengthened you and enhanced all the attributes of being a troll, but suppressed all other talents - including the Ulfhednar powers. Roghald had wanted a curse, but Mother Bestla had suggested a blessing instead.

"Curses can be broken," she had cackled, *"but who has ever tried to remove a blessing?"* There is no Shaman on Jotunheim who can remove it."

He almost laughed out loud at the look on Ash's face when he was pressed by two thursrs, running and weaving through trees to keep away from them at the normal speed of a human. Having had enough of the cat-and-mouse game, one thursr drove a massive knee into the young tree Ash had just ducked in behind, snapping the tree and sending it into him.

He saw Ash flying through the air and landing in a rolling heap before coming to a stop against another tree. A fierce shriek rang out, and Roghald turned to see the shieldmaiden running to the boy's rescue. The thursr she had been fighting was already a lump of stone, her spear protruding from where its neck had been. She leaped into the air and, landing on the back of one troll, pulled her seax from her belt. She raised the blade in both hands, ready to stab down into the neck of the beast, when something slammed into her back with a slap. Roots and vines sprouted from between her shoulders and wrapped around her body in a crushing embrace. Roghald heard her grunt as the force pushed the air from her lungs and caused her to topple off the troll. She landed on her back, with only parts of her face and a hand exposed, while the writhing mass of plants enveloped her.

Blodheid, holding a thin, softly glowing string that led to the bundle that encased Yrsa, laughed in triumph. With her other hand, she reached into a satchel on her hip and pulled out a fist-sized ball of roots. Smiling, she held it up to her lips and whispered to it. The ball moved and twisted in her hand. She took two quick steps forwards and launched it with a great overhand throw, trailing another string that she held in her hand. Roghald followed the projectile as it slammed into the chest of the unsuspecting Berserker who, busy fighting two thursrs of his own, never saw it coming. In seconds, a tangle of roots enveloped the raging warrior, but he stayed on his feet, straining against his bonds. For a second, Roghald thought the man's immense strength would actually tear the restraints, but a knock on the head by one of the thursrs sent him to the ground, where he remained.

He turned back to Ash, who still lay against the tree where he had landed. He had lost his sword when he was thrown, and Roghald watched the two hulking thursrs advance on him with confidence. Ash was scraping at the moss next to him, but when he lifted a fistful of black soil to his face, Roghald saw all hope leave the boy's eyes. No stone there, you lout. Roghald thought with glee. At least he could take some pleasure in watching Ash defeated, even if it wasn't by his hand. As the trolls lumbered to a stop in front of him, the boy fumbled with something at his belt.

"I don't think your tiny seax is going to help you right now," he chuckled to himself.

Ash raised his hand and threw something at the feet of the thursrs. With a green flash, the ground opened beneath the trolls who fell in, their surprised grunts cutting through the silence that had set upon the camp. With another flash, the ground sealed back up, and the trolls were gone.

A portal! He opened a portal! Roghald didn't know if he should laugh or cry at the boy's talent for last-minute saves. He heard a cry of rage from Blodheid a moment before one of her bundles of roots hit the boy in the chest. He did not fight it as it wrapped around him, but the look Ash shot the Shaman just before the vines covered his face was one of pure defiance. Then Roghald felt a firm hand close around his neck and lift him up.

"You said they would be easy to overcome," one of the battle trolls grumbled at Blodheid. "Five thursrs are now missing from Mogthrasir's ranks, and you will have to answer to her for this."

"Bah," Blodheid spat at the troll. "I am not responsible for their incompetence." She pulled herself up to her full height, standing a head and shoulder above the thursr.

"And you dare question me, little troll?" The jotunn's voice was like ice. "If you have forgotten your place, I will gladly show it to you."

The thursr met her gaze, but only for a second, before her will overcame his and he looked down to the ground and bowed his head in submission.

"Put the warriors in the baskets. That soft one can be carried. He is no threat." She nodded her head at Roghald.

One of the four remaining thursrs ran off between the trees, only to return with three wicker baskets. Roghald watched as the others, squirming against their restraints were stuffed into them and the lids shut and sealed. When they were safely locked in, Blodheid released the strings from her hand and the bonds of the others withered and disappeared. Two long leather loops on each basket allowed the trolls to carry the baskets on their backs, leaving their hands free to hold their weapons, and soon they were all loaded up. The thursr holding Roghald simply hoisted him into the crook of his massive arm and stood ready to depart with the others.

"Towards Utgard," Blodheid barked, and the trolls set off in a steady, bouncing jog. Roghald's ribs were already sore from where he hung, uncomfortably close to the thursr's armpit. His only comfort was that the others in their baskets would be even more uncomfortable than he was.

He considered for a moment simply changing into his troll shape and escaping in the confusion that would ensue, but that would mean that he would lose Ash again. Also, he was uncertain how many of those root bundles Blodheid held in her bag, not to mention any other magic at her disposal. As the trolls ran through the night, he decided he had no option but to go along for the ride.

By the time the sun rose the next day, Roghald was sore in places he didn't even know he had. His only relief had come when the troll's arm tired out and he swapped to the other arm, slightly changing Roghald's position. It did not surprise him to find that the trolls jogged tirelessly through the day and into the following night. Thursrs had incredible stamina and did not tire easily.

With not much else to do, Roghald had kept an eye on the sun through the day and knew they were running east. In the afternoon, they turned south. He gathered they had rounded the tip of the Great Lake before changing their direction southward, and heading toward Utgard. They should reach the town in a day or two, he thought, although he wasn't sure he could take it for much longer. He hadn't been able to feel his legs for hours.

When night had settled around them, Roghald heard one of the thursrs speak, "I am hungry."

A chorus of assent from the other trolls followed this.

"We could make camp and eat one of the prisoners," one suggested. "Utgarda-Loki and Mogthrasir are only interested in the wolf pup, anyway."

Another chorus of agreement.

"I am sick of carrying this one," the troll carrying Roghald rumbled, jiggling him. "He is soft and puny and surely is not important to the chieftains."

"No," Blodheid said firmly, "I will bring all the prisoners back, and if you mention it again, I will cut off your arm for you to eat."

They ran in silence as the hours of the night stretched out into what felt like days to Roghald. Utterly exhausted, he was just slipping into sleep when a thursr in the front called out, pointing.

"There is a fire ahead of us."

All the trolls stopped and looked to where he was pointing. Roghald raised his head from where he was hanging and could indeed see the flicker of a fire in a stretch of trees in the distance.

"Let's see if there is something to eat there," one suggested.

Blodheid stood silent for a moment before shrugging. "Fine,

since it is on the way. But we must not linger, and we will not risk the prisoners."

All the trolls agreed, and they set out toward the lone fire. The trolls, all eager to fill their bellies, ran at a much faster pace and only slowed down as they got within earshot of the fire. The troll carrying Roghald leaned out from behind a tree to scout, giving Roghald a clear view as well.

On a small grass-covered hill, in the middle of a large clearing, a lone figure sat wrapped in a shaggy pelt, leaning in towards the campfire they had seen. The figure sat unmoving, looking into the flames, and appeared to be unaware of the five battle trolls eyeing it from behind the tree line. The thursrs drew back, and a whispered conversation ensued.

"It is just one small creature," one said, rubbing his hands together. "It cannot oppose us."

"Not much eating on it, if we are all hungry," said another.

"It is a vaettr, by the size of," a third said with a grimace. "Tastes terrible and always upsets my guts. Even if you eat quickly, they turn to stone halfway to your stomach."

"You don't have to eat any, Bragnir," the first one said. "More for the rest of us that way. I am starving and could eat a rock."

They all turned to look expectantly at Blodheid.

She rolled her eyes. "Fine," she sighed. "Eat your fill, if it will stop your complaining."

The thursrs grinned, all except Bragnir who made another grimace and stuck his tongue out. At a signal, the trolls spread out and circled the clearing, before stepping out around the lone creature, all escapes blocked.

CHAPTER 20

JARL ASTRID STOOD OUTSIDE THE MAIN GATE OF GJALlarholm. She was listening to the builder with only one ear as he swept his arms excitedly, explaining the different options of expanding the walls to encompass most of the town. He was also strongly advocating for the addition of a moat.

The world is changing, she thought. And those who cannot change with it will perish.

Her left hand was resting on the hilt of the sword strapped to her waist. The reassuring weight of the weapon and the chain mail shirt were a comfort in these trying times. She couldn't believe that she had worn nothing but dresses since she had hung her sword up to govern her people a decade ago. Never again, she vowed to herself.

Since the recent battle with the draugr, she had felt as if the years had fallen off her and she longed for the next opportunity to be swept away into a battle frenzy again. Thinking of the draugr reminded her of Ash and his Jomsviking companions. They had shown more bravery than most and had nearly paid with their lives, all in the service of ridding Midgard of the draugr infestation. And now they were in Jotunheim, seeking the source of the infestation.

She doubted she would ever see them again, and the thought filled her with sorrow. She liked Ash. Something about his boyish innocence and naivete had endeared him to her. She had never had children; she always felt it would have been cruel to have a shieldmaiden for a mother, as the child would likely be orphaned at some point. Ash was one such orphan. Maybe the sisterly bond that existed between all shieldmaidens made her feel motherly towards the child of one who had fallen. Either way, she didn't think she would see him again. Hopefully, she would never have to see another troll, either.

A shout from the wall above her interrupted her thoughts. She looked up to see one guard pointing beyond her, and she spun around, her chain mail jingling. Thirty yards away a green circle of light was expanding on the ground.

"A portal!" she cried. "They are returning!"

She smiled and readied herself to welcome the heroes. She was glad that she had been wrong in underestimating the Jomsviking trio. Meanwhile, the wall and gatehouse were filling with warriors, guards, and townspeople who wanted to see what all the commotion was about.

Two enormous creatures emerged from the hole in the ground. They hung suspended in the air for a second while the portal closed beneath them with another flash of green. Then they dropped unceremoniously to the ground with two loud thuds. For five endless seconds, the two thursrs and the humans could only stare at each other in utter confusion. Then all hell broke loose. The humans shouted, some screamed, and the two thursrs bellowed and roared, raising their weapons to the sky.

As she pulled her sword from the scabbard, Jarl Astrid couldn't help but laugh. She alone saw the humour in the situation of two trolls being dropped in their midst. The trolls had seemed as surprised as they were. She pulled back towards the wall as a rain of arrows fell on the two advancing beasts. At this close range, the longbows bit deep and the trolls were already staggering. She saw movement in the corner of her eye and looked over to see the remaining Jomsvikings spill out from the fortress.

"To me!" Astrid called to them, raising her sword.

The battle-hardened warriors moved in and closed around her, the Berserkers forming a shield wall in front of her, while the Ulfhednar moved to her sides, preparing to flank the trolls. The Berserkers had begun their battle chant, stomping their feet and beating their weapons against their shields. Astrid felt goosebumps on her arms as the ancient rhythm washed over her. The already sizeable and sturdy warriors seemed to grow even larger. She breathed in deeply, savouring all the sensations. She felt so alive! Then the battle trolls reached them and the fight started in earnest.

The thursrs had already taken damage from the arrows, but these were trolls bred for war and had a lot more fight left in them. One jabbed its long spear straight through a shield, impaling a Berserker and lifting him up in the air. The warrior, in the thick of his battle rage, didn't even slow down. Instead, he chopped at the spear shaft with his axe over and over until it snapped and he fell to the ground.

The Berserkers had all launched forward at the trolls, their axes cutting deep and their war hammers cracking bones. The warrior who had been impaled got up, with the large spearhead embedded in his guts and protruding out his back. He raised his axe and staggered towards the enemy. Then, the Ulfhednar swept in from the sides and back, moving in a blur, their spears flashing, cutting the heel tendons of the two trolls. The thursrs fell forwards as their feet gave out and with curses and battle cries, the Jomsvikings and Astrid closed in, their weapons hacking. It didn't take long for the trolls' bodies to fade to grey stone.

With a triumphant roar, the defenders raised their weapons into the air.

The impaled Berserker lowered his axe and turned to the warrior standing next to him. They looked at each other and smiled, clasping their right wrists. Astrid heard the uninjured one speak and nod to his friend.

"It is a good death, Bjorn."

The impaled man nodded happily, then his eyes glazed over and he fell backwards. He was dead before he hit the ground.

"Alvhilda," Astrid called to the acting leader of the Jomsvikings in Torsten's absence. The Berserker woman turned to meet Astrid's eyes. Astrid was fond of Alvhilda. She was a blunt and no-nonsense kind of woman, but also reasonable and competent. Having just seen the woman growling and foaming at the mouth as she attacked a troll twice her size only added to Astrid's fondness of her. "We need to talk. I don't think things are going very well in Jotunheim."

CHAPTER 21

ASH FELT SICK. THE JOSTLING AND BUMPING AROUND inside the small enclosed space while the troll jogged along had made him nauseated. Fortunately, the vine and root that had wrapped around him had fallen off and disintegrated as soon as the lanky troll had let go of the string.

He found himself in some kind of wicker basket, made of thin branches. It seemed flimsy enough, but it must have been infused with magic because he couldn't tear the branches no matter how hard he tried. They were like iron. When he had thrashed about in frustration, trying to force the lid up, the troll carrying him reached around and gave the cage a couple of hard smacks. This jolted Ash around even more and he hit his head on the side of the basket, making the nausea much worse, so he settled down. He intended to escape as soon as the lid was opened. Probably in the presence of Utgarda-Loki and his entire horde, he thought bitterly.

What worried Ash more at the moment was that he could not Shift. When he searched within himself, he could no longer feel the part in his chest where his powers stemmed from. The space beneath his heart just felt... empty. He touched the bracelet on his arm. It had to be this bracelet. Hagan had been almost obsessed with him receiving it and had forced it upon him in the end. Ash did still have a lingering sense of euphoria, similar to the feeling he had when the bracelet first clasped his wrist. And somehow this euphoria persisted despite his unfortunate current fate of being trapped in a basket and feeling nauseated.

He closed his eyes and reached out with his Stonesight. He could feel the rock beneath him, and he could paint a picture in his mind of what the immediate landscape looked like. Anything made from rock, anyway. He hadn't lost his Stonesmithing powers, just the Ulfhednar abilities. Which was worrying indeed.

He put his forehead against the wall of his small prison. There were plenty of gaps in between the branches that made up his prison, and he had a clear view of another thursr running behind them. It had a basket on its back too, and he wondered if it was Yrsa or Torsten in it. He hoped his friends were unhurt. He couldn't help allowing a little snort of laughter to escape when he imagined how angry Torsten would be, bumped around in his basket. Ash almost felt sorry for whatever troll would open up the Berserker's basket later.

They had been running along for an entire day and into the night, before the battle trolls spoke at all. When they started talking, he could hear that they were complaining of hunger, and he felt a pang of worry. What if they ate one of them? He was relieved when he heard the tall, skinny Shaman forbid this very idea and almost felt grateful to her.

She made his skin crawl, and whenever he had glimpsed her through the gaps in his basket, he could not take his eyes off her. She looked like a large, pale spider as she kept up with the jogging thursrs by simply taking great strides with her long legs. Her long, red hair swayed from side to side as she swung her head with every step, and she had a myriad of strange amulets and bones pinned to a surprisingly well kempt green tunic. She wore a determined expression on her face, and her intelligent eyes seemed to take everything in.

He heard the trolls discover a campfire and set their course towards it. Another whispered conversation and they all split up. Although Ash was on the back of the troll and couldn't see the fire directly, he could see the soft glow of a fire reflected from the surrounding tree trunks and canopy.

"Good evening, fellow travellers," It sounded like a human voice. Ash felt sorry for the man. He would be dead and devoured in no time. "You are all welcome to sit by my fire if you like."

Ash's troll took a few steps forward and then his basket tilted to the side, followed by a thud that rattled his teeth. The troll evidently had slipped him off his back and set him down on the ground. A quick look through the branches revealed that the enormous troll had sat down next to the fire with Ash's basket next to him.

Ash looked straight ahead and across from the fire, indeed sat a human. It was a stocky man, wrapped in a bearskin. He had bright red hair in two long braids, and a bristling red beard. He had scars on a face that was dominated by a broad nose and thick eyebrows. Ash thought the man resembled a Berserker and felt saddened because even so, he would have no chance against five thursrs.

He looked at the trolls, who all sat around the fire, grinning maliciously at each other. They were going to toy with the man before they ate him. The troll who had been running behind him and had initially opposed eating what they thought was a vaettr cheered up significantly and began licking his lips. There was no sign of the jotunn Shaman, he realised.

"What are you doing in Jotunheim, little human?" the largest of the thursrs asked of the man.

"I am hunting." The man smiled kindly at the troll.

He must be stupid or mad, Ash thought. Poor man.

"You have no bow or spear," the thursr said, signalling with his arm toward a small pack that appeared to be the man's only belongings. "You come to Jotunheim to snare rabbits?"

The trolls chuckled at their friend's comment. Ash thought the ginger man must be daft indeed, because he laughed along with the trolls, not realising they were mocking him. He even saw one of the thursrs use a finger to make a twirling motion at his temple to the amusement of the troll next to him.

"I have all I need with me," said the man, patting his waist area on the outside of his bearskin. Ash noticed that the man wore an iron gauntlet on his hand. "And I hunt for larger quarry than rabbits," he continued in good nature.

"And what is that?" The glee was radiating off the large thursr, who clearly was enjoying this cat-and-mouse game.

"Trolls," the man said cheerfully.

Everything fell quiet for a second before the thursrs all burst out laughing. They were slapping their thighs and one even fell over backwards, holding his belly as howls of laughter echoed out over the forest.

Meanwhile, the man sat there smiling, but for a moment his piercing blue eyes landed on Ash's basket and he could have sworn the man had winked. The laughter went on and as the trolls were wiping their tears, the largest one spoke.

"I will remember this meeting for a long time," he chuckled. "Tell me your name before I kill you, so that I may remember the biggest fool to ever set foot on Jotunheim."

"My name is Thor Odinsson,"

The laugher stopped. The trolls all visibly paled.

"If this is a joke, you will regret it," the large thursr said as he held up an enormous fist at the man. He put up a good front, but he did not keep the tremor out of his voice when he spoke.

The man smiled and stood up, letting the bearskin fall to the ground. He had a powerful build, with broad and muscular arms and legs. His shoulders were so thick that there was hardly a neck to speak of. He wore a simple woollen tunic, but around his waist sat a hefty iron belt, the green runes carved into it glowing with a soft light. As Ash had noted before, the man's iron gloves were intricate, covered in swirling patterns and runes, but they paled compared to what he gripped in his right hand.

Thor's hammer, named *Mjolnir*, was legendary. The dwarves, who had created the masterful weapon a long time ago, crafted Mjolnir out of a strange metal that they had picked from the stars. It was short-handled, and it crackled with power as thin tendrils of lightning reached out from its surface, dancing over the metal belt and gauntlets of the man holding it.

The trolls sat frozen, staring at the Thundergod in front of them. The god known as the Trollslayer. Thor's eyes became aglow with white light as he spoke in a voice echoing with power.

"LET THE HUNT BEGIN."

A bolt of lightning shot out from the hammer, slamming into the largest thursr, the one who had been mocking him. It burned a hole the size of a barrel through the troll's chest and a second later, what was left of him fell as crumbling stone to the ground.

This sprung the rest of the trolls into action, but not to attack the god, simply to run away. Thor laughed as he threw his hammer straight through a retreating troll's back and watched the weapon turn around in the air and return to his hand. On its way back, it had smashed through the now-dead troll's stone body before it fell to the ground, crushing it and sending a cloud of dust into the air. Lightning and thunder filled the clearing and although Ash covered his ears and closed his eyes to the blinding light and deafening booms, he could still hear the screams of the trolls as they fell one by one.

Then all fell silent.

Ash opened his eyes and, peering out of his basket, witnessed the devastation in the clearing – the ground had turned black, a tree was snapped in half and ablaze, and the air carried a scent of tin and smoke. Thor the Thundergod was whistling a cheerful tune as he hung his hammer back onto a hook on his belt.

"Thunder-Thor, stay your hammer and hear my words!" Blodheid's voice rang out over the clearing. Ash saw her stride out from the line of trees, holding her head high, but he recognised the fear in her eyes when she looked at the man in front of her.

"A jotunn," Thor chuckled, reaching for his hammer. "I haven't killed a jotunn in ages."

Blodheid blurted out, "I am Blodheid, daughter of Utgarda-Loki. You are oath-sworn not to harm him or any of his line."

The look of disappointment on the Thundergod's face was palpable.

Seeing the god take his hand off Mjolnir, she continued with more confidence, "When you lost your challenges in my father's hall, you took an oath on your honour that you cannot breach and now I demand that you leave me and my property be," she said, pointing to the baskets containing Ash and his friends.

Thor's face turned absolutely sour and if looks could kill, Blodheid would have been mincemeat, but he held still, bound by his oath.

"Ha," the Shaman cackled once and strode past the god toward the baskets.

Ash's grandmother's words returned to him. Utgarda-Loki had tricked Thor.

"It was a trick!" He yelled out. "Utgarda-Loki tricked you!"

Blodheid picked up speed and reaching Ash, gave the basket a good kick that sent him and the basket tumbling backwards.

"Begone, Thor." She told the god, her voice now high pitched. "There is nothing else for you here."

Thor's eyes narrowed as he took a few steps towards Blodheid.

"I want to hear what the lad has to say." He walked up to Ash's basket, righted it, and ripped off the lid at the same time, causing a shower of sparks as the magic holding it shut faltered.

"Go on," he told Ash who looked up at him, blinking.

"Eh- hello," he said nodding to the god of lightning. "Utgarda-Loki tricked you with his magic. The horn you were given to drink from contained the entire ocean, and no one could drink all of it. The cat that you had to lift was Jormungandr, the world serpent, and even the strongest giant couldn't have lifted it. Finally, the old woman you wrestled was none other than Old Age, which no one can defeat, even the gods."

Thor looked deep into Ash's eyes for a long while before swivelling his head around to Blodheid, who had sidled further away from him as Ash was speaking.

"Is this true?" His voice was only a whisper, but it carried across the clearing.

It was the flicker in her eyes that gave it away, Ash thought later. It was the very briefest of movements, away from the god's eyes for a split second, but it spoke volumes. They both moved at the same time. Thor grabbing his hammer and Blodheid throwing something she held in her hand. Whatever it was, it landed on the ground between them, exploding in billows of smoke. A heartbeat later, Mjolnir flew through the smoke to where the Shaman had stood, before returning to the Thundergod's hand.

After the smoke cleared, there was no evidence of the jotunn, and no mound of stone to show her demise.

"Damn it," the Thundergod muttered.

Ash turned to his saviour, only to find Thor scrutinising him.

"I owe you thanks, lad. Utgard has been a thorn in my side for centuries, but that ends tonight," Thor said, attaching his hammer onto his belt again.

"As I owe you," Ash replied, trying to keep the awe out of his voice. He became thoughtful for a moment. "I thought the gods could not interfere in this?"

Thor looked mischievous when he replied. "Well, they found me, not the other way around. Besides, I have been hunting trolls in Jotunheim since I learned how to walk, so nothing unusual about that."

"Quite a coincidence that they came across you then," Ash remarked. "I mean, Jotunheim is a vast land."

"Yes, quite a coincidence," Thor replied, looking Ash square in the eyes.

"Nothing to do with Odin or Freya, then?"

"Well," Thor said, busying himself throwing a few logs on the fire. "It may have been suggested to me that it would be a fine night for hunting."

"In this particular area?"

"Around here, yes."

"Ah," Ash replied, mirroring the god's deadpan face. "Well, alright then. I see. Thank you."

"Think nothing of it," Thor replied.

They both spun around as one of the other baskets fell over.

"We best release your friends," said the god, happy to change the subject.

The Thundergod walked up to the nearest one and ripped the lid off with ease. A flash from the basket lit up the clearing and a blinking Yrsa gazed out at them.

"Care to join us?" Thor asked her. Yrsa nodded once and clambered out, stiff from the confined space.

Several thuds rang out and jostled the third basket as it fell over. Then the lid was straining on its bindings for a moment before it snapped open in a flash of sparks and two large feet popped out. There was a bit of muttered swearing as the rest of Torsten wriggled out backwards. Red in the face from the effort, the berserker stood up, squared his shoulders and with his eyes on the Thundergod, he closed his right fist and placed it over his heart in a sign of the Hammer.

"Thor, Odin's son, my axe belongs to you," he said in a deep, formal voice.

The deity gave Torsten an appreciative nod. "Hail Berserker Torsten Grimsson. You have filled my father's hall with your dead enemies, who all sing your praises."

Torsten's face turned even redder at the God's words and the Berserker stammered out his thanks, his eyes aglow with pride.

Ash heard Yrsa sigh and mutter, "We'll never hear the end of this."

Soon after, Thor went back to the fire and picked up his bearskin, which he once more wrapped over his shoulders. He reached into the small pack that had been sitting next to him and pulled out an ornate horn. He lifted it to his lips and blew three quick notes.

Ash looked around expectantly but saw nothing. He was just about to ask the god what that was all about when an enormous bulk flew into the clearing and landed in front of them, startling him and his friends.

The Sagas and stories about the gods always described Thor's chariot as being drawn by two goats; *Tanngrisnir* and *Tanngnjóstr*. Sure, these two creatures in front of them had horns, but that's where the similarities ended with any goat Ash had ever met. The two beasts tethered to the crude, rune-covered and battle-scarred wooden chariot were built like bulls, had claws instead of hooves, and drooling mouths filled with long, sharp teeth. Their eyes glowed red and when the nearest one turned its scarred, white head to look at Ash with the same intensity as a wolf looks at a rabbit, he saw nothing but madness in its eyes. When it snorted loudly, sending a cloud of steam towards him, he couldn't help but take an involuntary step backwards.

"Oh, don't mind him," Thor said, patting the goat's flank. "He is harmless."

"If you say so," Ash replied, his voice full of doubt.

"I wasn't talking to you," Thor rumbled, swinging himself into the back of the chariot.

As he grabbed the reins, he looked over at Ash and his friends. "Farewell."

"Where are you going?" Yrsa asked.

"I have a score to settle," the Thundergod replied, his face a strange mask of glee and anger.

"Until your death or Ragnarok, whichever comes first," he said winking, before flicking the reins. The goats set off and clawed their way into the air, with the chariot soon disappearing over the treetops. Ash and Yrsa heard a choking sound and turned to see Torsten, his fist over his heart again, staring at the point from where Thor had disappeared.

"The proudest moment of my life," the Berserker sniffed, eyes brimming with tears. "I wish my old dad had been alive to hear this."

"For the love of Freya," Yrsa muttered, putting her palm over her eyes.

A little while later, as they sat around the fire Thor had built, a thought struck Ash.

"Hey, where did Hagan go?"

"Probably took the opportunity to run away." Yrsa said, in between mouthfuls of the dried meat Ash's grandmother had given them.

"Probably still running," Torsten chimed in.

They could hear the rumble of thunder coming from the south. They all turned to see the horizon lit up in a spectacular show of lightning as bolts repeatedly hammered down from the sky.

"What's over there?" Ash whispered in awe.

"I think the question is 'what was over there?'" Yrsa said. "And the answer would be Utgard."

CHAPTER 22

ROGHALD CHANGED INTO HIS TROLL SHAPE, ALLOWING him to take long strides away from the raging Thundergod. He had been so close to finishing his quest before Blodheid and the Mogthasir trolls showed up. It was clear that Utgarda-Loki had sent them to foil Burrugandr's plans. And now they were all likely dead. It was just as well that Roghald had got away amid the chaos. He doubted that his human form would have fooled the god for very long.

The lightning and thunder that had erupted in the camp behind him stopped, and he slowed down to a walk. He didn't think that the God of Thunder would linger for long, so he just had to bide his time, then circle back. Hagan could simply return, saying that he had run away in fear, and he would be free to resume his plans where he left off.

He could hear running feet behind him. He spun around just in time to see Blodheid emerging from behind a tree. The spindly Shaman's eyes widened when she spotted him and she came to a stop in a crouched position, ready to fight. They stared at each other for a moment before Roghald spoke.

"It seems your efforts were futile."

The pale jotunn scowled at him, "You were following us?"

"Something like that."

"Get out of my way," she hissed at him, her eyes narrowing. "I need to get to Utgard to warn them right away."

A whooshing sound came from above their heads, and they both flinched, ducking down low. The treetops swayed as the chariot swooped past overhead. They stared at it as it climbed higher in the sky, before disappearing into a bank of clouds.

Blodheid paled even more.

"My father...," she whispered. "My clan... Thor found out my father had deceived him. The half-blood knew somehow and told him. He's going to destroy Utgard."

A thought struck Roghald, and he assumed a graver composure. "Ash ruined my life," he began.

Blodheid looked up at him.

"He humiliated me and took everything from me. I have hunted him across the worlds. And soon, he will be responsible for your loss too."

Blodheid stared at him, confusion and indecision mingled in her expression.

"Like me, you will soon find yourself all alone in this world, and it is all because of Ash the Ulfhed. We have good reason to join forces because neither of us will find peace until we make the Ulfhed pay for his actions. And who better than Burrugandr to mete out a torturous punishment? He alone can ensure we get our vengeance."

As if to punctuate what Roghald was saying, a tremendous lightning storm erupted on the horizon. The flashing lights lit up Blodheid's face as it twisted into a grimace of horror.

"Join with me," Roghald said, holding out his hand. "Join with me and I will give you your revenge."

A single tear ran down the Shaman's face as she turned back to Roghald. She looked from his eyes to his hand.

"We go to Utgard first. I have something I need to retrieve," she said. "Then, we hunt for the Ulfhed."

Roghald grinned and stretched his hand out further.

"Agreed," she whispered, and clasped his hand.

They reached what had been Utgard late the next day. As they crested a rocky hill, they caught their first sight of the bay that had been the centre of trade in Jotunheim. The ground where the city had been was now nothing but a large cluster of blackened craters. Debris lay scattered everywhere and smoke was rising in columns from smouldering timbers. The devastation was total and even Roghald was taken aback by the sheer magnitude of it.

Blodheid let out a blood-curdling shriek at the sight. She fell to her knees and tore at her chest. Roghald left the Shaman with her grief as he took in the view. Everything lay in ruins. Only small parts of the once great walls and some jetties remained, everything else was crumbled, melted or charred. He reminded himself to stay well clear of the gods if he could help it.

"Come," he said to the kneeling Shaman. "The sooner we finish, the sooner we can leave all this behind."

Blodheid took a deep breath and staggered to her feet. Without a word, she squared her shoulders and set off down the hill. It was even worse when they got into the city proper. The stone shapes of trolls lay spread out everywhere. Roghald even thought he could make out looks of horror on some of them.

It took them the better part of an hour to pick their way around destroyed buildings and craters to reach the spot where Utgarda-Loki's hall had been. The damage was more concentrated here, and everything was blackened. An unmistakable gigantic pile of scorched stone lay where Utgarda-Loki had sat the last time Roghald was here. The pile had melted and fused, as if it had been hit by lightning again and again.

Blodheid pulled out a long dagger and chipped at the base of the pile until she broke off a piece. She rolled it in her hand while staring into the distance with unseeing eyes. After a while, she stopped and slipped the piece of stone into the bag on her hip.

"This way," she said to Roghald as she walked around the mound that had been her father. She took a long stride over a crumbled wall into what had been a large room. She bent down and began clearing away rocks and debris, revealing the stone floor beneath.

Roghald clambered over the wall and helped her without a word. Soon they had cleared an area of the room and Blodheid held her hand up, signalling for Roghald to stop. She bent down and humming a wordless song, she drew a series of runes in the dust on a stone block the length and width of Roghald's arm. A glowing red outline appeared around it, and the massive block slowly lifted out of the floor with a grating sound. Now entirely out of the floor, Blodheid gently guided the stone to the side, where it settled with a thud.

Roghald watched as she reached into the hole and lifted out a bundle wrapped in aged grey cloth. She set it down on the ground next to her and unwrapped the fabric with great care. The cloth was so brittle that parts of it broke away despite her effort to preserve it. Upon removing the wrappings, a twisted face was revealed beneath, causing Roghald to involuntarily step backwards. At first he thought it was a large head, but soon realised it was a mask made of some kind of hardened leather. It had a thick swell of hair made from braided ropes. At the end of each rope, there dangled a stone or a piece of twig intricately engraved with minute runes. A horrible grimace distorted the mask's face. Roghald couldn't quite determine if it was an image of pain, fear or anger. Maybe all three, he thought. The face had hundreds of small runes carved into it, swirling and bending around its features.

"*Sjaldrikkir*," Blodheid spoke in a voice thick with reverence. "It grants the wearer tremendous powers, amplifying what magic they already have, but at the cost of their soul, slowly stealing it away until only an empty husk remains."

She caressed it almost lovingly. "My mother made it a long time ago. She gave it to me when she died. Not even my father knew about it. He would never have allowed me to possess such a weapon, capable of casting him from his throne." A cruel expression came over her face. "It is the perfect vessel for my revenge."

Roghald felt jubilant. Blodheid's blind thirst for revenge had made her a formidable weapon for him to use. She is even prepared to sacrifice her soul for it. He had to stop himself from chuckling at the turn of events. He had a jotunn Shaman at his disposal. That was better than a dozen thursrs!

"I may not be able to kill the Thundergod, but I will lay the gods' plans to ashes. Their Ulfhed will die in pain." There was a fervour in her voice as she spoke, and Roghald knew the thirst for revenge had blinded her.

"We will go back to my master," Roghald said. "Ash has eluded me on the road twice now, and we cannot risk attacking them in the open again, while Thunder Thor is in Jotunheim. He seeks the source tree in Burrugandr's hall. We will meet him there on his arrival and have a warm welcome ready."

Blodheid stood up and walked over to a pile of debris. She pulled out a sack from the rubble and after emptying it of some roots and tubers, wrapped the mask in it. She tucked the bundle under her spindly arm and turned back to Roghald.

"Lead the way."

CHAPTER 23

I JUST CAN'T DO IT." ASH'S VOICE WAS THICK WITH FRUS-tration. "It's like there is nothing in my chest where I usually feel the power."

Yrsa was watching him intently. "But you feel well otherwise?"

"I feel great," Ash said, his voice climbing an octave. I am stronger and there is a... harmony in me I didn't have before."

Yrsa tried to cut the bracelet with her dagger for a third time, with the same result. She threw her dagger to the ground and threw her hands up in the air.

"Curse that slimy Hagan and his tricks! If he was still here, I would have beaten how to remove it out of him." Her eyes flashed with anger and she stood up and paced around the camp muttering and swearing.

Torsten, who was lying on his blankets, his legs stretched out and his head on his pack, opened one eye.

"Although the boy is missing his powers, he can still hold his sword and fight. He also has a good head on his shoulders, so I am sure he will be fine,"

"He will not be fine, Torsten! The next time we have to fight another of those damn thursrs, he will die. Not to mention that bastard Roghald and what he might have in store for us."

"The Gods will protect us. We are merely tools in their hands, acting out their will. If we are to die, we are to die," Torsten added in a lecturing tone.

"What, are you some kind of Seidman now?" Yrsa spun to face Torsten. "You meet Thor once and you suddenly know the will of the gods?"

"I was deeply touched here, by the honour of meeting Thor, yes," Torsten said, as he placed his hand on his chest.

"You've definitely been touched by the gods, alright," Yrsa muttered, rubbing her face. "But not there."

"Let's just go," Ash cut in. "The sooner we get to my father's mountain, the sooner we can end this part of the ordeal. Besides, we might figure out how to get the bracelet off on the way. Worst-case scenario, we can ask my grandmother about it when we return my father's body to her."

Both Yrsa and Torsten assented to this, and they made quick work of packing their things up and were soon on their way. The Mogthrasir trolls had taken them off course, but not too far off, and it only took them another day to find themselves back on track and heading east towards Jordr's mountain. Another day later and they looked out over a broad mountain peak which sat much lower than the surrounding summits. A still lake wrapped around the mountain's base on one side.

"That must be it," Yrsa said.

Ash could only nod in silence as he took in the sight. Jordr's mountain was nestled between the other mountains, surrounded at the base by a lush, purple forest and its little lake. He could see a red tinge to all the surrounding mountains, signalling that they had a high iron content, but the smaller mountain was much darker, more concentrated. Considering the easy access to iron ore, this is where he too would have set up a home and workshop. He was happy that, as a Stonesmith, he would have chosen the same spot as his father.

They clambered down the rise they were on and were soon trekking through the forest towards the base of the mountain. His grandmother had told them that the entrance was on the western side, close to where the forest and the lake met. They wound their way through the forest to the base of the mountain, and once there, they simply circled around it towards the still water. At last, they saw an opening in the mountain.

Ash and his friends looked at the doorway in wonder. Around it, carved in minute detail was a relief so beautiful and intricate that it was hard to believe it had been carved in stone. It depicted animals and flowers, woven together in an incomprehensible pattern which arched around the opening. The carvings were so lifelike that Ash half expected the animals to leap out any moment and scatter into the forest beyond.

He reached out and touched the doorframe in awe. His father had carved this. He had worked the stone with his hands, creating something so beautiful with the same power Ash had been gifted, but with a skill he couldn't possibly match. This same power Jordr had given to Ash, as the only legacy he could give to the son he had never met.

Ash's eyes were drawn to the stone doors, which lay shattered and broken a few steps inside the doorway. They had been of equal beauty and craftmanship, but now only fragments of the carvings could be seen among the rubble. It tore Ash's heart to see them broken, and he viewed them as a testament to the violence brought to this mountain in the name of power and greed. To capture Jordr.

Ash felt overwhelmed by guilt. If his mother had not been pregnant with him, Burrugandr wouldn't have sent his trolls to attack this mountain. The sound of his father's smithing hammer would have echoed inside these halls, competing only with the laughter and joy of his mother. These doors would have remained whole. He felt warm tears run down his cheeks, and bending forward he placed his forehead on the cool stone carving. He felt Yrsa's powerful arms gently wrap around his upper body as she hugged him from behind. She laid her chin on his shoulder and spoke softly.

"It is not your fault, Ash. How could it be?"

They stood there for a moment, as Yrsa squeezed some of his broken pieces back together with her warm embrace. Then she stretched up and kissed him on the cheek before letting him go and slapping him on the side of his head.

"Now let's go. We mourn, then we move on. We are Jomsvikings, not milkmaids."

The slap jolted Ash back to the present. She was right. He would serve his family best by action, not by thought.

They stepped through the entrance and into the darkness of the mountain. Ash was still amazed that he could see perfectly in the dark, with no need to use his Stonesight. That's the reason he was nearly blinded when Yrsa spoke the word "Lyse" next to him, and her lightstone lit up the passageway. Shielding his eyes from the blinding light, it took a moment for his eyes to adjust, but when they did, he looked out over the long passage. The walls were smooth, far smoother than any tools could make them, and the tunnel stretched straight into the mountain, wide and tall enough for a large wagon to pass through.

They didn't have to walk far into the tunnel to see the first signs of a battle long past. There were scorch marks on the walls and several stone shapes on the ground marked the spots where trolls had fallen, with spiked clubs and nasty looking spears next to them.

They picked their way around the detritus and pushed deeper into the mountain. Before long, the tunnel opened up into a cavern, and the rough surface of natural rock formation replaced the smooth walls. It was cold and still, the wind not reaching this far into the mountain. Stalagmites reached up from the ground, and in some places met with the stalactites above, forming glistening pillars of what had once been moisture seeping through the mountain for hundreds, if not thousands, of years.

Although the cavern was large, the many natural outcrops and formations obscured the view ahead, only allowing them to see a short distance in front. There was a once cleared, twisting path in the middle of the grotto, now strewn with fallen rocks and debris.

"Keep your wits about you," Torsten rumbled. "These caves have lain empty for a long time and we don't know what has taken possession of them."

Ash heard the familiar rustle of leather straps behind him as Yrsa armed herself with her small shield and spear. Torsten already held his axe in two hands. As they ventured deeper into the mountain, Ash felt increasingly at ease. Having spent so many years underground in Eikinri's foundry, he had become accustomed, even comfortable, with being surrounded by stone. He closed his eyes and let his Stonesight sweep out around him. An image of dozens of passageways and caverns, some natural, some carved, branched out in his mind. The network was vast, and even though he stretched his ability to its utmost, he could not see the entire labyrinth under the mountain.

"This place is enormous," he told his friends. "We could walk for days and still not cover all of it."

"Well, it was getting late in the day when we entered anyway and I'm hungry," Torsten said. "Let's find a defensible place to camp, then continue our search tomorrow."

Yrsa and Ash agreed, and when the tunnel opened up into a broad cavern, they called it a day. The area, being close to the opening, seemed to have been used as a stable of sorts. There were leather harnesses, half rotted, either hanging on the walls or on the ground where they had fallen. Two carts, smashed to pieces lay in heaps along one wall and three wide stalls, equally ravaged by the battle, had once stood along the opposing wall. Whatever beasts of burden had occupied them were long gone, either escaped or carried away by Burrugandr's trolls when they had attacked the mountain.

"Let's eat," Torsten said, rubbing his hands.

A few crates in one corner, having miraculously survived the destruction, served as a table and chairs once a thick layer of dust had been brushed off. They unpacked a simple but tasty fare of dried meats, stale but edible bread, and a tightly sealed jar of honey. As they ate, Torsten spoke at length about all the mead and ale he planned to drink upon their return to Midgard. He went into great detail reminiscing about feasts he had attended in the past and how he now regretted not drinking more when the opportunities had presented themselves. He recalled one particular Yule feast, years ago, in the King's own hall in Hammershall. As he told Yrsa and Ash that the King had challenged all present to drink their own weight in mead over seven days, tears ran down his cheeks and into his beard. Even Yrsa seemed to wish for something stronger, giving her cup of water a sour look as the Berserker spoke.

After finishing their meal, Ash took the first watch while Yrsa and Torsten laid down on their blankets. The shieldmaiden left her lightstone on the crate, the eerie blue-tinted light washing away most colours. Ash remained seated on his crate, his sword in his lap. He ran a stone across the edge, just to keep his hands busy. He could sharpen the edge in a few seconds, simply by running his fingertips over it, but he enjoyed the mindless task.

A few hours crept past and his sword now rested on the crate next to him. It would be time to wake Yrsa for her watch, but he thought he would let her sleep a little longer. The middle watch was always the worst one, and he was determined to ease her burden a little. His eyes were tired and gravelly, and he just needed to rest them for a second.

He snapped them open a second later. He had nearly fallen asleep. That was a very dangerous game, deep in enemy territory, and he should know better. As much as he wanted to be nice to Yrsa, he was dangerously tired and needed to sleep. He stood up intending to walk over to her when he noticed a thin mist on the ground. Ash scanned the cavern, sword in hand, when he saw a movement from the passageway leading deeper into the mountain.

He opened his mouth to call a warning to his friends but stayed himself in the last second.

Rani stood in the passageway. She looked old once again, not the youthful self she had been when he had last seen her. She stooped, burdened by old age, with her grimy robes swaying in a breeze he couldn't feel. A wave of comfort washed over him, and he relaxed. She smiled at him and held up a bony finger to her lips. He looked at his two companions briefly before turning back to Rani. If she wanted him to be silent, who was he to argue?

She turned her hand and motioned him over with her index finger. I really should wake Yrsa because she needs to keep watch while I go with Rani, he thought. As soon as he took a step towards the shieldmaiden, another warm wave of comfort washed over him, and he turned back to Rani. She had her finger to her lips again.

I'm sure this won't take long, he thought as his feet steered him towards her, almost of their own accord. His mind felt foggy and clouded. He shook his head, trying to clear it, but the haze didn't budge. He tiptoed toward the old Seidwoman, careful not to wake his friends. When he moved towards her, she seemed to drift backwards, deeper into the tunnel. He walked faster, but somehow she stayed a few steps away from him, always smiling and keeping her finger on her lips, urging him to be quiet.

Rani disappeared into a small side passage, and Ash followed her through. He walked down a much narrower tunnel which went steeply downward for a short while before it opened up into a small chamber. Old shelves stacked with jars and bundles lined the walls, everything covered in a fine layer of dust.

Rani stood in the middle of the floor, smiling at him. Ash noticed casually that there were a few piles of stone on the floor in the shape of trolls. He even saw a few dried and dusty smaller skeletons scattered around the place.

Rani pointed to an empty area of floor in front of her, and a wave of comfort and fatigue filled him. He was so tired. Maybe he should just have a quick nap before he talked to Rani. He walked over to the Seidwoman and laid down on the floor. She stood over him, still smiling, as he closed his eyes.

"Ash,"

He drifted in a storm. Angry clouds rolled around him as if he was in a vortex, a violent wind tearing at him. For some reason, it was difficult to breathe. It was as if a great weight had sat on his chest. He tried to move a little to shift it, but it wouldn't budge.

"Ash,"

There was the voice again, ringing out over the storm. It was a voice he had heard with warmth and loving, but now it sounded angry. A fierce woman on a winged horse broke through the storm clouds. It was his mother. Her usually loving face was furious, and her eyes flashed with lightning. She sat across the horse, her back straight with a spear and shield raised as if for battle. She wore a gleaming suit of armour, but no helmet, her blonde hair blowing around wildly in the storm.

"Not like this!" she raged, her anger as relentless as the storm surrounding her. "You will not reach Valhalla, Ash! Wake up and fight!" She held her spear high above her head and a bolt of lightning leaped from the clouds above, striking it. She shone as bright as the sun for a moment before the bolt shot from her spear and slammed into him.

The world turned white and his body twisted with pain. Ash opened his eyes. The creature sitting on his chest was something out of a nightmare. It was short, with ghostly white skin over nothing but bones. Matted, ashen hair hung down in tufts, partially obscuring a face which was composed only of tightly stretched skin over a grimacing skull. It had an elongated jaw with an open, toothless mouth revealing a leathery black tongue. It squatted on Ash's chest, with its bony knees by its ears. The creature's unnecessarily long arms stretched out in front of it, with long fingers wrapped around Ash's neck.

The pressure on his chest and throat was tremendous, and the creature made a high-pitched keening sound as it throttled him, its thin arms shaking with the effort. Ash's vision swam, and his thoughts became murky. In desperation, he grabbed the creature's arms and tried to pull them, but they remained clamped around his throat like a vice, refusing to move even an inch.

In a cloud of haze, he let go of the creature's arms and ran his hands along the ground in front of him. His fingers closed around a shaft, and Ash brought it up, striking the monster's head with all his remaining strength. He had grabbed a thigh bone from some unfortunate creature and it struck his attacker across the temple. The top of the bone shattered in a cloud of dust, but beside rocking the creature slightly to the side, the strike did not seem to have any significant impact on his tormentor. Ash's vision darkened, and he felt himself fading out of consciousness.

The bone in his hand was now reduced to a short handle, but with a sharp point. Summoning his last strength, he slammed the point into the creature's head. The hands let go of his throat and air rushed into his burning lungs and his vision cleared. Ash brought his hand back for another strike, but the creature was much faster than him in his dazed state and grabbed his wrist with both hands.

The icy fingers were tremendously strong and even though Ash pushed with all his might, the monster slowly bent his wrist, turning the point towards Ash's throat. The creature pushed with all its weight. As the jagged point drew nearer, it began its eerie keening sound again.

The few breaths Ash had taken had cleared his mind, and he could think again. He concentrated and sunk himself into the stone beneath, taking the creature with him. Just as Ash felt the cold stone floor close over his nose, the creature started thrashing wildly and he felt a burning pain in his throat. The creature let go of his wrist, but Ash shot his hands out and grabbed its arm with an iron grip. Holding the monster, he pulled himself deeper into the stone. When they were several feet beneath the floor, he let go of his attacker, who froze as the stone solidified around it, no longer in contact with Ash. With his Stonesight, he could see a hole in the stone the exact shape of the creature. It wouldn't be able to move a hair's width again. Ever.

The pain in his throat intensified, and Ash drifted to the surface. He rose from the floor, back into the chamber just as Yrsa ran into the room, her glow stone casting a bright light around her. She visibly paled when she saw him.

"Ash," she said, but her words fell away.

Torsten entered behind her, his eyes also widening as he saw Ash.

Raising his hand to his neck, Ash now felt an icy bolt of fear in his heart. The bone was stuck into his throat. As he ran his hand over the back of his neck, he could feel it protruding through on the other side. His hand came away, covered in bright red blood.

"Oh," he rasped, his voice hoarse. He felt his mouth filling with blood. He grabbed the shaft with his hand.

Yrsa's "No, don't!" came too late as Ash tore the bone from his throat. It came away with a sickening sound and a spray of blood. He felt lightheaded and dropped to his knees. Yrsa's arms wrapped around him and her hand pressed against the wound on his neck.

"Torsten, help me!"

Ash had never heard her voice so high pitched before.

CHAPTER 24

ROGHALD STOOD AGAIN IN FRONT OF THE RED DOORS leading to Burrugandr's great hall. The dried elven head fixed on the door had a different expression of horror compared to last time he was here. Roghald wondered if the elf was still aware, its suffering unending as it served as a magical ward to the chieftain's inner sanctum. Knowing Burrugandr's talent for cruelty, he would have been surprised if it wasn't. Behind him, he noticed Blodheid's breathing was faster than before. No doubt she knew that her fate would be decided beyond these doors. Roghald almost felt sorry for her. Almost.

Placing his finger on the elf's forehead, he spoke. "Burrugandr."

The elf's eyes glowed red, and the doors swung open with a tremendous rumble. Cold, humid air washed over him as he stepped over the threshold, Blodheid following close behind. The hall looked the same as when he last stood before the jotunn only a few weeks ago. Flickering cold blue light from torches along the walls did little more than cast long shadows from the carved pillars holding up the roof.

Roghald could see the chieftain, sitting where he always sat, but his stone chair was gone, replaced now by a sprawling throne. Carved from black obsidian with glimmering golden inlays, the throne depicted monstrous faces over the jotunn's shoulders and beneath the armrest where his hands lay. The throne signalled the jotunn's ambitions clearer than anything else could; he would one day soon declare himself the Troll King.

To his right, sitting on a bench, he saw Grinbodr. Roghald got a foul taste in his mouth as soon as his eyes fell on the Shaman. She was watching him approach the throne with a smugness that rang alarm bells in his mind. Beyond her, he saw the twisted stem of the source tree, reaching up towards the rough ceiling of the hall. It seemed to have grown even taller since he was last here.

Roghald advanced to a spot in front of the throne where the flagstones were worn to a slight hollow from trolls and thursrs falling to their knees in front of the chieftain over centuries. Roghald's knees hit the ground and the rest of his body followed, as he laid himself prone, with his arms straight out from his sides, prostrating himself before the jotunn. He hated this. The humiliation always burned him, and he reminded himself that it was only a means to an end. A rustle behind him suggested Blodheid had followed his lead. He laid there on the cold floor as the seconds became minutes, but he knew better than to speak before being addressed. He could feel their eyes on him, treating him like a dog as he laid still, subjugated.

After what seemed like an endless time, Burrugandr's voice rang out over the hall. "Rise."

Roghald pushed himself up and stood before his chieftain.

"Thursr Roghald," the jotunn's voice was like iron. "You dare return without the Ulfhed?"

"Great Burrugandr," he began. He had rehearsed his speech during the long walk back to the mountain. "The Ulfhed, along with two Jomsvikings, are on their way here as we speak, all according to my carefully laid plan. You see, I have weakened him, removing his powers and-"

"Enough, Roghald," Grinbodr held up her bony hand to cut him off. Roghald could see the glee in her eyes as she continued.

"I have scried your journey day and night since you left. I have followed you in failure after failure, watching your inability to perform this simple task set for you."

Roghald wanted to slap himself. He should have realised that the old bat would have had a way of spying on him. His lie now staring him in his face, he grappled for words that would not come.

"You are useless, Roghald. I had my doubts spending the precious soul from Muspelheim on a mere human, and I should have listened to myself," the Shaman continued.

Roghald's eyes flashed with anger. The Shaman noticed and smiled at him, daring him to challenge her. He knew she was far more powerful than him, and he could not fight her in the open. After a second, he let his eyes fall to the floor, and Grinbodr's snigger grated on his nerves.

"Not entirely stupid," she mumbled.

"You have failed me," Burrugandr's deep voice cut in. "The only thing of value in your entire existence is the soul that lives in you. Know that you would have died the second you returned, was it not for that."

Roghald felt the world open up beneath him. He had lost his standing with Burrugandr and by that, the means for his revenge.

"You will live only as long as it takes for us to find a new vessel for the soul," the chieftain continued.

He knew then that he had to escape. The red doors had remained open since they had entered. They opened and closed slowly and if he sprinted, he could slip out before they shut. If he ran as fast as he could, he could escape from the mountain before the alarm reached the front gate. Roghald spun on the spot, but as he did, the floor disappeared beneath him. He fell forwards and landed on all fours knee deep in what felt like mud. Shocked, he glanced behind him and saw Grinbodr on one knee, her palm pressed against the ground. A trench of liquid rock reached across the floor from her hand all the way to Roghald.

He scrambled to get up, but she removed her hand from the ground and the floor solidified again. With Roghald in it. His hands and legs were trapped in the floor. She is a Stonesmith, he thought in shock. How had he not known? This marked her as an even more formidable foe than he had given her credit for. Roghald cursed the very existence of Stonesmiths.

"You look like the fool that you are," she cackled.

Roghald cursed and swore as he tore at his limbs, but they were anchored in the ground.

"If you don't keep quiet, I will melt some stone around your head," the Shaman warned and Roghald fell quiet.

"Now as for you," Grinbodr started, turning her malicious eyes on Blodheid. The jotunn seemed taken aback by the turn of events, but she kept her head high and her shoulders squared when she faced the Shaman.

"I am jotunn Blodheid, daughter of Utgarda-Loki, Shaman of the Nine Moons, and I find myself clanless since the Thunder-god destroyed Utgard and everyone in it. I will serve the great Burrugandr if he finds me worthy and does not judge me on the company I have kept." Blodheid spoke with a firm voice, her eyes never leaving Burrugandr. Roghald couldn't help noticing that she implied him to be the poor company. If he could, he would have strangled the ungrateful bitch there and then.

"Word has reached us of the fate of your father," Burrugandr's face lit up with joy as he spoke. "His arrogance became his undoing, and thus fate has removed another obstacle from my path. Although it pleases me to no end that Utgarda-Loki's clan is no more, and some would say I would be wiser to strike you down where you stand, it would be a terrible waste to end your bloodline and all the magic that comes with it. I will find a place for you in my ranks, but you must swear your allegiance and your soul to me and my clan."

Burrugandr lifted his right hand and held it down and open in front of him. Blodheid had stiffened at the jotunn's words, but only hesitated for a moment before she bent low to the ground and scuttled past Roghald and up to the throne. She had never looked more like a spider than right now, he thought. When she reached the chieftain, she lifted her head and licked the palm of his hand with her long, black tongue, before pressing her forehead to his feet. Burrugandr reached down and placed his enormous hand lightly on the back of her head as he spoke.

"So be it. Grinbodr will see to the ritual."

Blodheid crawled backwards from the giant, keeping her head low until she reached her original place behind Roghald. As she rose back onto her feet, she shot Roghald a smug look, and he found it difficult to contain himself. I will crush that spider, he thought.

"Put the human away," Burrugandr spoke to Grinbodr. "and let us prepare for the Ulfhed."

Grinbodr bowed her head to the chieftain before turning to Roghald with a cruel smile. "Hope you can hold your breath," she told him before she sunk into the floor and disappeared. Roghald flinched as he felt a hand grip his ankle, and the stone beneath him soften once again. He thrashed about in panic as he was dragged into the floor. As he was pulled under, the last thing Roghald's wide eyes saw were the corners of Burrugandr's lips going up into a grin. It was the first time he had seen the jotunn smile.

He entered a nightmare world of darkness and pressure all around him. The only sensation was that of moving deeper underground. His lungs burned, but he feared opening his mouth lest it should fill with liquid stone. He sunk deeper and deeper until at last the movement stopped. The iron grip around his ankle was released, and he found himself suspended in the stone, pressure all around him. Panic rose again within him as he feared he would be left embedded in the stone and suffocate to death.

But between one heartbeat and the next the pressure disappeared. Roghald was lying on his back, staring up at a stone ceiling only just beyond his nose. He raised his head until his scalp scraped against the stone above and looked down. He was in an enclosure that only gave him a hand's width of space in any direction. It was like he was lying in a coffin. A waft of fresh air blew across his face, and he saw a small hole open up at his feet. Turning his head to his side, he saw that another hole had opened up next to his head. It was small; he doubted he would've been able to fit his arm into it.

Peering through the hole, he saw it stretch into the mountain, only to curve upwards, disappearing out of sight. He was trapped in the middle of the mountain, with barely any space to move. He couldn't even bend his legs more than a few degrees before his knees scraped against the stone. His mind reeled when he thought of the tremendous weight above him. Despite the fresh air blowing through, he found it difficult to breathe as the panic spread through his body. He flinched as Grinbodr's ugly face appeared in the stone in front of his.

"Make yourself comfortable," she told him. "You'll be here for a while."

"You can't do this," Roghald's voice was strained, and he found it difficult to speak, the panic felt like a tight knot in his chest. "I will go mad."

Grinbodr smiled at him. "We just need you alive, little thursr. It does not matter if you are sane or not."

He roared and reached up for her face with his clawed hands, but she sunk back into the stone, her laughter abruptly cut off as she disappeared. He put his hands against the ceiling and pushed, but the stone was unyielding. His panic turned to overwhelming terror, but there was no one to hear his screams.

CHAPTER 25

IN A DETACHED SORT OF WAY, ASH WATCHED THE BIG BERserker pull the knife from his hip and begin cutting off the sleeve of his own tunic. He noticed that the big man's hands were shaking. He also felt a tremor in Yrsa as she held him tight. Looking down, Ash saw the front of his tunic absolutely soaked in the blood dribbling out between Yrsa's fingers. So much blood. He realised that the pain had faded and gone away. A wave of warmth filled him, and he felt relaxed. This must be what dying feels like, he thought. At least I will have died fighting, not just strangled in my sleep, so I will still reach Valhalla.

Ash prepared himself to die and to meet his mother again. Guilt overcame him about not completing the task Odin had set him. Humankind would fall to Burrugandr's schemes. The source of the corruption would find its way to Midgard again, and the draugr infestation would begin anew. The destruction of everything he loved awaited him, and when Ragnarok came, the trolls would conquer the worlds, leading to the demise of all that was good. All because he had let his guard down.

But that's out of my hands now, he thought. I am dying,

Except he didn't.

"What?" Yrsa's voice was almost a shriek. "Where is the wound?"

Ash felt her fingers probe his throat, wiping away the blood with Torsten's cut off sleeve. She sat back on the ground and stared at him.

"How?" she whispered.

Ash brought his hand up to his neck. He could feel only smooth skin and the tiniest of scars where the piece of bone had entered.

They sat back at the stable cavern. Yrsa had brewed some tea, and they drank it sweetened with a good dollop of honey. None of them thought they could sleep any more that night, so they sat up talking.

"It sounds like it was a *mara*," Torsten rumbled. "Foul creatures that control people's dreams. They can give you terrible nightmares, just for their own wicked pleasure. But I've also heard they can use someone's dreams to kill them and feed on their life force."

"Which means," Yrsa said, a dangerous look in her eyes, "that you fell asleep on your watch."

Ash shamefully remembered what he thought was a moment's nod, and now realised it was likely a proper sleep.

"Just know that if you fall asleep on watch again, you don't have to worry about a mara getting you, because I will kill you with my own hands." She emphasised her words by pointing her seax at him.

Ash looked to Torsten for support, but the bearded man raised his hands to the heavens and looked away, showing there was no aid to be found in him.

"I'm terribly sorry," Ash mumbled, his face flushed with shame. "It will not happen again."

"You best see to it," Yrsa spat. Having considered the matter dealt with, Yrsa's attitude changed. "Now, let's discuss why you are still breathing and there is not a mark upon your neck."

"Your guess is as good as mine," Ash said, although he had his suspicions, glancing down at the bracelet Hagan had forced on him.

"I just wish we had discovered it before I ruined my good tunic," Torsten muttered, running his hand over his bare left forearm.

"I have seen you wipe your nose a hundred times on that sleeve," Yrsa told the Berserker. "You do realise that any wound you tied with that grimy snot-rag would fester and kill the person anyway?"

Torsten snorted indignantly at this and ignored her.

"Cut your arm," Yrsa told Ash.

"I don't see the point of inflicting more pain on me tonight."

"Just shut up and do it."

Ash sighed and pulled out his seax. He drew the sharp edge across his forearm, leaving a thin red line.

"Properly," Yrsa said in her no-nonsense voice.

"Fine," Ash grumbled, and cut deeper into his arm. A trickle of blood seeped out of the wound and dripped to the ground. Then, before everyone's eyes, the wound closed, and the bleeding stopped, leaving only a thin white scar.

"That could come in very handy," Torsten said in a low voice.

"It is a poor trade off if it has come at the cost of not being able to Shift," Yrsa said. "Especially while we are in Jotunheim. I'm sure having his head ripped off by a thursr will still kill him. It is that damn bracelet, I'm sure of it."

All eyes fell on the bracelet made of twisted twigs, but no one could know for sure.

While they sat around and Torsten and Yrsa fell back into a longstanding argument about how the Jomsvikings should be rebuilt to their former glory upon their return to Midgard, Ash used his Stonesight to explore the mountain. From Rani's and his grandmother's stories, he knew that his father had been cast down a deep chasm. As Ash mapped out the tunnels and caverns around them in his mind, he noticed one deep shaft that stood out to him, reaching down beyond his range. His heart skipped a beat when he sensed something strange, yet familiar, from the chasm.

"I know where my father is." He had spoken softly, but his

friends fell silent as he spoke. Without another word, they stood, packed their belongings and it wasn't long before they were following Ash's lead as he picked his way through the labyrinth of tunnels and caverns.

The mountain became more lived in as they delved deeper into it and beautiful furniture, carved from stone appeared in what would have been comfortable rooms. Ash never strayed from his path, but whenever a carved object or piece of furniture came within reach, he ran his fingers along it, leaving trails in the dust.

They entered a wide cavern, and Ash stopped to take it all in. Workbenches stood along the walls, and piles of stones lay in the corners. An assortment of tools and devices hung on hooks above the benches. In the middle of the cavern stood an enormous hearth. It was made from a white stone Ash had never seen before and had four openings around it, one for each corner of the world. It was round and squat, its thick chimney disappearing into the ceiling of the cave, and troll runes were carved around the base. There was no doubt that this was his father's workshop.

It had also been the scene of a battle. Blackened spots and broken benches lay scattered around the place, but also large piles of stone where trolls had fallen. At the end of the cavern, a stone bridge spanned a chasm leading into a tunnel in the rock face on the other side. The closer they got to the chasm, the higher the piles of stones on the floor. Broken weapons lay scattered around them. They had to climb over several large mounds to get to the bridge, and as soon as Ash set foot on it, something caught his eye.

Snapped in two and blackened as if burned, he recognised an Ulfhed spear. His mother's spear. He bent down and picked up the shortest piece. The timber of the shaft was so brittle that he could break it with his fingers, but when he drew his thumb across the spearhead, wiping away the soot, gleaming metal shone beneath. It looked as if it had been forged only yesterday. A wolf's head, with its teeth bared towards the point was delicately etched into the metal. He wiped it on his tunic as best he could before placing it in his bag. Then his eyes fell on the chasm beside the bridge.

He closed his eyes and sent his Stonesight down the shaft. It was deep. Very deep. When his mind reached the bottom, he felt the same strange familiar sensation. The stone there felt different. He knew that this was where his father's remains lay. Ash turned to his friends as he rested his pack against the balustrade of the bridge.

"I have to go alone. It is too steep and far down for you to climb."

His friends both frowned, but couldn't argue with him.

"We will be here when you get back," Torsten said. "Do what you have to do."

Ash pressed his chest against the balustrade and swung his legs over the ledge. He concentrated and let the front of his feet sink into the rock face. His hands followed next, as he pushed them in up to his wrists. He gave his friends a smile and began descending the shaft, his hands and feet flowing through the stone. The chasm was so deep that even with his newfound night vision, the bottom was still lost in darkness. He looked back up and could see Yrsa's outline in the slowly disappearing opening. Soon, she too, disappeared.

As he lowered himself deeper and deeper, the world around him seemed to take on a surreal quality. It felt like he was drifting through the dark of the world, utterly alone, and if it hadn't been for the occasional luminescent mushroom drifting past, he could have sworn that he was not moving any closer to the bottom. The air got colder and more humid as he descended and a thin layer of moisture coated his exposed skin, making the chill seem worse. Time lost all meaning, and when he reached the bottom of the chasm, he couldn't say for sure if minutes or hours had passed since he'd swung his legs over the ledge. Looking up, he could see the wall he had come down disappearing into the obscurity above.

He looked around and saw that the chasm opened up at the bottom, forming a large grotto to one side. There was a large mound of boulders inside the grotto where a piece of the wall had broken away at some point. The surrounding floor was littered with smaller stones and boulders and Ash realised it would take a long time to examine them all individually in search of his father's remains. A shiver went up his spine, unrelated to the cold. It felt like he had entered a tomb. Ash closed his eyes and used his Stonesight. He might be able to find what he was looking for that way.

"Why have you come to this place of sorrow?"

Ash's eyes snapped open. The voice had been deep and sounded like rocks being ground together. His hand fell on his sword, the reassuring feel of the hilt strengthening him. He stood silent for a few long heartbeats.

"Erh... hello?" his voice echoed in the still air.

"Why have you come?"

Ash took a few steps back. "I am not in the habit of talking to shadows," he said, eyes scanning the dark corners. "Show yourself and I will tell you why I am here."

At first there was no movement, but soon several smaller boulders rolled past his feet. A grating sound filled the space as the boulders in the grotto shifted and piled themselves together. More boulders rolled towards the structure and added to the pile as it shifted and grew taller. Ash's mouth fell open as an enormous creature started taking shape from the rocks.

It stood four times taller than Ash, towering over him. Ash's sword, now forgotten, fell to his side where it remained hanging in a loose grip as he stared wide eyed at the monstrosity before him. A boulder swivelled around its body, finally settling into place on its shoulders. Ash saw it comprised dozens of smaller rocks, giving it some facial features. The only thing worse than the uneven jagged shards that were its teeth were the two dark hollows it had for eyes.

Ash tried to swallow, but his mouth was as dry as old leather.

"Why have you come to disturb my mourning?" As it spoke,

its mouth remained unmoving, with the voice echoing all around them. Which was so much worse.

"Has the world not taken enough from me already that you would steal what little peace there is down here?" The voice was louder, with wrath seeping into its words.

Anger blossomed within Ash's chest. He had come this far, within physical reach of his father's remains, and here was this pile of rocks standing in his way. He didn't care if he got crushed into a pulp by those massive stone arms, this thing would not cow him.

"I am Ash Jordrson, the last Wolf of Odin." He straightened himself and levelled his sword at the creature. "I am sent here by Gundaganr, seeking the remains of my father, her son, and I will not be opposed. Grant me leave to do so or suffer the consequences." He stood tall and firm, eyes locked on those horribly dark voids the creature had for eyes, determined not to give an inch.

The creature stood silent and unmoving for what felt like forever. Ash wondered if whatever ward or magic powered it had ceased working. He was just about to speak again when the creature broke the silence, its voice now so low it was almost a whisper.

"I am Jordr, son of Gundaganr. It is I that you seek."

CHAPTER 26

ROGHALD LAY IN A DAZE. HE DID NOT KNOW HOW LONG it had been since he was put in this grave. It could have been weeks or only hours. He had switched back to his human shape, which had provided a little extra space to move and stretch, but the feeling of the walls and ceiling closing in had not changed. Looking up at the bloodied ceiling above his face, Roghald could see where he had beaten his fists against the unyielding stone. Gamir filled the silence, forcing Roghald to listen to its rantings and ravings uninterrupted. There was no way to get away or distract himself from this torment.

At some point, it must have rained outside, because a trickle of water found its way in through the air tunnel Grinbodr had created to keep him alive. Just. Parched with thirst, he had slurped the water off the rough stone before it reached the mess he'd made when in his horror he lost control of his bodily functions. He sobbed, alone and trapped, drifting in and out of consciousness as his body ached and his mind tortured him. Twisted scenes of humans and trolls flashed before his eyes, while behind them the world burned. Their screams washed over him and he covered his ears with his hands, but there was no escape from their laments.

The pressure from the stone above felt unbearable, and it was difficult to breathe. He pushed and clawed at it, leaving bloody trails on the dark granite, but it did not yield, the pressure never ceasing. The mad troll was there in his mind, laughing or sobbing ceaselessly. When Roghald screamed, the troll screamed with him, their voices merging into one.

The hours stretched into days, and his suffering stretched out into eternity.

CHAPTER 27

ASH STARED AT THE STONE CREATURE IN FRONT OF HIM. "How...?" was all he could say.

The stone monstrosity lowered itself down to the ground. Several boulders and stones fell off the thing, crashing to the floor.

"Forgive me," it rumbled as it settled down, looking more like a pile of boulders again, but the face remained. "Maintaining this shape depletes my energy."

"I was told you were dead," Ash whispered. "I... I would have come sooner if-"

"I am not dead, no. But nor am I alive," There was a mournful tone emanating from the creature as it spoke. "My body broke and shattered when I was cast down here, but in my last seconds of life, I used my powers to merge my soul with the stone I landed on. I entered it with my mind and let go of my broken body, hoping to return to the fight above." The creature raised an arm from the mound, made up of stones and a hand with pebbles for fingers. "These make poor tools for climbing, and I could not get out of here. Soon I realised that all had gone quiet and my beloved Gunnr had fallen." His father's voice was thick with sorrow.

"She lived," Ash whispered. "She lived, and I am the testament of proof."

"Gunnr is still alive?"

The hope in the creature's voice broke Ash's heart. Tears ran down his cheeks as he shook his head. "She died by Burrugandr's hand years later, back in Midgard. She thought you were dead too, or she would have returned, I am sure of it."

They sat in silence for a while. Ash tried to make sense of his tumultuous emotions.

"You have your mother's face." His father said. "I wish I had seen you grow. I would have taught you to be the greatest Stonesmith of them all."

He gave his father a weak smile. "Although I am not the greatest, I am a Stonesmith."

Another stretch of silence before his father eventually spoke, now with more warmth.

"Blood will out. Who taught you the craft?"

"I trained for ten years with Eikinri of the dvergir," he announced with pride.

"A dwarf taught you?" His father asked slowly, the pebbles making up his face assuming an almost comical expression of being flabbergasted.

Ash nodded.

"Which runes do you use for your wards and enchantments?" There was an edge to his father's voice that made Ash hesitate for a second before answering.

"Well, mostly Esh, the dwarven runes, but I can read both Futhark and the Kerach,"

All the stones that made up his father's body ground and twisted against each other.

"Enchanting stone was born from Kerach, did your dwarf teach you that?" There was anger in his father's voice. "Did your dwarven master teach you that enchanting in his runes is a mere mimicry of the true power of Stonesmithing? Trolls ARE stone! Kerach and stone are as one, and enchanting in other runes is a hollow imitation compared to the real craft."

Ash was taken aback by the ferocity of his father's voice. Eikinri had taught him that a rune was merely a binding and a focal point of the power within oneself, that the designated rune for an enchantment only needed to be relative to the desired outcome. For example, when he had crafted the trollhelm, he had used the runes for 'invisibility', 'disguise' and 'change'. These runes had only acted as channels and seals to the stones within as he shaped the helmet and its abilities according to his will. Surely, the type of runes he had used did not matter.

"I'm sorry, but I don't see what difference it would make?"

Ash took a step backwards as a wave of almost palpable anger radiated from the mound of stone in front of him. Long seconds passed, and soon his father's calm voice filled the cavern once again.

"I should be grateful for your master's mis-teaching, because it will allow me to bestow a gift upon you I otherwise wouldn't have been able to give you." After a long pause, Jordr spoke again. "You best be seated and heed my words."

Ash sat down on the cold, hard ground.

"You would be familiar with the story of Odin hanging himself from the world tree Yggdrasil for nine days and nine nights in order to learn the wisdom of the runes, yes? The wisdom of the runes was revealed to him in recognition of his suffering and sacrifice, and with this wisdom came a lot of Odin's powers. What he learned was the Futhark, the runes used by the gods and humankind. The fact that Odin understands the very essence of the runes has granted him extraordinary abilities, because there is power inside runes themselves, if you know how to harness it. Odin has always closely guarded the magic in the runes, sharing only snippets with the Seidwomen of Midgard who do his bidding. Eventually the dwarves got their hands on them, but never fully understanding the power within the runes, they used them more as a tool for enchantment, channelling their intrinsic powers through the runes and into whatever object they were enchanting."

What his father said made sense to Ash, at least from the dwarven point of view, as this was how Eikinri had taught him.

"Kerach," his father's deep voice rumbled, "is different. A long time ago, the greatest troll Stonesmith who ever lived, Finnbolgr, felt the calling of the stone beneath him. He burrowed deep inside a mountain and sealed himself in. Here he went into a deep slumber that lasted a thousand years, and as he slept, the mountain whispered its secrets into his ear. When he eventually awoke, Kerach had been revealed to him, and the true power of enchanting stone was borne into the world.

"Each of the runes holds its own power and can be built into staves or patterns of endless complexity, allowing the enchanter to shape spells that stretch the stone to the end of its ability. There is a lot of power within stone; fire from when it was formed, the icy cold of Ginngunnagap, the great nothing, that has seeped into it over millennia, the wind that has withered it away, and stone is also the very earth itself. Whereas Esh and Futhark use the enchanter's own power in order to fuel the enchantments, Kerach draws its powers from the stone itself, making the runes more powerful, durable and less taxing on the enchanter. This is why any troll who knows them can make powerful wards. But if that troll is a Stonesmith, one that has the power to see into stone and shape it to their will, the power of Kerach can be tremendous."

Ash sat in silence for a moment, allowing what his father said to sink in. He thought of Beli, who had been a simple vaettr, and the wards he had made that prevented a company of Jomsvikings and the undead draugr from approaching his cave.

"Show me," Ash whispered.

A chuckle rang out across the shaft. "I am glad you are eager to learn," Jordr said. "Pick up a stone next to you."

Ash reached out and closed his hand around a rock the size of his fist.

"Take your finger and carve the dwarven rune for 'fire' into the stone. As you do it, gather the energy within you and pour it into the rune, like the dwarves do."

As he carved, Ash let his energy fill the rune to power it, and the effort made beads of sweat erupt on his forehead. He dropped the stone when he realised with a shock that it had emitted fire, burning his fingers. It fell to the ground with a clack. Opening his eyes, he saw it sitting in front of him with thin blue flames racing across its surface, spreading an eerie glow inside the cavern.

"Fire from stone," he whispered to himself. "Amazing!"

"How do you feel?" his father asked.

Ash felt tired, as he always did after enchanting. Part of why it had taken so long to finish the trollhelm was that he often had to stop and rest for a day each time he had exhausted himself.

"Tired," he told his father.

"Now take another stone and do it again, but this time you will use the Kerach."

Ash hesitated. Eikinri had taught him the dangers of over-stretching oneself enchanting. You could use up your life force and never wake up if you overdid it.

"Do it." Jordr's voice was firm.

Not wanting to disappoint his father, Ash reached out for another stone.

"Look into the stone and find the fire within it. Search its memory, back to the day it was spewed from a volcano. The fire is still there, it has merely gone cold."

Ash closed his eyes and let his Stonesight flow into the rock. He had never looked at stone this way, but he did as his father commanded and as his mind permeated the minerals that made it up, he sought for heat and fire. Deep inside the stone he found it, a trace of heat that wrapped around and bound the granite particles together. It felt thin and fragile, but it was there, in every part of the stone. "When you have found the fire, gather it together with your mind and hold it while you carve the rune onto the surface," his father's voice was no louder than a whisper.

Ash searched his memory and found the troll rune for 'fire' and carved it into the surface. It was almost as if the heat leaped eagerly towards the rune as soon as he carved the last stave, and a red flame burst from the stone, singing his beard. He yelped and threw it away from himself. More a raging fireball than a rock, it rolled away and came to a stop against the cavern wall where it burned steadily, dwarfing the wispy, blue flames from the first stone. He looked at his father, his eyes wide.

"How do you feel now?"

Ash blinked a few times before answering.

"No different,"

"Because the rune is powered by the fire within the stone, not by the energy you put in. The stone knows Kerach because it is the very language of mountains."

Ash stared at the merrily burning piece of rock that was now blackening the wall.

"How long will it burn?" he asked.

"If a normal troll who knew what they were doing had carved it with a chisel, probably a day or two. Since you are a Stonesmith, it will burn for maybe five or even ten."

"Stone burning for ten days?" Ash asked incredulously, unable to conceal the scepticism in his voice.

"Not days," Jordr said. "Years."

Ash turned back towards his father to see if he was joking, but found it hard to read a pile of stone.

"You need to practice enchanting with Kerach until it becomes second nature. Remember that the power will come from within the stone, not from you. All you need to do is guide and shape it to meet your will."

"Yes, father." As Ash spoke, a warmth filled his chest. He had longed his whole life to say those words. Somehow, it felt like a broken piece of him fused back together. Jordr paused at his words and fell silent. Ash fingered his bracelet, now feeling slightly awkward, looking for something to break the silence between them, when a thought struck him.

"Do you know what this is?" he asked, holding out the bracelet towards his father. "It seems to prevent me from using my Ulfhednar powers, but I heal almost immediately when injured, and my strength has more than doubled. I cannot remove or destroy it."

Jordr, relieved to move on as well, answered Ash. "I am not a Shaman, but I have inherited a touch of it from my mother; at least enough to know a spell charm when I see one," he started. "It is either a blessing or a curse, they can have different effects on different trolls, depending on who you are. Healing all but mortal wounds is a troll trait, and since you have been granted that and can no longer Shift as your mother did, I would say the spell enhances your troll side, at the expense of your Ulfhednar side."

Ash looked down at the bracelet and pulled at it for the hundredth time, but it remained as unbending as before.

"So, how do I remove it?" he asked.

"As these spells and curses go, it is usual for only the person who placed it on you to remove it."

Ash felt as if a pit had opened up under his feet. If the only person who could remove the bracelet was Hagan, he was in deep trouble. The chances of the plump servant even being alive after running off into the wilderness of Jotunheim were close to non-existent he estimated. He could never Shift again unless he could find a way to break it. Surely Odin could remove it? Although that meant that he would be directly aiding Ash and perhaps he was not willing to pay that price. Ash feared that in being foolish enough to allow Hagan to trick and force the bracelet on him, he had now doomed himself and his friends to failure. He doubted they could even reach the source tree, let alone destroy it. Midgard would fall, and all because he was too trusting.

"It is time to go."

Jordr's words pulled him from his thoughts and he pushed his worries to the back of his mind.

"I better go up first and warn my friends about you, or they will get a terrible fright," he told his father.

"I am not coming." There was a hint of sorrow in his words again.

"I know you can't climb in the shape you are now, but I'm sure I can move you through the stone and all the way up," Ash said, reassuring his father.

"No." There was a finality in Jordr's words. "This life I have is not living. I can feel nothing but my own thoughts. I have no powers to speak of, short of moving the stones that my soul now occupies, and this existence is... painful in certain ways."

"But" Ash began, but was cut off.

"I stayed alive to mourn, so that the love I shared with Gunnr would never die, that it would exist in me until Ragnarok, when the world is finally destroyed." He paused for a moment. "But now that I know of you, I know that our love will live on in the greatest of vessels; a loved child. I can let go and leave this world with a sense of peace."

Ash's throat felt tight. He wanted to rave and protest, but he knew he would only shame himself in front of his father.

"Bergbrakkr." The word rang out from his father and echoed around the cavern. Ash could feel the vibration of the word in his very bones.

"What is that?" Ash asked.

"That is one of two gifts I wish to bestow upon you as we part," Jordr rumbled. "It means 'mountain breaker'. It is a word that, like the great Finnbolgr, the mountain has whispered in my ear since the day I fell into this shaft. Often have I wondered what it meant, but now in my last moments, it has become clear. The mountain has whispered your name this whole time."

Ash remembered that Rani had told him that trolls didn't name their young until they came of age, and in respect for his father, his mother had never formally named him. Eventually, Jarl Eric named him Ash because the first time the Jarl saw him, he was covered in soot.

"Since the mountain has named you, it is not just a powerful name, but also a prophecy."

Ash bowed his head.

"The second gift I wish to give to you, you will find inside my hearth, where none but a Stonesmith could find it. With this, my duty as a father is complete, and it is time that I go to rest."

It was as if an icy hand had gripped hold of Ash's heart. He had just discovered that he had a father, only to lose him again moments later.

"Father, please don't. Surely we-"

"No." Jordr's deep voice silenced him. "I am pleased to have met you, and to see your mother's strength lives on. Knowing that we will both carry on in you completes my lifespan. To linger any longer would be... undignified. All that lives must die, it is the order of all things."

Try as he might to appear brave in front of his father, treacherous tears started running down Ash's cheeks.

"Well met, my son. Know that I am proud of what I have seen in you."

"Well met, father. Rest easy."

And with those words, Jordr the Stonesmith was gone. There was a clatter of rocks and pebbles as the pile collapsed and settled in front of Ash. He stood quietly, staring at it for a long time, but it did not move again.

CHAPTER 28

Roghald's mind was chaos as he was thrown from one tormenting dream to another. Gamir's screams and laughter filled his entire existence as horrible images flashed before his eyes.... Occasionally, he would wake from the dreams, only to find himself trapped in the mountain, and he would beat his bloodied hands against the rock until he drifted off into his nightmares again. Whether he was awake or dreaming, that damned troll was always there, making the torment so much worse.

In one wakeful moment, when he was certain he could take it no longer and that his mind was about to shatter, without warning the voice suddenly fell silent. Roghald opened his eyes and stood on a grey dirt road in a dark landscape. The worn road was perfectly flat, with dark mountains spanning the entire horizon beyond it. Above him, countless frozen stars glittered, and the cold air on his skin sent a shiver down his back.

He sensed someone next to him and spun on his heels. It was the bargemaster from his dream in Utgard. He had the same terrifying grin and his eyes glowed as if they were of molten brimstone. A robe of swirling shadows and smoke wrapped the troll, revealing only its face with that horrible smirk.

"Where am I?" Roghald asked. His voice had a strange echo as he spoke, and he realised that Gamir's voice spoke in unison with his own.

"You stand on *Helvegen*, the Trail of Sorrow. Your destiny lies at the end."

A movement in the corner of his eye made him turn his head. A strange shape drifted just outside of his field of vision. He stared at it, but it twisted and warped, moving away from his line of sight. Try as he might, he could not get a good look at it. He noticed several more shapes just like it, gliding out of his view.

"They have not fed on the living for a thousand years and have grown hungry. I would make haste if I were you," the bargemaster chuckled, and then he was gone as if he had never been there at all.

Roghald spun around again and caught glimpses of the creatures. While his back was turned, they had drawn even closer. He set off down the road. At first, he was walking at a brisk pace, but as the surrounding shadows moved ever closer and he thought he could hear them whispering, he started running. Soon, the whispers turned into words of hunger and lust for his blood and soul, and Roghald sprinted as fast as his legs would carry him.

A square shape appeared far ahead on the road. A glimmer of hope entered Roghald's heart as he made for the construction. The shadows came even nearer, and he panicked when he felt icy fingers scratch at his back and neck, claws scraping at his skin. The shape ahead of him revealed itself to be a lone timber archway straddling the road. Having no other hope to cling to, Roghald made a mad dash for it and threw himself through it, landing hard on slick cobblestones.

Disappointed shrieks erupted behind him as he lay panting just beyond the archway.

The laments of the shadows died away, and Roghald raised his head. A thin mist surrounded him. He looked back towards where he had come from but could see nothing but billowing fog on a grey landscape. There was no sign of the archway or the wraiths that had chased him.

He stood up and looked down at his hands, scraped from sliding along the cobblestones. His breath caught in his throat when he realised he was looking down on the human hands he had always known, before he was turned to troll. Big, firm hands, calloused and scarred by years of toil, but very much human. His actual hands. He lifted them up and felt his face. It was broad with a prominent brow and a thick, short beard, and as familiar as a thing could ever be. He was in his real form, as he had been before Havbodr had swept him out to sea and killed him. When he looked down, he noticed he was wearing his old, torn red tunic, the one he had on when he transformed into a thursr in Jarl Eric's hall before slaughtering the Jarl and his hird.

It was clear to him that this couldn't be real. He looked around and, peering through the mist, he could see that the cobblestones ended abruptly a dozen paces ahead of him. Roghald took a few cautious steps towards the ledge and looked down to find his own reflection staring back at him, reflected by dark waters. He was standing on some sort of quay next to a perfectly still body of water.

A gentle movement in the water below caught his eye. Soon he glimpsed it again, a flowing pale motion deep in the water. He kneeled down on the cobblestones to get a better look. His eyes widened when a skeletal face, skin stretched tight over bone, rose from the depths to gaze at him from just below the surface before sinking back down into the dark. Several others slowly swam into its place, all staring at him with dead empty sockets.

A gentle ripple on the water blurred the vision, and the ghosts disappeared from wherever they'd come. Roghald raised his head and peered into the mist ahead of him. A soft, yellow light appeared in the mist and Roghald jumped back when he realised it was only a few arm's lengths away, hidden in the thick fog. His stomach dropped when a fierce dragon's head appeared from the haze, staring directly at him. He wanted to run, but his legs wouldn't obey him and he stood frozen on the spot.

The light he had seen sat behind and to the side of the head, casting its face in eerie shadows. The dragon started turning slowly to its right and when it was in profile, he could see its shape in full. It was a ship, not a dragon.

The Norse carved dragon or wolf heads on the prow of their ships to strike fear into the spirits of the lands they were raiding. Roghald had, in his youth, sailed on several dragon ships but had never seen a more frightening or well-carved head than the one before him. The ship was long, with room for at least twenty rowers on each side, and wide enough that they could sit two abreast. But there were no oars to be seen, nor anyone to row it; the ship was empty.

Amazed by the size and craft of it, he gingerly stepped forward to lay his hand on the neck of the dragon. The timber felt rough and strange to touch, and he bent down low under the single lantern to inspect. It took him several seconds to realise what he was looking at, but when he did, he flinched. The ship was not made from timber, but from human fingernails and toenails. With disgust, he wiped his hand on his tunic.

"Neither fingernail nor toenail on the dead, no nails for the giant. No nail for the giant, no nail for the *Naglfar* ship," he whispered. It was an old saying about the troll ship Naglfar. The ship was made from the untrimmed fingernails and toenails of the dead. Vikings were always careful to trim their fingers and toenails before going into battle, so if they died their nails would not be added to the legendary ship. The ship that belonged to Muspelheim, the world of fire.

"Beautiful, isn't it?"

Roghald spun around and found the bargemaster standing next to him again.

"The great Surtr, Destroyer of Worlds, must see potential in you, thursr. He has sent the greatest of ships to ferry you across."

"Ferry me to where?"

The troll's face remained distorted in that horrible smile as it turned its burning gaze from Naglfar to Roghald.

"To get here, you travelled on the road Helvegen and this is the river Gjöll. I think you must know what lies on the other side."

Roghald stared into the mist beyond Naglfar. His mouth had gone dry, and his heart was beating like it was about to burst from his chest. When he spoke, it was more of a croak;

"Helheim."

The bargemaster said nothing, but his grin seemed to widen even further. Helheim, the land of the dead. An afterlife for those who died in bed from sickness or old age, but also oath-breakers and the dishonourably fallen, forever denied a seat in Valhalla. A grim and drab world ruled by the fearsome goddess Hel where the sun would never shine, nor would any shoots grow.

"Why must I go?"

"There is something you must understand,"

"And what is that?"

When Roghald's words remained unanswered, he turned back towards the bargemaster, only to find that he was gone. He stood for a long time at the edge, staring into the distance, trying to penetrate the fog to see what awaited him on the other side, but the mist did not lift or yield its secrets. Roghald closed his eyes for a moment, took a deep breath and when he opened them again, he stepped forward and placed his foot firmly on the deck of Naglfar.

As soon as he embarked, the great ship drifted out into the river. Roghald did not sit down on the boards or shelter himself. He stood at the prow, determined, with his back straight like a proud captain, with one hand resting on the dragon's head. Without oars or rudder, Naglfar turned away from the shore and headed into the mist.

CHAPTER 29

ASH LOOKED AROUND THE BOTTOM OF THE CHASM UN-
til he found what had to be his father's original body. A pile
of rocks, different in composition from the surrounding stone, lay
in the rough shape of a man sprawled out on the ground. Realising that he couldn't possibly carry it all, he reached into the stone
where his father's heart would have been and carefully removed a
lump of rock the size of his fist. He placed it in his pack to return
to his grandmother. Then he drew his sword and rolled the burning stone from earlier over to the remnants of his father.

"I will leave a light in the dark for you, father," he whispered. "If
I am still alive five years from now, I will return to renew it before
it burns out." The last thing he did was to place his mother's spearhead on top of what would have been his father's chest. With that,
he turned back towards the wall of the chasm where he had come
down. He sunk his arms and legs into the rock, and concentrating,
he drifted upwards.

As he ascended, he would occasionally look down at the light
of the burning stone, and each time, as it grew smaller and further
away, his heart ached. Ash was awash with emotions, and his mind
was racing. The sorrow of knowing that both his parents had lived
for years believing the other to be dead was conflicting with the joy

of having met his father before the mourning of losing him again rose in his chest.

He thought about the name his father and the mountain had given him. Bergbrakkr. Why had he been named mountain break-er, and how was that a prophecy? His mind went to the bracelet. If what his father had said was true, Ash was now a full troll, the human side of him suppressed until he could find Hagan to remove the damned thing. But Hagan was likely dead, so he would have to find another way to break the charm.

For a moment, he considered remaining a troll, and following in the footsteps of his father, but then remembering his mother, a pang of guilt clutched his heart. He could not deny the side of him that came from her. Besides, he never felt like he belonged anywhere until he joined the ranks of the Jomsvikings. With his Ulfhednar powers now gone, he doubted they would count him as their equal any longer. Also, when he had reconciled the two sides of himself, he finally felt complete. And now he felt imbalanced. That settled it, he needed to remove the cursed bracelet.

These thoughts were all-consuming, distracting him so much that he hadn't even realised he'd made it to the top of the chasm until his hands came free and he almost toppled backwards.

A firm hand caught his wrist and pulled him back towards the edge at the last moment.

"Wolves have no business climbing."

The unfamiliar voice made him snap his head up and when he realised he was staring into the almost white eyes of the dark elf as she smiled at him with sharpened teeth, he nearly fell backwards again.

Ash looked at Agash across the fire. He found her fascinating. Her smooth, black skin glistened in the firelight and her swell of straight white hair framed her strong yet delicate features in a very interesting way. Her tight, black leathers seemed to be glued to her and enhanced her athletic shape when she moved. He remembered how it had felt to press up against her when they fought, and his heart skipped a beat. He looked to the side to see Yrsa staring at him with a scowl on her face. She shook her head ever so slightly in a way that spoke volumes, and Ash looked down at his feet as he felt his cheeks flush.

"So, what does the Troll King want with us?" Torsten's voice rumbled, drawing Ash's attention back to the conversation.

"I am merely a messenger," Agash said in an almost bored voice. "But I do know that he does not like change, nor anyone challenging his power. If it is as they say that my enemy's enemy is my friend, then I guess you have a friend in Thrym."

"How do we know that this isn't a trap?" Yrsa's voice was full of doubt.

"You don't," Agash replied, fiddling with the bandages on her hands. Ash had wondered why both her hands were wrapped up, but hadn't felt comfortable asking her questions yet. "But can you afford to not have any friends at this point?"

You can only destroy the source by getting beyond those doors. Odin's words came unbidden to Ash. He had assumed that the Troll King, with all his hatred for humankind would be the enemy, but perhaps it was the opposite?

"Damn the gods and their riddles," he muttered.

The group fell silent and stared at him.

"We will go," he said, his eyes on Agash. "Take us to the Troll King."

The dark elf gave him a wicked grin, sharpened teeth and all, but there was a mysterious look in her eyes. "As you wish," she said with a mock bow.

Yrsa and Torsten both spoke at once, raising their concerns, but Ash held firm.

"We leave at first light."

Ash stood and left the fire. Still in his father's smithy, he walked across the rough floor and came to a halt in front of the round forge in the middle of the vast cavern. He paused as he took in the band of runes that wrapped around the base of the hearth. He could feel the eyes of the others on his back as he placed his hands on the smooth stone. Letting his Stonesight permeate the forge, he saw the runes and the spells his father had set to keep the fire burning hotter than any normal fire. He let his mind drift across the weave of the runes and the spells that remained, like an empty shell, now that the runes' power had long worn out, with no one to recharge the wards. It had been almost twenty years since the attack on his father's mountain after all.

Having just learned from his father how the power of troll runes worked, he gave in to his curiosity and sought all the runes carved around the forge with his Stonesight. There were a dozen runes, all connected in a network of enchanted tendrils. He frowned at the complexity of it. Of course, a Stonesmith's forge, as powerful as it was, wouldn't rely solely on one simple fire rune. As he mapped out the tendrils in his mind, the network all seemed to converge on one rune. The spindly stave, with a bit of imagination, resembled a lightning bolt, the rune for power. He placed his hand on it, examining the surrounding stone, and saw the small tendrils and minute channels that stretched out to the sides and connected to other runes. All tendrils but one. One stretched into the stone, away from the surface. Ash followed it with his Stonesight as it delved about a foot into the rock. At the end of the tendril was a patch of stone about the size of his fist that felt... lifeless. All the power had been drained from it. This rune was the catalyst, he realised, the one that powered all the others.

He concentrated on an area of stone next to the dead patch and looked deep into it. When he found the fire buried within, he gathered it and guided it back to the rune to bind it. His heart skipped a beat in excitement as he waited for the forge to roar back to life any second. But nothing happened. He frowned again, confused for a moment, then he wanted to smack himself on the forehead. It was the rune for power, not fire, so of course he couldn't bind the fire in the stone to it.

Releasing the fire back into the stone, he delved deeper into it. The stone comprised a myriad of small particles, and they all spread out before him. Some sparkled like diamonds, others were dull and bland as they crowded close to each other in the make-up of the rock. Ash didn't know exactly what he was looking for, but he had a vague idea he was searching for power.

He found a small part that seemed to pulsate with minute sparks. He concentrated on that pulsation, let his whole being permeate it and suddenly his mind filled with thunderstorms, pelting the iron-rich mountain with countless lightning strikes, century after century, flashing through the stone, carried by veins of iron ore. In his mind's eye, Ash saw the mountain move and shift in response to pressures from below as Yggdrasil grew and twisted over millennia, the friction building up within the rock itself, lodging there as energy, trapped between the grains of minerals.

An image of a lumbering troll climbing to the very top of a mountain came to him. The troll carved off the highest point of the mountain with his bare hands, the part most commonly struck by lightning, and carried the tremendous weight down the steep slope. His father had known to build his forge from the most powered stone.

Ash swept his mind through the untouched section of the stone, next to the spent part, and led the energy there back to the rune. It flashed once, and the tendrils flared to life and all the other runes surrounding the forge lit up. The wall of heat slammed into him as the fire, long dead, reignited and forced him back a step.

When he heard the others gasp behind him, he turned to them and winked. Torsten laughed while Yrsa, who didn't like surprises, shook her head at him for the second time that night. When he looked to Agash, he saw her eyes were wide, and her mouth was slightly open. She recovered immediately when his eyes fell on her, assuming a disinterested expression, and returned to fiddling with her bandages.

The fire roared in the forge, and Ash took great pleasure in watching the runes pulsate with power. He had let himself get distracted by the forge, but now returned to his original task. Ash let his Stonesight expand to include the whole flaming stone construct, and that's when he saw it. In the floor below the forge, something shone like the sun in his mind's eye. He took a breath and sunk into the stone, bending down and reaching towards the luminescent spot through the rock.

His hand came to an abrupt stop against a flat solid surface. Perplexed, Ash concentrated on the barrier he didn't seem able to penetrate. He ran his hand over it and found it to be a square block about an arm's length in all dimensions. Something about it felt familiar, but he couldn't put his finger on it. The object he was looking for was within this very block, still shining brightly to his Stonesight. Ash concentrated on the firm barrier before him, delving deeply into its smallest components. That's when he realised where he had seen it before. It had surrounded him in Eikinri's smithy, above his head and below his feet. The block was made from Yggdrasil, the world tree, and was infinitely harder than any stone in existence.

How his father had carved out a block from the world tree he did not know, but it had made the most impenetrable strongbox in the world. Still submerged inside the forge's stone, Ash rested his hand against the block and sang the low, deep song of creation. His voice vibrated through the surrounding stone, and he felt every syllable pulsate through his body. Slowly, the walls of the block yielded to his touch and his hand pushed through, inch by inch.

The wall of the block was only a hand's width thick, and soon he felt open air around his fingers. When his hand had pushed through the block, he released the part of the spell he had been building and the stone pulled away from him, leaving a hole in the block big enough that Ash could have slipped his whole body through if he wanted.

He smiled as he reached down to the bottom of the space and closed his hand around his father's smithing hammer.

CHAPTER 30

ROGHALD'S FOOT LANDED ON THE COLD, DAMP FLAG-stones. No sooner had he stepped off Naglfar did the ship drift out into the river again and disappear into the fog. This side of the river looked much the same and he could see Helvegen stretch out ahead of him through the same sort of archway he had fallen through while running from the wraiths. For a second, he wondered if he had returned to the same place, if Naglfar had turned around in the fog without his knowledge, and if he was about to walk through the archway into a horrible death, with the wicked spirits consuming him. It seems like a lot of effort for a cruel practical joke, he thought, and dismissed the idea.

Roghald squared his shoulders and set out through the archway. As soon as he crossed its threshold, the mists lifted, but the view did not improve in the slightest. He was looking out over the bottom of a dreary, grey ravine with jagged rock walls that stretched out ahead of him. A light drizzle fell from low, grey clouds, just enough to dampen everything. The ground beneath his feet was slick with moisture, and brown puddles had formed along the path. Gone were the flagstones from the riverside, replaced by a thin layer of cold mud and silt over rough rock.

He examined the surrounding walls, seeking a way out of the

ravine, onto the high ground, but they were far too steep and slippery. One mistake could mean a fall to his death. Never had he seen a more miserable place. Roghald sighed and started picking his way around the deepest puddles, but despite his best efforts, cold moisture soon found its way inside his boots, which were caked in slippery mud. A shiver went up his spine. His clothes clung to his body in a cold, damp embrace. It wasn't freezing, but combined with the drizzling rain, it was cold enough that his fingers hurt, and he had to frequently rub them together to get a bit of warmth and movement. The ravine twisted and wound its way across the landscape, and Roghald had no option but to follow it.

When he turned a corner, he stumbled and nearly fell over as he came face to face with a man sitting on a rock only a few paces away from him. Roghald reached for a sword at his waist that was no longer there and had to resort to clenching his fists, preparing for a fight.

He relaxed when he realised it was an old man, stooped over from age. He was bald, not a hair on his head, his eyes sunken deep into a wrinkly face. The man huddled under a grey blanket, shivering in the cold as he slowly rocked back and forth. Roghald thought he looked sickly, and his suspicions were confirmed when the man's body was racked by a long, wet coughing attack that almost toppled him off the rock he was sitting on. The man spat out a thick, green gob and returned to his shivering.

"Hello?" Roghald said, but the man ignored him.

Roghald walked up to the man and stood square in front of him.

"I said hello. What ails you, old man?"

The old man raised his head and looked up at Roghald. Old cataract eyes met his.

Roghald was astounded at the morosity in them. There wasn't a trace of hope in him, all he saw was an utterly dejected creature whose existence was a drawn-out suffering with no end. Without a word, the old man lowered his head to his chest again and resumed his gentle rocking as if Roghald wasn't there, or it didn't matter whether he was.

Died in bed from illness, Roghald thought as he turned his back and continued along the path. Another coughing attack rang out across the ravine, and Roghald hurried along to get away from the sound. Before long, the ravine opened up into a broad valley, skirted by tall mountains. The muddied ground lay in rolling hills and in the middle of the valley stood a sprawling building.

The structure was black and grey, and as gloomy as the land. It must've had some warmth inside it because Roghald could see a strand of smoke rising from the roof. He would give anything to sit by a fire right now. Looking around the valley, he could see people on the rolling plain. Some sat huddled in groups, while some paced aimlessly back and forth.

"You have a glow to you, seldom seen around here,"

Roghald turned towards the voice. A man stood leaning against the rock wall where the ravine had opened up. He was young, no older than twenty summers, and had probably once been handsome, with chiselled features. Now, his skin was grey and his eyes sunken, his wet hair plastered to the sides of his face. His eyes, although more alert than the old man's, still held nothing but misery. The young man wore leather armour and had a shield on his arm, but the most noticeable adornment was the spearhead that protruded from his chest. It seemed the wound was still bleeding as Roghald could make out a black trickle down the man's torso where it slowly dripped to the ground.

"Because I'm not dead," Roghald replied. Then he considered his situation and added, "Yet."

"Well, lucky you."

"Why are you here?" Roghald asked. "Clearly you died in battle, so shouldn't you be drinking with the other warriors in Valhalla?"

The man gave him a long stare before answering. "No. I am a coward. I ran from battle and in doing so, caught a spear with my back. There is no seat for me in Odin's hall. The Norns found it best to weave me such a fate." His voice was full of bitterness.

"Is everyone who did not reach Valhalla here on this plain?" Roghald asked, steering the man away from his personal lamentations.

"No. Only cowards and adulterers are damned to this wet and cold existence." He raised his hand and pointed to the building in the middle of the valley. "We are denied a seat at the table in Hel's hall. There sit those who the goddess deems to have lived well and honourably, but lost their life to old age, illness or murder." The man raised his hand even higher, pointing towards the end of the valley. "Beyond the hall lies the shore of *Nastrond*. There you'll find the worst of those who have died; the murderers and the oath-breakers. Their bodies are chewed by the dragon *Nidhogg* and they are bathed in snake venom as punishment for the lives they led."

"I have an errand in the hall, and must be on my way," Roghald said, turning away. The dead man made him uncomfortable. There was longing and jealousy in his eyes when he looked at Roghald, and he wasn't sure if the dead could hurt him or not.

He couldn't help but to feel an anguish in his heart as he left the man behind and steered himself towards the hall. Roghald had never considered his afterlife, but it was staring him in the face right now. He had taken a sacred oath when he, as a young man, joined Jarl Eric's father's hird; an oath that he had broken when he attacked and killed the Jarl. It could be argued that his dismissal from the hird released him from his oath, but he had a feeling that it would still not be looked upon favourably. Besides, he had murdered aplenty. Every person he had turned to draugr would no doubt count as part of that tally. Even worse than murder since he had denied them an afterlife. When his time came, Roghald was sure they would stick him in the deepest pool of venom in Nastrond.

He weaved around groups of drab people, young and old, as he made his way towards the hall. Their eyes followed him with greed and envy, and some called out after him, but he ignored them and hurried along.

Hel's hall was an impressive building. Built from black timber, every corner and awning was decorated with fierce dragon heads and the skulls of men. Bones tied to strings dangled from every cornice. They rattled and clunked softly whenever a cold gust of wind swept past.

Roghald stepped up to the closed doors, tall, grey things of ancient oak, studded with rusted iron. He put his hand on them and pushed. They swung open readily on light hinges, surprising Roghald. He had expected some resistance, or at least an ominous creak.

The hall inside was gloomy, but Roghald could see that it was impossibly large, considering the size of the building. He could barely see the end of the hall. Row after row of tables stretched out toward the distant walls where people sat, with food in front of them. There must have been thousands upon thousands of people at the tables, yet no one spoke above a whisper, leaving the hall eerily quiet. It was lit by a fire pit in the middle of the floor and torches along the walls and sparsely spaced candles on the tables, however the light struggled to penetrate the darkness, leaving the hall in shadows.

To his delight, it was warm inside. Roghald gratefully opened up his tunic to allow some of the warmth closer to his body, and he revelled in the warm pinching sensation on the skin of his cheeks. Looking around, he saw the people seated at the tables were a mixture of young and old, in bed-shirts and armour. All sat bent over their meals or talked softly amongst themselves.

An old woman wearing a stained apron walked up to him. Without a word, she grabbed his arm and pulled him down the middle aisle between two rows of tables. Roghald didn't resist and allowed the old woman to lead him to a table with an empty spot. She pointed to the seat until Roghald complied and sat down.

Before him on the table sat a bowl of soup and a cob of bread, as well as a cup of what appeared to be ale. There were people seated all around him, but having no interest in talking to any of them, he ignored them, looking only at the food. He realised he actually felt hungry, and carefully sampled the soup and bread. They were a little bland, but the warmth of the soup was delightful.

Roghald could feel the person seated in front of him staring across the table but continued to ignore him, his eyes on the food. He would eat, then get up and look around the hall. He didn't know what he was supposed to understand here, but whatever it was, he suspected it would be inside this hall. The sense of the person across the table blatantly staring at him got worse and was irritating Roghald. Finding it difficult to concentrate on the task at hand, he snapped his head up, ready to tell the person to keep their eyes to themselves when he choked on his words.

Roghald was looking into a face he had known and loved his entire life.

"Hello, son," his father said with a joyless smile.

CHAPTER 31

THE FIRE HAD ALMOST BURNED OUT. ASH HADN'T BOTHered to add more fuel to it, since the horizon was already a dull grey as the sun made its way up. Chirps and croaks replaced the silence of the night as animals ushered in the early morning.

He had been allotted the last watch of the night as his friends slept. None of the Midgardians trusted Agash, so no watch had been assigned to her. She had been awake for most of his watch, pretending to sleep. Since Hagan had placed the bracelet on Ash, he had been able to see in the dark, as trolls do, so he had seen her watching him when she thought her face was hidden in the shadows. He was aware of her eyes on him, and he felt torn between liking the attention and fearing whatever she was plotting. He almost spoke to her on several occasions, but stopped himself every time. To distract himself from her icy blue eyes, he took out his father's hammer and placed it on his lap.

The hammer was a thing of beauty. Bands of runes swirled on the hammer head in an intricate pattern. The handle, wrapped in leather, bore the marks of years of use by his father's hand. When he first picked it up, he had felt the same elation as he did when he picked up Beli's hammer, a long time ago on Midgard. Though, Beli's hammer was a child's toy compared to this. It radiated raw power, ready to bend to the will of a skilled Stonesmith. He studied it with his Stonesight, but could not make sense of the intricate weave of runes and spells that spun and twisted throughout. There were even metals and minerals in there that he had not encountered before and had no name for.

Before they left his father's mountain, he had smelted some ore in the reignited furnace and had set to work the iron on one of the many anvils in the workshop. Holding the hammer in one hand, he discovered that when he used his Stonesight on the lump of iron, he could see its composition with such clarity that every component stood out to him, making the smithing almost effortless. He had hammered the glowing iron into a perfect rod before plunging it in a cooling vat, sending a cloud of steam billowing to the ceiling. When it had cooled sufficiently, he heated it again and set upon it with powerful blows of the hammer. Under normal circumstances, to bend iron, he would have heated it again, then bent the hot steel around a round point of a vice, but now he simply willed it to the desired shape as Jordr's hammer struck it, sending sparks flying around him. It reminded him again of Beli, and how he had been smithing a delicate piece with hefty blows of his hammer. This was the true magic of trolls. Ash had been impressed back then, but now realised that Beli had been comparatively unskilled and though he didn't know where he had gotten his smithing hammer, he likely hadn't made it himself.

Ash worked and bent the piece of iron, and while doing so, moved the minerals within to make his enchanting easier and more powerful. Once he had cooled the metal in the vat again, he held it up to his eye for a closer inspection. He bent the rod into a loop, about a foot across, crossing over itself at the bottom with the ends curling back on themselves in sharp points. Spaced out along it were three runes, stamped into the metal.

"A troll-cross?"

He hadn't heard Yrsa coming up next to him. Startled, Ash almost dropped the thing.

"It wasn't necessary, but I had to shape it like something, and it seems kind of appropriate," he said.

It was an old Norse superstition. People believed that hanging a troll-cross over your door would deter trolls from entering, similar to how blacksmiths hang a horseshoe over their door to keep evil spirits out.

"And what do you intend to do with it?" she asked.

"You'll see." He smiled at his friend. "Get ready to leave."

She shrugged and walked over to where Torsten was sitting, cleaning and oiling his axe, and began packing up their little camp. Agash bent down to help her by rolling up a blanket, but Yrsa gave her an icy stare and pulled it from her hands. Ash had remained by the forge, turning his creation over in his hands, when he saw Agash abandon any attempts to help and approach him instead.

"You will forgive us for not trusting you," he said, not taking his eyes off the trollcross. "After all, your arrows nearly killed Torsten, and you tried to kill me."

Agash placed her hands on her hips casually. "Nothing personal," she said matter-of-factly. "Just as there is no loyalty in me joining you now. I am a sell-sword and assassin. I work for the highest bidder, and at the moment that is the Toll King."

"Why is the Troll King interested in us now? I assume you were working for him when you tried to kill us?" Ash asked, meeting the dark elf's gaze.

"At first, you were unimportant. My job was to keep an eye on Burrugandr and his scheming. Thrym, although he never leaves his frozen fortress, likes to stay abreast of events, especially those regarding his enemies. When I had reported back enough information that the Troll King deemed Roghald a genuine threat, and you a possible asset, my orders changed. I was to kill Roghald and bring you to Thrym." Agash concluded, her voice revealing no emotion.

"Roghald is dead?" Ash burst out.

Agash's eyes narrowed. "No. I failed." Her words dripped with bitterness. "He is cleverer than I gave him credit for." Her eyes fell to Ash's wrist. "I see he outsmarted you as well. How did he do it?"

Ash's arm flew up, and he held it in front of Agash's face. "This is from Roghald?" he demanded. "Another man placed this on me, not Roghald. I know what his human shape looks like."

"Short and plump with an annoying nasal voice?" she asked, one eyebrow raised.

Ash nodded.

"That's him," she confirmed. "I don't know what he used to look like, but that is the shape he takes as a human."

Ash groaned and sat back on the anvil, his palm on his forehead.

"That bastard," he muttered. "That dirty, rotten bastard."

"I see I am not alone in being bested by the thursr." Then she added, "Temporarily."

Ash sat staring into space for a moment before sighing and looking up at Agash, "Why are you here, anyway?" he asked her. "I mean, why did you leave Svartalfheim?" Ash knew very little of the world of the dark elves, beyond that they preferred to keep to themselves, staying out of the business of gods and trolls.

Agash shrugged. "My clan was defeated by another, greater clan. Had I remained I would have been trapped into slavery and servitude to the other clan's chieftain. I was a bodyguard of our clan's Warlock, a spell caster, and I knew he had saved a portal stone to allow escape when things turned sour. I needed it more than he did, so I cut his throat and took the portal stone. I have been stuck on Jotunheim ever since." When Ash's eyes widened at her words, she revealed her pointed teeth as she flashed him a grin. "Look to your own house first, Ash of the Ulfhednar, and burn the rest."

She turned and walked back to collect her belongings, leaving Ash to ponder her words.

She even walks like a predator, he thought as he watched her back walking away.

THURSR

They stood at the opening of Jordr's mountain. Ash told the group to stand back a little before placing his hands on the frame of the opening. He closed his eyes as he began singing the deep song of creation and entered the stone with his mind. He pulled at the ancient rock, shaping it and moulding it, until it had shifted to cover the opening completely.

Once he sealed the opening, he knew he had to work quickly, before the spell ended and the stone returned to its original shape.

Turning his attention to the troll-cross in his hand, Ash delved into it with his mind.

He focussed on the first rune he had stamped into the iron, the rune for 'fear'. Ash had to pause and think. There was no obvious source for 'fear' naturally in the stone, yet the rune existed. He frowned as he pondered how to solve this problem.

Father said that Kerach allows us to shape the power to meet our will, so my will must go into the rune. Ash placed his thumb on the rune, letting his Stonesmithing power fill it. He closed his eyes and thought about the day he had come across the draugr on the road to Gjallarholm. He remembered icy fear in his belly as he had looked up and saw the monster stare at him from the side of the road with its dead eyes. The fear of running wildly through the forest as a horde of the undead snapped at his heels and finally bore down on him as he fell into the stream. When the fear he had felt that day permeated him, he spilled all of it into the rune, letting it absorb his terror. When he could sense a density around the rune that hadn't been there before, he knew he had succeeded.

He moved on to the second rune, the one for 'strength'. This would hold the stone in place, leaving it sealed from the world as long as it had power. He took the image of what the opening looked like now and infused it into the rune.

Satisfied that the rune was bound, he raised it level with his chest and placed it in the middle of the stone that sealed the opening to the mountain. A slight push and it sunk in to sit flush with the wall.

Then Ash moved on to the third and final rune, the same rune for 'power' that he had rekindled in his father's forge. He reached into the stone now surrounding the troll-cross and gathered the power there the same way he had done previously. When he bound the power to the rune, it flashed a bright green, and he saw the energy racing down the tendrils he had drawn to the other two runes. When it reached them, they lit up in the same way, and soon they all pulsed green in unison.

A wave of fear swept through his body. The sound of weapons being drawn behind him made him turn and he saw his friends armed, looking around in confusion. He gathered that the first ward he had ever created worked well. Not only would the ward keep the entry sealed until Ash's return, but the fear would drive away anyone approaching. The last thing he wanted was for another mara or goblin clan to take up residence inside what was essentially his inheritance.

"Sorry," he told the group who were now giving him suspicious looks. "I wanted to see the effect to make sure it worked."

Yrsa rattled off a curse at Ash that made Agash raise her eyebrows and Torsten laugh out loud.

"Let's get out of here," the Berserker said, bemused.

CHAPTER 32

ROGHALD STARED AT HIS FATHER AS HE WRESTLED WITH the tumultuous emotions that arose within him. The last time he had seen the man, Jarl Eric's men had dumped his arrow-riddled body overboard after that fateful night so many summers ago. Roghald's father had gotten drunk while on watch, allowing them to be ambushed in the night in an attack that saw over half of Jarl's warriors slaughtered. Most of them in their sleep.

Roghald had always loved and respected the man growing up, idolised him even, although his actions brought unspeakable shame on Roghald and cost him his place in the Jarl's hird. He had always blamed the Jarl for the unnecessarily harsh punishment, and lay no fault at his father's feet.

Roghald smiled broadly and was about to reach over and clasp his father's arms, but then he took in the man's ashen grey appearance, slouched shoulders and the shame written all over him. Gone was the powerful man who had always held his head high, who had fought bravely in countless battles against stronger foes and won. In his stead sat a broken man, resigned to his fate, waiting out the end of the world in this gloomy hall. He was forever bereft of the feasts and flowing mead of Valhalla, sitting next to great men and women of equal rank. He had forfeited his place in

Ragnarok, the last battle, as would have become him. All this was for one mistake that a petty Jarl could not forgive.

For the first time in a long time, Roghald felt sympathy for another human and reached out his hand to rest it on his father's. "I killed Jarl Eric, father. I crushed his body to a pulp with my bare hands and tore down the gates of his fortress. The wrong done to you has been avenged."

His father's eyes, sunken and tired, looked into his. "You always were a fool, Roghald."

Roghald froze.

"To what end?" his father continued. "To share this bench with me when your time comes? The shame and dishonour was mine alone to bear, no matter what the Jarl said. You could have moved away from Hornsborg after my death. Had you only asked, the Jarl would have given you leave. It would have spared him the rash decision he made while grieving his own father that he would later come to regret. You were young and strong and more skilled with a sword and shield than anyone your age. Any Jarl would have been glad to have you, but you wallowed in self-pity in the stables, growing more bitter every year. Now you are an oath-breaker," his father's face was a grimace of disgust, "and your fate will only take you to Nastrond, no further."

Roghald sat with his mouth open, staring at his father. He could find no words to respond. Einar Halvarson turned his attention back to his soup. "Get out of my sight, boy. You are too painful to look upon."

Roghald sat in silence for a moment as his world crashed down around him, and his stomach filled with ice. His father's words and the undeniable truth they held had torn down everything he believed in in a flash. He stood up slowly and clambered out from behind the bench, his mind reeling. As if drunk, he staggered down the aisle between the tables and hurried toward the entrance of the hall. He had to get away, away from his father and the fate he had created.

Roghald ran aimlessly, the drizzly rain on his face making his eyes blur. He ignored calls from the miserable souls in the field as he darted past, splattering them with mud. How had he been so misguided? How had he gone so wrong?

But it isn't my fault! He raged inside as the injustice of his fate dawned on him. Jarl Eric was the one who shamed me for the actions of another, and Ash's actions led me to be cast away from Hornsborg and thrown into the clutches of the trolls to begin with. And now I am to face damnation because of them!

He came to a stop at a sight that tore him from his internal conflict. Roghald stood at the top of a gully, looking down on a nightmare that spread out before him. On a beach of black, jagged rock, stretching the entire width of the valley, a mass of writhing bodies crawled and twisted. The sea that met the beach was not water, but churning and bubbling venom, sizzling and burning the flesh of the people that fought one another to get out onto the land. When they succeeded, their skins mended, and flesh grew back. The people crawled out of the burning waves and staggered towards the walls of the gully. Roghald looked down on the steep wall under him which led down to the beach and saw it was littered with snakes, their heads sticking out of hollows and cracks. The people would start a horrifying climb up the walls where the snakes would bite them and spit burning venom into their eyes. Most fell, crashing onto the rocks below as they clutched their eyes and bites against the burning pain.

Roghald watched one woman persevere, climbing through the torment, her eyes bleeding and blinded. As she came within feet of the ledge, he saw a bubbling frenzy in the sea of venom as a reptilian head the size of a wagon rose from the burning depths. The dragon's head extended from a long, glistening neck and shot up to pluck the woman from the wall. It crunched her body a few times as she screamed in pain before spitting her out into the swirling waves. Then the dragon fell back beneath the waves again, landing with a splash that sent a wave crashing over the writhing bodies on the beach. The wave carried forward and slammed into the cliff walls, the spray rising halfway up the wall he was standing on, and taking a few climbers with it. A wail of anguish arose from the people as it burned them anew.

Roghald cried out with burning pain on his hand and looked down to see that a few drops had splattered him and were sizzling his skin. The pain from the droplets was almost unbearable, and he shook his hand to get them off.

The dragon resurfaced a moment later and repeated the process with another climber who drew close to the top. Roghald took a few steps back, clutching his stinging hand in the other. The laments and screams of the damned souls filled his ears, and no one reached the top.

Nastrond, he thought. Roghald pictured himself among the writhing bodies, suffering eternally. He watched the dragon rise from the acid again and crush and throw another climber down. This time it didn't submerge, but held still for a moment. Roghald realised to his horror that this was because it had caught sight of him. Black, soulless eyes stared at him as the head started moving forward slowly. The beast tensed as if to strike. Roghald yelped, staggering backwards and after slipping in the mud a few times, set off running as fast as his feet would carry him.

He ran until he once again stood at the hall in the middle of the valley, and only then did he dare to look behind him. Nothing but the muddy plain with its miserable inhabitants. Bending down, placing his hands on his knees, he drew deep breaths to soothe his burning lungs.

He sensed more than saw that someone was near. It was as if what little joy remained in Roghald got sucked out of him and the world darkened as all colour fled. He looked up and saw a naked woman standing only two steps away, watching him.

She was slender, with her right side covered in soft skin, ghostly white, yet beautiful, but her left side more akin to a corpse, blackened in rot where the skeleton was not visible. Her eyes, one green and the other cloudy white, as of the draugr, watched him from an expressionless face. He knew it was Hel, the goddess of the dead.

I don't see many warm ones within the boundaries of my Queendom. Her lips did not move, but Roghald heard her voice inside his head. Gamir roared in protest.

"W-why was I sent here? Was it only to torment me with my father and with Nastrond? Will there not be enough time for that after I'm dead?" Still gasping for breath, Roghald was torn between fear of the goddess and the anger he felt.

You are at a crossroads, Roghald Einarsson. You were sent here to understand what awaits you should you stay on your path, a path that leads only to Nastrond.

Roghald stared at the goddess' unmoving face for a clue as to what she meant, but it was cold and dead. "I don't understand," he croaked. The chill radiating out from her seeped into his bones and he couldn't help but shiver even though he was still sweating from running.

Ascension can only occur with a living sacrifice. Just like Odin sacrificed himself to himself when he hung himself from the branches of Yggdrasil, so must you.

"That makes little sense!" he spluttered. "If I die, I will only end up back here again to be your plaything!

Only humans reach Helheim, trolls do not. You must burn, Roghald Einarsson. Burn your human soul and embrace the troll within.

Roghald's mouth fell open, and in his head he heard Gamir laugh with joy.

"But... but he is mad," he whispered. "I will be surrendering to his madness. For years I have fought to keep him at bay, lest it consume me too."

For the first time, a slight look of bemusement crossed the goddess's face.

I know souls like no other, she said, *and souls cannot be mad. They are merely the essence of existence, while madness is of the flesh and the minds of the living. The madness was always in you, Roghald Einars-son. It is yours and yours alone.*

Roghald felt like he had been struck in the stomach. His own madness? That voice in his head that haunted him was from his own mind? He first heard it when they placed the troll's soul in him and the voice has been with him ever since. Was it possible that he had been tipped over the edge and driven mad when Gurmr and Grundr had tortured him in the ritual? He did still have nightmares about it from time to time.

"So, what do I do?" he pleaded with Hel.

Her lips parted in a horrific smile that showed perfect white teeth on one side and horrible, rotten stumps on the other. *Burn, Roghald. Burn.*

CHAPTER 33

ASH PULLED HIS CLOAK TIGHTER AROUND HIS SHOULders. Agash had led them through a broad crevice where two mountains met and they were now descending into a wide tunnel. The further down they went, the colder it got, and Ash could see small icicles forming on the tunnel's ceiling.

"I have always said that bearskins come very much handy in these situations." Torsten's voice billowed in the cold air as he happily patted the skin draped across his shoulders. "Not only do they make a warrior look fearsome, but are comfortable to sit on and most importantly, they keep the cold out."

"These situations, eh?" Yrsa was giving him a sidelong glance. "How often do you descend into a frost giant's fortress, pray tell?"

"I have fought with the Jomsvikings since before you filled your first nappy and could not possibly disclose all my adventures to you." The Berserker winked at Ash, who, despite the gravity of their situation, couldn't help grinning back.

"Perhaps your aging brain is making up stories for you?" Yrsa countered. "I guess it won't be long until we will have to put nappies on you."

Torsten stumbled on his next step, but recovered quickly.

"I'll be long dead before then," he muttered as Ash and Yrsa's laughter filled the tunnel.

"I would keep quiet if I were you." Agash snapped from the front. "The Troll King's guardians are unpredictable, and it would not be wise to test their patience." With that, she turned to keep walking.

"Fine," Yrsa said, loud enough for everyone to hear. "We'll just go back to watching Ash stare at your behind."

The dark elf's back stiffened for a second before she stomped off down the tunnel, this time followed by Torsten and Yrsa's laughter. Ash didn't laugh as he was too busy hiding his burning cheeks and looking anywhere but Agash's disappearing form.

They continued forward, down the forever descending path. There were many dark hollows and alcoves along the tunnel, and several times the path split into two. Agash continued onwards without ever hesitating when taking a turn as they weaved their way down and under the mountain. Yrsa's lightstone illuminated their path, casting long shadows in the icy underworld. Several times as they passed an alcove, Ash sensed movement in the corner of his eye. Thrym's guardians, watching them as they drew nearer to the hall of the Troll King. He knew they could not turn back now, they had to continue on no matter what.

Soon they came to a stop in front of a jagged wall of ice blocking their path. Agash reached into her belt and pulled out a large metallic coin. She held it up high above her head and toward the wall.

Ash had time to exhale three cloudy breaths into the freezing air before anything happened. With a crack, the part of the wall in the middle of the tunnel broke off and moved forward, towards them. Ash took an involuntary step backward when he saw that what had been a solid part of the ice wall a moment ago had arms, legs and a head.

It was a creature made of ice, faceless and featureless beyond its limbs and torso. Standing twice as tall as Torsten and just as wide again, it had long arms that reached almost all the way to the ground. It bent forwards only slightly to rest on them and as granules of ice fell glittering to the ground from its frozen shoulders, it lumbered to the side, revealing a hole in the wall.

"Hurry," Agash said to her companions, "The thing is about as intelligent as a beetle and can decide to fill the hole again at any moment." Stepping through the hole in the wall, she added: "Or crush us."

Ash and his friends exchanged brief glances before hurrying after the dark elf.

Beyond the ice wall, the surroundings changed. Perfectly fitted paving stones covered the floor, and the walls were smooth and straight. They stood in a room large enough to be called a town square, and Ash doubted he could throw a rock from where he was standing and reach the other end. Dozens of doors inside intricately carved frames lead off in every direction. A myriad of icicles made the walls and the distant ceiling glitter, while a fine layer of frost covered everything else. Braziers were placed along the wall, lighting the space with cold blue flames, which seemed to emit no heat at all.

The grandness of the immense hall was not enough to distract Ash from what stood before them and caused his friends to draw their weapons with an echoing hiss. Only a few steps ahead of them stood three rows of trolls, four abreast. These were unlike any trolls Ash had ever seen. Towering over him and his friends, they seemed bred for battle. Their broad shoulders and backs sprouted sharp icicles that merged seamlessly with their white, frosty skin. They wore no clothes, but their long, muscular arms held oversized swords and axes of a strange black metal with ease. At first, Ash thought the creatures were carved from ice, but as he watched the closest troll in front of him, it drew a slow breath and looked him up and down with curious, intelligent eyes.

"Frost thursrs," Agash breathed to her companions. "Thrym is not taking any chances with a Wolf of Odin inside his home. It is probably best if you sheath your weapons and not make any more sudden moves."

After a quick glance and nod at his friends, Ash sheathed his sword, and the others followed suit, however a reluctant muttering could be heard from Torsten.

On a wordless command, the trolls split down the middle and formed two rows of three on each side, revealing three creatures, one so wrapped in furs that they seemed almost spherical. The other two were tall and slim, and although they were of similar build, that was where the similarities ended. The one on the left was a woman, tall and slim, wearing only a thin, but luxurious, green robe, richly embroidered with gold thread. She was fair, with high cheekbones, and her long hair fell in ringlets over her shoulders. Her large almond-shaped eyes shone with intelligence. She was beautiful, yet it was obvious to Ash that she was not human.

The creature on the right seemed her complete opposite and Ash's eyes widened when he saw his second dark elf ever. He was a head taller than Agash, and he wore his long white hair tied back with the sides of his head shaved. Like her, he had smooth, black skin and piercing icy-blue eyes, but where she was graceful and almost feline, he exuded power and strength. He wore leathers of the same cut as Agash, however his were much more luxurious, with silver inlays and seams. Ash always felt that Agash had an air of danger and mystery about her, but all he sensed from this dark elf was malice and superiority. He, like the woman in the green robes, seemed unaffected by the cold that was seeping deeper and deeper into Ash's bones. Ash glanced sideways at Agash and saw that her eyes were looking everywhere except at the other dark elf.

The two taller creatures stopped when they drew level with the first row of frost thursrs, while the middle, fur-covered one waddled forward toward Ash and his friends. Two thickly mittened hands reached up to pull back a thick fur hood, revealing a few inches of a pink, bearded face.

"Greetings and welcome to the court of the great Thrym, Troll King and ruler of Jotunheim."

Ash's mouth fell open and at first he could only stare at the rosy-cheeked man that stood before him. Even with small icicles in his moustache and eyebrows, there was no doubt that he was human.

"I see that you have been taken aback by my eloquence and good looks." The man had a pleasant, deep voice and warm eyes. "My name is Frode Halfdansson, skald and poet by trade, and currently an advisor to King Thrym on all things Midgardian. His Majesty, in his infinite wisdom, wishes to put you at ease with a greeting from one of your own."

Meeting a human here, let alone a skald, had taken Ash by surprise. Everyone respected and prized skalds, who were warrior poets of Norse society. Any Jarl, and even the King in Hammershall, would rejoice at having one as a guest.

Introductions were made, and Ash had to bite his tongue to hold back the dozens of questions he had for the man. Frode pointed to a pile of furs on a bench and bid them to dress warmly, since the Troll King's chamber was even colder. Ash and Yrsa, who had already been shivering for some time, hurried over and selected large pelts that they wrapped around themselves. Torsten shook his finger when Yrsa offered a fur to him and patted his own bearskin.

"Dire wolf," Frode said, nodding at the furs. "Nothing better to keep the chill off your bones."

"There is no creature greater than the mighty bear," Torsten said in a lecturing tone, "and nothing warmer than its fur."

The dire wolf fur was soft, if a bit musty smelling, and weighed pleasantly on Ash's shoulders. Soon, he felt some warmth creeping back into his body. He noticed Agash hadn't taken a fur either and like the other dark elf, it seemed as if the cold didn't affect her.

"The King has been expecting you and will see you promptly. Please, follow me." Frode said, turning around to lead the way.

"I would like to talk with my friends first," Ash said. He wanted to discuss a strategy for their meeting with the Troll King.

Frode stiffened and turned around. Ash could see the panic in his eyes, and the man's otherwise warm smile looked more like a grimace now. "Erh," he started. "His Majesty, the great Thrym, has very, very little patience in these matters and any delay would benefit no one involved, including myself."

Ash saw the desperate pleading in the man's eyes, so he nodded, signalling the skald to lead the way. He caught sight of Yrsa who raised an eyebrow in warning. They better tread lightly from here on.

When Ash and his friends reached Frode's side, the man started walking again, a relieved smile on his lips. The thursrs surrounding them set off in unison on another wordless command, flanking them as they walked down the length of the hall. The other two that had accompanied Frode did not move to follow. When they passed them, Ash saw the dark elf turn his head towards Agash.

"Clanless," he hissed and spat at her feet. She ignored him and continued past, but Ash saw her jaw clench.

At the end of the hall, opposite to where they had entered, there was a broad archway leading into another long tunnel. It was wide enough that their escort could maintain their double rows on each side and still give them a wide berth. Detailed carvings depicting raging trolls in gruesome battles adorned every inch of the arched stone tunnel.

Frode saw Ash staring at the frosted wall and spoke. "The first Troll War," he offered. "This is where Thrym defeated the other chieftains and crowned himself king of Jotunheim."

Seeing how they seemed free to talk, Ash quickly changed the topic. "How did you end up here, Frode?"

The skald hesitated for a second, casting a glance sideways at the nearest thursr. Lowering his voice slightly, he replied, "I was recruited from Midgaard by one of Thrym's Shamans. In my home. In my sleep." A look of anguish came over him. "I have a family in

Midgard, who know nothing of me. The King brought me before him and offered me to serve for ten years. He promised I would be returned to Midgard with any amount of gold I could carry after." He paused and pursed his lips for a moment. "Had I declined, I would have been killed. I have four years left to serve in this frozen mountain, then I will go home, richer than most. Overall, I made the best choice I could at the time. My fellows back there are in the same boat, taken from their worlds and forced into servitude to act as Thrym's advisors in all things from their worlds. The feisty one is Grimnash from Svartalfheim, and the short one is Hamugi, a light elf from Alfheim."

The tunnel opened up into a large chamber, and Ash found himself in a familiar place. He took in the large pillars and walls covered in similar scenes he had just observed in the tunnel's carvings. The immense stone doors with enormous iron hinges dominated the space. Ash read the band of runes above the doors; Only Winter is Eternal. Last time he was here had been in a dream.

"You can only destroy the source tree by getting beyond those doors." Odin's words came back to Ash as the doors swung open with an ominous rumbling, revealing the frozen keep of the Troll King.

CHAPTER 34

ROGHALD OPENED HIS EYES. IT TOOK HIM A MOMENT TO realise that he was staring at the blood smeared ceiling of his coffin-shaped prison deep within Burrugandr's mountain. Had it been only a dream brought on by his madness? He raised his hand to his face and stared at the angry burns. Although he was looking at the short fingers of Birk, not his old, firm hand, the burns were definitely new. He remembered the lancinating pain when the acid had splashed him at the shore of Nastrond.

He let his hand fall to his chest. Hel had said the mad troll's spirit was actually his own, that the spirit had not been implanted into him when he received the soul. But the voice felt so... foreign to him. Mad or not, he knew he was destined for Nastrond. He rubbed the burns on the back of his hand. The pain from the acid had been tremendous. He couldn't imagine the horror of being bathed in the acid over and over for eternity. Actually, he could, and that was the problem.

The bargemaster had told him he'd have to go to Helheim because there was something he needed to understand. And now he understood. He knew what he had to do. Others had snared him into his fate, but there was still a way out. An opportunity which he would seize and use to rise far above those who had forced this fate upon him. Then he would wreak his revenge on them all; on Ash, Burrugandr, Grinbodr and all the people of Midgard. They would all feel his wrath.

The feeling of the mountain pressing down on him returned as his mind cleared, but now he raged against it, pushed back against it. Never again would he allow himself to be weak, to be overcome by fear. He had seen Nastrond and he would fear nothing else again.

The sensation of pressure disappeared, and the mad troll in his mind cackled. For the first time ever, Roghald laughed along with it, in a harmony of madness.

A long time passed. Roghald lay in the mountain scheming, and soon he had a plan. Days went by, maybe even weeks, he wasn't sure. A few times he woke from slumbers to discover someone had dropped food through the ventilation hole by his head. Stale bread mostly, but once there was also a lump of raw meat. He threw it to his feet and kicked it out of the other hole, his resolve made.

As days and weeks went by, Roghald watched Birk's plump body slowly wither until he could see his ribs. He knew this was the best he could achieve and set to work. When Grinbodr had trapped him, she had made his prison just large enough to accommodate his thursr body. She had made the ventilation holes small, so that he could only place his arm into them. She hadn't accounted for Roghald's human shape and that when sufficiently emaciated, it was about the size of his thursr arm.

He crawled over to the hole and stared into it. Soon after leaving his little chamber it turned up and out of sight. Roghald turned onto his back and, raising one arm above his head and placing the other flat along his body, he wormed into the narrow tunnel.

It was a tight fit. The stone passage wrapped closely around him, but inch by inch he wriggled in. When he reached the bend upwards, he got stuck, and panic threatened to overtake him once more. He summoned the rage within, and it again burned his fears away.

He took shallower breaths and pushed with his toes against the walls of the narrow shaft and pulled himself through the bend a hair's width at a time.

As he cleared the curve, he again found it easier to move and returned to inching along. The problem was that he now had to work his way straight up and needed to bend his knees and press them against the walls to prevent him from sliding down in between pushes. The stinging on his back, knees, and toes told him he had lost a lot of his skin, but the pain fuelled him onward and kept his mind sharp. Roghald did not know how long the shaft was, since there wasn't even room to tilt his head back to have a look. He didn't care if it was a mile. He just pushed on, fuelled by the rage and vengeful fantasies of the tortures he would unleash upon his enemies with every painful scrape against the rock.

After what must have been hours, Roghald thought he could see a little light filtering down from above his head and he redoubled his efforts. A short while after, he felt the scrape of the stone on the fingers of his raised arm give way to open air. A draft played across his hand and Roghald revelled in the sensation, wriggling like a madman the last bit.

Soon his head cleared the hole, and he looked around. There had been no way to peek out of the hole before getting out, since he had no option but to go in with one of his arms raised in order to fit into the tight enclosure. If someone out here had seen his arm emerging, they would have had plenty of time to sound the alarm.

His heart soared with joy when he looked out over purple treetops. The usually muted daylight that reached Jotunheim seemed almost blinding after his long confinement in the dark. He blinked against the light and once his eyes had adjusted, he confirmed he was indeed alone, somewhere on the side of Burrugandr's mountain. He wriggled through enough so that he could free his shoulder and drop his arm down and push. The pain in finally lowering his numb arm nearly made him scream out, but he clamped his mouth shut.

After resting for a few moments and allowing blood to circulate through the arm, the pain subsided. He could now squirm out enough to bend at the waist and pull his other arm free. His chest clear of the hole, he took his first deep breath in many hours and became giddy with the sensation.

Roghald changed back to his thursr shape. His whole body tingled as he observed his torn and scraped skin healing and knotting itself back together. He stretched and rolled his shoulders as the stiff and damaged muscles repaired themselves. Revelling in the sense of power, he flexed his muscular arms. Yes, this was his true form, not the weak human one.

Another quick look around confirmed that no one was watching him and Roghald started making his way down the mountainside towards the trees below. He cursed when he realised he was on the north side of the mountain, the opposite of where he wanted to go. It would take a long time to make his way around, increasing the risk of him being discovered.

Roghald didn't know how far the news of his fall from grace had travelled. Burrugandr's thursrs were aware and sure to be on the lookout for him, but had word gotten out any further? Did the watchers know? He wondered, eyeing the treetops with suspicion. No doubt I'll soon find out.

He jogged along the moss covered forest floor, making his way around the mountain while giving it a wide berth. He tried to look inconspicuous in doing so, like he was just going about his business.

A shrieking wail from above confirmed that the watchers indeed knew of his fate and banishment from the clan. The shriek was answered from a little further away by several others only to be drowned out by the roar of a thursr. He cursed the watcher and all its ancestors before setting off in a sprint.

Running fast, Roghald leaped over logs and boulders, but he soon heard something crashing through the forest behind him, drawing closer. As he darted along, more shrieks erupted from above, and he could hear new pursuers not only from behind him but also from his side and up ahead. As he ran to get around the mountain, he would collect every damn thursr posted along the way.

He caught a movement in the corner of his eye and ducked just in time to avoid the sweeping arm of a battle troll as it shot out from behind a tree trunk. He glanced behind and saw the thursr as it ran out behind him, missing him by only a step. It was a large, green-mottled beast with yellow tusks and an angry sneer. Its cruel little eyes homed in on him as it spun around to change its trajectory. Roghald recognised the thursr but had never spoken to it. There would be great honour in capturing or killing an enemy thursr, so Roghald knew he would find no quarter. Beyond the troll, he saw another that had been on his heels.

He dipped down as a massive spear shot past his head and slammed into a tree in front of him, splitting it with a loud crack. Roghald sped up even more, his lungs burning with the effort, his legs pumping, tearing up the moss beneath his feet. If they caught him, he wouldn't stand a chance. He might fight and defeat one battle troll, but against several, there was no hope.

CHAPTER 35

ASH STARED AT THE TROLL KING. THE TEMPERATURE had dropped further once they entered the hall, so much so that he gasped when he drew a breath and it felt like his lungs filled with icy needles. He knew that the frost giant was Ymir's first son, and therefore thousands of years old, but that did not prepare him for what he saw.

King Thrym was the largest creature Ash had ever seen. Despite being seated on a throne of ice, the King was still as tall as a three-storey building and just as broad. The hall was massive, larger than the first chamber they had entered, and still the king filled a good portion of it. A thin dusting of frost covered his skin, which had a mottled appearance of white and light blue. Thrym's head seemed to be carved from a block of stone, his features rough and dominated by a broad nose and a wide jaw, where icicles hung like a frozen beard. The Troll King's eyes were pitch black, like pools of ink, glaring with the contempt and loathing that Ash knew the jotunn felt for all things warm and living.

"Bow down when I do," Frode whispered out of the corner of his mouth.

The thursrs that had escorted them in drew to the sides of the hall, leaving the group exposed in the middle of the hall as they approached the throne. Ash noticed that they kept their weapons in their hands, however, and their eyes followed them closely as they stopped before the king.

"All hail King Thrym!" Frode bellowed and bent low at the waist.

Ash quickly followed his lead, but a sharp rattle of weapons from the thursrs made him turn his head.

Neither Torsten nor Yrsa had bowed. The shieldmaiden stood with her back straight and her arms crossed, while the Berserker was leaning lazily on his axe.

"ALL hail King Thrym," Frode bellowed, his voice now an octave higher.

Torsten began picking his nose. Ash straightened up and noticed how the skald had visibly paled. Yrsa raised her hand in the open-handed gesture of peace used by the Norse.

"Hail King Thrym, ruler of Jotunheim," she called in a steady voice.

"Hail," Torsten echoed, raising his hand as well.

"We do not bow," she continued, loud enough for the entire hall to hear. "Not to our jarls, king or even the gods." She paused for a second. "... and certainly not to a Jotnar, king or otherwise."

Frode's eyes were bulging out of their sockets, and Ash noticed that the man had stopped breathing. Ash could feel the oppressive tension in the hall for several long heartbeats. Then Thrym lifted a massive hand from the armrest of his throne and held it up in the same gesture Yrsa had made. Ash could feel the collective sigh of relief in the hall.

Feeling sheepish for having bowed, he squared his shoulders and raised his hand as well. "Hail King Thrym, ruler of Jotunheim." He tried to keep his voice as firm as Yrsa's. "I am Ash Jordrsson, of the Jomsvikings, Wolf of Odin. These are my companions–"

"I know who you are," The king's voice rolled into them like a wall of sound. It was deep, yet piercing, like two glaciers grinding against each other. "All of you."

With his words came an aura of hatred and scorn so strong that Ash imagined he could almost touch it.

"I would not tolerate your presence leeching the cold away from my hall, but we have a common enemy."

The king's eyes bored into Ash, who had never felt so small and insignificant as when he had the Troll King's full attention. He rested his hand on his father's hammer as it hung from his belt and drew some courage from it.

"Burrugandr has hunted you since you arrived in Jotunheim. He has schemed against me for centuries, seeking to usurp my throne from beneath me. I believe you know something of his workings."

"What is it you wish to know?" Ash asked.

Thrym's black eyes narrowed. "Everything."

Ash spoke at length with the Troll King. He told of the draugr attack on Midgard, of the corruption of Roghald, and of the source tree. He told the king about how he'd used Aesir fire to burn the tree in the cave, but yet the source tree remained, likely inside Burrugandr's lair. The king listened as he spoke, asking only a few questions, and when Ash had finished his tale, the king sat in silence, eyes staring into the distance. When he finally spoke, his voice was grave.

"Burrugandr has no interest in Midgard. No, it is more likely that he is on an errand of another. The power to grow such a source and to corrupt souls in order to build an army of undead lies only with a few, myself included. Burrugandr is also too cowardly to rise against Midgard and the Aesir in this way of his own design. His ambition has always been to claim the throne of Jotunheim, and no doubt this is what he has been promised for his servitude. The king paused to gather his thoughts before continuing.

"That a servant such as Burrugandr is being used suggests one of The Great Ones is the mastermind. Someone who is bound by the prophecy of Ragnarok and therefore is forbidden to act against it. I know of only one who would dare oppose me and promise my throne to another. My brother Surtr of Muspelheim, the Fire Giant destined to burn the world."

Ash remembered his vision of flying to Jotunheim and the large hand of lava reaching up from the world of fire.

"Fate has given you a terrible enemy, Ash of Midgard, one I doubt you will overcome."

"The enemy of my enemy is my friend," Ash started. "Those were the words of the dark elf when she asked me to meet with you. As such, King Thrym, surely you could offer us some aid?"

The Frost Giant sought Agash in the back of the hall and shot her a murderous look. "You are no friend of mine or Jotunheim, Ulfhed." Thrym's voice was full of disdain. "And even if you were, as king, I am bound by the prophecy and cannot help you directly without paying a great price. A price I am not willing to pay."

"Even to keep your throne?" Ash demanded. "If you are so much more powerful than Burrugandr, send your armies against him." He swept his arm out towards the thursrs lining the walls.

"If only it were that easy. Openly attacking Burrugandr with no other proof than the words of a Wolf of Odin would cast Jotunheim into another Troll War. No, you are on your own, Ulfhed."

Ash slumped his shoulders. What a waste of time it had been to come to the Troll King. Time he didn't have.

"What I can do, however, is to send a peaceful envoy to Burrugandr as his king and ruler. Perhaps I can instruct my thursrs to not pay close attention to who joins their ranks."

It took Ash a second to understand, but when he did, he smiled.

"Frode will see to all the preparations. He will also act as my envoy to Burrugandr."

At this, the skald visibly paled, and his mouth started moving in protest, but a glare from the Troll King silenced him.

"Now begone from here and know that if you ever return, it will be as an enemy. To me, you are an abomination, a half blood." Thrym's enormous face twisted into an expression of disgust before he averted his eyes from Ash.

Ash nodded. He knew that any parting words would be wasted on Thrym, so he simply turned around and marched out of the hall, followed by his friends and Frode. He noticed that the thursrs still took no chances with him and followed them in the same manner going out as they had gone in.

When the doors to the hall sealed shut behind them with a resounding boom, Ash took a deep breath in the relatively warmer room. The large wolf skin had kept him warm, even in the well below freezing temperature of the king's hall. He noticed Torsten was shivering next to him and had stuck his hands in his armpits to warm them a little.

"How's the great bear skin holding up?" he asked the Berserker, but the only response he received was a murderous stare. He heard Yrsa snicker behind them.

"How do you stand the cold?" Torsten asked Frode as they walked further through the tunnel.

The skald looked miserable when he answered. "I don't."

They entered the first hall, and the thursrs fell behind and lined up in front of the tunnel entrance, blocking any return to Thrym's hall.

"He doesn't take any chances, does he?" Torsten rumbled, looking back at the dozen battle trolls standing by with their weapons still in their hands.

"That's how he's held his power for a thousand years," Frode muttered. "I imagine we will set out shortly. The King wastes no time. If you so wish, to escape the cold, you may wait for us outside."

The group nodded eagerly, and Ash handed his wolf skin to Frode. The skald then turned to Yrsa and held his hand out.

She only stared at him.

"Erh, these are quite rare. Extremely so, as a matter of fact. Dire wolves are almost extinct, even on Jotunheim, and to track and hunt one down takes extraordinary.." His words trailed off as Yrsa's eyes narrowed and she pulled the fur tighter over her shoulders.

But Frode was a skald, and a warrior poet was always quick of thought and an excellent judge of any situation, so he hesitated for only a heartbeat before continuing with a resigned expression, "...but no doubt a parting gift would be in order, and let no one say that the Great Thrym is not a generous king."

Yrsa nodded once, and turning around, swept the fur through the air and around herself as she marched out of the opening in the wall of ice.

"Smart man," Torsten muttered as he followed her.

Ash shrugged at the skald and turned to leave as well. He noticed Agash remained standing next to Frode.

"Are you coming?" he asked the dark elf. For a moment, he thought he saw a sad expression flash across her face, but maybe he had just imagined it.

"No," she said. "I have fulfilled my obligation for which I was paid. Besides, I doubt I'd get a warm welcome inside Burrugandr's mountain."

"Oh," Ash said. "So, what now?"

"I'll lie low while this business blows over. Shame that Utgard is no more, otherwise I would have gone there and enjoyed Utgarda-Loki's peace for a while. Alas, there are other mountains and other chieftains that would pay well for my services," she said.

"Oh," Ash said. He didn't know what else to say. He had hoped that she would stay around for a while, that he would get to know her better. She fascinated him. She was fierce and violent, but he had sensed something vulnerable in her too, something that called to him. As frightening and dangerous as she was, he knew he was attracted to her from the very first time he had seen her, and he thought she might have felt the same. His heart sank when he realised that may not be the case.

"Well, farewell then," he said, sounding more bitter than he had intended to.

"Farewell, Ash." There it was again, that hint of sadness that disappeared as quickly as it had arrived. "Try not to get killed," she said as she turned around and walked away through one of the side doors.

Frode looked between Ash and the dark elf. "Did I miss something?"

Ash just shook his head. "No. You missed nothing."

Ash caught up with his friends in the long tunnel up to the surface.

"Isn't Agash coming?" Yrsa asked with a sidelong glance as he drew level with them.

"No," Ash said shortly, unable to keep the sullenness from his voice.

They walked in silence.

"Just as well," Torsten said after a while. "A love bite from those teeth and you'd risk bleeding out."

There was a clang as Yrsa drove the butt of her spear into the side of Torsten's helmet.

"What?" he said in an indignant voice, as he stopped to rub his head.

"Sometimes, your stupidity baffles even me," she hissed as she walked away.

"Oh, come on," the Berserker called after her and Ash. "That was funny!"

CHAPTER 36

ROGHALD TRIED TO GULP DOWN BIG LUNGFULS OF AIR AS he weaved his way through the trees and rocks. The closest thursr was only a step behind him and he felt the swish of its claws close to his neck, followed by a roar of anger. Roghald was tiring, his legs were burning, and his chest felt like it was about to explode.

Just when he was ready to give up, admit defeat and turn to fight his assailants in a hopeless battle, he caught a scent of sulphur on the wind. He looked up and tried to pinpoint where he was. Burrugandr's mountain was visible to his right through an opening in the canopy above. The familiar shape of the south side of the peak confirmed Roghald had made it around to the other side. Ecstatic, he feigned stepping right towards the mountain before shooting straight left. Angry roars followed the surprised grunts behind him. Hope, having given him renewed strength, fuelled his legs in a last, desperate push.

It wasn't long before the sulphurous stench of rotten eggs became almost unbearable and Roghald shot out of the forest and the hazy, barren valley spread out before him. He sprinted the last stretch, with thundering footfalls behind him, and when he reached the ledge overlooking the valley, he simply leaped from it.

But it was a long drop, and he slammed into the black rock below. Roghald tried to roll to break his fall, but his foot slipped when he landed and a loud crack was followed by a sharp pain in his ankle, as he came to a sprawling stop.

He pulled himself up to the sound of rocks and pebbles sliding down the bank behind him and he turned to see five thursrs scrambling down the ledge, all eyes on him. Roghald started limping away, hoping to lose them in the haze, but soon he heard laughter only a few steps behind him.

"Roghald!" a deep and raspy voice called out. He turned around and saw the five thursrs walking towards him in a line, victory written all over their ugly faces.

"I was going to give you a quick death," the green one with the tusks barked at him, "But for making me run and breathe this filth, I am going to make it slow. Very slow." The other thursrs laughed in response, offering him nothing except cruel grins. Some of them flexed their clawed hands in anticipation.

Roghald, out of breath and out of luck, had no snide remarks to offer in response. He backed away from them, but his broken ankle made it a painful and ineffective retreat. He needed a few more minutes to let it heal. The battle trolls seemed to enjoy his torment and simply walked forwards slowly, maintaining their distance.

"We are going to rip your arms off, Roghald, then let you heal and set you free." The green troll continued. "It will be great sport to chase you back to the mountain, armless, like a chicken." This was met with another round of laughter from the battle trolls.

The thursr took a few quick steps towards Roghald and raised his arms to grab him. The ankle had not yet healed, so he couldn't turn and run. He would have to fight the troll and all his friends. Roghald raised his arms in a gesture of hopeless defiance as he hobbled backwards. Then his back hit a wall of heat. He glanced down and saw that only one step behind him was a short drop into molten rock.

Gamir spoke a few coherent words for the first time ever: Burn, Roghald. Burn. His face split into a wild grin, and Roghald laughed, making the thursr hesitate for a second.

"What's so funny?"

"Life," Roghald said, then he stretched his arms out to his sides and fell backwards into the burning pool of lava.

The pain was beyond measure. Roghald felt his skin and flesh melt away in seconds. His world became one of blinding agony. As his eyes burned out of his skull, his world became black, but the pain continued as his flesh and bones dissolved. Instinctively, he fought the pain, pushing against the fire that burned his body, when a deep voice resounded in his mind. *"Embrace it. Embrace the flames. Let your humanity burn away."*

The gravity of the voice was tremendous, and it shook Roghald's very soul. He stopped fighting the pain and opened himself to it, letting the pain and fire fill his existence. Everything that was human in Roghald burned away, consumed by the blistering fire. What little joy, compassion, and empathy remained in his twisted soul was dissolved into the molten rock. However, his bitterness, cruelty, and hunger for vengeance remained because those were prized qualities in Muspelheim, as the soul belonging to one of its sons displaced the human soul and took its place.

Krakr looked down into the pool of molten rock where Roghald had disappeared. He had to shield his eyes from the intense heat that radiated from the fissure.

"What an idiot," he muttered, shaking his head. He turned around and walked back to the other thursrs. "We better tell Burrugandr that we threw him in during battle," he said. Krakr's head would be on a stake if he admitted to the chieftain that Roghald had evaded them by jumping in himself. "We all better tell the same story," he said, raising a warning finger, "Agreed?"

But the thursrs didn't answer him. He realised they were all staring over his shoulder, their mouths open. He turned around to see a creature standing at the edge of the crevice. It seemed to be made entirely of molten stone, with lava dripping off it into a pool at its feet. Krakr squinted in the haze and saw that it was Roghald.

"W-what-" was all he uttered before Roghald launched forward and grabbed him by the throat. It took only a couple of seconds for Roghald's hand to burn through his neck and for Krakr's head to hit the black ground and roll away. The body stood still for a moment before realising that it was dead and falling into a heap as it turned to stone. The other four thursrs had paled and stood as if frozen on the spot. Roghald smiled at them.

"Run," he said.

This broke the spell, and they all turned and fled. They didn't even make it out of the valley.

CHAPTER 37

Ash had once again donned the trollhelm. He received some curious looks from the frost thursrs when he joined their ranks. A joyous Frode had slapped him on the back when he realised who it was. The skald was in a cheerful mood since he'd been placed in charge of the delegation to Burrugandr.

"First time out of that frozen mountain in years," he told Ash, with his eyes closed, and his face raised towards the gloomy light of the Jotunheimian sky. "Fantastic!"

The skald had shed the many layers of fur and wore a well spun blue robe and a leather cap. He had thick leather bracers around his wrists and had revealed a luxurious brown beard, rivalling even Torsten's.

"Yeah, fantastic," The Berserker's voice cut in. Torsten looked miserable, standing next to them, but this was because his hands were bound in front of him. As were Yrsa's.

"I'm sorry, Torsten, but I can't think of any other way of getting you inside the mountain," Ash said. "If Roghald is there, he will easily recognise you and all the plans will be for nothing. Besides, the knots are loose, and you could free your hands in a heartbeat if you had to. And your weapons are on the back of this thursr," Ash pointed to the closest troll, who turned to show Torsten's axe and Yrsa's spear where they hung, "So you can grab them in a flash."

Torsten still looked indignant and harrumphed.

"The plan is what it is," Ash told his friend.

"It's goblin shit, is what it is," the Berserker muttered. "Why must we be tied up already? It's a long way to Burrugandr's mountain. And I don't trust these trolls, especially not with my axe. My one way of defending myself against them, should they turn against us."

At this, the frost thursr turned its head and glared at Torsten. Cold smoke ran off the troll upon being struck by the pale sunlight, like the trickling of water, but there were no signs that being out in the relative warmth bothered the creature.

"Yeah, I'm talking about you, snowflake," he spat at the frost troll and stared at it until it looked away.

"Look, I can't do this without you two," Ash told his friends. "This is the only way we could think of."

"Don't worry about him," Yrsa said. "The plan is good; we go in, you sneak away and find the source tree and destroy it somehow. Then we try to leave with the delegation, but failing that, we fight our way out before finding some way to get back home. Easy."

"Yeah," Torsten said. "What could possibly go wrong?"

This was met by silence from everyone until Frode broke it by slapping his hands together.

"Well," the skald said. "Let's set out then, shall we?"

Two dozen frost thursrs stood in two rows in front of them. They held a motley assortment of weaponry; spears, swords, and axes. The only armament they all held in common was a large rectangular shield, made of dim ice. Behind them stood a group of vaettrs, in a haphazard arrangement, loaded high with various packs, parcels and implements.

Frode signalled to a particularly large thursr at the front of the procession. The pale ice troll swung a great horn from his back and, putting it to his mouth, he blasted two piercing notes. All the trolls fell in line and a moment later, when a third note rang out from the front, the procession set out.

Ash and Frode walked behind the battle trolls, and in front of the vaettrs. Torsten and Yrsa walked just in front of the last pair of thursrs. This way, they could still talk to Ash and Frode while upholding the illusion of being captives.

"That really is quite a remarkable disguise," Frode told Ash. "I have seen more trolls than most people from Midgard and I would never have guessed."

"Well, it sounds like you have been here long enough," Ash replied. "Where in Midgard are you from?"

Frode sighed longingly, and his eyes became distant. "I travelled around a lot in my youth, but in my last few years on Midgard, I had more or less settled in the town surrounding Hammershall. Have you been? No? Well, the southern part of the kingdom is beautiful, and the marketplace outside the king's keep is a vibrant, exciting place, with people and curious items from all over Midgard. And it is not without its rewards to be a skald in proximity to the king, let me tell you. King Ulfgar drinks only the finest mead, and he is more than generous with it, as well as his silver, to a skald who reads poetry to him at a feast."

Ash hadn't missed the yearning in Frode's voice as he spoke. The skald seemed thoughtful for a moment, then he cleared his throat and spoke in a deep, clear voice.

"In a frozen peak,
Far from friends and cheer,
A skald's heart will bleed.

For his world is bleak,
And he sheds a tear,
Dreaming of his king's mead."

After his poem, Frode fell silent and spoke no more that day, but walked in gloom with his shoulders slumped. Ash felt sorry for the man. Yes, the Troll King would reward him in gold for his service, but at what cost? Ash had been in Jotunheim for a much shorter time than the skald, and his longing for his home world was almost a physical ache. Frode had been here for seven long years. Ash couldn't even imagine how lonely the man must feel.

They travelled slowly through the landscape, walking the shortest route along prominent ridges, not worrying about concealment. After all, Ash thought, what could the Troll King's forces have to fear?

Ash often saw creatures scurrying away from their path, or trolls staring at them from behind boulders as they passed. For a while, dark birds circled them from above. Ash wondered if they were regular birds or the vildvittras he had encountered on his arrival to Jotunheim, but they were too high up to tell. They would camp out under the stars, sleeping safely behind a perimeter of watchful battle trolls. Ash and his friends would wake feeling well-rested in the mornings.

On the sixth night of travel, Frode cleared his throat and spoke. "We will arrive at Burrugandr's mountain tomorrow, the thursrs tell me." He was speaking around mouthfuls of a hearty stew he had prepared for the group. The skald had surprised everyone by revealing himself to be an accomplished cook and Ash was savouring the rich and flavoursome meal of tubers, roots and some sort of meat. Frode told him that a warm meal was the highlight of his day inside the frozen mountain, and so he always kept a bag of spices and dried herbs on his person.

"When we arrive," he continued, "Burrugandr will leave us to wait for a while. Long enough to show that he doesn't fear the Troll King, but not long enough to show insubordination. If you have the powers that you claim," he was looking at Ash, "this will be your opportunity."

Ash nodded. The plan was that Ash would disappear into the stone at his first opportunity and search for the source tree.

"I still don't like it," Torsten growled. "Anything could happen to you and we would be none the wiser. Besides, the tree is most likely well guarded."

"Well," Frode interjected. "Burrugandr is also quite arrogant. He has secured and warded his mountain well. I doubt that even a Stonesmith could enter the mountain undetected from the outside, nor could anyone approach unseen. However, once inside, I don't think there will be a lot of spells or watchful eyes as Burrugandr believes himself safe within it."

Then the skald's face turned grave.

"Beware the chieftain's Shaman, however," he warned. "Grinbodr is as cruel as she is cunning and she sees more than most. Her magic is powerful, and she too is a Stonesmith of some renown."

Ash paused with the spoon halfway to his mouth. Another Stonesmith? He felt a pang in his stomach when he realised his one advantage was matched by his foes.

"This changes things," Yrsa said, staring at the skald with disdain. "Why did you not tell us before?"

Frode shrugged. "Shaman, Stonesmith," he said dismissively between mouthfuls. "What's the difference?"

Yrsa took a deep breath and Ash recognised the early warning sign of an upcoming sharp tirade and quickly cut her off before an argument broke out.

"It doesn't matter," he said. "It wouldn't change the plan anyway, I just have to be more careful."

Yrsa exhaled and remained silent, but she showed her displeasure with eyes like knives trained on Frode. The skald, having lived under the constant threat of the Troll King for so many years, made a grimace and stuck his tongue out at her. However, when rage flashed across Yrsa's face and her hand fell to her seax, Frode coughed and looked down, turning his full attention back to his food.

They finished their meal and spread out their blankets for the night. As Ash laid down, resting his head on his knapsack, he couldn't help but worry about the skald's words. He had said she was a Stonesmith of some renown, while I am only a Journeyman. How can I possibly defeat her? And she is a Shaman as well.

He ran his hand over the bracelet on his wrist. Without it, he would have a weapon she did not, levelling the field somewhat. It had to be removed voluntarily by the person who placed it, his father had said. That person turned out to be Roghald, and there were no circumstances under which he could see his old stable-master, the person in all the worlds that hated him most, extending him that kindness. Have I lost my Ulfhednar powers forever?

His worries chased him around for hours and gave him no peace, twisting and turning on his blanket. Eventually, he felt a firm hand on his shoulder. He opened his eyes to see Yrsa sitting down next to him. The shieldmaiden gave him a sad smile, and he was just about to apologise for keeping her up when she put her finger to her lips.

She stroked his hair gently in slow, soft movements, and Ash closed his eyes. Something about the way she soothed him seemed familiar, and he remembered the old adage that 'A shieldmaiden's child belongs to all shieldmaidens'. Even though Ash was now a grown man, he surrendered to her motherly touch, and as a warmth spread through his body and calm through his mind, he fell asleep.

He opened his eyes. He was standing in a flowery green field drenched in sunshine. It was a beautiful summer's day, and he looked up at the blue sky of Midgard. His heart filled with joy at the sight, and he took a deep breath of the fresh air. The smell of the surrounding flowers was almost intoxicating.

A raven cawed by his side, and he turned to see Odin in his tattered grey robes standing next to him. The tall god with his long, grey beard had a serious expression on his face and his one, icy blue eye stared so deeply into Ash that he felt he was looking into his soul.

"You have changed since we last spoke," Odin said.

"A lot has happened since then."

"You met your father," the god continued, a hint of surprise in his voice.

Ash nodded, but offered no words on the subject. He felt slightly torn between his loyalty to Odin and the gods as an Ulfhed, and his father's lineage as the troll and Stonesmith that he also was.

"Not all trolls are our enemies, but those who are, are," Odin said, as if he had read his mind. "Some trolls want the Aesir and Midgard no harm, but the forces of chaos that seek our demise are all trolls. Surtr in Muspelheim seeks to destroy us, but do not think that King Thrym wouldn't do the same, given the opportunity. Your father was different, but I think his love for your mother had a lot to do with that. The scars between the trolls and the Aesir run too deep, Ash. As foretold, we will ultimately destroy each other at Ragnarok. This is all well and as it should be. The world will be born anew from the ashes of the final battle and a kingdom of eternal peace will emerge. However, in this new world, there will be no trolls. Only two humans will survive Ragnarok and they will repopulate the worlds. Humankind will live on, and trolls will be gone forever. Some trolls think they can change the prophecy and destroy humanity instead."

"Can they?" Ash asked.

Odin shrugged. "Ragnarok is yet far off. If too few warriors have gathered in Valhalla by then, and trolls have populated the worlds, the battle will be uneven. Maybe they will win without destroying the world. This is why the gods, and the troll equivalents, cannot act directly against each other. Too many things that have been foretold are yet to occur, and the Norns, who determine the fate of even the gods, might cut our webs short and bring Ragnarok upon us too soon. The outcome would be too uncertain for us or the trolls to want to see that happen. It is possible that all the worlds could be permanently destroyed, without a new world to rise from the ashes. This is why we have to act through champions. The Wolves of Odin have always been the champions of the Aesir.

Your mother was the champion before you. You see, if a human is the champion, then it is not the gods who are challenging the trolls, is it? It is for the same reason that the champion of the trolls is-"

"Roghald," Ash cut in. "Roghald is their champion." It only dawned on Ash as he said it.

Odin nodded, a thin smile on his lips. Ash could feel nothing but pity for his old stable master. He knew the man was a petty, right bastard, but not to such a degree that he would turn against and destroy all of humanity. Along the way, someone must have corrupted the man somehow, using magic or trickery.

"Equally important to destroying the source is destroying the champion," Odin told him. "Like you, he grows more powerful with time. He has now made a sacrifice, the greatest one, and has been rewarded for it. He will not be easy to vanquish."

Ash had known for a while that he had to kill Roghald, if only just to cease the relentless attacks by the old stable master; but now the act would serve the higher purpose of protecting Midgard.

The sunlight faded and Ash turned to see dark clouds roll in. Looking around him, the landscape had changed, and he was now looking out over the mountaintops and purple forests of Jotunheim. The earth rumbled beneath his feet and a round mound sprung up in front of him and the god. From it sprouted a tree, and as it reached up and widened, Ash saw that its bark was dark and glistening with reptilian scales. Large, bulbous black fruits hung down from its twisted branches, and where the fruit had split, dark sap leaked out, burning the ground it splattered on. It was the source tree.

A movement behind the tree made him reach for the sword at his waist. The head of a gigantic wolf appeared from behind the sickening trunk. To call it a wolf, Ash realised, was an understatement. The creature was twisted and grim, with black fur and eyes that glowed like fire. Teeth like swords crowded its enormous mouth, and its shoulders were as broad as a wagon.

The wolf stepped around the tree and its massive paws clawed the earth where it trod. It stared at Ash, hunger in its eyes, and leapt forwards. Ash drew his sword and crouched to meet the creature's attack, but the wolf was yanked back mid leap and fell hard to the ground, before getting back up immediately. His heart racing, Ash straightened to see that a thin silver chain, looped around the creature's neck, anchored it to the tree. The beast strained against its bond, eyes fixed on Ash, but the chain held.

"I-Is that...?" Ash left the question hanging.

"Fenrir, the wolf." Odin said calmly.

Ash remembered the story of Fenrir from the sagas. The creature, of troll blood, had been raised by the gods from a cub. But as the years passed, the wolf had grown larger and more vicious, forcing the gods to restrain it. Under the guise of testing the wolf's strength, they attempted to chain the wolf with various ropes and chains. The gods tried magical ones, inscribed with powerful runes and forged by the best smiths, but Fenrir broke his shackles with ease each time, mocking the gods' folly. So, the Aesir tasked the great dwarven smith Sindri to craft an unbreakable chain. Sindri laboured and enchanted in his smithy for seven days and seven nights before bringing the fetter Gleipnir to Asgard. It was thin and silken, seemingly more like a ribbon than a chain, but when Sindri challenged the gods to break it apart, even Thor, with all his strength, could not do it.

The gods brought the chain to Fenrir, but when the wolf saw it, he became suspicious. As it was so thin and smooth, he feared trickery. Unless one of the gods placed their hand in his mouth, he refused to let the chain be placed around his neck. That way, he could make sure there was no foul play. None of the Aesirs were willing to sacrifice their hand to fetter the beast, until Tyr, the god of war, famed for his bravery, strode forwards and without a word placed his hand in the massive wolf's maw.

Thus placated, Fenrir allowed the gods to place Gleipnir around his neck and they bound it to the roots of a mountain. Fenrir pulled and strained against the binding, but try as he might, he could not tear it. Reluctantly admitting defeat, the wolf demanded to be released, but none answered his call. As the wolf looked into Tyr's eyes, he saw the truth and, without further delay, bit the god's hand off. Fenrir was thus forever chained, where he will remain until Ragnarok, when he will break free and is prophesied to devour Odin himself in the last battle.

Ash stared at the snarling beast who had not taken its eyes off him for a moment.

"Fenrir isn't really chained to the source tree, is he?" Ash's voice was just above a whisper.

Odin chuckled. "No. No, he isn't."

"Is this another riddle?"

The god looked at Ash and smiled. "Isn't everything?" Then the Odin faded away and vanished, leaving Ash to stare at the wolf alone.

"Damn the gods and their riddles," he muttered.

CHAPTER 38

Roghald stood on the bank of the valley, gazing at Burrugandr's mountain. As he cooled in the breeze, Roghald could hear little pings and cracks. He looked down on his new body. He had maintained his thursr shape and features, but his usual mottled green skin was now a coal-black, hardened crust. Moving his limbs, Roghald saw cracks appear at every joint, revealing a bright fiery glow beneath. He felt stronger and more powerful than ever. As he revelled in the sensation, he realised that, for the first time in a long while, all was quiet.

The mad, blabbering voice in his head was gone, burned away with his human soul.

Roghald closed his eyes and savoured the silence of being alone in his mind at last. Only one thing gave him some cause for concern as he explored his changed body and mind; his memories seemed... vague. He remembered everything, but in a very detached sort of way, like he had had the story of his life told to him, and had not experienced it himself. But he felt like his old self too, the person he had always been.

He thought of Ash and the familiar loathing filled him again. There was a fire in his chest, as always, but this time it took a physical shape. Flames burst from the cracks in his arms and shoulders and he looked down to see the ground blacken beneath him.

Roghald laughed as his mind flooded with memories that felt like his own, but were not. He saw the great fire giant Surtr sitting on his throne, his flaming sword in his lap. He saw himself engaged in battles with trolls and beasts for centuries, with fire his foremost weapon. Images of long-lost battlefields, where Surtr's fire reigned victorious as Roghald destroyed all who would dare to oppose the hordes of fire thursrs. He willed the flames to gather in his hand and watched as they swirled around, tighter and faster, until a glowing orb filled his palm.

He drew his arm back and threw the ball at the forest in front of him. Striking a tree, it burst into an explosion of fire, and splattered the surrounding trees, setting them ablaze as well. Roghald roared with malice and set off in a sprint towards Burrugandr's mountain. Underneath his footfalls, the moss and grass smouldered, leaving scorched footprints. He knew what he had to do, his instructions were as clear as the flames in his heart.

Roghald reached the opening to the mountain and found the doors sealed. The alarm had been sounded and Burrugandr had not hesitated to seal off his mountain. He snickered and placed his hands on the grey doors. Old, petrified timber like this might not burn in a conventional fire, but Roghald's flames were much hotter. He concentrated. Blinding flames burst outwards from around his hands, the wood charring and glowing as the fire ate away at it. Soon both doors were ablaze and Roghald could hear calls and shouts from behind them.

The heat and fire slowly spread through the ancient wood, and when a shot of flame burst through to the other side, he was rewarded with the sound of someone yelping in pain. Roghald aimed a hard kick at the smouldering timber, and the bottom quarter of the left door broke off in a shower of embers.

The gloom beyond echoed with shouts and grunts, and Roghald narrowly ducked a broad-bladed spear that someone thrust at his head through the opening. He took a step back and, holding his hands in front of his chest, he let the flames build between them. Within seconds, a fiery ball the size of his head was roaring in front of him, but he closed his eyes and pushed harder at the flames, willing them to grow hotter and hotter. He felt something slam into his thigh, but ignored it, his mind filled with Surtr's fire, until the ball was glowing white. When the roaring mass was so hot that it became difficult to contain it in his now shaking hands, Roghald opened his eyes.

With both hands, he slung the fiery ball through the opening. The blast threw him backwards, and he relished in the wall of flame that washed over him. He landed hard on his back and came to a sliding stop dozens of paces from where he had been standing. Raising his head, he looked around at the devastation. The explosion blew the doors clear off the opening, leaving the surrounding area scorched black and a large crack in the stone to one side. Black smoke billowed out of the entrance and rose in a great plume toward the grey sky. Beside a few crackles emanating from spot fires, it was eerily quiet.

Roghald pulled himself up, which was difficult since he had a spear lodged in his thigh. He pulled it out with one hand and let it fall to the ground. His tarred flesh knotted back together, and Roghald realised that he had healed even faster than before. He walked to the opening and saw only scorched stone beyond. A dozen blackened rock mounds lay as evidence of where the guards and thursrs had fallen once consumed by the flames. He hoped it had been agonising for them.

With no one else to oppose him, he set off through the wide tunnel, heading straight for Burrugandr's hall. He followed the familiar path, deeper and deeper into the mountain, which now seemed deserted. He saw no one and could only hear the fall of his feet echoing inside the network of tunnels. They are wise to hide, he thought. No one can stand against me.

He arrived at the doors to Burrugandr's hall. The dried elven head on the doors was grimacing at him as it always had. With a sense of humour, Roghald placed his finger on its forehead and spoke "Burrugandr." The eyes of the elf glowed and Roghald couldn't help laughing out loud when the doors began swinging inwards. Burrugandr is a fool, he mused as he pushed in when the doors were wide enough to let him pass. He started building flames in both hands, ready to rain death on the jotunn at first sight.

The hall was empty. Burrugandr's massive throne sat unoccupied, and the entire space was cast in darkness. The flickering blue torches he was expecting to see along the walls were not lit, and the only light was the glow from the fire in Roghald's hands, but this was enough for his dark vision to allow him to see the entire hall. He eyed the great cavern with suspicion, holding the flames at the ready to be used at the first sign of movement. His eyes ran over the tattered banners and rusty weapons of war that crowded the walls, but all was still.

He stood for a long moment, scanning the hall from the entrance, but when nothing appeared, he moved inside. Roghald crept forward with great care, gingerly placing one foot in front of the other, trying to look everywhere at once. Behind the throne, the source tree reached its boughs towards the distant ceiling, casting shadows on the rough wall behind it. After making a full lap of the hall and revealing no one, he let the flames in his hands die and darkness filled the room again. By the soft light of a few luminescent mushrooms along the walls, he walked up to Burrugandr's throne.

Has he really fled? Roghald felt disappointed, having looked forward to extracting his revenge on the jotunn and his inner circle, in particular Grinbodr. He had imagined searing the flesh off her bones one limb at a time, making her suffer as long as possible.

When a blinding light burst from all the walls in the hall, he instinctively raised his arms to shield his eyes. A second later, he felt something painfully clamp around his wrists. With a roar, he threw himself forwards, clawed hands outstretched, but with only air in front of him, Roghald fell to the ground with a grunt. He stumbled to his feet, blinking to get his vision back.

"Your arrogance will be your death," Grinbodr's voice echoed through the hall.

As his eyes adjusted, he saw the Shaman standing only a few paces in front of him, leaning on her staff, a grin on her face. The torches along the walls were now all lit, casting their usual cold blue light across the hall. A weight around his wrists and a clinking sound made him look down to see manacles of some dark metal linking his wrists together. They were locked tight, pressing into his skin, with about a foot of chain between them.

Rage filled him and he summoned the flames, ready to burn Grinbodr to a crisp, but his hands remained black and cold as no fire sprung up between his fingers. An intricate band of red runes had appeared on the shackles and glowed with a flickering light, as if holding his fire within the runes. He concentrated, willing the flames to appear with all his might, pushing at the binds to melt them, but the runes only glowed stronger and the manacles remained cool.

"We expected the fire giant to betray us and knew it was only a matter of time, so we took precautions," said Grinbodr. "I am surprised at the means Surtr has chosen, and it appears that I gave him more credit than he deserved."

She tapped her foot and Roghald sunk down to his waist into the stone floor. He thrashed and raved, tearing at the manacles, but they held firm and the stone enveloping his legs remained solid.

"Save your strength," Burrugandr's deep voice filled the entire hall. "You'll need it. I intend to make your suffering legendary in all of Jotunheim."

There was a shimmer in the air and the previously empty throne was now filled with Burrugandr's bulk. The massive giant had its eyes locked on Roghald in an expression of barely concealed anger. Leaning against the side of the throne stood the spindly Blodheid, her arms crossed and a flat expression on her face. Her pale skin looked ghostly in the lambent light of the torches, but even the dim light could not dampen the deep red of the swell of hair spilling down her shoulders.

Roghald cursed himself. He should have filled the hall with flames as soon as he entered. He should have expected trickery and illusions from the jotunn. The troll chieftain slapped a meaty hand on the armrest of his throne, sending his thick gold bracelets clanging.

"We have what we want from Surtr." The giant spat a gob to the side after uttering the fire giant's name, and his eyes grew distant. "We have the source tree and the magic to wield it. Once the shoot regrows to Midgard, I will turn all of humankind to draugr. With such an army at my disposal, I will start the Troll Wars again and conquer Jotunheim. With the pesky Utgarda-Loki already ground to dust by Thunder-Thor, only Thrym can stand against me now. Once he is cast from his throne, I, Burrugandr, will be Troll King and rule forever!"

The jotunn smiled from ear to ear and leaned back on his throne. "Midgard will be but a wasteland, Jotunheim will be mine, and Surtr can only watch with impotent envy from his fiery throne."

Grinbodr shrieked in delight at the jotunn's words. Roghald couldn't help but notice that when her father was mentioned, Blodheid frowned and glared at the chieftain.

"You, my ungrateful and deceptive thursr, will be sent back to Muspelheim in shards and pieces," Burrugandr said as his gaze fell back on Roghald. "Except your head," he added thoughtfully. "I think it is time for a new doorknob."

Roghald swore and cursed as both the trolls laughed at him. Grinbodr tapped her staff three times on the stone floor. Even though the taps were only light, they resounded in sharp booms. The doors opened and a large thursr lumbered in. Without a word, the troll walked up to Roghald and uncoiled a long whip that fell in ringlets on the ground. Roghald didn't miss the unmistakable clicks of sharp metal tips hitting the floor.

When the whipping started, Roghald desperately tried to summon the fire, but he was again only rewarded with glowing runes on the manacles.

CHAPTER 39

Ash nudged Frode in the ribs. "There is a small troll staring at us from up in that tree," he whispered to the skald.

Frode glanced up into the canopy before replying. "Burrugandr's watchers. They keep guard throughout this entire forest," Frode whispered back. It is almost impossible to approach his mountain unseen."

The troll in the tree whistled three sharp notes that were taken up by others closer to the mountain.

"They don't seem too alarmed by our arrival," Ash pointed out.

"Burrugandr must already know that we are approaching, since that was not a distress call. He has eyes all over Jotunheim and his arm is far-reaching. He most likely knew we were coming almost as soon as we set out."

No sooner had he spoken than the trees that encroached the well-trodden path they were on opened up to febrile activity. A large group of vaettr were scurrying around, removing debris and slabs of charred timber scattered in front of a large, blackened square opening at the base of the mountain. The opening itself was guarded by a dozen thursrs, all heavily armed. Ash sensed the tension among the frost thursrs as they came to a halt. Although they did not draw their weapons, their hands were resting on them.

The smaller trolls scurried out of the way, clearing the field between the battle trolls, and a strained silence settled around them. Ash caught a movement out of the corner of his eye and noticed several big trolls peering out from behind the trees off to their side. They were effectively flanked.

The leading frost thursr raised his fist into the air and bellowed. "Hail Burrugandr, Chieftain of the Wasteland Mountains! King Thrym, Ruler of Jotunheim, sends his regards!"

Some of the tension left the guardians in front of them, and an old, gangly troll stepped out of the opening. Long, tangled white hair covered her face, and she wore dirty, red robes with frayed ends that dragged behind her. She also carried a tattered satchel over one shoulder. The thursrs parted to let her pass and although she used a gnarled staff to lean on, she had a vigour in her step that didn't match her apparent age. Ash glimpsed olive-green skin as she raised her head to peer out at the delegation from behind her hair.

"Grinbodr," Frode whispered so low that Ash barely heard him. Ash straightened and looked with concern at the Shaman and Stonesmith. She seemed ancient, but that only meant that she had had a long time practicing her arts. He really hoped that he wouldn't have to face off with her.

"Hail King Thrym, Ruler of Jotunheim," she spoke in a level voice. "What brings you to Burrugandr's doorstep?"

Frode squared his shoulders and stepped out in the open.

"My name is Frode Halfdansson," Although he was small compared to the trolls, his voice carried well across the clearing. "I have been sent as an envoy by King Thrym, in the spirit of friendship, to discuss some slight matters with his chieftain, Burrugandr." Ash didn't miss the connotation Frode placed on the words 'his chieftain.'

"I know who you are, Frode Halfdansson," Grinbodr replied as she narrowed her eyes. "One can only wonder why King Thrym would send his only Midgardian advisor."

"I begged the great Thrym to select me for this envoy as the cold of his fortress has seeped into my bones." Frode replied, but Grinbodr seemed unconvinced.

She scrutinised the group behind Frode, and Ash was relieved when her eyes swept past him after only a cursory glance. Her eyes widened when they fell on Torsten and Yrsa.

"You have humans in your company?" There was a pleasantly surprised tone in her voice.

"We caught them trespassing on the outskirts of King Thrym's personal domain," Frode said in a well-rehearsed voice, "and we will bring them back and deal with them upon our return."

Grinbodr's eyes remained locked on Ash's friends and she slowly moved forwards. When almost standing on top of Frode, she stopped and squinted down at him.

"They don't have any troll blood in them," she muttered in disappointment.

"Erh, no," Frode said in feigned confusion. "That's what makes them human."

Grinbodr gave Frode a murderous glare. Ash glimpsed two cruel eyes, and a shiver went down his spine.

"We are not prepared for visitors," she told the Skald. "You may camp out here until we are better prepared."

"You deny shelter from Thunder-Thor to the envoy of your king?" Frode's voice was full of indignation.

Grinbodr stared at him, but to Frode's credit, his eyes met hers calmly and didn't flinch once. The Shaman grimaced and the following words seemed to cause her physical pain as she uttered them, "Of course. I apologise. You may enter with your thursrs but the vaettrs must stay outside."

Frode must have been willing to concede her this minor victory, because he nodded. "This is acceptable."

"Give us a moment to prepare," she muttered before spinning around and stomping off, disappearing into the mountain.

Frode let out a long breath. "I really hope you know what you are doing," he told Ash.

So do I, Ash thought to himself.

They did not have to wait long until a tall, gangly and pale troll emerged from the mountain. An icy lump settled inside Ash's stomach when he saw the unmistakable long, red hair and recognised the Shaman who had captured him and his friends. She approached their group and as soon as she laid eyes on Torsten and Yrsa she froze on the spot, and her mouth fell open. Ash glanced at Torsten who was already loosening his bonds to prepare for the fight. Her eyes darted across their group several times before settling back on Torsten and Yrsa. A long moment passed as she stood silently staring at them. Then she turned to Frode.

"The humans may not enter," she told him in a curt voice.

"They are my prisoners and, as you well know, are very valuable and can fetch a very good price. They will go where I go," he replied, crossing his arms.

"Our thursrs will guard them for you with their lives,"

"Pfft," he replied. "The day I set another to watch my wealth is the day I lose all of it."

She looked at him with a curious expression for a moment. "Come this way. Bring your wealth." Her voice revealed nothing of the conclusion she had come to in her mind. Without waiting to see if they would follow, she turned around and walked back to the opening.

Frode yelled out a few instructions to the vaettrs in the back, before hurrying after Blodheid, followed closely by Ash, his friends and the frost thursrs. Burrugandr's guards parted as they approached and let them pass. They entered the dark opening. Blodheid led them through a network of broad, well carved tunnels. The air inside was cool and damp as she took them deeper and deeper into the mountain.

When they entered a large cavern, supported by broad pillars placed unevenly across the floor, Blodheid stopped.

"You may wait here. Burrugandr will send for you when he is ready," she said. With a final strange look at Yrsa and Torsten, she walked back out the way they had come.

"We might as well settle in and have something to eat," Frode said, swinging his knapsack off his shoulder.

"How long will it be?" Ash asked him.

Frode shrugged. "A day, maybe two, depending on how far Burrugandr wants to push the insult."

Torsten groaned behind them. They unfolded their blankets in a corner whilst the frost thursrs spread out across the cavern in groups of three or four.

After a simple meal of bread and honey washed down with water, and accompanied by Torsten's muttered complaints, they all laid down to get some rest. They'd been walking for days and all felt the effects. Ash sat leaning against the cold rock wall and decided it was time. After a quick glance to ensure no one was watching him, he sunk backwards into the wall.

The cold stone closing around him felt like diving into a fresh lake. He had come to enjoy the sensation of the stone flowing around him, and he hung suspended for a moment, calming his mind. Then he concentrated, pushing his Stonesight to its limits as it painted a complex network of tunnels and caverns that made up the underground settlement.

Ash realised the enormity of it and understood that he could never explore all of it in the limited time he had. He wondered where Burrugandr would keep something as vital and precious as the source tree.

Close, he thought. He would keep it close. Knowing that the chieftain would most likely live in the deepest part of the mountain, where he was protected, Ash made himself sink down, going deeper and deeper. He was careful to avoid most tunnels or open areas in his path steering around them. He saw trolls moving through the space of the tunnels, like outlined shadows, as he drifted past, the stone in their blood visible to him. When he needed to, he would push his head into an empty tunnel to draw a few deep breaths before drifting downwards again, moving towards the depths of the mountain lair.

Ash came to a stop above a vast cavern. Below him, he saw the shapes of several trolls and one of them was immensely large, sitting on a throne of stone. Burrugandr, he thought. He moved down to the ceiling and let his face emerge from the stone. The sight of Burrugandr made his heart skip a beat.

The jotunn chieftain sat on his throne, every inch of his grey, fat body carved with runes. Thick gold bands encircled his fleshy arms. From this angle, Ash couldn't see his face, only a bulbous, fleshy nose protruding from a thick mane of white hair, so long that it fell in ringlets on the floor next to the throne.

Ash swallowed as he noticed what stood right behind the intricately carved throne. There was no mistaking the source tree with its glistening, scaled bark and twisted branches laden with deathly fruits. It was much larger than the one that had grown in the two-headed jotunn's cave in Midgard, and it seemed to sway in a wind Ash could not feel.

Ash's eyes wandered to the small gathering in front of Burrugandr. He saw Grinbodr and the spindly red-headed troll standing a little to the side. Before them, half sunk into the floor, was a dull black troll, large as a thursr, hands bound in front of him, his shoulders and head slumped. Behind the black troll stood another, even larger, with a long whip in his hand.

At a signal from Grinbodr, the larger thursr pulled his arm back and in a swift movement cracked the whip on the black troll's back. A long mark, seemingly aglow, tore the bound troll's skin and a shower of embers swirled out from him. Its roar echoed inside the cavern, but it wasn't a roar of pain, but one of anger. He watched as the wound on its black skin healed over, the glow disappearing, only for Grinbodr to raise her hand again before another crack rang out. As before, it was followed by a roar and another burst of embers.

His eyes went back to the tree. As he looked at it, it dawned on Ash that he had not come up with a means to destroy it. Last time, Odin had given him the Fire of the Aesir to burn the tree down, but there was a distinct lack of deities here now to help him. He had no extraordinary weapon to use against the tree. Only his father's hammer.

"Odin corrupted him, tempted him with the fire of the gods, which he placed in his hammer." Remembering his grandmother's words, he almost laughed aloud. Of course! He could use it to strike the tree, setting it on fire. But would it even work, and would it be enough? Even if he came out of the rock right beside the tree, he would only have one chance before the jotunns and thursrs were on top of him. *I could just strike the tree once or twice and then sink into the rock again. That would only leave Grinbodr who could follow me.*

The thought of the far more experienced Stonesmith catching him deep in the stone made his stomach hurt. Besides, he doubted the trolls would just let it burn, even if he somehow set it alight.

Ash had seen enough. He sunk back into the stone and hovered for a while. He needed a distraction. If he could draw their attention away for a moment, he might have a better opportunity to destroy it. Concentrating with his Stonesight, he took in the whole cavern. Behind Burrugandr's throne and the tree, there was a small opening. Ash drifted around the massive hall and saw a short tunnel leading into a series of three smaller chambers. This piqued his curiosity, and he moved closer.

A quick check told him that no one was in the chambers, at least not any trolls, and he stuck his head out in the first one. It was a smithy. A small forge in the corner filled the room with a stifling heat, and Ash broke into a sweat after just a moment. A blackened anvil stood before the forge, and many familiar tools hung on the walls in neat rows. His attention was caught by the hammer resting on the anvil. It reminded him of Beli's hammer. Just like on that occasion, this hammer called to him too, urging him to pick it up and wield it. Ash stepped out of the wall and walked up to the anvil. He picked up the hammer and examined it. It was a tool of quality, and although it did not surpass any of Eikinri's many hammers, it was a far cry beyond what Beli had used. He returned it to the anvil and walked towards the next chamber.

The room he entered was the opposite of the neat organisation in the smithy. Where the smithy had order, here reigned chaos. Animal skulls, bones, and twisted branches crowded the walls, while strange patterns of bound animal feathers and colourful runes and symbols covered the walls and ceiling.

A Shaman and Stonesmith. This must be Grinbodr's rooms. Swirls and symbols were painted on the floor, with small skulls placed in various locations within the pattern. All the swirls originated from a central empty spot in the middle of the room, where the stone had been well worn and had a slight groove. Grinbodr had clearly practiced her arts for a long time. Ash was very careful not to step on the pattern as he made his way through the room and into the last chamber.

It was a simple room; a pile of furs were accompanied by an old chest in a corner. Opposite the furs stood a simple table and a short bench, all made of plain stone. The only concession to comfort was a piece of fur on the bench. Some rocks and sticks lay on the table, but otherwise he saw nothing of interest.

He had just walked up to the table to investigate the items when he heard a clank from the smithy followed by footsteps. Ash threw himself into the wall and sank into the stone. He turned around and his Stonesight revealed a lanky troll had entered the room only a moment after he disappeared. The creature stood in the room for a second and reached out towards the table before turning around and moving back through to the first chamber.

His heart was beating so hard that he feared Grinbodr could hear it even through the stone. The thought struck him it might have been possible for the Shaman to see him with her Stonesight even when he hid in the stone. The thought made him sick, and he thanked the gods that she hadn't been using her ability.

A dull rhythm vibrated through the stone, and he turned his attention back to the first chamber. Grinbodr stood where the anvil was, her arm moving up and down in great strikes. What had she done at the table?

Ash's curiosity got the better of him and after ensuring that she was occupied at the anvil, he drifted closer to the table. He emerged with his head right above it and his ears filled with the rhythmic clangs of metal striking metal from the first chamber. Looking down, Ash saw the Shaman's satchel resting on the table in front of him. Reassured by the sounds of her work, he stuck his arms out from the wall and gingerly lifted the flap with two fingers and peered inside.

There were several things inside the satchel; a stone knife, some feathers and several small animal skulls, but what caught his attention was the soft glow of runes in various colours. Half a dozen portal stones glimmered at him. Knowing that they needed a way home, Ash's hand reached into the bag and, carefully avoiding the other items, he picked out one and held it in his hand. Although he had never created a portal stone, he could see that the flat, round stone as long as his thumb clearly had the troll rune for 'move' carved on it.

Concentrating, Ash looked inside the stone. He could see how the rune powered the spell, and he followed the rune's tendrils as they twisted into themselves. As the worlds rested on the boughs of Yggdrasil, all stones interconnected. In the middle of the portal stone, surrounded by a fine web of spells was a glowing ember. He focused on it, and an image flashed into his mind. He could see a grove of purple leaved trees somewhere next to a burbling stream. The image was crystal clear, and he could even smell the trees and hear the running water.

The image is the central part of the enchantment, he thought, but how can I make this stone take us home? Is it a memory? He stared at the image, but it revealed nothing else. I wonder... Ash brought up one of the clearest memories in his mind; the stable in Hornsborg, where he had spent so much of his youth. He imagined how it had looked on a warm summer's day, the smell of the horses and the feel of the floor inside the stables. When the picture was clear in his mind, he moved it on top of the image of the grove in Jotunheim, displacing it. He could almost hear the 'click' as the image of Hornsborg slid into the enchantment and the red rune flashed once.

He had found a way home.

CHAPTER 40

The humiliation hurt Roghald more than the physical pain from the whip. Pain didn't bother him much anymore. After what seemed like an eternity, the whipping had stopped, and the thursr dishing out the punishment was sent away. Roghald made sure he committed the troll to memory; he would take vengeance on all who had crossed him. He remained upright throughout the beating, his last bastion of defiance, and he could see that it had grated Grinbodr.

"The thursr soul in him is strong," Burrugandr rumbled thoughtfully. "Very strong."

He turned his massive face to Grinbodr. "We need to trap it for our own needs."

The shaman bowed her head to the giant. "It can be done, my chieftain, however, it will kill him."

Burrugandr only shrugged his massive shoulders. "I have grown bored with his suffering, anyway."

Grinbodr turned to Blodheid. "Watch him," she hissed. "If he as much as opens his mouth, have the thursr with the whip return."

Blodheid bobbed her head once and watched the Shaman disappear behind the throne. Before long, the rhythmic clang of metal being worked on an anvil rang out in the hall. Roghald watched Burrugandr turn his attention to Utgarda-Loki's daughter.

"I always despised your father," his booming voice startled her. "He was deceitful and a coward at heart."

Roghald didn't miss Blodheid grinding her teeth when the chieftain spoke ill of her father.

"But there is no denying the magic and strength in his blood-line. Therefore, I will not accept your request to serve me as a Shaman. Grinbodr is more than enough. Instead, you will serve me by bearing my offspring."

The already pale Blodheid blanched even more at the giant's words.

"But, great Burrugandr," she started, her voice an octave higher than normal, "surely my powers are-"

"Quiet." The giant had spoken softly, but there was a finality in his tone. "Once I conquer Jotunheim, my offspring will serve as my chieftains throughout the land. They must be strong to keep their power and your blood will assure it. This is the best way you can serve me. You may do it willingly or in chains."

Blodheid stared at the giant for a moment. Roghald could see a myriad of emotions flashing across her face before she squared her jaw and let her head drop to her chest, "As you command." Then Blodheid lifted her head. "But allow me to make one request, great chieftain."

Burrugandr raised one massive eyebrow.

"Let it be me who takes this worm's life." She turned towards Roghald, fire in her eyes. "If not for him, my father would still be alive, and I would be Shaman of Utgard. Let me be the one who ends his miserable existence."

She spoke with such hate and passion that Burrugandr burst out in laughter.

"A small favour to grant," he said. "His life will be yours to take."

Roghald found himself surprised at this turn of events. It wasn't really his fault that she found herself in this situation. True, he had brought her to Burrugandr's mountain, but her father's death and the destruction of Utgard had nothing to do with him.

He watched as a large, roasted beast of some sort was carried in on logs by four vaettrs and placed before Burrugandr. The giant reached down with his meaty hands and tore large chunks from the animal, shoving them into his mouth while smacking his lips loudly, with grease and juices running down his chest. Roghald watched in disgust as the giant devoured his meal, bones and all, while the metallic clangs rang out from behind the throne, every strike bringing him a step closer to his demise.

Eventually, the metallic clangs stopped, and a smiling Grinbodr emerged. She held up an iron spike for the chieftain to examine. The soft glow of runes all along the metal caught Roghald's eye, and a sense of foreboding overcame him.

"This spike, driven into his heart, will ensnare and trap his soul. We may then use it to forge a powerful weapon, or even a fire thursr of our own, if I can corrupt it first," Grinbodr declared with triumph.

"As always, you have served me well," Burrugandr said.

Grinbodr took a few quick steps towards Roghald, the spike held out in front of her and a manic glow in her eyes. Roghald tensed, his eyes searching the room for any means of escape, but finding none.

"Hold," Burrugandr rumbled, and the Shaman stopped, confusion written on her face, as she turned towards the chieftain.

Roghald exhaled a slow breath he hadn't even realised he was holding.

"Bring in the envoy from Thrym. Let them witness the destruction of the fire thursr.

Word will spread across Jotunheim and the Troll King will have a warning about what happens to those who oppose me."

"Of course," she mumbled, bowing her head. "Your wisdom knows no match, my chieftain."

Grinbodr turned to Blodheid. "Fetch them," she snapped, and turned back to stand next to the throne.

The spindly jotunn set off with long strides and Roghald heard the large doors swing open, then shut behind her. The minutes felt like hours as he waited for his execution.

CHAPTER 41

Ash drifted back from the depths of the mountain. He had lingered almost too long at the Shaman's dwelling, lost in the enchanting, only realising the clanging had stopped when it was almost too late. The sound of footsteps drawing near had made him quickly shut the flap of the satchel and draw back into the wall a heartbeat before the Shaman re-entered her bedchamber.

His heart threatened to burst out of his chest when his Stonesight showed him the silhouette of Grinbodr, only a foot away from him, reaching out towards the little table. Ash was sure that she had spotted him when she stood still for several long seconds in front of the table, but relief flooded him as she turned around and left her sleeping quarters.

Moving through the stone, back towards his friends, he berated himself for not finding a way to destroy the source tree. Unsurprisingly, it was not a straightforward task. If an opportunity did not present itself, he would have to create one.

He arrived back at the group's camp and slowly emerged from the stone. A quick look around told him that no one had spotted him, or if they had, they seemed to ignore him.

"I gather from the lack of alarm and urgency that you were unsuccessful?" Yrsa teased.

He shook his head.

"It's too well guarded," he whispered. "Right behind Burrugan-dr's throne. The Shaman is there, as well as that skinny jotunn. I couldn't even get close to the tree."

Yrsa frowned, while Torsten just shrugged.

"Well, there is always the option of attacking head on and hoping for the best," said the Berserker, who had somehow gotten his axe back and was busy running a stone over the edge. "It is a fine thing to go to Valhalla with the tale of falling in a troll chieftain's hall."

"That is all fine and well," Yrsa snapped. "But it does not help Midgard in the slightest."

"So, what do we do?" Ash asked.

Yrsa rubbed her face. She seemed older than usual. "If nothing else comes up, we do what Torsten said," she sighed.

"Ha!" the big man exclaimed triumphantly, before boxing Yrsa in the shoulder. "Finally, you have come to your senses,"

She grimaced and was just about to reply when the sound of the frost thursrs jumping to their feet made them all turn their heads.

"Burrugandr awaits you," Blodheid's voice carried across the cavern from where she stood in the doorway. "Don't make him wait."

"That was quick," Frode mumbled. "Something must be going on. I expected us to wait a lot longer."

They stood and Torsten reluctantly handed his axe back to the frost thursr. Frode handed Ash a stack of wooden tablets, crowded with runes.

"Hang on to them. You are now my assistant."

The lanky jotunn awaited them outside the chamber. When they joined her, he noticed she wore a thick but frayed cape draped over her shoulders. She set off down the tunnel without a word, and they had to hurry to keep up with her long strides. They went deeper and deeper into the mountain before coming to a stop in front of two massive stone doors. Ash stared at an old died head, making a horrible grimace, suspended where the doors met. He cringed when the jotunn reached out a long finger to its forehead and muttered "Burrugandr". The eyes became aglow with a pale light and the doors swung inwards.

For the second time that day, he looked out over Burrugandr's hall. The chieftain was still there, as were Grinbodr and the black troll in manacles. He checked to make sure the trollhelm was firmly on his head before he stepped over the threshold.

As he entered the massive hall, he noticed the addition of several large thursrs along the walls. They faced even greater odds than he had initially thought. He heard both his friends breathe in sharply as they took in the bulk of Burrugandr where he sat. He was almost as large as the Troll King.

"Maybe we can draw the frost thursrs into a fight as a distraction," Yrsa whispered after a while. "If they are all busy fighting, we can slip behind the throne and set fire to the tree. Do you have the hammer handy?"

Ash nodded and patted the side of his belly. Having placed the hammer under his clothes, the trollhelm's illusion hid it.

As they approached the throne, the frost thursrs stopped and Ash saw them place a heavy hand on each of the 'prisoners'. Ash swallowed and adjusted his bundle of wooden tablets as he alone followed Frode towards the jotunn chieftain.

"King Thrym, ruler of Jotunheim, sends his regards to his loyal chieftain, Burrugandr," the skald bellowed as he came to a stop halfway between the jotunn and their group.

The jotunn sneered at the obviously pointed remark. "Hail Thrym," Burrugandr boomed, leaving out 'King' in an act that made Frode stiffen. "Will you forgive me if I settle something before we continue to exchange pleasantries?" the jotunn asked of the skald.

"Of course," Frode replied, his voice thick with suspicion and his eyes darting around the hall.

"We have captured a fire thursr who schemed against Jotunheim," Burrugandr said whilst raising his hand to point at the black troll.

Ash looked at the troll up close, and saw that although its skin was a black crust, there were cracks in all its joints where an angry fire glowed with a dull sheen. There was something familiar about the shape of it, and when he looked closely at its face, the wooden tablets slid from his fingers and fell to the ground with a loud clatter.

Roghald!

The spikes on his arms and shoulders were missing, but he still had his horns and that unmistakable face that Ash had seen in so many nightmares. When Ash dropped the tablets, Roghald turned his hateful eyes on him. There was a fire in his eyes that sent a shot of fear through Ash. He fell to the ground and mumbling apologies, collected the tablets, careful not to look up at his old stable master. By the time he stood back up, Roghald had turned his attention back to Burrugandr.

Why was Roghald here? What had happened to him? Odin had warned Ash that Roghald had grown in power and this... change must have been it.

"This fire thursr will die here, in an act I am sure will not only please myself but also Thrym, on his frozen mountain throne." Burrugandr said, his eyes never leaving Frode.

Ash saw how Grinbodr, her face eager, took a step forward, raising a spike of some sort.

"No," Burrugandr rumbled. "Blodheid will do it," he continued, tilting his head towards the skinny red-haired troll.

The Shaman hesitated, her eyes flicking between the two jotunns, but when Burrugandr gave her a look of steel, she hissed and pushed the spike into the younger troll's hand. The eyes she gave her said that this was far from over. Grinbodr walked back and stood next to the throne again.

Blodheid pulled her cape tighter over her shoulders and walked up to Roghald who stared at her in open defiance. She stopped so close to him that their heads were almost touching and rested the point of the spike against his blackened chest. Her lips moved as she said something to Roghald. Ash strained his ears to catch what was said, but he stood too far away. Roghald gazed into her eyes for a moment before nodding once.

That's when all Helheim broke loose.

Chapter 42

The humiliation burned inside Roghald. His death was to be paraded in front of some envoy from the Troll King. He had underestimated Burrugandr's cunning and now he was about to pay the ultimate price. He had allowed his anger to take control of him again, and he had been ensnared like a mindless beast. Looking up at Grinbodr, he saw she was toying with the spike she had aimed at him earlier. There was no mistaking the glee in her eyes when she looked at him.

He heard the doors behind him open, and he let his gaze fall to the floor. Many heavy footfalls could be heard behind him before coming to a sudden stop. Sounds like quite a gathering, he thought. Then the hall filled with a distinctly human voice that called a greeting to Burrugandr. Roghald lifted his head, his curiosity piqued.

It was indeed a human who had addressed the chieftain, one that Roghald had never laid eyes on before. An ugly little vaettr stood next to the man and Roghald realised that the little troll was staring at him, transfixed. Roghald raised an eyebrow, and the troll dropped some wooden tablets that fell clattering to the floor. Had he seen this troll before? He didn't recognise it, so why did it look at him in such a knowing way?

Burrugandr's booming voice cut through his reverie. As expected, the chieftain declared Blodheid would be the one to cause his demise. The look of disappointment on Grinbodr's face gave him some comfort, and he rejoiced in the fact that his death was denied her. The Shaman reluctantly handed the spike to Utgarda-Loki's daughter, who had never taken her eyes off Roghald. Her face was a mask of determination. There was no way out now. At least he had cheated Helheim of his soul and instead of eternal suffering, he would simply turn to stone and cease to exist.

The lanky troll strode up to him, stopping so close he could feel her breath on his face. She was breathing heavily, and he wondered if she was nervous or excited about the impending act. He noted she had wrapped a worn cape over her shoulders. With a strange sense of fascination, Roghald inspected the strands in the woven cape and where they had broken from long wear and tear. It felt incredible to be taking in the tiniest details in these his last moments, as if his mind was desperately holding on to life.

She rested the tip of the cold spike against his chest and looked into his eyes. Roghald felt surprised at how calm he was and at the slow and steady beat of his heart.

"Will you give me my revenge as promised?"

Her voice was barely a whisper, and it took him a moment to understand what she had said. He looked into her yellow eyes and the black pinprick irises in them. As she gazed deeply into his eyes, he could see hope and desperation plainly written in them. And he understood.

Roghald nodded once, and Blodheid sprang into action. She dropped the spike and before it had fallen to the floor with a clang, she had thrown open her cape and pulled a bulky item from under her arm. She raised it towards Roghald and for a moment his world went dark. Something wrapped around his face and after a moment of panic, his vision returned, and he was looking out of two small holes. The thing pulled tight around his face and neck and he felt a surge of energy come over him.

Sjaldrikkir, he thought. She had put her mother's mask on him. The mask that would amplify someone's power at the cost of leeching on their soul. Well, as it happened, Roghald had had enough of souls and was happy to feed the mask some of his.

He tensed and called forth his fire again, but where there was previously a steady flow, now roared a firestorm. He watched as the manacles on his wrists glowed intensely for a second before the light fizzled out and they splattered to the ground in melted globs. Chaos reigned throughout the hall, and he was the eye of the storm. Screams and shouts echoed, and trolls were running to get away from him as waves of heat and flames radiated out from his body.

His eyes sought Burrugandr who sat wide-eyed on his throne, with his mouth open and hands clutching the armrests. Roghald stepped towards the chieftain, leaving molten footsteps in the stone where he'd trodden. But Burrugandr was an old hand and had fought countless battles to reach his status, and after the initial shock, a grimace of rage engulfed his face. He stood slowly to meet Roghald, standing twice as tall as the thursr. He reached behind his massive frame and pulled out an enormous block of stone.

The grey stone had the same shape as many of the standing runestones Roghald had seen throughout his life in Midgard. It was about the size of a man, but in the jotunn's hand it looked small and rested comfortably in his fleshy palm. Roghald's eyes fell on the myriad of runes carved into its rough surface as it radiated with power.

They both roared and met with a thunderclap as Roghald's flaming fists and Burrugandr's stone collided. All present were knocked from their feet as the hall shook, causing pebbles and dust to fall from the ceiling. Bones snapped in Roghald where Burrugandr struck him. The smell of Burrugandr's seared flesh filled the hall whenever Roghald reached him as they traded powerful blows and roared in anger and pain. Around them, humans and trolls alike ran for cover, as shock waves and swaths of red flame filled the hall. The mask strained against Roghald's face as he grimaced with the exertion of battle. Burrugandr was tremendously strong and Roghald feared that if the jotunn landed just a few blows in the right place, the battle would be over.

But Burrugandr had grown fat sitting on his throne for centuries and Roghald's broken bones healed almost immediately as the Sjaldrikkir mask flooded his body with might. Before long, the chieftain tired and his movements slowed enough that Roghald could push past his reach and grab his wrist, feeding a fury of flames into it. The jotunn howled in pain as the fire came close to burning through his wrist, and he lost his grip on the rock. In desperation, the giant threw himself at Roghald, but the fire thursr met his assault with a leap up and an embrace around the giant's wide neck. Roghald closed his eyes and pushed the flames as hard as he could, his entire body erupting in the fire of Muspelheim.

The jotunn's screams reverberated through the hall as thick, billowing smoke rose from his body towards the distant ceiling. As Burrugandr screamed and tore at his body to cast him off, Roghald only pulled his deadly embrace tighter and forced the flames hotter, so that the giant's hands came away as charred stumps after grabbing at him. The troll chieftain's cry died in his throat and within seconds, the giant's body fell, as a half-melted lump of rock, to the ground.

Roghald felt the last of his injuries from the battle heal and took in the chaotic scene around him. A group of white thursrs were crowding around the door, lined up for battle with their weapons drawn. Burrugandr's thursrs cowered against the back wall, fearfully watching him. He turned around to see Grinbodr leaning on the throne with one hand, her face ghostly white as she stared at the smouldering lump of what had been the chieftain. Her mouth was opening and closing, but not a word escaped her lips.

A movement on the other side of the throne caught his attention, and he turned to see a group of people running to the back of the hall. One turned its head to look at him as they ran.

It was Ash.

CHAPTER 43

Ash watched as the lanky troll threw open her cape and pulled something out of it. At first, he thought it was a severed head, but as she slipped it over Roghald's face, he realised it was a mask. It was an ugly thing, with ropes for hair and a patchwork of leathers making up the face.

As soon as it was firmly on his head, dozens of runes flared to life, and Ash watched the pale troll dive away from Roghald as a blast of shimmering heat exploded from him. The manacles melted away, and Roghald easily pulled his feet out of the bubbling pool of melted rock that had formed beneath him. Ash stood in shocked awe as Roghald clashed with the chieftain in a scorching battle.

"Move, you idiot, this is our chance!" Yrsa had grabbed his upper arm and pulled him towards the back of the hall.

Trolls were milling about everywhere in confusion and disarray and Ash saw Torsten, who was in front, slam his axe into the side of a thursr's head, when he had blocked their way.

"Move! Move!" Yrsa called, pulling him along, and they were halfway to the throne when a stray blast slammed into them, sending them all sprawling on the floor. Ash had been unprepared for it and fell hard, the trollhelm knocked off his head and tumbling off to the side. His ears were ringing from the blast, and he felt dizzy as he stood and turned to collect his helmet. Strong hands seized his shoulders and spun him around. Yrsa was staring into his face with an irritated look.

"Leave it!" she seemed to shout. He could barely hear her over the ringing in his ears. Then her facial expression softened into something akin to worry. "Are you okay?"

The ringing in his ears subsided, and he nodded to the Shield-maiden, who once again pulled him along. Torsten and Frode had also gotten back on their feet, and they all hurried along. They were almost at the throne when Ash spun his head around to find Roghald, still wearing the horrendous mask, standing over the fallen Burrugandr.

He saw the look of surprise on the thursr's face when he recognised him. Roghald seemed to mouth 'Ash'.

Expecting to be attacked, Ash halted in his tracks and pulled out the only weapon he had at hand; his father's hammer.

Roghald's face twisted into a grimace of rage, and he took a stride towards Ash. But then he stopped. Roghald seemed to stare into space for a moment, and then a strange expression came over him.

"Oh, no" Frode's voice had been little more than a whisper, but the hall had fallen deathly quiet.

Roghald's body spasmed, and his arms flew out to the side. Flames shot out from every crack in his shell-like black skin and with the flames, Roghald grew.

"H–he's ascending," Frode stuttered.

"Explain," Yrsa growled, grabbing the now pale man by the collar.

"He killed a jotunn chieftain in battle," the skald's voice was hoarse with fear and he was unable to take his eyes off Roghald.

"So?" Yrsa demanded, shaking him..

"So, he is about to become one."

They all turned to stare at Roghald, who had now doubled in

size. The spikes which Ash had noticed were missing from the troll's body earlier, now regrew, but they were glowing spikes of heated metal. His face distorted, his jaw widened, and the mask he had been wearing was torn to shreds before falling to the ground in singed pieces. Glowing embers replaced his eyes and his mouth, filled with fanged, blackened teeth, burned like a furnace.

"We are about to be trapped in here with a fire giant," Frode whispered.

"MOVE!" Yrsa shouted and pushed the skald in the tree's direction. Ash and Torsten didn't need telling twice as they all sprinted towards the source.

When Ash reached the tree, he risked a glance behind him. Roghald stood like a nightmare behemoth in the middle of the floor, flames licking his enormous body. All of Burrugandr's trolls in the hall had fallen on their knees, including Grinbodr. Her long hair hid her face, but Ash imagined she wore a worried expression. The lanky troll who had placed the mask on Roghald was nowhere to be seen. Roghald turned his burning eyes back on Ash. He wasn't sure if he had imagined it, but they seemed to burn a little hotter when he looked at him.

Something slammed into the back of Roghald's head with a hiss and a shower of white sparks. Ash leaned over to look down the side of the throne and saw that the frost thursrs were moving forward, weapons at the ready. One of them bellowed and the first row of thursrs threw their icy spears in wide arcs that slammed into Roghald.

"STOP THEM AND YOU MAY SERVE ME," his voice, like a roaring forest fire was directed at Grinbodr. The Shaman's head shot up and hope glimmered in her eyes.

"Yes, my chieftain," she called back and leapt to her feet with a vigour that betrayed her years. She slammed her staff into the ground, sending a wave of stone toward the frost trolls.

That was the last Ash saw, because Roghald took two long strides towards them, blocking the view.

"We'll hold him off! Go!" Torsten shouted a second before he faced the giant and began the Berserker chant.

Ash threw himself at the source tree, hammer raised in the air, and slammed it into the slick bark. The hammer sunk in, almost to the hilt, but nothing happened. He pulled it out only to see the bark knot itself back together as if it had never been damaged. He could hear his friends shouting in rage and pain behind him.

No, he thought, raising the hammer again, but as he did, he entered it with his mind. A complex network of enchantment tendrils spanned out before him. He had seen the fire of the gods before, and he scanned the complex network for it, because he knew he could not destroy the cursed tree without celestial fire. He found it at the very centre of the hammer's head. The amount was pitiful, only a tiny spark, but it fed dozens of enchantments and the whole spell network of the hammer was built around it. He dove into the spark and forced it out along the bundles, up to the surface of the hammer. Then he tried striking the tree again and drove his hammer down with as much force as he could muster. It slammed into the trunk, biting deep. The whole tree shook and a few black leaves fell around him. But beyond that, nothing happened. As soon as he pulled the hammer out of the dark wood, the scaly bark closed over again.

No! It has to work!

He raised the hammer a third time, tensing his muscles and hitting the tree as hard as he could. Just as the hammer fell towards the trunk, something slammed into Ash's ribs, sending him tumbling across the exposed roots of the tree. He landed on his side and looked down to see tendrils of smoke coming from what remained of his tunic, his scorched flesh visible beneath it. The pain was tremendous, but subsided as his body healed.

He had landed next to Torsten, whose arms were bound tightly to his chest by a bundle of roots and branches. The Berserker was red in the face as he struggled against his bonds, to no avail. Beyond the big man stood the lanky troll, Blodheid, holding strings in her hand that led to the tangled roots that enveloped his friends.

"We've been here before," she cackled at Ash.

He rolled onto his back to see Roghald bent over him.

"Since you can heal, this is going to take a long time," Roghald spoke in an omnipotent voice, crackling like a fire. Ash didn't recognise him anymore. He was now so altered that if Ash had not seen the transformation himself, he wouldn't have known that it was his old stable master that stood before him. Ash saw how Roghald's body and soul had been consumed and incorporated into this monster, and a strange sensation came over him. He felt sorry for Roghald.

"I'm sorry this happened to you, Roghald."

The fire giant paused, his burning eyes looking deep into Ash's. For a moment, Ash believed he had struck a chord with Roghald, that there was a sliver of humanity remaining in him that could be reasoned with. But then the giant let out a thunderous laugh and pressed his flaming hand down onto Ash's body.

Ash screamed as his skin was singed off along with his clothes and most of his beard. In desperation, he tried to Shift, but his powers remained elusive and beyond reach. He struggled to get to his feet, but again Roghald's burning hand came down, flattening him and searing his flesh.

Ash's world became one of blinding pain as the hand came down repeatedly, his body healing in between. He could sense his mother nearby, and knew she had come to collect him, but every time he was on the cusp of death, Roghald stayed his hand long enough for Ash to heal and return from the brink. Then he would start again. Ash's screams mingled with the fire giant's laugher and the screams of frustration from his bound friends. Through the pain, Ash longed for the release of death that lingered just beyond reach.

"*Sacrifice.*"

The word came unbidden into his mind. It was his mother's voice.

"Odin sacrificed himself to himself."

His mind was murky from the pain.

"Roghald sacrificed his soul."

He didn't understand.

"Tyr, the god of war, sacrificed his hand."

Another blow from Roghald and the searing pain sent his mind reeling.

"This is your Fenrir."

And Ash understood.

CHAPTER 44

Roghald felt jubilant. He had felt nothing like the power that coursed through his body right now. The transformation had been painful, but now his mind was clear and he was faster and stronger than he ever imagined possible. And now he had Ash at his mercy.

But no mercy shall be granted, he thought with glee as he slammed his burning hand into the man's broken body. He sent a warm thought to Mother Bestla who had fashioned the bracelet that now kept Ash alive, allowing Roghald to burn and torture him over and over. He paused for a moment to watch his antagonist's skin slowly repair as he drew ragged breaths. His beard had been burned off and he looked more like the boy he used to be. Like the boy who had humiliated Roghald and beaten him in the stables a long time ago. The memory seemed blurry, like it belonged to someone else, but the hate blossomed anew inside Roghald's chest and he pressed his burning hand down onto Ash again. Ash's muffled screams were like music to his ears. Roghald roared with laughter.

By his side, Blodheid laughed with him, her eyes bright with joy as he tortured the human. She held the three strings in her hands that bound the other humans. Their turn would come. She turned her head and looked at him. Roghald realised she was quite striking in her own way. Yes, she had helped him only in pursuit of her own revenge, but that was something no one could understand better than Roghald. Besides, very few had stood on his side since all this had begun and he found he enjoyed having an ally.

He smiled at her, and she returned the smile. But then her face lost all expression as an arrow slammed into her throat and she fell forwards and the strings fell from her hand. Roghald spun his head around to see the cursed dark elf standing next to the throne, knocking another arrow. He roared in anger and swatted at her with his enormous hand, slamming into the base of the throne where she stood. When he removed his hand, she was gone.

Ash.

He had to finish the boy for good, to kill him and his friends. He turned back just in time to see Ash lying on his side, skin still burned, but healing. The boy had somehow got hold of the Berserker's axe and raised it over his head with his left hand.

Ash's friends were just getting to their feet, now free as Blodheid's spell failed. Roghald laughed again. The idiot thought he could take on a fire giant with an axe. His laughter died in his throat when Ash brought the axe down on his own right wrist. Blood shot out of the stump as the boy's closed fist rolled away from him. He hadn't even cried out.

Ash slid the bracelet off his wrist.

CHAPTER 45

Ash stared at his clenched fist as it rolled away from him with a mixture of determination and shock. Part of him couldn't believe what he had just done. The other part looked coldly at the bleeding stump, counting the seconds until the blood flow subsided as the vessels, muscles and skin healed enough that he would not bleed out.

He had seen Agash shoot Blodheid, breaking the spell holding his friends and buying him a few precious seconds to act. It was both with a sense of relief and loss that he slipped the bracelet off his wrist, and with it, his ability to heal.

But the Shifting burst forth from his chest like an animal that had been caged too long and washed any doubts away. He felt the Ulfhednar power move throughout his body and his heart soared with joy. Everything around him slowed down and came into incredible focus. He spent a second or two looking at the glistening sheen of moisture on a root of the source tree next to him and marvelled at the roof of the cavern reflected in it.

Ash felt a radiant heat on his head and shoulders and looked up to see an enormous, flaming fist, slowly but relentlessly moving towards him. He rolled away to the side as the fist crashed into the ground where he had been lying. The impact sent flames and burning rocks flying with a dull, prolonged crash. The fist pulled back up and he saw his father's hammer lying half buried under smouldering gravel next to what was now a small crater. Ash dove for the hammer, snatching it up with his one hand and turned to face the fire giant.

Roghald's body was aflame with rage, waves of heat radiating off him. Ash saw him move slowly as he pulled his fist back, preparing for another strike, his burning eyes locked on Ash. A spear flew towards the jotunn's face, but as it hit his cheek, it bounced off and fell to the ground. On Roghald's side, Ash could see Yrsa, Torsten and Frode, throwing stones and whatever they could find at the flaming giant.

What are they thinking? They could never take him on!

Worried for his friends, Ash knew he had to hold Roghald's attention, so they didn't come to harm. As Roghald's swung his fist down at him again, Ash ran forwards, ducking underneath it and slammed the hammer into the giant's left kneecap.

There was a deep crunch as sparks and embers burst out from where the hammer had shattered the dark crust that was Roghald's skin. Roghald's bellow of pain and anger drew out over long seconds in Ash's state of slowed time. The heat that radiated off the jotunn this close to him was made so much worse by the cracking of the crust, exposing the flames beneath. Ash's skin felt raw and singed, just from being near the flames, and he had to squint as they pained his eyes.

The giant's knee buckled slightly, and an idea came to Ash in a flash. He sent a quick prayer to any god who would listen and slammed the hammer into the outside of the same knee. The enormous leg buckled in a blast of sparks and heat, and Ash quickly leapt up into the air and slammed the giant as hard as he could in the ribs. The hammer struck Roghald's chest with a thunderous boom and a flash of light, pushing him to his left side. When more weight was added to the already buckled knee, a loud crack, like a giant tree snapping in a storm, echoed inside the cavern.

Roghald, unable to stop himself as his leg gave out, fell and landed against the source tree. The tree shuddered and some of the bulbous, black fruits fell to the ground, where they burst.

Ash cursed. The tree had held.

Roghald, his face a grimace of pain, rolled to his back and leaned against the tree, holding his broken knee that was already healing. Ash could see that the flames off his back were licking the bark behind him, making the tree shiver and twist in pain. The fire of Muspelheim burned like the fire of the gods. Ash stopped Shifting. Roghald's pride and anger had always been his weakness. This had saved Ash before, and he hoped that his old stable master had not learned to control his anger yet.

"I was always better than you Roghald! Prepare to die in disgrace, just like your father did!" he called to the giant, smirking.

The fire giant's eyes widened for a second, as if he couldn't believe what he was hearing. Then his rage exploded in a wave of heat that forced Ash to shield his face, even at the distance he was at. Roghald roared, his body bursting with flames and fists slamming into the ground to push himself up.

A piercing shriek filled the cavern as the source tree was engulfed in flames. The fire of Muspelheim, destined to burn the world, ate away at the tree, and only a moment later, it cracked under the weight of its own boughs and fell to the ground in a cascade of flying embers. Ash saw it reduced to ashes and glowing cinders in a matter of seconds.

Roghald hadn't even noticed, he was so focussed on Ash. He tried to stand but staggered sideways as his leg would not yet carry him.

Time to get out of here, Ash thought. Instinctively, he reached down for his pouch where he had put the portal stone he stole from Grinbodr; their only ticket back to Midgard. But when Ash checked, there was nothing where his belt had been, the pouch gone along with his burned-through belt and tunic.

"Run!" Ash shouted as he turned to his friends, but he saw their backs were already disappearing behind the throne. He sprinted and reached them as he passed Burrugandr's throne. The rest of the cavern was now revealed as a battlefield.

Grinbodr stood next to the throne surrounded by dead frost thursrs, their now stone bodies, even in death covered in a layer of frost. She looked battered and bruised and had a deep cut on her forehead that bled profusely. Despite her injuries, she swung her staff with vigour, sending flashes of green light as the remaining three frost trolls launched a desperate attack against her. Several of Roghald's battle trolls flanked them on both sides.

Ash steered his friends towards the wall of the cavern, hoping the Shaman was too distracted by the battle to notice them.

"Grinbodr," Roghald's voice filled the cavern.

Ash turned to see him leaning on the throne with one hand, a mad expression on its face.

"Collapse the entrance! Do not let them leave the mountain!"

Grinbodr spun to look, first at Roghald, then Ash and his friends who had almost reached the entrance to the hall. She backed away from the remaining frost thursrs, leaving her own trolls to fight them. Then she rummaged inside her satchel for a second before pulling something out and holding it above her head. When she threw it on the ground, Ash recognised the familiar flash of a portal stone. The band of runes started small but expanded out into a wide circle.

"They will not leave the mountain, my lord!" Grinbodr called to Roghald. Then she threw herself into the portal and disappeared.

Roghald laughed and tried his leg with a few stomps. "Nowhere to run," he bellowed as he started limping towards them.

Neither Ash nor his friends needed any more encouragement, and they sprinted into the broad tunnel exiting the hall.

"Stop them!" Roghald called to the thursrs who now stood over the fallen frost trolls.

The big battle trolls lumbered towards the exit, but they were built for strength, not speed. As Ash entered the tunnel, something whistled past his head and he heard the thud of an arrow behind him, followed by a moan and the sound of a massive battle troll hitting the ground.

"What took you so long?" Agash grinned at them with her sharpened teeth and Ash had never been happier to see anyone in his life.

"There are four thursrs and a furious fire giant right behind us," Yrsa said through gritted teeth as she ran, dragging a huffing and puffing Torsten along by his arm. "I suggest we catch up later."

Nothing else was said as they ran along the maze of tunnels and caverns. Vaettrs jumped out of their way as they came through and those who didn't got shouldered by Yrsa, sending them tumbling to the ground. A few times, as they tired and a thursr drew nearer, Agash would spin around and still running, shoot an arrow that would be followed by a thud as the troll stumbled with an arrow in its eye or foot.

"My arrows won't kill them," she called out in between breaths. "I'm only slowing them down."

They felt a wall of heat wash over them as they heard some kind of fiery explosion close behind them.

"He's catching up!" Frode yelled and picked up his speed, pulling slightly ahead of the group.

"If the Shaman has collapsed the entrance to the mountain, we will have to make a last stand, prepare yourselves." Yrsa called.

Torsten, jogging along, red in the face, snot and spittle running down his beard called out between breaths like a bellow. "Stop and fight... now. Otherwise... only going.... to die... tired."

"No, we run!" Ash called out, pushing the big man in the back to encourage him along. "She won't be there!"

Yrsa gave him a strange look as she grabbed the Berserker's arm again to drag him.

"How do you know?"

"I have a hunch," Ash replied. "Now run."

Relief flooded Ash when, at the end of the last tunnel, he saw the flood of daylight.

They ran out amongst the vaettr still cleaning up outside, and the small trolls ran from them. But the ten thursrs guarding the entrance did not. They turned to look at the group with confusion. Then a thursr burst out of the tunnel behind them and Agash spun and shot it in the face, sending it tumbling to the ground, clutching at the arrow. The guarding battle trolls growled and drew their weapons, an array of blunt and sharp, large implements, and closed in on the group.

Torsten, now purple in the face from the run, bent over and vomited while he searched his belt for an axe that wasn't there. It was left behind in Burrugandr's hall. Yrsa drew her seax, having thrown her last spear at Roghald. Frode clutched a short sword in his hands and Ash raised his father's hammer. Agash knocked her last arrow. They faced fresh battle trolls, outnumbered and virtually unarmed, while being worn, tired, and out of breath. But Ash felt nothing but joy.

We did it, he thought. We destroyed the source tree. His heart soared. As he looked at his friends, he felt sorrow that they would die for his cause, but he knew they would be rewarded in Valhalla. Heavy footsteps rang out from the tunnel behind them, and he could see the flames licking the walls in the distance as Roghald drew nearer.

A drop of rain fell on Ash's nose, followed by another.

"It is going to rain," Torsten said in his most bitter voice, still drawing heavy, ragged breaths. "Could this day get any worse?"

Yrsa burst out laughing. It was a hearty belly laugh, driven by exhaustion and relief of tension, in this, their last moment. It was contagious and set the others off, first in chuckles, then side-splitting roars as tears ran down their faces and they struggled to hold whatever weapons they had aloft.

The thursrs paused for a second and looked at each other. Through his tear filled, blurry vision Ash saw a pinprick of light flash behind the battle troll in front of him. He thought it was a trick of the light at first, but when it broadened to the size of a plate, he saw several leafy tree branches poke out of it, suspended in the air.

The laughter died in his throat, and he reached out to squeeze Yrsa's arm. The branches moved apart, stretching what was now a ring of green-hued light wider and wider. Ash's jaw dropped as a portal opened with three Seidwomen holding the branches, their faces painted white and lips blackened. The Seidwomen stepped out behind the thursrs, and when they moved to the side, broadening the portal, the sweetest music that had ever fallen on his ears flowed out of the rift; the battle song of the Berserkers.

Broad and powerful men and women, their shoulders draped in bear skins and their faces tattooed, spilled out of the opening and slammed into the trolls from behind. Axes flashed and mighty blows, fuelled by their Berserker rage, saw the battle trolls cut down. More and more warriors spilled out of the portal into the clearing. Ash and his friends, too stunned and tired to fight, could only watch as the trolls were decimated around them in just a few moments. Then firm hands seized Ash and his friends by the shoulders and dragged them back towards the Seidwomen. Someone sounded a horn, and the warriors all backed away towards the portal.

While he was whisked away and the Berserkers and the Seidwomen stepped back into the ring of light, Ash's last sight was Roghald stepping out of the tunnel. The fire giant wore an expression of pure hatred and drew his arm back, a massive orb of flames forming in his palm. Then the Seidwomen dropped their branches, and the portal disappeared, and Roghald with it.

For the first time in what felt like an eternity, Ash felt warm sunshine on the back of his shoulders and he looked up at a blue sky.

CHAPTER 46

Ash laid in bed in his chamber in Gjallarholm. He had slept for what felt like days, and his thoughts felt murky. Everything hurt.

Lifting his blanket, he saw that someone had bandaged up the parts of him that were covered in burns, which were most of him. He held up his right arm and looked at the stump. It was dressed in clean bandages, but there was a dull throb beneath. He tried to move the fingers he no longer had, and a stab of pain shot through him.

Sacrifice. He lowered the arm to rest on his blanket with a sigh.

"How are you feeling?" Yrsa stood in the doorway, looking at him, a sad look in her eyes.

"Don't look at me like that."

"Like how?"

"With pity," he replied with a grimace. "I don't need it and it won't make me heal up any faster."

Yrsa shrugged.

"I just came from Jarl Astrid. She sends her well-wishes."

"How did they know to come for us?" Ash asked.

"Apparently, they interpreted your act of dropping a couple of battle trolls at her gates as a distress call," Yrsa smirked.

"I can see how people would perceive it that way," Ash said. Is everyone else fine?" Ash asked her.

"As fine as can be," she said with a shrug. "Torsten is recovering from his damaged pride of being too winded to fight. The day after we returned, he started the morning by running around the training yard."

"Really?" Ash said, raising his eyebrows.

"Yes," she said. "But only on that one occasion. Since then, he has spent all his time in Jarl Astrid's hall decimating her mead supply. He says that next time he is just going to stand and fight, not run."

Ash chuckled, but he must have had a broken rib or two, because it really hurt.

"Frode mourned his loss of payment from the Troll King, but soon remembered his family and left for Hammershall,"

"And...?" Ash left the question hanging in the air.

"I haven't seen her since we entered the portal," Yrsa sighed.

Ash pressed his lips together.

"Look, Ash," Yrsa started. "She's a dark elf. Although she proved herself in the end, the complication of you two.." she stopped and left it unsaid.

Ash nodded. He didn't know what he had hoped for exactly, but he had hoped for something. A goodbye, if nothing else.

"Try to get some rest," Yrsa said. "I will have some food sent up to you."

"Thank you, Yrsa." Ash whispered. "For everything."

She gave him a penetrating look for a moment, then she smiled and reached for the door. Just before she shut it, she paused and opened it slightly again. "Something has been bothering me," the Shieldmaiden said.

Ash raised his eyebrows.

"How come you were so sure that Grinbodr would not seal off the exit?"

"I found her portal stones when I went looking for the source tree. I may have altered them somewhat."

Yrsa gave him a thoughtful look.

"Good thing you did," she said before shutting the door.

Ash listened to her footsteps disappear down the stairs beyond.

"I thought she would never leave."

Ash looked up at the window above his head. Even though he was looking at her upside down, there was no mistaking the dark elf in her tight leathers.

"Agash," he exclaimed. "I thought you had left."

"No, I just laid low," she said as she leapt from the window and landed in front of the bed without a sound. "I don't think most humans would take too kindly to my appearance, so I figured it was best if I stayed out of sight. By the darkness, the sunlight here is uncomfortable," she said, rubbing her exposed skin.

"Well, I'm glad you're here," he said.

She looked around the room.

"What will you do next?" he asked her.

She tilted her head and pursed her lips. "I don't know," she said. "New world, new opportunities. I thought I might follow you for a while. Seeing how trouble always finds you, I'm sure there won't be a dull moment."

Ash's face darkened. "Well, this business with Jotunheim is far from over," he said, his voice bitter. "Roghald will be back, it is just a matter of time. I fear he is a far worse enemy than Burrugandr was."

"Stop thinking about it," Agash scolded him. "You will drive yourself mad and lose the battle before it even begins."

"I guess you're right," Ash sighed, leaning his head back against the pillows. "I'll have to distract myself."

When Agash didn't answer, he looked up to see her standing next to the bed. He became acutely aware that under his blanket, he was wearing nothing but a few bandages.

He watched wide eyed as she unlaced her leather jacket and let it fall to the floor, revealing her smooth, pitch black skin.

"W-what are you doing?" Ash asked in a much more high-pitched voice than he had intended.

Agash grinned, revealing her sharp white teeth as she looked at him, a strange hunger in her eyes. "I'm distracting you."

She climbed onto his bed and pressed down on him.

"Be careful," Ash groaned, as everything hurt at once.

"Not a chance."

CHAPTER 47

Felp bent down over his boat and pulled his meagre catch onto the rickety jetty. Looking at the two tiny fish, his stomach rumbled, but he knew it wouldn't be enough to fill him. He sighed and with his hands on his hips, leaned backwards, stretching his sore back. It was getting worse every week.

He'd had a terrible year, and it was going to get worse. He thought his luck had changed when he sold the strange troll that came wandering over the hills a while back. Even what he sold him for was a pittance compared to the gold the troll had had in its knapsack.

He had only just rowed the treasure home when those stinky humans had appeared. The bigger one was more animal than human anyway, and they had beaten him black and blue until he had told them what had happened. As if that wasn't enough, they took all the gold he had stolen honourably.

He was pulled away from his self-pity by a red light appearing on the otherwise calm water of the red lake. It was maybe twenty yards out from his jetty, and he squinted to see it better. He took a few steps back when the light flashed once, then expanded to a wide circle sitting just on top of the water.

The water inside the circle disappeared for a second and Felp yelped when a creature shot out of the hole. The circle closed in on itself with a flash, and the creature splashed into the water. An angry face broke the surface, spitting and coughing water.

"W-what...?"

By the sound of her voice, it was an old woman. And big enough to be a jotunn, he thought.

"You!" she shrieked at him. "Throw me a rope."

Felp didn't bother. He saw the blood running from a cut on her forehead and knew there was no point.

Sure enough, the water started churning near to her. He counted under his breath and didn't even make it to three before a long, slimy body rose out of the water behind the woman. The creature had no eyes, only a mouth that opened into four separated jaws. It looked a bit like a flower, he always thought. Except this flower had countless razor-sharp teeth covering its petals. The eel crashed into the old troll and pushed her under the water. Felp stood there watching the water churn and splash for a while, before all fell silent again.

A clonk from the jetty below made him look down and he saw a long, gnarled staff bobbing against one support. It had glowing runes covering it, pulsating with a life of their own, and if there was one thing Felp knew, it was that magic was worth its weight in gold.

Maybe this year would not be so bad after all.

THE END

The saga continues in the third and final book 'Jotunn'.

ACKNOWLEDGEMENTS

First, as always, I need to acknowledge my editor-in-chief,
my grammar police, beloved and mother of my child; my wife
– Hasna Ameti - without her endless support and patience this
book series would only be a pipe dream.

Furthermore, I would like to thank Vikram and Swati Iyer, Corey
Crossin, Matt Carson, Anders Stromfeldt and Gemma Kelly for
their invaluable input into the creative process.

I would also like to thank Johnny Greenteeth for the cover art
and Scott Colliver for the Yggdrasil illustration. Without them
this book would not look as great as it does.

It is with joy that I also give a warm shoutout to Eammon Jamie-
son and the coolest book club in Australia - Fiction Addiction -
for their love and support.

Last, but certainly not least, I would like to thank you, the reader,
for making it all the way to the end. This is my very first publica-
tion, and as an indie-author I am highly dependent on reviews,
so please, if you have enjoyed it, leave a review on your favourite
reading platform or Goodreads. Or why not both?! You might

not think so, but every single review makes a big difference and I will send a spiritual hug and kiss to everyone who posts one.

If you would like to leave me any personal feedback, drop me a line at afnjansson@gmail.com.

Thank you,

A.F. Jansson

A.F. JANSSON